DARKNESS TRIUMPHANT

BOOK FOUR OF
THE CATMAGE CHRONICLES

BY
MERYL YOURISH

COVER ART BY JULIE DILLON

MAY PUBLISHING

FOR MY MOTHER

Text copyright © 2017 by Meryl Yourish
Cover art copyright © 2017 by Julie Dillon

All rights reserved. Published by MAY Publishing.

No part of this book may be reproduced by any means, electronic, mechanical, or otherwise, without first obtaining permission from the author. For information regarding permissions, contact the author at www.merylyourish.com.

ISBN 978-0-9881804-6-8

First printing March 2017

CONTENTS

ONE: Many Happy Returns • 1
TWO: Razor's Edge • 14
THREE: The Other Side of the Story • 32
FOUR: Sunday School • 40
FIVE: Lighten Up • 54
SIX: Tuesdays with Nafshi • 63
SEVEN: Parents Night • 74
EIGHT: Junior Year • 80
NINE: Mischief in the Night • 97
TEN: Halloween • 107
ELEVEN: Double Exposure • 124
TWELVE: Licking Their Wounds • 141
THIRTEEN: A Midwinter's Night Scheme • 149
FOURTEEN: Fiye for Fighting • 164
FIFTEEN: The Enemy Within • 173
SIXTEEN: Rid Me of This Troublesome Catmage • 180
SEVENTEEN: Catsoyer • 187
EIGHTEEN: Mouse Trap! • 202
NINETEEN: Cat Trap! • 221
TWENTY: Parental Consent • 242
TWENTY-ONE: Fathers and Daughters • 253
TWENTY-TWO: Campfire Boys and Girls • 261
TWENTY-THREE: East yersus West • 275
TWENTY-FOUR: Exultations and Lamentations • 293

ONE: MANY HAPPY RETURNS

Andy lay on his back, snoring slightly, sound asleep. On the night table beside him lay two leather bands. One, a thin band in the shape of a doubled-crossed sideways X, held a charred and empty metal clasp. The other, a thick, wide band, held a glowing green stone.

Andy's snoring stopped as he drifted into a dream he'd had many times before. He found himself once again in Principal Saunders' cellar, choking smoke rising as fire spread. Saunders aimed a pistol at Goldeneyes, the paint thinner exploded, and Andy fell to the ground as the gun went off. He looked toward the remnants of Nafshi's cage, expecting to see her bleeding at the bottom of it.

"Not this time," dream-Nafshi said, sitting beside the cage and lashing her tail. "Aren't you tired of reliving those painful moments?"

Puzzled, Andy tried to speak, but all he could do was splutter wordlessly.

I'm dreaming, he thought. *It's just another nightmare.* Nafshi faded, and he fell into a dreamless sleep. Dawn was breaking, and sunbeams shone into his bedroom from the window next to his bed. Andy sighed in his sleep.

As the light grew, it revealed a small tortoiseshell cat sitting next to Andy's pillow. The cat wore a leather collar that looked exactly like the empty one on the night table except for a green stone inside the clasp. The

CHAPTER ONE

cat reached out a paw and tapped Andy on the nose once, twice, three times. Andy continued to snore. The cat's tail switched irritably. The light in her collar flashed. Andy's Magelight in its leather band rose from the night table, flew through the air, and smacked him soundly on the side of his head.

"Ow!" he said, sitting up and looking about groggily. "Wha—what? Leilei? What are you doing here?" He rubbed the side of his head and blinked. "Did you just hit me?"

The cat's ears swept back, the morning sun dappling the many colors of her fur.

"Get up," she snapped as her tail beat a noiseless tattoo on the bed. "We've a lot of things to do today."

Andy's mouth dropped open. "That's—that's Nafshi's voice. Not funny, Leilei." His eyebrows drew together in a scowl.

"I am not Leilei, child. I *am* Nafshi. Now get out of bed."

Andy sat unmoving. "Not possible," he said. "You're dead. I'm dreaming."

"Well, yes, I died," she said, "but I am also here. Child, you need to stop lazing around and get out of bed. We have a lot to do today."

"I'm dreaming," he said again. "I'm having a really strange Nafshi dream. Maybe I shouldn't have had that last slice of pizza before bed." Andy shook his head and lay back down. "Go away, Nafshi-dream," he said, yawning.

Nafshi's tail switched. "If you don't get up, I'll smack you with that Magelight collar again. Andy, you're not dreaming. It's me. I never left you. But it's taken me this long to find a way to contact you."

Andy sat back up, looking even more confused. "I don't understand."

Nafshi sighed. "The Magelight, Andy. The Magelight. Think. How many times were you able to do things with my Magelight that you hadn't been taught? Remember those waves of power you used to stop the Wild Ones? Where do you think they came from? It was me! When you really needed help, I was there."

"Nobody ever knew why those surges kept happening," Andy said. "*You* were behind them?"

"I just said that. Pay attention. I do not like repeating myself." She gazed out the window. "Think back. On the day I gave you my Magelight, I didn't know it but I also gave you a part of myself." Her voice grew soft as she thought back on that day years before. "At first, it was like being in a long, dark room. I could sense everything that happened to you, and I could see what you saw, but I couldn't get out of that benighted room! I spent ages wandering around in the dark. And then, at long last, I saw a crack of light. I followed it and found myself here with you." She purred. "I must admit, it's nice to be out and about."

"But how? You're dead, and either I'm totally insane or I'm talking to the spirit of the Catmage who used to own my Magelight. And she's answering back."

"Not quite my spirit. I'm not really sure what I am, actually. I only know that on the day I died, I found myself, well, inside you. As if I were looking out from behind your eyes. But I couldn't get you to hear me until today."

"That is so weird," Andy said. "You—you're really Nafshi?"

"Of course I am. I told you that. How is it that in three years you have not yet learned to listen?"

Andy grinned. "I listen. But it's kind of hard to believe I'm sitting here talking to you. Really talking, not just wishing." His face lit with joy. "You're really here! Wow! Oh, Nafshi, I've missed you so much!" He reached out to scoop her up in his arms and fell face-first onto the bed.

She laughed. "I have no physical form anymore. I found that out when I tried to wake you. I can't touch you, and you can't touch me."

Andy sat up with a rueful smile on his face. "I guess seeing and hearing you will have to be enough," he said. He couldn't stop smiling. "I'm really glad you're here."

Nafshi lifted her paw and began gnawing at her claws. "It's definitely better than being stuck inside your mind screaming my head off at

CHAPTER ONE

you. I'm amazed you never once heard me. Although, come to think of it, perhaps it's just as well. Some of the things I shouted … Well, that's neither here nor there, as I am here and not there."

Andy laughed out loud. "I can't believe you're back."

"I am. Now get out of bed," she said. "We have a lot to do today."

"We do?"

"Yes. Since you are no longer training at the Compound, you will take lessons with me."

"Uh—what?"

"Just because you stopped training with Zahavin doesn't mean I'm going to let your education lapse. If you're going to use my Magelight, you're going to learn how to use it properly."

Andy narrowed his eyes at the image of Nafshi. "Hey! How come you have a Magelight around your neck when I have your Magelight right here?" He picked up the thick leather band that lay on his bed.

"Because this is how I looked in life. I was a pale shadow of myself when I died." She looked down at her body. "This is much better. This is how I looked before Saunders got his hands on me." She looked away, and her head drooped.

"Nafshi, I'm so sorry!" Andy said. "I tried to save you. I tried so hard!" He went to scoop her up again but stopped himself in time.

"Well, you can make up for it now. Get up, get dressed, and let's get to work."

"It's Sunday."

Nafshi stared at him without saying a word. At that moment, she reminded him of Goldeneyes when she got angry.

"Uh, I'll just go take a shower," he said. He jumped out of bed and grabbed some clothes on the way to the bathroom. He came out a few minutes later, dressed and rubbing his hair dry with a towel. Nafshi sat in the window licking her shoulder.

"Why are you washing yourself when you're not real?" Andy asked.

"Would you stop the habits of a lifetime if you suddenly found

MANY HAPPY RETURNS

yourself non-corporeal?"

Andy shrugged. "I never thought about it."

"Well, I don't see any reason to change my routines just because my physical form has changed a bit."

"A bit?"

"All right, a lot. But the point remains."

"Andy!" his mother called from downstairs. "Breakfast!"

"Be right there!" he called back. "I guess you shouldn't come downstairs with me," he told Nafshi.

"I could but I suspect no one but you can see me. We can test that later. But you'd best remember to use your mind-voice only to me."

"Yeah, or people will think I'm nuts," he sent.

"Well done, Andy. Your talents are coming along nicely. I was right to give you my Magelight."

Andy brightened at the compliment.

"I'll meet you in the yard after you've eaten. You have much to learn if you want to defeat the Wild Ones."

Andy's grin disappeared and his expression hardened. "I quit. I'm not watching any more of my friends die."

"We'll see about whether or not I let you quit," Nafshi snapped. "But in any case you will still learn how to use my Magelight properly. It's the least you can do for me after all I've done to help you."

"Wait a minute. *You* were the one who caused the power surge that hit Taylor. You're the reason I almost killed him."

"Oh, pooh. He didn't come close to dying. All we did was knock him down. He deserved it. He attacked you."

"Taylor hit his head. He could have been really badly hurt. Head wounds are dangerous!"

"They didn't seem to care so much about hurting your head when they captured you and put you in the cellar with me."

"That's not the point! I'm not going to use my power to kill anyone."

"Your Magelight is *my* power, Andy," she said, staring steadily at

CHAPTER ONE

him. "I gave it to you. And I won't let anybody do anything to harm you—or it."

Something in Nafshi's tone chilled Andy. "My breakfast is getting cold," he muttered. He turned his back on her and left the room. Nafshi continued her bath, unconcerned.

Hakham walked through an empty field toward a small stand of trees—the wood where the previous Council had met, the place where they had been betrayed by his brother, Niflah. Three full cycles of the sun had passed since Hakham was last here. He thought back to the day he and Zahavin were late for that Council meeting in the wood. It had started out so well. He was bringing his apprentice with him to see his fellow Councilor, Niva, invested with the *Chai* award. She had served eighteen cycles on the Council, both the number that means life in the ancient language, and the number of toes on a Catmage's paws. That correlation amused Hakham. So did the declaration by Letsan, his other apprentice, that it discriminated against the polydactyls in the Catmage family—those who had extra toes on their paws. But *Chai* was an important milestone. Normally there would be a brief Council meeting, followed by a celebration in honor of the Councilor. But that night the meeting had ended in tragedy before Hakham arrived.

The Council had been taken by surprise by the Wild Ones, working in concert with the human, Saunders, and his dogs. They had defiled this formerly sacred place by killing all of the Council members and stealing their Magelights. All but one, he corrected himself. His brother Niflah had perfected a spell that made him appear to be dead.

They had buried the Council nearby in shallow graves. Hakham could only presume that Niflah used his Magelight to dig his way out of his grave after they left. But the tale of the Council's violent end had frightened his people. The Council Wood was now considered unlucky and even passing Seekers—Catmages who searched out half-breed Catmages living outside of Compounds—walked around it. The Wild Ones would not return to the wood, either. There was no need.

MANY HAPPY RETURNS

Hakham sighed as he thought of the task that still lay ahead. Ten of the eleven Magelights the Wild Ones had stolen were still in their possession. Razor had recovered and destroyed one of them during the battle at Saunders' house only a few weeks ago. Too many were still in the Evil One's hands, not to mention the Tilyon, the most powerful of all Catmage artifacts.

He trotted into the trees, ears twitching and senses extended by his Magelight. The Council Wood's current bad reputation made it a perfect place for a secret meeting. There in front of the ancient oak where the meetings used to take place sat two striped tabbies, one slightly larger than the other.

"Greetings, Hakham," said Aryeh, the smaller tabby, as Hakham drew near.

"It is good to see you. Are you ready?"

"We are," he said.

"Can't let my sisters have all the fun," Levavi, the larger tabby added. He dropped his glance at Hakham's sharp look.

Aryeh saw the look and blinked at Hakham. "My son understands the seriousness of our mission, Hakham," Aryeh said. "You don't know Lev. This is just his way."

"I don't think the Wild Ones would appreciate it. We won't be able to help you if things take a bad turn. Your lives depend on the Wild Ones not knowing you're ours."

"The Wild Ones won't find out from me," Levavi said, "and don't worry. I can be as serious as Razor when I need to be. I didn't think I'd have to be around you."

Aryeh gazed at Hakham and decided to change the subject. "Where is Razor?"

"At the Compound. Hakham taking a walk alone is not unusual. Hakham and Razor taking a walk together is noticed. We had a spy in our midst—Kel, one of Roah's kits. You'll meet him, I'm sure. He assaulted our Compound while we were attacking the Evil One's house." Hakham

CHAPTER ONE

paused, pushing down the anger he felt at the betrayal. "It was Kel's duplicity that set Razor's mind toward turning the tables on our enemy. We have the perfect cover for you. Hed was killed in battle this spring. He was one of their scouts and often away on missions. Refer to him as the one who recruited you."

"I will," Aryeh said. "And I'll keep my eye on this Kel character as well." He changed the subject. "How are my daughters?"

"They are well. Silsula is a very happy—and excellent—Nanager. She's quite good with a Magelight as well. Do you remember my teacher, Methuselah? He chose both your daughters and Leilei for special tutoring last year. As for your other daughter—well, you know Zahavin. You should be very proud, Aryeh. And you, Levavi. Leilei is showing all the signs of being a true scion of Nafshi. I'm giving her private lessons now. She outgrew the Teaching Rings ages ago."

"Good for her, doing what I never could," Levavi said cheerfully. "The First knows I couldn't wait to get out of the Rings and become a Seeker."

"Which is a very honorable profession," Aryeh said gruffly.

"I must ask you again, Aryeh. Are you certain you want to do this? What if Roah recognizes you?"

"I'm sure. I haven't been back to the Council Compound since—well, since Lev, Silsula, and Zahavin were kittens. Roah was already gone, and Lev became my apprentice as soon as he could talk his way out of the Teaching Rings. We've both been on the road ever since. There's always the possibility that some of the Wild Ones saw us at some point or another. But what can they say? That they saw two Seekers doing their jobs? Hed won't be around to contradict me when I tell them how tired I am of Catmages like that tyrant, Hakham."

Hakham chuckled. "Don't forget to insult Razor. They loathe him over there."

"Now that will be fun," Levavi said.

Hakham twitched his ears back. "It won't be fun. If the Wild Ones

MANY HAPPY RETURNS

suspect you, they'll kill you both. And then I shall have to tell your daughters. That is not a task I want."

"Well, that's a cheerful thought," Aryeh said. "Hakham, if there's nothing more to be said, it's time for Levavi and Aryeh to disappear. Call us Lev and Ari from now on. We're leaving our old names behind."

"Lev and Ari, then. Your scents must be left behind as well," Hakham said, whiskers twitching. "Especially after this meeting. The Wild Ones can't know you've been around me recently."

"But we haven't touched you," Lev said.

"We still don't dare chance that my scent is on either of you. The risk is too high."

"The things I do for my people," Lev said, his Magelight flashing.

"What did you just do?" Ari asked as they heard the sounds of a creature coming toward them through the wood. A skunk emerged from between two trees and he and Hakham backed away from it. "Did you just call a skunk?" he asked incredulously. "Lev, are you insane?"

"I'm taking care of our scents. Nothing from the Compound could possibly survive—"

"You idiot! We don't need skunk spray! All we have to do is roll in mud to remove the scents of home!"

"Oh," Lev said, chagrined.

"I'll take care of it," Hakham said, trying hard not to laugh. His Magelight flashed and the skunk turned and disappeared into the woods. He gazed at Lev.

"Well," Lev said, "now you know why I became a Seeker. Zahavin got the brains in the family."

Hakham gave up trying to hold in his laughter. He and Ari roared as Ari swatted his son affectionately.

"Indeed she did, boy. But we've got a use for you yet. Let's be off to the stream to rid ourselves of the scent of civilized Catmages, and any possible remnants of Hakham." Ari turned to the ancient Catmage and blinked at him. "We're ready."

9

CHAPTER ONE

"Have you any questions before you go?" Hakham asked.

"No. We know what we need to do. We've rehearsed our story. The last time we saw Razor he got impatient and told us to get on with it or he'd give us a few scars to take with us to impress the Wild Ones. Don't worry, Hakham. We'll get a leg up on them for a change."

"May the One hear your words and bring them to pass. Take care of yourselves," Hakham said. "Send me a message when you can get away."

"We will. You *will* see us again, Hakham. Trust me on that. May the First bless both our paths in the days to come," Ari said. He and Lev turned and melted into the trees.

Hakham watched them go. The irony of meeting Lev and Ari in the Council Wood was not lost on him. But it felt right to begin the plan for the downfall of the Wild Ones in the place where Roah and his accomplices had murdered the Council. That was the other reason he'd chosen this wood. It was a form of defiance, a way to remove the disturbing feelings that came with being here. Hakham sighed as he thought of the friends he lost that day. Then he shook himself and headed for home. Now to concentrate on the next part of the plan. It was time to meet the current Council—time to take the lead into his own paws again. He set his path for the East Woods Compound. Yes, it was long past time to take control.

Goldeneyes lay on the edge of the meadow, paws tucked under her breast, watching the Teaching Rings. A pang of loss hit her as she realized it had been weeks since she'd seen Andy. There had been one furious meeting at his house a few days after the last battle with the Wild Ones. They'd ended up shouting at each other and Andy had flown off in a rage, slamming the door behind him. Goldeneyes vowed she'd not see him again until Andy came back and begged her forgiveness. Letsan had tried a few times to bring up the subject, dropping it quickly at her furious responses.

"I can't speak to you when you're so angry," he'd said before he left.

Goldeneyes was still annoyed at Letsan. Why shouldn't she be angry? Andy had a role to play that he had no right refusing. Razelle, the

MANY HAPPY RETURNS

Council Prophet, had brought herself back from the edge of death to utter the words that Andy would be the help they'd need to defeat the Darkness. Who ever heard of the subject of a prophecy quitting? No one. Because the ones who quit were not worthy, and the prophecies forgotten—as all failed prophecies should be. That thought frightened her the most. Andy, not worthy? She could barely stand to think it. Her ears flattened and her tail switched. She'd spent so much time training him. How could she have been so wrong about the boy?

"You were not wrong, Zahavin," Hakham said. She turned and saw her ancient teacher walking slowly toward her along the edge of the meadow. "Andrew is still a boy. He is lost right now. He needs help finding his way back."

"Let someone else lead him," she growled, rising as Hakham came near. "There is no excuse for his behavior. He is old enough to put aside sadness and move on."

"And he is young enough to be deeply hurt," Hakham said gently. "The young feel things differently than we do. Andy suffers each loss profoundly."

"We have all lost friends in this war!" she shouted.

"There's my girl," Letsan said cheerfully as he approached from across the meadow. "The Wild Ones' Compound might not have heard you, can you shout a little more loudly next time?"

"Oh, be still," she snapped. "I'm not in the mood for your jokes."

"I am," Hakham said, grateful for the interruption. "Have you any new ones for me?"

"As a matter of fact," Letsan said, "Mike told me a few the last time I saw him. What time is it when an elephant sits on your fence?"

"What's an elephant?" Hakham asked.

"I'm not sure. It's either a fat bird that people eat or it's some kind of large monster that could flatten a house. Oh, wait, it must be the last. Because the end of the riddle is 'Time to get a new fence.' That bird I'm thinking of is a chicken. I've had it, and it's delicious."

CHAPTER ONE

Hakham chuckled. Goldeneyes turned away, but they could both see Letsan's mood was affecting her for the better. "Have you seen Razor?" Hakham asked.

"My brother was watching Zohar train the new recruits when last I saw him."

"Tell him to meet me in my bayit when he's free. The two of you come as well. It is time to make our next move."

"Good," Letsan said. "We don't want to give the Wild Ones too much time to recover."

"It's not that kind of move. But you'll find out." He nodded and left.

"I'll get Razor and meet you at Hakham's," Letsan told Goldeneyes. "By the First's whiskers, it wouldn't hurt you to listen to a few jokes now and then." He left and Goldeneyes resumed her position on the ground, closing her eyes against the sunlight and tucking her paws beneath her chest. She'd rest for a few more minutes and then go to Hakham's. Perhaps this new mission would take her mind off Andy.

Kel trotted past the bayits in the West Woods Compound, tail arched high over his back, followed by his brothers and sister. "Hurry it up, you three. You know what happens when you disappoint me."

"No kidding," Dalet muttered.

Kel stopped, forcing his siblings to come to a halt. "What was that, sister dear?" he asked sweetly. "Did you have something to say to me? Or perhaps I should say, something you want me to report to Roah, or maybe to my friends Imri and Inbar?"

Dalet's heart pounded at the mention of Kel's large, angry guards. He was quick to set them on his siblings when they displeased him.

"Nothing," she said sourly. "I didn't say anything important."

"Of course you didn't," he said. "You never do. Now, get back in line and keep up!" he snarled. As she stood, his Magelight flashed and she screeched in pain. "And remember never to talk back to me again," Kel said.

MANY HAPPY RETURNS

His brothers glared at him, but that was all they ever dared nowadays. Things had changed a lot for young Kel since he had infiltrated the Catmages and helped in the spring battle. His father, Roah, included Kel in most meetings and made it plain that he was a favored son. Alef, his siblings' sire, could do nothing more than seethe privately as he watched Kel elevated above his own kittens.

Alef didn't dare try to stop him from treating his sister and brothers the way they'd treated him for two cycles. Everyone knew you crossed Roah and Niflah, the leaders of the Wild Ones, at your peril. Well, Roah, anyway. Niflah was soft. Kel had the feeling that Niflah might not be in favor much longer, but that was one of the pieces of information he would keep to himself until needed. Information, he had found, can be as powerful as a Magelight. And Kel thrived on it. He had made friends with the Wild Ones he singled out as the smartest and most well-informed and flattered the duller ones until they adored him. Kel's network was starting to show dividends already. For instance, not many knew how out of favor Niflah was becoming, but Kel had divined it from a story here, a few words there. Yes, information was a powerful tool, especially to those who could interpret it correctly. On the other hand, a Magelight also had its uses. It could cut flesh and bone, as his siblings could attest.

Kel turned and trotted down the path, not bothering to see if they followed. He knew they would. And they knew what would happen if they went against his wishes. Yes, events had definitely turned in his favor. His tail arched high, Kel quickened his pace. There were important things going on, and now he was in the thick of it.

TWO: RAZOR'S EDGE

Hakham sat on his haunches in his bayit before the East Woods Council. In addition to the elders, two of Razor's captains were present. Katana, a grey and white female, sat silently next to Zohar, Letsan's son who had lost his right front leg in battle with the Wild Ones. Ranged in a semicircle around Hakham were Letsan, Razor, Goldeneyes, Silsula, and Zehira.

"I am going back to the Council to ask them to restore Razor as head of the Shomrim," Hakham said. "The void left by Matanya's death must be filled."

Letsan laughed. "What makes you think that Kharoom will do as you wish?"

Hakham's eyes flashed and he flattened his ears. "What makes you think he will not? Do you doubt my abilities, Letsan?"

"No sir," Letsan replied. "But I know Flathead. He is stubborn and unwilling to admit mistakes."

"I know Kharoom, too. I have known his type since long before you were born. And I also know what I am capable of. Zahavin and I will be leaving for the Council Compound at dawn."

"What about me, sir?" Letsan asked.

"You are unable to control yourself around Kharoom. I can't afford to alienate any of his allies on the Council. You will stay here. And I will not brook any arguments," Hakham said, eyes glinting. Letsan lowered his head and blinked at him.

"Katana is in charge in my absence," Razor said. "Zohar will assist her. It's about time he took on more responsibility." Razor swished his tail at Zohar, who remained still as stone.

"I hesitate to bring this up, but has anyone spoken to Andy lately?" Zehira said. "It's been ages since I last saw him."

Hakham glanced at Goldeneyes, who looked away and shifted uncomfortably.

"I was with him not long ago," Letsan said. "He hasn't changed his mind."

"We're wasting time discussing Andrew. He's not coming back," Goldeneyes said angrily. "He has left us for good. You heard what he said."

"We heard him, sister," Silsula said gently, "but we're waiting for him to heal and return to us."

"Heal from what?" she asked. "That little cut he got from Taylor? It's gone. There's nothing wrong with him!"

"Some wounds are not of the body," Silsula said. "Zahavin, Andy is still a boy. Matanya's death, and the death of so many other Catmages, hit him hard."

"And we feel their deaths less?" Goldeneyes said. "You and I, and Zohar here, mourn our friends and we fight on."

"Zahavin, we are all grown. If Andy were a Catmage, he'd still be in the Teaching Rings. Don't forget he lost his father when he was quite young," Letsan said. "By the First's whiskers, he still blames himself for Nafshi's death!"

"I lost Nafshi, too. My mother died when I was a kitten." Goldeneyes said coldly. "You were there, Letsan." He lowered his eyes as she glared at him. "Yet here I am, working as hard as ever to defeat the enemy. Andrew is not. Don't speak to me about loss, Letsan. You saw my mother waste away to nothing." Her tone grew steely. "I overcame my grief. Andy

CHAPTER TWO

must, too." She looked away from the sympathy in Letsan's eyes.

"You do not have a monopoly on grief, sister," Silsula reminded her. "I lost our mother, too." She glowered at Goldeneyes. "You are too hard on Andy."

"This is pointless," Razor said. "I am tired of hearing this from you, Zahavin. Argue on your own time. Andy will come back when he comes back. Subject closed. Is there anything else, Hakham?"

"No. Zehira will be in charge while I am gone. Zahavin, Razor, Letsan, remain behind. The rest of you, may the First guide your paths."

Hakham waited until the others had left and turned to Goldeneyes. "They're right. You *are* too hard on the boy. And you seem to forget that the prophecy states we will not succeed without Andy's help."

"It said we will not succeed without a Son of Aaron. There are other sons of Aaron in the world."

"*The* Son of Aaron," Hakham said. "Razelle's prophecy was quite specific. *By his aura you will know him,* she said. There are no others like Andy. He has a Catmage's aura. He wields Nafshi's Magelight now like he was born to it. He is a student at the Evil One's school. Any one of these can be called coincidence, but all of them together are the hand of fate."

Goldeneyes' tail switched. "It has been almost two moons, and still he stays away. We must go on without him, Son of Aaron or no Son of Aaron."

"For the present," Hakham said.

"He'll be back," Razor said.

"I think so, too," said Hakham, "but I am surprised at your patience in this matter, Razor."

Razor looked at the old tabby and twitched his tattered ears. "Like you said, he's a boy. He needs time. Andy will come back. And if he doesn't, I'll go get him myself. We all have work to do."

"Indeed we do, my friend," Hakham said. "Let us tend to it." He led the way out of the bayit. Letsan held back for a moment, thinking.

"He'll come back when he comes back," he repeated to himself.

RAZOR'S EDGE

"But maybe we can hasten that along." He hurried after them, his mind now on other things.

The following morning Letsan joined the three of them as they traveled down the path that led out of the Compound. Four of Razor's Shomrim ranged ahead and behind, eyes and ears alert for anything.

"I told you to stay here, Letsan," Hakham said.

"I know. I'm going to town to see how Andy is doing so I thought I'd see you on your way for a bit."

"Ah," Hakham said. They both glanced at Goldeneyes, who marched a few feet ahead of them. If she heard, she showed no sign. "That's a good idea," Hakham told Letsan privately. "Stay with the boy as much as he will allow. Make him homesick for us."

"Now *that* I can do." When they reached the road, they separated. "Send Kharoom my love," Letsan said as he headed toward Coreyton. "Or throw a rock at him. Whichever is easiest."

"Watch your back, brother. The Wild Ones are still in town as well as in the woods."

"Watch your tail, Razor," Letsan said. "If you lose it, however will you balance that great ugly head of yours?" He laughed as Razor sent a light jet flashing into the ground near his paws and trotted away.

"You're wasting energy," Goldeneyes said. "We have a long journey ahead of us."

"And it will seem even longer if she's in this mood the entire journey," Razor sent privately to Hakham, who held back a laugh. "Did you meet with them?" Razor asked privately.

"Yes. All is well. They joined the Wild Ones two nights ago. I had one brief message from Ary—Ari early this morning."

"What did he say?"

"Just two words: *It's done.*"

Razor grunted. "Good." He looked toward Goldeneyes. "Will you tell her?"

CHAPTER TWO

"No. Nobody but you and I know that Ari and Lev are here."

"Let's keep it that way. Their lives depend on secrecy."

"Yes. And ours depend on my persuading the Council that it is time to throw off the rule of the incompetent."

"You won't succeed, old one. Kharoom has had a full cycle to tell the world you're a washed up old Catmage who hasn't been able to do anything about the Evil One."

"Thank you for the compliment," Hakham replied drily.

"I am only saying what my spies have reported. You know I'm on your side, always."

"I do, my friend. And we shall see about getting my reputation back. I think I've had quite enough from this young, ignorant upstart."

"Good. Because if you don't take care of him, I will."

"Razor, I forbade your brother from coming for that very reason."

"No, you told him not to come because he can't control himself around Kharoom. I can. And I can also tell Kharoom he's an idiot in front of the entire Compound without distracting from the issues at hand."

Hakham laughed, remembering that Razor did exactly that the last time he stood in front of the Council. "I see your point. Oh, this is going to be a meeting to remember."

They caught up with Goldeneyes and set a steady pace for the Council Compound. Razor's Shomrim arrayed themselves around them, ears twitching as they scanned the trees.

Hakham and his companions reached the Compound without any trouble and made their way to the central meadow in the late afternoon. They greeted friends as they moved among Catmages sunning or grooming themselves in the grass. The Teaching Rings had finished for the day, as evidenced by the number of kittens romping around the meadow.

A young British shorthair, his fur so grey he was almost blue, caught sight of them and left a group of adolescent Catmages playing. "Razor is back! Razor, is there news? Will you be staying long?" he shouted, running up to the battered Maine Coon. For a moment it was almost like seeing Matanya alive again.

"You're Tzuri?" Razor said.

"Yes! How did you know?"

"You look just like your father," Razor said. "Go tell your mother we're here. Quietly, now, don't broadcast it to the world."

"Yes sir!" Tzuri ran off.

Razor's attempt at privacy was a wasted effort. A crowd gathered quickly, many Catmages shouting questions at Razor and Hakham. Soon they were surrounded by dozens of them wanting to know how things were going in the East Woods since Matanya's death.

"I shall be happy to tell you all the news I have," Hakham told them. "Send word to gather in the north end of the meadow. We'll be there shortly."

Word flew from mind to mind. Razor laughed as in no time at all the north end of the meadow was filled with Catmages young and old, and more were streaming in. "Was this your plan, Hakham? To address the entire Compound?"

"As a matter of fact, it's turned out better than I'd hoped," Hakham replied. "I wanted a public meeting, and wasn't quite sure how to go about forcing Kharoom's hand. It looks like I underestimated the concern of our average Catmage. Matanya was well loved. His death hit this Compound hard." He paused as he thought of the captain of the Shomrim killed in the last battle with the Wild Ones.

"He was one of our best," Razor said. "Another death we owe Roah."

"I promise you, Razor, he and my brother will pay for every last one of them!" Hakham's ears flattened and his voice sharpened. Some of the Catmages heading for the north end of the meadow paused to look back. Hakham, aware that he was being observed, calmed himself. He raised his ears and stopped his twitching tail. "That's a subject for another day. Today, I need you to go find our friends on the Council and send them to the meadow. Organize the crowd as you would for a Council meeting.

CHAPTER TWO

I'm going to let Kharoom know we're here."

Hakham watched him leave, then trotted toward the largest bayit in the Compound. It stood a little away from the others. A large calico cat sat at guard in front of the door.

"Greetings, Hakham," she said. "Tzuri just left. You look well."

"Ufara," Hakham said pleasantly. "I gather Kharoom is within?"

"He is asleep and may not be disturbed." Her eyes glinted with mischief.

Hakham laughed. "Don't worry, you won't disturb him," he said. "I, on the other hand, suffer from no such restriction. Kharoom!" he bellowed, "I would speak with you. Awake!"

From inside the bayit came a dull, heavy voice. "Eh? What? Who is it?"

Hakham moved past Ufara into the bayit. "It is I, Kharoom," he said. "Get up. There is work to be done."

Kharoom stood and yawned. He slowly stretched his ponderous body. He was fatter than ever, Hakham noted with distaste. Ruma rose next to him, also stretching, watching Hakham steadily.

"I see your manners have not improved since we last met," Kharoom grumbled. "You are no longer on the Council, Hakham. I do not take orders from you." He glared at Ufara. "Why did you let Hakham in?"

"Sorry, sir, but he didn't listen when I told him not to disturb you."

"So you just let him in?"

"He pushed past me, sir." She could barely hide the amusement in her voice. "He *was* a Council member, sir. Protocol dictates—"

"To Sheol with protocol!" Kharoom said. "You are *my* guard, and it is your duty to follow my orders."

"You may sit here debating protocol," Hakham said. "Or you can join me. I'm sure you didn't want to sleep through a Compound gathering. Come to the meadow with everyone else and hear what news I brought. I hear there is quite a crowd already."

Ruma glanced sharply at Hakham. "What do you mean, join you?"

she said. "What are they doing in the meadow? Ufara? Do you know what he's talking about?"

"No, Ruma. I've been at my post all afternoon."

"A meeting is taking place, or there will be as soon as I get there," Hakham said pleasantly. "The members of the Council Compound seem eager for news from the East Woods. You should attend. But if you prefer to stay here and rest, don't worry. We will go on without you."

"What?" Kharoom spluttered with anger. "*I* call the meetings at this Compound. *I* am the head of the Council!" he thundered. "No Council meeting will take place without me!"

Ruma glanced from her mate to Hakham. Then she moved closer to Kharoom and rubbed her cheek against his.

"It won't hurt to see what he wants, dear," Ruma said in soothing tones. "Let us go to the meadow." She licked her mate's ear.

"Very well," Kharoom said. "But make it quick. I don't have much time these days."

"Yes," Hakham said, watching Kharoom stretch again, "it's obvious you lead quite a busy life."

Kharoom's ears flattened at the sarcasm. Hakham ignored him and left the bayit without looking back. His voice echoed in both their heads.

"I'd hurry if I were you. The meadow is getting quite full. You may not find a spot to sit." Chuckling, he hastened through the gathering Catmages. When he glanced back Hakham saw Ufara parting the crowd for Ruma and Kharoom waddling a short distance behind.

As he neared the edge of the meadow, he was pleased to see the rest of the Council sitting in a semicircle at the north end. Razor and Goldeneyes sat in front of the Council facing the crowd. They greeted him cheerfully.

"Looks like everyone wants to know what you're doing here," Razor said. "I think they miss you." He blinked at the old tabby, who took his place between the two of them. Catmages in the crowd peppered them with questions.

"Be patient, my friends," Hakham broadcast to all. "The meeting will begin soon."

CHAPTER TWO

Many in the crowd muttered as Kharoom and Ruma made their way to the front. They looked none too pleased and shoved past Hakham, taking their places at the center of the Council semicircle.

"I call the Council meetings here," Kharoom growled. "What is the meaning of this? Who authorized this gathering?"

"Well, it was rather spontaneous," Hakham said. "I was approached by many asking for news of what happened in the East Woods this past cycle. In fact, so many Catmages wanted information that I thought it would be easier to tell them all at once, like we used to do at Council meetings. Surely you still use your meetings to inform the community of current events," Hakham said, knowing that was not the case. His spies had told him that in the past cycle, Kharoom had held only one public meeting—to announce Matanya's death.

"What important news could you possibly have since we sent the last message?" Kharoom asked. "I was told you have done nothing since. We know you failed—again—to retrieve the Tilyon. We know that Matanya was killed in the last battle. Have you come back to apologize for your failures?"

"No, Kharoom, for yours," Hakham said. The crowd, which had quieted as Kharoom spoke, began to murmur. "Your actions since I left the Council have done little good, and indeed, some have caused us harm!"

"How dare you!" Kharoom shouted. "You and Razor are the ones who allowed Matanya to be killed in battle last spring!"

"Just so, Kharoom," Ruma purred. "Hakham and Razor did everything they could to inhibit Matanya's attempt to regain control of the East Woods Shomrim. It was their hindrance that caused our losses, not your leadership."

"Must I point out to you that every Compound is independent of every other? Razor had the right to keep the Shomrim he recruited to fight our common enemy!" Hakham responded. "Matanya interfered with *our* battle preparation at your bidding! But he saw his mistake and joined us long before he died. Matanya secretly transferred leadership of the Shomrim back to Razor after the fiasco of the Halloween battle."

RAZOR'S EDGE

"You lie!" Kharoom said.

"No he doesn't," Razor said gruffly. "Give the word and I'll transmit the image of that meeting to everyone here."

Ruma and Kharoom were momentarily silent. Every Catmage knew that Magelights can only show scenes that have actually occurred. The crowd would see Razor could not be lying.

"Oh, nicely done," Goldeneyes whispered to Razor.

"What is it you want, Hakham?" Ruma asked, her voice dripping with sweetness.

"Restore Razor as Captain of the Shomrim."

Cries of assent came from all over the meadow. Even some on the Council were agreeing.

"No," Kharoom said. "Ufara is acting Captain. We planned to promote her at the next Council meeting. What say you, Council? Shall we promote her now?"

"Just a minute, Kharoom," Razor said. "Maybe we should ask Ufara what she wants first."

"Nonsense," Kharoom said. "No Catmage would turn down such an honor."

"Then you won't mind asking her."

Kharoom looked puzzled. "Of course not. Well, Ufara?"

All eyes turned to Ufara. She looked over the crowd, her gaze lingering on Tzuri, her eldest son with Matanya, who sat behind Razor, flanked by his brother and sister.

"I thank you for the honor, but I must refuse," she said. There were scattered cheers and gasps from the crowd. "I have no wish to command the Shomrim. I wish to remain here with my kittens. They never had the chance to meet their father. I won't risk them losing their mother as well."

Many in the crowd murmured in sympathy.

"You expected this," Goldeneyes said privately to Razor. "You're not surprised at all."

"My messengers have been busy these last two moons. Now we see

CHAPTER TWO

if all our hard work pays off." Razor glanced over at Tzuri, blinking. "Matti would approve."

Goldeneyes couldn't bring herself to look at Tzuri for long. The resemblance to his father made it too painful as the scene played out in her mind of Matanya sacrificing his own life for hers. "I'm sorry," she whispered, her head drooping.

"Don't be," Razor said gently. "I would have done the same if I'd been next to you. So would Ufara."

Ufara twitched her ears and blinked at them. Goldeneyes sat up straight, blinking back at Ufara.

When the crowd quieted, Kharoom was still sputtering at Ufara's refusal. He looked helplessly at Ruma.

"I empathize with your reasons for refusing," she said loudly enough for the crowd to hear. "But Ufara, dear, sometimes our duty to our society comes before our duty to our kits."

"Sometimes it does," she agreed. "Nevertheless, I will not accept the position."

"Since Ufara has refused you twice," Hakham said, "I ask once again that you restore Razor to the position of Captain. He served ably in the East Woods. Matanya himself yielded to Razor's superior abilities and transferred command to him. With all due respect Kharoom, you and Ruma do not constitute a majority. I ask the Council to consider Razor."

The crowd in the meadow concurred. There were many shouts of approval and some started chanting Razor's name.

Ruma stepped forward and waited for silence. "This is too great a matter to be entered into lightly. We must discuss it, set a date to vote, and move forward with Council business as our customs dictate—not drop everything and do as Hakham commands."

"I do not command, Ruma, I merely suggest."

"You are no longer a member of this Council!" Kharoom cried.

"But I am," Adin said, "and I say the Council should ask Razor to return as head of the Shomrim."

RAZOR'S EDGE

"And I!" said Levana. "Let us vote on it now!" She was echoed by many of the other Councilors. Hakham noted with pleasure that even some of Kharoom's faction were calling for a vote.

"Very well," Kharoom said sourly. "We shall discuss whether or not we should bring back Razor as Captain, or find another candidate in the ranks of our Shomrim."

"May I speak first, Kharoom?" Ruma asked sweetly.

Hakham and Razor exchanged quick glances. Nothing good would come of this, but they knew no way to prevent her from talking.

"Let her do her worst," Razor sent privately. "She's nearly as big a blowhard as Flathead. I can handle her."

Hakham blinked at him.

"My fellow Councilors, Catmages, and visitors to this Compound," she said, looking at Razor as she spoke the last phrase. "I would urge you to remember that Razor quit his post after refusing an order from the Council last summer."

"I would remind the Council that it was an illegal order," Hakham responded. "They wanted Razor to take Nafshi's Magelight away from the Son of Aaron. They had no basis under the Laws to do so. Further, you all know of Razelle's prophecy. We will not defeat the Evil One without the Son of Aaron's help."

There was much murmuring from the listening Catmages. The prophecy was now well known throughout all the Compounds. Hakham's allies on the Council had made sure the real story of Razor's resignation got out, not the distorted one that Ruma and Kharoom tried to pass along as truth.

"Andrew has been a great help in our battle against the Wild Ones," Hakham continued. "He saved many of our Shomrim on more than one occasion."

"Yet you have not recovered the Tilyon, nor the stolen Council Magelights," Ruma countered. "I understand you had the Evil One's apprentice out cold on the ground during the last battle, and not one of Ra-

CHAPTER TWO

zor's Shomrim thought to grab the necklace from him. This is the Catmage you want back as Captain?"

Hakham looked sharply at Ruma. She seemed to know an awful lot about the battle. He knew Razor hadn't given her much information. Who had been talking to Kharoom and Ruma? There was a spy in their midst. He made a note to discuss this with Razor at the earliest opportunity.

"We were in the middle of a battle," Razor said. "You've never been in one, have you? Or you, Kharoom?" He paused to let that sink in to the listening Catmages. "It's easy from the safety of the Council Compound to say what you would have done in our place. It's harder to be on the ground, ducking Magelight attacks and charging dogs as your comrades are falling all around you. 'Grab the necklace,' you say? How? The boy was at the gate with Andy. The rest of us were inside the yard and the house, fighting the enemy. Although if you'd like to direct the next battle yourself, Kharoom, it would be my pleasure to escort you to the Evil One's lair."

"My place is here, directing the Council," Kharoom mumbled. The shot had obviously hit home.

"You are a warrior, Razor, and you have failed—again—to bring back so much as a single Council Magelight."

"That's because we destroyed the one we recovered," Razor said. "We killed the dog that was wearing it and brought the Magelight to the East Woods to identify it before we smashed it."

There were gasps from the crowd. "Dogs! Dogs with Magelights?" someone shouted. "How can this be?"

"Yes, how can this be?" Ruma echoed. "We've had no report of this!"

"We did not want to risk this information getting out until we could present it in person," Hakham said. "Although we hadn't intended on presenting it in so public a fashion," he said, glancing at Razor, "but our fellow Catmages have the right to know. During the last battle, a young Catmage known as Patches sensed an aura coming from one of the dog collars. Upon examination, it was proven to be a Council Magelight. Now we know why the dogs were acting so strangely. It wasn't only that they were being

RAZOR'S EDGE

directed by the Wild Ones. Roah and my brother have done something to them—something that makes them far smarter than any normal dog."

"Another failure by Razor and his Shomrim!" Kharoom shouted. "And you want us to reinstate him? Why, so he can miss even more and put us all in danger? You didn't even know your own brother was a traitor. Why should we accept your recommendation of Razor?"

Kharoom's points scored with some of the crowd. There were worried whispers and grumbling. The tip of Ruma's tail twitched toward her mate. Razor looked around the meadow and at the Council. He stepped forward and faced the crowd until it quieted.

"My turn to talk," Razor said. "Yes, I quit last year, because I was given an order no decent Shomrim would carry out. And yes, we've seen defeat after defeat. The Wild Ones are strong. They've been recruiting heavily and finding many Catmages who are unhappy with the way things are run. They're being fed lies by Roah and Niflah. Even some Catmages here found something they liked in those lies. Who's missing from this Compound? You know which of your companions have gone. Did you try to stop them? Or did you just let them go to join the enemy in this battle?"

Many in the crowd looked around uneasily.

"That's not our way and you know it, Razor," said a large black cat with white socks. "No Catmage tells another what to do. We are free to come and go as we please."

"I know that, Ronit, and I'm not blaming anyone. I'm trying to tell you that nothing is easy. Or simple. I know what Roah and his allies want to accomplish. I've been working to defeat them for three cycles of the sun. This isn't about ego, or finding fault or blame! I want to be Captain for only one reason: I want the authority to raise an army of Catmages to counter the army of Wild Ones. I don't give half a whisker about what makes Kharoom happy. By the First's Pendant, Matti died trying to stop the Wild Ones! He died saving Zahavin! Give me back my office and I'll avenge him. Give me back my office and help me! Ronit, come to the East Woods with us, and bring your friends. My Shomrim could use a few more

CHAPTER TWO

good warriors. Roah's not going to win. I'll keep going after him and after him until he's dead. And if I have to die in this fight, I'm taking him with me, I promise you that! Now. Who will stand with us?"

The crowd roared. "Razor! Razor! Razor!" The chant went on for a while. Adin stepped forward.

"Call the vote, Kharoom. We have heard enough."

Kharoom glared at him. "All those in favor of Razor as Captain, step forward."

Adin, Levana, and Sharonit—all members of Hakham's faction—stepped forward, followed by Benzi, Tigra, and Dar. For a moment, every Catmage who could count tried to work out if Hakham or Kharoom had won. Kharoom glared at Hakham, all but gloating. Seven Councilors were on his side. Hakham had lost!

Then Yeshana, the ancient calico who had been chosen to replace Hakham, stepped forward.

"Nothing went right without Razor," she said. "I want him back."

Before Kharoom could react, and to the surprise of many, Keres and Talma came forward as well.

"Razor is a great captain," Talma said. "We need someone like him in the fight ahead."

Nimrah, a short-haired black-and-white female, looked from group to group. "They are right. We need Razor." She stepped forward, followed by her son Naftali. Now only Kharoom and Ruma remained. Eleven Councilors stood with Hakham.

Kharoom spluttered incoherently. Ruma rubbed her shoulder against his. "Very well," he said sourly. "Ruma and I agree. Razor is reinstated as our Captain. Unanimously."

"Way to save face at the last second," Razor sent privately to Goldeneyes, who laughed out loud. The noise from the crowd covered her laughter. Once more a chant arose, and soon everyone was shouting "Razor! Razor!"

Razor moved to the front and faced the crowd, waiting until they quieted.

RAZOR'S EDGE

"Thanks," he said. "Here's the rest of my speech: Everyone get out of here while I meet with my Shomrim."

Peals of laughter followed his remarks as the crowd began to break up. Hakham nudged Goldeneyes. Razor and Tzuri were deep in conversation as his sister Usheret, a calico like Ufara, and his brother Eitan, a lighter grey Russian Blue, listened. When Ufara approached, Razor tapped Tzuri with his tail. "Find me later tonight, when I have time. I'll tell you stories about Matti until your ears fall off. Bring your sister and brother. Now your mother and I have work to do. Get!"

The kittens ran off, Tzuri in the lead.

Hakham watched Ruma and Kharoom as they headed back to their bayit. Ruma looked back over her shoulder as she passed, her look long and thoughtful.

"That's one to watch out for," Razor said. "I've never liked her."

"I've never liked either of them," Hakham responded.

Soon only a handful of Catmages remained in the meadow. Ronit and a few others approached Razor hesitantly. "You have something to say?" Razor asked.

"We want to help," Ronit said.

"Excellent. New recruits." He nodded to one of his Shomrim. "Take them aside and tell them what being one of my fighters will entail. If they still want to enlist after that, we meet at the meadow tomorrow at dawn." The warrior blinked and led the others away. Now only a young, all-black female remained.

"Hatzot, isn't it? Your grandmother was Razelle?" Hakham asked.

"Yes, Councilor," she said shyly.

"I am no longer on the Council," he said.

Hatzot's eyes darkened as her pupils widened. Her voice deepened and grew strong, echoing in their heads.

"You will be on the Council once more, Hakham, and lead us to the resolution of this war. But you must beware the two-headed serpent."

"What? Hakham, is she prophesying?" Goldeneyes asked.

CHAPTER TWO

"Hush!" he said. "Hatzot, what do you mean?"

Hatzot's all-black eyes gazed past the three of them, looking to something none of the rest could see.

"The Son of Aaron is in danger from the one who came before. You must restore the balance, or he will fall."

Hatzot blinked, and her eyes returned to normal. "What—what did I just do?" she asked, breathing hard.

"It appears you have just made your first prophecy," Hakham said. "Hatzot, you have inherited your grandmother's special ability."

"I did?" She seemed confused. "That's never happened before. Did—will what I said help?" she asked.

"It will if we can figure out what it means," Razor said. "Of course it was too much to ask that you speak plain Catmage."

"I'm sorry, Razor," she said softly, blinking.

"Don't be, young one. I'm just teasing."

"Hatzot, your grandmother would be very proud. It is good to see the talent being passed to another generation," Hakham said. "Now, if you will excuse us?"

She nodded and left.

"Hakham, Andy is in danger!" Goldeneyes said. "But from what?"

"I have no idea who 'the one who came before' can be. But we've a long walk home and now we'll have something to talk about."

"We're leaving now?" she asked.

"Tomorrow. I have a few more things to do. And I believe Razor has as well."

"Yes," he said. "I'm going to stay here for a while to set things up. I don't trust Kharoom not to work against us in my absence."

"He can try, but you heard our people. They're scared. They want you, not Kharoom. Don't spend too much time worrying."

Razor laughed. "I always worry about being stabbed in the back. It's what's kept me alive all these years. I'll see you later."

He trotted off to meet Ufara.

RAZOR'S EDGE

"But Hakham, we must help Andy!" Goldeneyes said.

"What, Zahavin? Not so angry with him anymore?" he asked.

"Of course I am, but not so much that I want him to be hurt!"

Hakham rubbed his shoulder against hers. "Don't worry, Zahavin. We'll work out what Hatzot's words mean. We'll take care of Andy. In the meantime, I have a private meeting to attend. I will find you later."

Goldeneyes blinked at him and made her way back through the crowds. She found Ufara watching her three kittens as they played with their friends. She sat down next to her.

"They're not babies anymore," Ufara said. "And Tzuri—he looks so much like—"

"Matti," Goldeneyes said. "Yes, he looks very much like him." Goldeneyes turned her gaze to Ufara. "I owe you a debt I can never repay. Matti gave his life for mine."

Ufara gazed at Goldeneyes. "He gave it willingly. Zahavin."

"Still, I must pay my debt," Goldeneyes said. "Tell me what I can do for you. Shall I teach your kittens as Nafshi taught me? How are they doing in the Rings?"

"Oh, they're all doing well. But Tzuri—all he wants is to follow in his father's footsteps. He wants to be in the Shomrim."

"He's too young."

"Razor told him he needs to get through all the Teaching Rings before he can even think of joining. He listens to Razor, thankfully."

"When this is over, then, if your other children wish it, I will teach them myself."

"I think Usheret would like that. She's advancing quickly. Nafshi's is not the only line of strong females in this Compound."

Goldeneyes blinked at Ufara. "Your reputation has spread among many Compounds. Ufara Unyielding, they call you. The one who never gives up."

Ufara dipped her head at the praise. "You don't give up easily, either. Go. Fight. Win this battle for all of us. And for Matti." Goldeneyes brushed her shoulder against Ufara's and turned away to find Hakham.

THREE: THE OTHER SIDE OF THE STORY

Ari and Lev paused as they neared the West Woods Compound. Their Magelights glowed and faded as they scanned the woods before them. "How many do you sense?" Ari said to Lev.

"Six in front. There are two more heading straight toward us from the Compound. Do you want me to count the ones along the border?"

"No need. I found them, too. Are you ready?"

"Yes."

"Let me do most of the talking. And remember, the less said, the better. They can't catch us in a lie if we're not speaking."

"If I wanted a life of talk-talk, I wouldn't have become a Seeker," Lev said. "Besides, this gives me a chance to do my Razor impression and be tough and silent."

"Just as long as it doesn't extend to imitating his habit of accruing scars. I like your face the way it is." Ari bumped shoulders with his son. "Be careful to speak to me privately from now on. We're not out on the road where it doesn't matter who can hear us. Guard your words, and speak only when necessary. Clear?"

"Clear," Lev said.

"Let's do this."

THE OTHER SIDE OF THE STORY

Ari steeled himself and headed straight for the guard post, Lev walking beside him. They immediately found themselves facing a troop of Wild Ones, fur fluffed and ears laid back.

"Who are you?" the biggest one, a black cat, asked, glaring at them.

"Which one of you is Kfir?" Ari asked. The Wild Ones parted, and a short-haired, cream-colored tabby strode forward, sides heaving with the effort of having run from the dwellings and looking none too pleased at the intruders.

"I am. Who's asking?"

"I'm Ari. This is Lev. Hed said you wanted Seekers. He sent us."

"We do need Seekers," Kfir said, "but I don't know you. How do I know you're not a spy for Razor?"

Ari let out a short bark of laughter. "Razor? Do I look like a fighter to you? Kfir, I've been up and down as many regions as the toes on two Catmage's paws, looking for half-breeds since I was old enough to hightail it out of the Compound. My son here joined me as soon as he could escape those ridiculous Teaching Rings. You know what you don't get when you're a Seeker?"

"What?"

"Killed in battle. We have no interest in fighting. All we want is to travel, meet new females, and find kittens who need to be brought up as Catmages. Hed told us you had no Seekers. We don't want to get involved in your problems. We want to find half-breeds."

Kfir studied the two of them for a minute. He was clearly discussing them with the small tuxedo cat who stood near. The tuxedo turned his attention to the newcomers and spoke.

"My name is Kel. Before we go any further, perhaps you can show us your abilities?"

"How?"

"There is a guard post on either side of us. Tell me how many warriors are nearby."

"I'll take the north. You take the south," Ari broadcast to Lev and

CHAPTER THREE

the Wild Ones. Their Magelights glowed. "You first, boy."

"Four."

"Same here. And how many in the next one?"

"Another four. There are only three in the farthest guard post, but I sense an aura not far away. Perhaps one of your guards is taking a bathroom break."

"There are four more in two more guard posts spread along the road. We could tell you how many Catmages you have in the Compound, but we can't count that high."

"Impressive," Kfir said. "And you're hardly even winded."

"We're Seekers," Lev said scornfully. Kel shot him an unfriendly look.

"Hed told you about us?" he asked Ari.

"Yes. Why don't you call him here instead of giving us tests? He'll vouch for us."

"We can't," Kfir said grimly. "He was killed in battle this spring."

"What?" Ari swore. "Hed told me things might get a little dangerous, but he didn't say anything about having to fight!"

"He was a soldier. You are a Seeker."

"So was Velvel," Ari said. "We heard he died."

"Then you heard he was murdered by Razor and his friends," Kel said.

Ari swore again. "Murdered? No, we didn't hear that. How? Why?"

"Who knows? A fit of pique, or perhaps Velvel didn't do what Razor wanted. If you know Razor, you know he has a temper," Kfir said.

"He gave me this," Kel said, pointing to the scar on his ear. "Razor's an unpredictable bully." He laughed to himself as Ari and Lev looked shocked. Kel would never tell them that scar came from being bullied by his siblings.

"I was never friends with Razor. I saw him once or twice on my trips to the Compound with half-breeds. This news bothers me," Ari said. "Hed didn't tell me Seekers were at risk. Maybe this job isn't for us after all."

THE OTHER SIDE OF THE STORY

"It isn't because he was a Seeker. It's because he was with us."

"So you're saying we're at risk if we join you? That's not a reason to stay."

"All life is a risk," Kel said. "Do you not have to take care in your journeys around dogs and humans?"

"That's true," Lev said. "Ari, we're not going to be here very much. We'll be on the road, like we always are."

"This Compound will be safe when you are home," Kfir growled. "We haven't had a single security breach. Razor's too afraid to show his face here!" He laughed harshly, echoed by his soldiers.

"Not one?" Ari asked. "But their Compound is a short walk away. They've never bothered you?"

"No." Kfir couldn't hide the smugness in his voice.

Ari tilted his head. "That's a different story. Well, Lev?"

"I'm tired of the rules the Council and their followers keep trying to throw over us. That's why we became Seekers, isn't it? So we can be free? I say we throw in our lot with Kfir and the rest. Give Razor a little jab, hey?"

Kfir blinked at him.

"You'll have plenty of freedom from Council nonsense here," Kel said. "Roah and Niflah are setting up a whole new way of life for Catmages. Why do you think the Council is trying so hard to stop us? They don't *want* us to be free. They want us to do as we're told."

"I never liked being told what to do," Lev said. "Right. If you'll show us around the Compound, we can determine your needs and get started on filling them."

"That's the spirit!" Kel said. "Come with me. Kfir, thank you." Not waiting for a response, Kel headed for the Compound, followed by Ari and Lev. Lev glanced at his father.

Not now. The words echoed in Lev's head. Yes, he had been about to say something privately, and yes, his father was probably right that his control was not as good as it could be. Best he keep his thoughts to himself.

CHAPTER THREE

They hurried to catch up with Kel. Phase one had gone well. They would soon be a part of the West Woods Compound.

Kel led them on a tour of the place. Ari noted there were far fewer females than was usual at any Compound, and almost no kittens. The predominant Wild One was a disaffected young male. Time and again, he heard them griping about their old Compounds. They couldn't do this, they couldn't do that. *By the First,* he thought to himself, *what a bunch of kittens. Did none of them have decent parents or Nanagers?* He had met some young Catmages like this in his travels, but rarely. Or perhaps he just hadn't asked the right questions.

"So what do you think?" Kel asked them.

"It's a fine Compound. Why so few females?" Ari said.

"Our last Seeker spent too much time in the Compound and not enough finding us females," Kel said. "We hope to see that trend reversed with the two of you."

"Count on it," Lev said. "There's nothing like the open road."

Kel glanced up at the sky. "It's almost time for the Telunah meeting. Would you like to watch?"

"Why not?" Ari said. They followed him into the woods, where he stopped at a small clearing with a large boulder at one end. Kel jumped onto the rock and waited as the Wild Ones gathered around him.

"Who would like to go first?" he asked.

A small, grey and white cat stepped forward. "Tzvi," he said, "formerly of the Swift Creek Compound."

"Tell us your tale, Tzvi."

"I was in the Third Ring and my leader was teaching us the message spell. I couldn't get it right. I was the last one in the ring to do it. He made an example out of me and gave me extra lessons. I was humiliated!"

The others murmured sympathetically.

Ari glanced at Lev and shook his head slightly. Lev steeled himself and returned his gaze to the speaker.

"You see how it is!" Kel said. "If you do not keep up to their strict

THE OTHER SIDE OF THE STORY

standards, they belittle you! I'm sure Tzvi's fellow students were laughing at him behind his back. Whereas here, I personally sat with Tzvi until he could send out a perfect message globe. Would you like to show them?"

"I would!"

"Come on! Up here with me!"

Tzvi jumped onto the rock and turned to face the crowd. Kel moved against him, brushing shoulders. "We need a volunteer to run back to the bayits." A dozen Wild Ones leaped up. "You," Kel said to an orange tabby. He raced out of the clearing and down the path through the wood.

"Now," Kel said. Tzvi concentrated. His Magelight began to glow. So did Kel's.

"What's he doing?" Lev sent privately.

"Keep watching. Talk later," Ari sent back.

Soon a green message globe formed at Tzvi's throat. Kel and Tzvi's Magelights flared one more time, and the globe shot out directly in the path the orange tabby had taken. The watching Wild Ones cheered.

"Well done, Tzvi! And that's how we do things in the West Woods. We work together, help one another, and defend our way of life from those who would take it from us."

Cheers burst out even louder than before. Ari and Lev glanced at one another and then back to the crowd. The orange tabby came running back.

"Why yes, I am hungry. Let's go hunting!" he said to great laughter.

"In a bit," Kel said. "Does anyone else want to share?"

Ari and Lev sat silently as another half dozen Wild Ones stood to complain about minor brushes with Catmages in authority at various Compounds. Kel sympathized with each of them, magnifying their trivial complaints and stroking each disaffected Catmage's ego. The last one finally stopped griping and Kel declared the meeting over. Kel leapt from the rock to rejoin Ari and Lev.

"Well?" he asked eagerly. "What did you think?"

"I think I know exactly what you're looking for," Ari said, glancing

CHAPTER THREE

at his son. "Thank you for that lesson."

Kel beamed. "You're welcome. I'm glad my meeting could help you. I look forward to meeting the new Catmages you will bring back to us."

Ari blinked at him. "Now if you could show us to a bayit?" he said. "We've journeyed far and could use a rest."

"Of course, of course. This way."

They followed him to a spacious bayit, where he bid them goodbye. They curled up on the bed of leaves side by side.

"Not yet," Ari sent privately. "Tonight, after we leave this place."

Lev blinked at him and closed his eyes.

Roah crept through the house. He knew Saunders wasn't home. It was a school day, but Roah trusted nothing to chance. He had one of his most loyal guards keeping an eye on the school to make sure there were no surprise visits home. He had made sure there would be no other Wild Ones around. There were only the dogs, and Roah had timed his visit when he knew they'd be napping. As long as he made no noise, there would be no problem.

The office door was open, and the locked box that contained the Tilyon sat atop the desk. Roah jumped lightly onto the chair and gazed at the lock. He concentrated carefully. His Magelight glowed, and the dial on the lock spun slowly. Fifteen left. Taylor had taught him left from right when he taught him his numbers. Three right. Eleven left. *Click*. The lock was open. He used his Magelight again and the bar sprang free of the slots. Roah eased the box open. There it was. The Tilyon. He half-closed his eyes and used his Magelight to lift it out of the box and onto the desk. Roah stepped softly onto the desk and placed his paw on the Tilyon. Its power flowed through him, a warmth reaching into every part of his body. He breathed deeply and forced himself to concentrate on the task at hand. As the Tilyon pulsed, the dark silhouette of a Catmage formed in his mind.

"I am here," he sent. "What news?"

THE OTHER SIDE OF THE STORY

"Nothing good."

The shadowy figure he could see in his mind's eye spoke sourly, informing Roah of the events at the Council Compound.

"It is a setback, but not a great one," Roah said. "One defeat is all it will take to remove Razor and put someone more favorable to us in charge."

"Ufara refused. She refused me!" the voice shouted.

"It is no matter. Kfir has proven time and again that he is a match for Razor. Is there anything else?"

"No."

"Then I must leave. We need to keep these messages short. I will contact you again when I get the chance."

Roah removed his paw from the Tilyon. He felt chilled and empty. He didn't want to put it back, but he dared not act before the time was right. He placed the Tilyon in its box, used his Magelight to fasten the lock and spin the dial away from its last number. He leaped carefully from the desk to the chair, then as softly as he could to the floor. He paused and listened intently. No, there was no movement from below. He hadn't woken the dogs. Roah left the office as stealthily as he had entered it and made his way out of the house. When he was clear of the yard, he paused to look back with longing. *One day, it* will *be mine.* He blinked and trotted off down the street.

FOUR: SUNDAY SCHOOL

The morning Hakham and the others left for the Council Compound, Andy took his seat at the kitchen table, where a plate of hot chocolate chip pancakes waited for him. "Thanks, Mom," he said as he poured syrup over the pancakes.

"Any plans today?" she asked.

"Nope," he said with his mouth full. "Not on a Sunday."

"He'll be training with me," Nafshi said. She manifested on the table in an empty place between Andy and his mother. Andy gasped and inhaled a piece of pancake. He coughed until his airway cleared.

"Are you okay?" his mother asked. She neither heard nor saw Nafshi.

He nodded, eyes watering. When his mother's attention was elsewhere, he glared at Nafshi. "Are you nuts? Don't do that around my mom!" he sent.

"I allowed you to ignore me before," Nafshi said. "Now, you will have lessons with me."

Andy glared at Nafshi. "No," he sent. Out loud, he said, "I guess I'll just hang around the house today."

"I'm going to do a little shopping," she said. "Do you need anything?"

SUNDAY SCHOOL

"Well, there's a new game I want."

"And you can buy it yourself with your own money."

"Then I'm good." Andy finished his pancakes and put his dishes and glass in the sink as his mother lingered over her coffee. He ignored Nafshi, who was still sitting on the table. "I think I'll go outside for a while," he said. "I'll see you later."

He went up to his room and retrieved his gaming device, clattered down the stairs and out the front door. Andy sat down on the porch seat and switched on the device. Nafshi materialized on his lap.

"I can't see my game. Move," Andy said.

"Make me."

"I don't know how!"

"That's why you need to train with me."

"No. I'm not training with anyone anymore. I'm done. I'm not watching another friend die."

"Have you considered that if you trained with me to the best of your abilities, you'd learn how to prevent anyone else from dying?"

Andy's eyes narrowed and he frowned. "You can't guarantee that."

"No, I can't. But I *can* guarantee you'll be in a much stronger position to defend yourself and those you care for. Andy, train with me. Let me help you learn how to wield my Magelight to the best of your ability. Let me turn you into the weapon that will defeat the Evil One."

Andy rolled his eyes at her. "Yeah, that stupid prophecy."

"Child, you try my patience. Every prophecy Razelle made came true. If she said I would stub my toe on a rock that afternoon, I stubbed my toe on a rock."

"Really? Did you ever stub your toe on a rock like that?" he said, grinning.

"No!" Nafshi snapped. "By the First, you have the attention span of a kitten. Andy, if Razelle said we can't defeat the enemy without your help, then we will lose without you. Saunders and the Wild Ones have already taken many lives. Do you want to lose Zahavin and Leilei as well?"

CHAPTER FOUR

"Of course not. But Nafshi, I—I hurt Taylor. He could have died! And he got me so angry—what happens if I lose control next time? What if—what if I hurt him even worse? How do I know I won't kill him?"

"Well, *that* I can guarantee. If you let me train you, we can rein in your temper. You won't do anything you don't want to do. I promise you that."

"You promise?"

Nafshi sighed. "Child, why do you make me repeat everything? Yes. I promise. Now, put that toy away and let's see what you can do with my Magelight."

"I can't do anything on the front porch!" Andy said. "The First Law, remember?"

Nafshi sighed. "Of course I know that. Let's go where you *can* show me your paces."

"Backyard," he said, rising through Nafshi's image. "Whoa, that's weird. Can you not do that, please? Can you just act like a normal Catmage and, like, just walk and stuff? And get off my lap when I stand up?"

"If you wish," she said, chuckling. "Right, let's begin. I have a pretty good idea of your current capabilities. What I want to know is what more we can do."

Andy hurried off the porch and around to the backyard. Nafshi followed him as if she were a corporeal Catmage.

"Better?" she asked as he held the gate open for her.

"Yeah. Much better."

She led the way into the yard and told him to sit down on the grass. "Let us start at the beginning," she said. "Breathing exercises."

Andy groaned. "Are you kidding?"

"No. We're going to do this right."

"But you already know what I can do! You've been inside my head all this time, or whatever."

Nafshi stared at Andy until he sighed, closed his eyes, and started the exercises.

SUNDAY SCHOOL

"Now I know where Goldeneyes gets it from," he muttered.

Two hours later, sweat poured down Andy's face as he tried to keep a canvas chair floating several inches off the ground. He clenched his teeth, waiting for Nafshi to tell him he could let go. The chair weighed only a few pounds but as Andy discovered, holding something even that light for long periods took a huge amount of effort. He breathed deeply and fought to keep the chair from descending. It felt like he was holding his arms out at full length, holding onto the chair. He could almost feel his muscles quiver. The chair dropped an inch, and Andy fought to keep it from falling. It landed on the grass with a light thump.

"Again," Nafshi said.

"I can't."

"Then quit."

Andy glared at her, took a deep breath, closed his eyes, and waved his right hand in an upward motion. The chair lifted from the ground.

"How long this time?" he asked.

"Until I tell you to stop."

"This is stupid."

"Then quit."

He shot her a look. "I don't remember you being this mean in the cellar."

"I wasn't training you then. Andy, you need to improve your skills. I won't let Saunders hurt anyone else I love."

"Neither will I," Andy said. He closed his eyes again, fought against the tiredness, and steadied the chair in the air.

"Andy!" Letsan called from the front of the house. "Andy, where are you?"

The chair fell with a thump and Nafshi's image disappeared. "Do not say anything about me to Letsan," she said.

"Why not?"

"We'll discuss it later. Tell him nothing!"

"Okay, okay," Andy muttered out loud. "In the back," he sent to

CHAPTER FOUR

Letsan. When the orange Maine Coon rounded the house, Andy was sitting on the chair playing a video game, his breathing almost normal.

"Hard at work, I see," Letsan said.

"Got to get past this level," Andy replied without taking his eyes from the game.

"We miss you at the Compound. Ranana said to say hello."

Andy felt a pang as he remembered how much fun he had with Silsula's kittens. He hadn't seen them in ages. They'd be well into the Teaching Rings by now. He turned off the game. "Tell her hello for me."

"Tell her yourself. She doesn't understand why you don't like her anymore."

"That's not true and you know it."

"Yes, but she's young. She thinks you're avoiding the Compound because you don't like us anymore."

"Explain it to her."

"You explain it, because I don't really understand why you quit. I know Matti's death hit you hard, but it's been two moons. Time enough to mourn. Matti would want you back with us."

Andy glared at Letsan. "Don't tell me what Matti would want. He's dead, you can't know what he'd think. He's dead, Nafshi's dead, lots of Catmages are dead. Maybe they'd still be here if it wasn't for me. All I do is screw things up. You're better off without me. Ranana's better off without me. Tell her that."

"So the lesson for today is self-pity, is it? I never learned that one. You'll have to teach me. You do seem to be quite expert in it."

Andy flushed at the sarcasm. "What do you want, Letsan?"

"I want you to come to the East Woods with me, but I'll settle for just spending the day together. Come on, Andy. I miss you, too." Letsan wound himself around Andy's legs. Andy reached down and scratched his ears.

"I've *really* missed that," Letsan said, purring. He leaped onto Andy's lap.

SUNDAY SCHOOL

"Oof. Now that's something I didn't miss. Are you gaining weight?"

"Bite your tongue!" Letsan said, lashing Andy with his tail. "I'm the perfect weight, whatever it is." He glanced down at his flank. "Do you think this fur makes me look fat?"

Andy laughed as Letsan twisted his head from one side to the other so Andy could scratch both his ears. He picked Letsan up so they were eye to eye. "I miss you. But I just can't do it, Letsan. I can't."

Letsan rubbed his face against Andy's. "Okay. We won't talk about it anymore today. Let's just go have some fun."

"Mom's out for the day. Let's get a ball and play Magelight catch."

"You're on!" Letsan said as he jumped to the ground. "Last one upstairs is a human."

Laughing, Andy chased Letsan into the house.

"No fair," he said. "You got a head start *and* you have four legs."

"It wouldn't matter even if you got the head start," Letsan said. "Catmages are faster than humans. Well, maybe not Flathead. He's too fat to run."

"That's the Council Catmage you hate, right?"

"I wouldn't say I hate him. I just despise him with every hair on my body."

Andy looked at the long-haired Maine Coon and whistled. "That's a lot of hair," he said, grinning.

"And every last one in perfect condition," Letsan said, striking a pose. "Aren't I gorgeous?"

Andy grinned as he opened a night table drawer. His Magelight flashed and a small sponge ball flew out of the drawer and straight at Letsan.

"Ha!" Letsan said, knocking it away with a shield spell. Before Andy could grab the ball, Letsan had cast a second spell and looped it out of his reach. "Magelights are faster than humans, too!" Letsan said. Soon the two of them were running up and down stairs, in and out of rooms and down the halls, knocking the ball back and forth as they went. Andy

CHAPTER FOUR

ducked behind the kitchen door to dodge Letsan's latest attack when they heard knocking on the front door.

"Anyone home?" Becca called as she pushed the door open.

"Fuzzypants!" Mike said from behind her as he saw Letsan. He grabbed Teresa by the hand and pulled her inside.

Andy frowned at Letsan. "Did you tell them to come over?" he sent.

"As a matter of fact, I did. I stopped at Becca's on the way over here and she told me you weren't spending much time with them, either. You need your friends."

"He's right, you know," Becca said.

Andy fumed at Letsan for broadcasting their conversation.

"Andy," Mike said, his face dead serious for once, "we all miss you. You can't hide out here all summer."

"I'm not hiding. This is my home. I live here."

"When's the last time you and I had an all-day gaming session? My finger muscles are getting weak. Look at them!" he said, wiggling his fingers in Andy's face.

Andy couldn't help laughing as he pushed Mike's hands away.

"It would be nice to spend some time with you," Becca said wistfully. "It's been a while."

"My grandfather invited everyone to a barbecue tonight," Teresa told them. "Parents, too. Wait until you try his chicken, Andy. *Abuelo* is a great cook."

As they stood eagerly around him, waiting for his answer, Andy realized he missed his friends as much as they missed him. It *had* been a long time since they were all together. "Yeah, I'd like that," he said. "I'll ask Mom."

"Great! Fuzzypants and I will continue whatever mayhem you were making when we arrived. Boy, we could hear you knocking around from the street."

"Magelight catch," Andy said. "Go for it." His Magelight shone as

SUNDAY SCHOOL

he raised the ball from the floor and knocked it up the stairs. Letsan went flying after it, followed by Mike. Teresa and Becca looked at each other.

"Nothing changes," Becca said, grinning. "Race you up the stairs!"

Andy followed them more slowly. He went to his room to send a text to his mother, grinning as his friends whooped with laughter and chased Letsan and the ball around the house. He read the text she sent back, put down the phone, and joined them. "Mom says yes. So, what are we going to do for the rest of the afternoon?"

"Games. Nothing but games," Mike said.

"I agree with Mike." Letsan's Magelight flashed and he sent the ball careening at Andy. Andy deflected it and aimed it at Mike, who caught it in one hand.

"Too bad we can't play outside. This is way more fun at the Compound." Mike stopped when he realized what he'd said. "Oops. Sorry, man, it just came out."

"It's okay," Andy said. "Let's just not talk about it."

"Okay."

"I'm hungry. You guys want lunch or did you already eat?"

"Well, as long as you're making it, sure!" Mike said.

"Nope, you're helping or you're not eating."

"Work, work, work." Soon the four of them sat in the backyard eating sandwiches while Letsan resumed his spot in Andy's lap. Every so often Andy pulled a piece of turkey out of his sandwich and gave it to Letsan.

"If Razor could see me now," Letsan sighed. "But let me tell you a little secret about my brother: He's been hand-fed by humans, too. Just ask him about his time with Kate."

"That's right, you both grew up in someone's house. I always forget about that when I think of Razor. He's such a Catmage." Andy grinned. "Did you both leave at the same time?"

"No. He grew dissatisfied with life with humans long before I did. I stayed a full year."

"Didn't that set you back in the Teaching Rings?" Andy asked.

CHAPTER FOUR

"No. I trained with my parents. Dad was a great Catmage. Is, I should say."

"Do you ever see him?" Mike asked with his mouth full.

Teresa rolled her eyes. "Gross," she said.

Mike chewed hastily and swallowed. "Sorry."

"I haven't seen my parents since the war began," Letsan said. "There's been no time. I wonder if I have any new siblings."

"That must be really weird, not knowing if you have new brothers and sisters," Mike said. "I've only got one brother, and I wish he was someone else's."

"You're so mean to him," Teresa said. "I'd love to have a brother or sister."

"Take mine!"

She rolled her eyes again.

Mike stuffed the last of his sandwich into his mouth, washed it down with the last of his glass of milk, and stood. "Well, I'm done. Who wants to play some more Catmage catch?"

Andy hastily finished his sandwich and joined him. "I'm in. Let's go, Letsan." They ran back into the house while the girls shook their heads.

"So he was always like this?" Teresa asked.

"Worse. You've calmed him down considerably."

"I don't think I want to know what he used to be like." They laughed and took their time finishing lunch. When they rejoined the boys, they were in Andy's room playing a computer game while Letsan watched, his tail twitching as things shot across the screen.

"You should teach Letsan to play," Becca said.

"How's he going to handle the buttons on the controller?" Mike asked, his eyes on the screen.

"With his Magelight."

"Maybe when things have settled down," Letsan said. "I think I'd like to try. Just don't tell Razor."

"Was he always so serious?" Becca asked.

SUNDAY SCHOOL

"No. He's gotten worse as he's gotten older. All joking aside, these are difficult times. And my brother is harder on himself than anyone else. Razor thinks it's his fault we lost Matti and his warriors. And Nafshi."

Andy paused the game. His brows drew level in a scowl. "It's not his fault." The others exchanged glances. Out of the corner of his eye, he saw Nafshi materialize on the windowsill.

"You're right, Andy," she said. "It's not his fault. The blame lies squarely on Principal Saunders. So what are you going to do about it?"

"I told you, nothing," Andy muttered.

"What?" Mike asked.

"Uh, nothing," Andy said. "There's nothing we can do about it right now."

"I thought we weren't going to do anything but games this afternoon?" Becca said.

"Yeah." Andy looked over at Nafshi. "Can you just leave me alone for now?" he sent. "I'm taking a break whether you like it or not."

"I like it not," Nafshi said, and disappeared.

"So where were we?" Andy asked.

"I was kicking your butt," Mike said.

"In your dreams."

Hours later, Mike looked at the clock in Andy's room and whistled. "Time to go!" he said. "Well, Andy, it's been fun. We must do this again sometime. How's tomorrow?"

"You do realize we're all going to see each other again tonight at Teresa's house, don't you?"

"Of course!" Mike said. "But I have a very busy schedule and you're going to have to call my assistant if you want to spend time with me. Or, you know, just text me and I'll come over." He grinned at Andy, who grinned back. A horn sounded outside.

"There's my mom," Becca said. "She's giving us a lift home."

"Get out of here," Andy said. "See you guys later!"

CHAPTER FOUR

"Bye!"

After everyone left, Andy went to the front porch to wait for his mother to get home. Letsan sat on the railing, his tail twitching as he watched a bird flit from branch to branch.

"Hungry?" Andy asked.

"No. Instinct."

"Oh, yeah. Are you going back to the Compound tonight?"

"In a bit. I'm waiting for someone."

"Who?"

"My squad. Razor doesn't want any of us travel alone anymore. They dropped me off here this morning. I sent a message to them a few minutes ago while you were otherwise engaged."

Andy felt a pang of concern at the news.

"It's nothing to worry about," Letsan said as he saw Andy's expression. "Purely precautionary. Most of the Wild Ones are in their Compound. Only a few stay in town these days. But my brother is right to be careful."

"Why they don't come after me?" Andy asked.

"The same reason as before, I suppose. Saunders will get into a lot of trouble if anything happens to you. Plus, they know you've left us."

Andy looked away from Letsan.

"I'm not criticizing, Andy. Just telling you the facts."

Andy's response was interrupted by his mother's car coming down the street. She pulled into the driveway, stopped the car, and got out. She greeted Andy and Letsan as she climbed the stairs to the front porch.

"Well, look who's here," she said, reaching out to scratch Letsan under the chin. He purred and twisted his head from side to side. "Where have you been, big guy? Andy, give me a few minutes to relax and then we'll head over to the Velezes."

"Why don't you relax right here?" he asked. "You never do that anymore."

"That's not a bad idea," she said, sitting down on the porch swing

SUNDAY SCHOOL

next to him. Letsan followed her. "Don't want me to stop, eh?" she said, smiling. He jumped onto the swing and sat between them, purring.

"This is nice," she said as they sat on the swing, quiet except for the sound of Letsan's purring and the breeze in the trees. "I can't remember the last time we did this."

"Me neither."

"You seem different this summer," his mother said. "Is something wrong? I don't see Becca and Mike around nearly as much as I used to. Come to think of it," she said, scratching Letsan under the chin, "I can't remember the last time I saw Goldeneyes. Where is she?"

Andy shrugged. "She likes to be outside when the weather's nice. Right, Letsan?" he said.

"Oh, like the cat is going to answer," his mother said, laughing.

Letsan chirruped at them and she laughed again. "I stand corrected."

"Anyway, I've been kind of busy with my summer schoolwork," Andy said. "You know they give us more and more work the closer we get to graduation."

"That's right, my little boy is a junior now. Two more years."

"And a big fat liar," Letsan said. Andy glared at him when his mother wasn't looking.

"Anyway, Becca and Mike and Teresa were here today and we're going to see them again tonight. Want to relax a little longer or should we get going?"

His mother sighed and rose, stretching. "Let's get going. I'm starving. Oh, wait. We should take the chocolate cake I baked last night. Would you run to the kitchen and get it, please?"

"Can I come too?" Letsan asked.

"No!" Andy said out loud.

His mother raised her eyebrows at him. "Did you just tell me you're not going to get the cake?"

"Uh, no, sorry, Mom. I was thinking about something else I almost forgot. I'll go get the cake." He glared at Letsan again.

CHAPTER FOUR

"It's not my fault you forgot to use your mind-voice."

Andy slammed the door behind him as he ran to get the cake. When he came back, Letsan was slipping under a car across the street. "Say hi to Becca for me!" he said before he disappeared. Andy got in the car and balanced the cake on his lap.

It was nice spending the evening with his friends. They hadn't seen much of each other since school let out, though that was mostly Andy's fault. He was the one who had backed away.

Soon they all sat down to dinner, talking and laughing as they ate their way through the barbecued chicken and side dishes.

After dinner, Teresa, Mike, Becca, and Andy brought their chairs to the other side of the yard. Their parents chatted amiably around the table while Mike's brother Kenny played on his hand-held gaming device.

"This was nice," Andy said.

"Yeah, dinner was great," Mike said.

"No, I mean hanging out with you guys all day. I've missed that."

"Well, then stop staying by yourself all the time and spend more time with us. Like you can come with us tomorrow."

"Where are you going?"

"To the Compound. Zohar wants us to work with the Shomrim on some new stuff."

"I'm not going to the Compound," Andy said flatly.

"Andy," Becca said gently, "it's been months. Don't you think you've had enough time to grieve?"

"That's not it," he said, glaring.

"Then what?" Mike asked. "C'mon, man, how long are you going to stay mad at them?"

"Is that what you think it is?" Andy said, his voice rising. "You don't know anything!"

"Guys, calm down," Becca said. "Andy, we're your friends. We're just trying to—"

"What? Force him to do something he's not ready for?" Teresa said.

SUNDAY SCHOOL

"You're not helping," Mike said.

"And you don't understand what he's going through. Neither of you do. Because both of your parents are sitting right there," Teresa said, pointing to the other end of the yard. "You don't know what it's like. You've never lost anyone, have you?"

"Well, my grandmother died when I was little," Becca said.

"Do you remember it?" Andy asked.

"No."

"Then Teresa's right. You don't know what it's like." He rose, knocking his chair over as he did. "I'm tired. I'm going home."

He stalked over to the adults. The others watched as he and his mother said goodnight and left.

"Nice going," Teresa said.

"What did we do?" Mike asked.

"Oh, never mind," she said, rising and walking away.

Becca and Mike looked at each other. "I thought the day was going so well," Mike said.

"So did I."

FIVE: LIGHTEN UP

Taylor Grant hurried through the gate at number 19 Oak Street, taking care to close it behind him. His hand reached out to touch his chest where the Magelight necklace lay beneath his shirt. Summertime meant more frequent lessons with Roah, and Taylor was glad to be out of the house. His twin stepbrothers didn't leave for college for another few weeks. In the meantime, they were doing their best to make his life miserable. But they had no idea Taylor had turned the tables on them. They didn't know why so many "accidents" kept happening to them. Items fell off shelves and hit them on the head as they reached for snacks in the pantry, or a framed photograph on the wall fell as they passed, and their father yelled at them for breaking the glass. Taylor smiled to himself. Roah was right. Using his Magelights in so subtle a manner not only gave him satisfaction against his stepbrothers, but it helped hone his skills. Taylor could stand in a doorway out of sight and move things as Matt and Nick passed by. They never suspected him, and most of the time they never even saw him. Roah taught him that secrecy was a powerful tool. He wondered if he could utilize these skills when he went back to school. Probably not. Too many people around. And then there was Cohen and his buddies, and—Becca. Taylor couldn't help smiling at the thought of her. But she was smart enough to figure out what he was doing, and she'd bug him about the

LIGHTEN UP

Magelights. Maybe. He shrugged and decided he'd think about it later.

At the back of the house a few of Principal Saunders' special Dobermans napped in their kennels. Shadow, the largest male, was awake and watching as Taylor climbed the steps and pushed open the screen door. Those dogs gave him the creeps. They were different from Catmages, though he couldn't say exactly how. Maybe it was because Catmages were born intelligent and these dogs were made that way by Saunders and Roah. Maybe it's because they always seemed to be watching him. Well, it wasn't any of his business. They could do whatever they want, so long as Taylor got to keep learning. No way Cohen was ever going to get the drop on him again. He felt a surge of anger as he remembered Andy tossing him to the ground with a flash of his Magelight. "I've got five to your one, Cohen," he muttered. "We'll see who hits who next time."

"That is a good way to think," Roah said as he strolled into the kitchen. "But you must not let your anger control you. An angry Catmage is a defeated Catmage."

"Andy keeps getting angry and kicking our butts," Taylor said.

"True. But there is something special about his powers. I have not been able to determine what it is."

"There's nothing special about Cohen. He's a loser."

"And yet he used his Magelight to fling you through the air. That is a significant accomplishment. No Catmage has ever been able to lift that much weight alone."

"Well, if he can do it, I can do it."

"That remains to be seen. But it may be a good topic for another lesson. First, tell me what you've been doing to your brothers."

"*Step*brothers," Taylor said.

"The report."

Roah actually chuckled when Taylor told him about the photograph. "Your skills are improving. That is good. Let us see what else has improved."

"I can't really let loose out here. Can't I come out to your Com-

CHAPTER FIVE

pound and practice sometime?"

"That's not a bad idea," Niflah said as he came into the kitchen. "Taylor could work with Kfir and some of the Tzofim. He could be a great asset in the next battle."

"When *is* the next battle?" Taylor asked. "I want to be in it!"

"We will inform you when you need to know," Roah said. "Let us go upstairs and test your control. Niflah, will you be working with the dogs while I train Taylor?"

"Yes, but I came to tell you that Saunders wants to meet with us in two hours."

"Then we have a timeframe for our lesson. Come, boy." Roah led the way upstairs to the room they'd designated for Magelight practice. The room was bare except for a single chair and a straw archery target that Saunders had had Taylor bring from school. The target was pitted and scarred with scorch marks. Straw and paper littered the floor beneath it. Taylor grinned at the thought it would soon have to be replaced. Yep, he was getting to be quite a good shot.

"You had better be," Roah said, "because your thoughts are as unguarded as a kitten's right now. You must learn to close your mind."

"Sorry," Taylor muttered.

"*Mind-voice!*" Roah hissed, firing a light dagger as he did.

Taylor reacted quickly, and the dagger bounced off his shield. He grinned slightly. Roah had a tendency to use surprise as a teaching tactic, and Taylor had the scars to prove it. He'd learned to expect anything at any time from this teacher. Niflah was a lot easier to work with, but Roah taught him more. Way more.

Roah blinked once at Taylor. "Well done. Now let's see how well you can fire your Magelights in sequence. I think that is going to be your best skill against the Son of Aaron."

Taylor gritted his teeth at the title Roah chose for Andy. He knew it was done to goad him, but it was working. So, today's lesson was going to be anger, was it? Yeah, Taylor could deal with that. He calmed himself,

LIGHTEN UP

concentrated on the target, and aimed light daggers in quick succession. Orange, green, yellow, green, yellow. He liked keeping them in order. The orange jet felt powerful and masculine. The greens and yellows seemed to have their own feelings to them as well, as if each Magelight had its own personality. Taylor shook off the distractions and concentrated on laying down a line of fire on the target. *Bam, bam, bam, bam, bam!* Puffs of smoke curled from the straw. He grinned at Roah.

"Well done, boy. Now let us review the basics. You allowed me to get you angry and only barely shielded yourself from attack. You must learn to fight without emotion, only conviction. Sit and practice the beginning breathing exercises."

Taylor sighed and sat on the floor. He closed his eyes and took a deep breath. Baby stuff again. When would he get past the baby stuff? He opened his eyes and glanced sideways at Roah. No, he hadn't heard him that time. Good. Pretty soon his thoughts would be as walled off as Roah's. He'd never heard a stray thought from that one, though every once in a while Niflah let one slide. Thinking about Niflah brought a surge of anger that surprised Taylor and reminded him he'd better start concentrating on his breathing. The last thing he needed was another shot from Roah burning a hole in his jeans.

Niflah alerted them when he heard the car in the driveway. He joined Roah and Taylor in Principal Saunders' second-floor office. Taylor took a seat as the two Wild Ones jumped onto the desk to wait. They could hear the door slam and heavy steps coming up the stairs.

Taylor recognized the look on Saunders' face as he marched through the door. Someone was in for it. He hoped it wasn't him.

Saunders swept around the desk and sat down, brows drawn, glaring at the Wild Ones. "I've just come back from visiting my associate. He won't let me buy Trudy's sister Tilda back." Saunders frown deepened. He slammed his hand down on the desk. "Three years! Three years we spent training Trudy, and *you let her die!*"

"We didn't 'let' her die," Niflah said. "She was killed in battle by

CHAPTER FIVE

the Catmages. We tried to stop her, but she went after them when Razor sent some of his fighters right under her nose. You can't stop instinct, and dogs have ever considered us their prey."

Saunders went on as if he hadn't heard a word. "Three years, wasted. I was getting ready to breed Trudy to Shadow. Now I'll have to settle for breeding him with the second-best bitch," he said, his lips curling in a sneer. "I don't suppose you have an extra Magelight to give one of Valda's pups?" he asked.

"There are five extra Magelights in this room," Roah said. "Take one of the boy's if you must."

Was this another facet of Roah's teaching him to control his emotions? If that was the point, it wasn't working. Taylor's breath caught at the idea that one of his Magelights might be taken away. His heart thumped as he thought frantically for a way to prevent Principal Saunders from taking his Magelights.

"We'd have to start all over again with a new puppy," Niflah said. "That would take time better spent on moving ahead with the plans we have. The dogs that remain will suffice."

Niflah was taking his side? That was unexpected. Another unexplained wave of anger washed over him. *Hypocrite.* Taylor flicked his attention back to the conversation.

"Perhaps you're right," Saunders said to Niflah. He glanced at Roah. "*Five* Magelights, you said?" he asked suspiciously. "Roah, have you learned to count?"

Roah watched Saunders, unblinking. "All Catmages can count up to seven, the number of our Laws. You had six dogs with Magelights. Now you have five. Why is this important?"

"It isn't," Saunders said through gritted teeth. "Exactly how long would it take you to train a puppy with one of Mr. Grant's Magelights?"

Taylor's heart beat faster. "Don't I get any say in the matter?"

"No," Saunders said. "The Magelights aren't yours. They are mine. They are merely on loan to you. Annoy me enough and I'll take them *all* back."

LIGHTEN UP

Taylor felt himself start to panic. Before any of them could notice, he felt a calming wave, almost a warmth, come down over his entire body. That was weird. But he was relaxed and didn't care why. Now he could concentrate on giving Saunders a reason not to take his Magelights. "But sir, I've trained for over a year with all five of them. If you take even one away, who knows how it will affect my powers?"

"The boy is right," Niflah said. "His Magelights seem to be complementing one another well. Removing even one will adversely affect him."

"Then he will adapt," Saunders said.

"Yes sir, I could do that, I suppose. But I've been working really hard these past two months. Ask Roah. Cohen is never going to beat me again!" He frowned as he remembered how Andy had knocked him out with a Magelight attack and rendered him useless during the most important battle yet. "If he hadn't hit me with that sneak attack, maybe we would still have all six dogs." That shot hit home. Taylor could see Saunders thinking it over. *Oh, good one* sounded in his head. Taylor dared not look at Niflah or Roah to see which of them had said it.

"Niflah is right," Roah said. "It will take too much time and effort to train a new pup. We have our hands full with the dogs we have left. It also takes time to run the West Woods Compound. Then there are all the hours we waste traveling to town every time you call us to you. Leave the boy's Magelights where they are. He is of more use to us with all of them."

Then why did you mention them in the first place? Taylor looked around quickly, but his thoughts had not been broadcast to the others. He allowed himself a small smile. *Of course they haven't. Because I'm that good already. They need me more than I need them.*

"If you'd had the brains to grab the Magelights off some of your dead, we would have many spares by now," Saunders said, his frown deepening.

"Razor's warriors moved quickly. They left us no opportunity."

"Can't you spare any of your own? Surely there are some weaklings who could be culled from the herd, as it were."

CHAPTER FIVE

Niflah stared at Saunders. "You would have us kill our own fighters and deplete our resources? Are you mad?" Niflah said.

Roah glanced at Niflah impatiently. "The weak create weak Magelights. We took the Council Magelights for you because they came from our strongest Catmages. That's why we spent nearly a whole cycle of the sun trying to get Nafshi's Magelight. She was a Magus. The boy has shown how powerful her Magelight can be. Unless you would rather we get you an inferior Magelight for your precious puppy?"

Taylor held his breath at Roah's sarcasm. He cringed inwardly, waiting for the explosion to come. But then his mood changed abruptly and he felt a surge of anger against Roah. His emotions were all over the place today. *What is up with me?* he wondered.

Saunders held Roah's gaze for a long moment. Then he shook his head slightly. "Keep your Magelights, Mr. Grant," he said. "And you, Roah, had best watch your tone with me." He stood quickly, his chair rolling backward to hit the wall with a thump. "Everyone can be replaced, Roah. Everyone." Saunders strode quickly from the room and stomped down the stairs. They heard the door slam and his car engine start.

"That was a risky thing you did," Niflah said.

"Life is risk." He turned to Taylor. "You may leave." They waited until the boy's steps faded and they heard the downstairs door close.

"You are too careless, Roah. We still need Saunders and his dogs. They are coming along well and will be a huge help to us in putting down the current leadership."

"You mean your brother and his allies," Roah said.

"Yes. We suffered a huge defeat at the recent Council meeting. The last thing we want is my brother's faction resurgent."

"We wouldn't have that if *we* had the Tilyon."

"The time is not right."

"That is always your excuse, Niflah. Timing. The time will never be perfect. We should strike, and soon!"

"No. We followed your plans and they led us to defeat. This time,

LIGHTEN UP

we wait until *I* say we go."

Roah gazed at Niflah unblinking. Niflah's ears went back.

"Don't challenge me, Roah. I am as powerful as my brother, when all is said and done. You will not defeat me." His Magelight glowed and his fur fluffed. The two stared at one another until Roah spoke.

"Calm yourself. There is no need to fight among ourselves. Save it for the enemy."

"Then do as I say for once!"

"This time," Roah said, dropping his gaze to let Niflah think he won.

Niflah's tail stopped lashing and his Magelight powered down. "Good. Let us go back to the Compound and see if our new Seekers have returned. I should like to take part in training the kittens this time."

"As you wish," Roah said. *But things will be as I wish soon enough*, he thought to himself. He followed the old tabby down the stairs and out the back door, fuming about the long walk back to the Compound. *Soon this will be unnecessary as well. No Niflah, no Saunders. Just Roah and his chosen few.* Their guards joined them as they left the house and headed out of town.

Outside the house, walking steadily down the street toward home, Taylor sighed with relief. His heart was still thudding.

Nobody is taking my Magelights away. Nobody.

He turned down the street and hurried away.

Saunders pulled into his space in the school parking lot, still fuming. How dare those *cats* talk to him that way? If he didn't still need them, he'd—well, he did need them, for now. He hadn't yet mastered the Tilyon the way they claimed it could be used. They were still a big help training the dogs. But not for very much longer. Saunders had been having his own private sessions with the dogs, and they were responding to him nicely. It was always good to have a card or three up your sleeve, and Stan Saunders was one to be prepared for any eventuality.

CHAPTER FIVE

His footsteps echoed as he walked down the corridors. His hand went to his chest as he reached for the Tilyon. *Why aren't you working for me? Work, damn you!*

The Tilyon did not so much as glow. He came upon the custodian in front of one of the classrooms opening and closing the door. Mr. Velez glanced up as Saunders came near.

"The door was sticking," he said as he opened and closed it again.

"I don't care," Saunders said.

Mr. Velez raised his eyebrows. "Having a bad day?"

Saunders frowned at him. "That's none of your concern." He swept past Mr. Velez and turned at the outer office door, slamming it behind him. The janitor grinned. A bad day for the principal was a good day for him and his friends.

SIX: TUESDAYS WITH NAFSHI

A week after Nafshi appeared, Andy was beginning to wish she had waited a few more months. Every day for the last week she woke him early, grumbled while he showered and ate breakfast, and then seemed to snap at him most of the day while she put him through his paces. She made him practice everything he had been taught by Goldeneyes and Zehira, and then she pushed him harder than either of them had ever done.

"And I thought Goldeneyes was hard," he muttered at the end of one morning's session.

"You'll thank me later."

"Maybe after lunch. I'm starving." Andy got up and made his way inside as Nafshi followed him. "Do you miss food?" he asked as he found some cold chicken and mashed potatoes in the fridge and put them into the microwave.

"I never thought about it," she said. "I suppose I'm just happy to still be here. I wasn't quite finished with my life."

"I barely got to know you. I'm glad you're here now, too."

"Even when I push you so hard?" she asked, eyes twinkling.

"Nope. But I'll take the bad with the good." The microwave timer went off. Andy piled chicken and potatoes on his plate and applied himself to lunch. Nafshi settled on the windowsill, the sunlight shining in her fur.

CHAPTER SIX

"It's so weird to see you like that," Andy sent, his mouth full of chicken. "You'd think the sun would shine through you or something."

"Like this?" Nafshi said, her image growing transparent.

"You can turn it on and off at will, huh? Neat."

"Eat. We have important work to do this afternoon."

"What?" Andy sent, still chewing.

"Auras. I want you to learn how to search for auras. Neither Zahavin nor Zehira has taught you that yet. I'll wait for you outside. Don't be long."

Five minutes later, Andy pushed open the back door and joined Nafshi on the lawn. He sat cross-legged and waited for her to start.

"Finding an aura is a difficult task," she said. "It's advanced magic, and it takes a lot of energy. Some Catmages instinctively sense auras."

"Like Patches," Andy said. "He's really good at it."

"Yes, like Patches. I'd like you to learn how to find an aura. It's too bad I can't tell any other Catmage that I'm back, or this would be easier."

"Yeah, why can't you?" Andy said. "You haven't really explained that to me yet."

"Because I'm afraid they might overreact to my existence. There's never been anything like this in Catmage history, as far as I know."

"But wouldn't they all be happy you're back?"

Nafshi's voice grew soft. "No, I don't think they would. I think they'd be concerned. Catmages don't like surprises that involve Magelights. No, it's best we keep this to ourselves. Maybe later we can let Zahavin in on the secret. But not now, Andy."

"Okay, I guess."

"Back to the auras. Wait, I have it. Taylor! That awful boy. Would he be home now, do you think?"

"No idea."

"Do you know where he lives? Is it far?"

Andy shrugged. "No, he's not all that far away. He's a few bus stops past mine. It's a long walk, maybe."

"Then we'll look there. Which direction?"

TUESDAYS WITH NAFSHI

Andy pointed.

"Let me try first."

Andy waited while Nafshi cast the aura spell.

"Yes, he's home," she said. "I can feel the Magelights of my old friends, drat the boy."

"Well, it's actually Saunders who should be dratted," Andy pointed out. "He gave them to Taylor."

"Drat them both, then. All right, cheeky child. Now it's your turn. Clear your mind of all distractions and let's see if you're up to this task."

Andy closed his eyes, breathed deeply, and waited.

"You have to search with your mind. It helps some Catmages to imagine the Magelights as colored points of light in the distance. I'll give you a hint this time: Two of Taylor's Magelights are green."

Andy thought of himself in a long, dark tunnel. He pictured two small green lights at the very end of the tunnel. Then he imagined himself getting closer to the lights. They grew in power and energy as he came near.

"Excellent," Nafshi said. "Can you feel them? Are they identical?"

"No," Andy said. "One of them seems—I don't know, more like a guy. And one feels like a girl's Magelight."

"You're right, Andrew. One of the green Magelights belonged to Ziv. The other was my dear friend Razelle's. She was the Council's prophet. Oh, it makes my blood boil to think that her Magelight is in the hands of a grubby little boy!"

"Hey!" Andy said, grinning. "I hope you're not including me with that grubby boy remark."

"Concentrate!" Nafshi snapped.

Andy stopped smiling and thought about the green lights.

"Listen. Think. Feel around the Magelights. Are there any more? Concentrate!"

Try as he might, Andy couldn't feel anything else. A wave of tiredness washed over him.

"That's enough for now," Nafshi said. "We'll try again tomorrow.

CHAPTER SIX

That was a good start."

"Thanks." He stood up slowly. "I need a drink. I'll see you inside. Or wherever." He went to the kitchen and poured a glass of fruit juice. He thought wryly as he drank it that the last thing he had expected to be doing this summer was Magelight lessons. He thought quitting the team would have ended that. Well, it just goes to show you. You can't predict the future.

"I can predict yours," Nafshi said as she reappeared on the table. "More lessons this afternoon. We still have to work on your messaging, your offensive spells—there is much, much more to do."

"But you said we'd work on the aura spell tomorrow!"

"Yes, we will. Today we work on some of the others."

Andy drained his glass and pushed his chair back from the table, turning away from Nafshi and putting the glass in the sink.

"I know you rolled your eyes at me, child. I'm still inside your head," Nafshi said, chuckling.

"There are definitely drawbacks to this partnership," Andy muttered.

A few days later, Andy sat cross-legged on the ground in the backyard. Nafshi sat nearby, grooming herself. He'd been unable to find the other Magelights yet. And to make it worse, each time they started aura training, he had to wait until Nafshi searched to make sure Taylor was home. He felt like a child waiting for a parent to give him permission to watch a show on TV. Nafshi could do it so well and so quickly! It was frustrating that this was so easy for her and so difficult for him.

"I've had many, many years of practice, Andy," she said. "But this would be so much easier if we could practice with a Catmage."

"Then let's tell someone about you so I can move forward!"

"No. I don't want you telling anyone about—" Nafshi's ears pricked up and she disappeared just as Letsan came through the bushes that divided Andy's property from his neighbor's.

"Hi, Andy! Wow, such a busy life you have these days. How can you stand sitting around in the yard all day?"

TUESDAYS WITH NAFSHI

"Hey, Letsan. What's up?"

"I've come to visit you, since you won't visit me. I was thinking of a round of Catmage catch. Are you up for it?"

Andy glanced over to where Nafshi had been.

"You bet I am. You get the window. I'll get the ball."

Andy grinned as Letsan's Magelight flashed and his bedroom window slid open. He half-closed his eyes in concentration, picturing his night table drawer opening and seeing the ball inside the drawer. He swept his hand upward and soon the small, red sponge ball was floating through the window. Andy let it drop to the ground. It bounced, and Letsan let out a sound that could only be described as *mrowr* and leaped after it, batting the ball with his paws. Andy laughed at him.

"That's not very Catmage of you."

"But it's fun," Letsan said. "Just don't tell Zahavin." He set his back legs, wiggled, and leaped at the ball. As he pounced, his Magelight flashed and the ball flew out from under his paws toward Andy, who put up his hand to catch it.

"You're supposed to use your Magelight," Letsan said.

"But this is fun," Andy replied, grinning. They spent the next hour running in and out of the house moving between Magelight catch and regular catch. Andy had never seen Letsan play like a cat before. He laughed a lot. At last, Andy collapsed on the floor of the kitchen, panting for breath. "I give up," he said. "I'm beat." Letsan joined him, purring, his sides heaving.

Andy stood up. "I'll get you some water," he said, filling a coffee cup and putting it on the floor for him. He took a bottle of water out of the fridge for himself. They rested for a few minutes.

"So why did you come to visit?" Andy said.

"For this. To make you miss me."

"Well, it worked."

"Good. I have to get back to the Compound." Letsan stood and walked to the front door and waited for Andy to open it for him. Andy

CHAPTER SIX

followed him out the door, standing on the porch to watch him go.

"We can play all kinds of games at the Compound when you make up your mind to come back," Letsan said.

"Don't ruin the moment," Andy told him. Letsan laughed.

"All right. Until next time, then."

"Seeya, Fuzzypants." Andy grinned as he used Mike's pet name for Letsan. His grin widened as Letsan waved his tail as he left. Andy caught a flash of sun on a Magelight as Letsan was joined by the Shomrim waiting for him under cars parked along the street. Andy turned to go back in the house.

"Not yet," Nafshi said as she reappeared. "Sit. Concentrate on Letsan. Try to feel his aura."

"Don't you mean his Magelight's aura?"

"No, *Letsan's* aura. Oh, be quiet and do as I say before he gets much farther away."

Andy sat down and cleared his mind. He pictured the dark tunnel, and placed Letsan at the end of it. That was easy enough.

"Now, try to sense the feeling of power that courses through Letsan. The Magelight is the focal point, and has a part of our *neshama,* our soul. But the fullness of our souls are in our bodies. Can you feel Letsan's power?"

"I feel the Magelight," Andy said. "It's different from the ones Taylor has."

"Probe around the Magelight. Look for Letsan's essence."

Andy tried to think of an image he could use to find Letsan's aura. He wracked his brain but came up empty.

"Just focus on Letsan!" Nafshi said. "Forget about anything else. Think of the Catmage you've come to know over the years."

Andy thought of Letsan sitting on his lap, or winding himself around Andy's legs. Sleeping on his bed, eating in his kitchen, telling him elephant jokes. Then he thought of the Letsan he'd seen in battle, strong, fearless, powerful. An orange light flared inside the imaginary tunnel, and Andy could *feel* Letsan's presence. It was like a warm, orange light had settled inside Andy. It was very different from the presence in Taylor's Magelights. They were like pale shadows compared to this. Andy smiled at the warmth. It felt like his friend.

"Now find his Magelight," Nafshi said softly.

Andy searched until he sensed a smaller, weaker version of the warm light. There. There was the orange light he'd seen so many times around Letsan's neck.

"No it isn't," Nafshi said wryly. "The stone Letsan wears is glass. He's Avdei Ha-Or. He wears his Magelight beneath his skin, just as I did, and just as Zahavin learned to do last year."

Sweat poured down Andy's face. "Can I stop now? This is really hard work."

"Yes. You've done very well, child."

He opened his eyes and wiped his forehead. "Thanks. But if you don't mind, I'm done for the day." He lay back on the ground, breathing as heavily as if he'd just finished running. "Why does it take so much energy?" he asked.

Nafshi moved next to him. "Because finding an aura is a difficult task. Most Catmages don't even bother to learn the spell. Seekers are truly gifted individuals. They perform extremely important work for Catmages. They find half-breeds like Patches and bring them to live among us. If not for Seekers, we would have many more untrained Wild Ones and the First only knows what might have happened. Who knows if our race would have survived without them?"

"I don't know much about your family, except for you," Andy said. "Goldeneyes and Silsula mentioned a brother and father, but they haven't said much about them."

"Zahavin has never forgiven her father for being himself," Nafshi muttered. "And she foolishly thinks little of Levavi."

"She didn't like *me* very much when we first met," he pointed out. "She changed her mind about me."

"That's true. Well, all this is just talk. You and my favorite grand-

CHAPTER SIX

daughter aren't doing much of anything these days."

"I know," Andy said sadly. "She's mad at me."

"I know," Nafshi said wryly. "I'm in your head, child."

"Yeah, how did that come to be?" he asked.

"I'm not sure. We've had no experience with this because we've never allowed a Magelight to survive its creator. And of course, I'm a Magus," she said proudly.

"Why was it so hard for me to find a Catmage aura?"

"Because you have to search past so many things to find the one small spark of light that is an aura, a Catmage soul."

"And if you know that Catmage, you can tell who it is from its aura."

"Yes. Each soul is unique, Andrew. No Magelight is truly like any other, just as no Catmage—or human—is truly like any other. The One Above Us All has gifted each of us with the ability to be unlike any other that came before or comes after. There is no other person like you in this world, and no other Nafshi. And that is a wonderful thing."

Andy was moved by her words. He sat up slowly. "I wish I could pet you," he said. A thought occurred to him. "Wait a sec—let me try this." He reached out his hand and imagined himself petting Nafshi's image. He moved his right hand in a petting motion. Energy crackled between his left hand and Nafshi as it moved along Nafshi's image.

"By the First, I can feel it!" she said. "Andy, you're brilliant! You made an image of your hand petting the image of me, and it's working!" She purred and rubbed her head against the hand, shifting from ear to ear.

"Not bad for someone who took so long to learn how to find an aura, huh?"

"Not bad at all, you cheeky thing." Nafshi purred as Andy lay back on the ground.

Rain pounded on the roof of the house and streamed down the windows. Andy sat on his bed and tried again to find all of the Magelights on Taylor's

TUESDAYS WITH NAFSHI

necklace. He thought about the lights in the corridor. He fixed his mind on just one, the light that had felt male. Now he could use what he'd discovered yesterday to help find the others. He knew the difference between a Magelight aura and a Catmage aura, and searched with his mind to find more of the Magelights. They were in the tunnel. All he had to do was shine the light in the right place, figuratively speaking.

His Magelight began to glow. He found the two green Magelights quickly and searched nearby. There! There it was! Andy felt a new Magelight near the first green Magelight. It glowed yellow in the imaginary tunnel. Closing his eyes, Andy envisioned himself searching the dark corridor with a flashlight. The beam fell on another yellow light. Andy grew excited and looked for the last one. He made his flashlight beam grow brighter, casting light more widely. At the very end of the beam he saw an orange glint. Five! He found all five Magelights. He couldn't wait to tell Nafshi.

"You always forget I'm right here," she said inside his head. "That's great work, Andy. You can call it quits for today. We'll pick up again tomorrow."

Andy opened his eyes, grinning at Nafshi. "I have a day off? Great!" He reached for his phone and texted Becca.

A few minutes later, Andy was pulling on his shoes. "See you later, Nafshi. I'm going to wait outside for Becca and her father. We're going to the movies."

"Enjoy yourself." Nafshi's image disappeared and Andy clattered downstairs to wait on the front porch. He hurried to the curb as soon as he saw Mr. Jefferson's car pull onto his block.

"What's the rush?" Mr. Jefferson asked as he got in the car.

"I've been working hard. It's nice to have a day to just goof off."

"Working on what? It's summertime."

"Oh, uh, they assign us summer reading and stuff," he said as he closed the car door. Becca rolled her eyes at him and he grinned.

Her father dropped them off at the theater and told them he'd be back to pick them up later. "I almost forgot," he said as he handed Becca

CHAPTER SIX

some money. "Popcorn's on me."

"Thanks, Dad!"

"Yeah, thanks!"

Becca's father waved and drove away. They got their tickets and stood in line to buy popcorn.

"This is nice," Andy said. "We haven't done this in a while."

"I would point out the reason why, but then you'd get mad at me," Becca said with the double-curved smile Andy liked so much.

"Not today. Today is about hanging out and eating popcorn and watching the hero beat the bad guys." Andy smiled back.

"Yeah, but who's the hero and who's the bad guy?" Taylor said from behind them. Andy groaned inwardly as he saw his nemesis standing with Pete and Tommy a little way back in line. Becca put her hand on Andy's forearm.

"Don't," she said softly.

"Okay," he sent. Then a thought struck him.

"Just once, can you leave us alone?" he sent to Taylor and Becca.

Taylor's head jerked when he got Andy's message. Andy sent him another.

"Becca can hear me, too."

At Taylor's glance, she nodded.

Taylor's eyes narrowed. He sent back two words: "For her."

Taylor ignored them while they got their popcorn and sodas. And though they were going to the same movie, Taylor made sure that he and Pete sat far away from Andy and Becca. To Andy's relief, they also left him alone as the crowd streamed out of the theater. Becca's father waited outside. They got in the car and drove away.

Taylor stood under the theater awning watching Becca go. "I feel like walking home," he told Pete and Tommy headed for their ride. "See you." They shrugged and walked away.

But Taylor didn't really want to go home. He wanted to hit something. He strode angrily through the wet streets until he stood in front of

TUESDAYS WITH NAFSHI

number 19 Oak Street. "Anyone there?" he sent. Roah's voice answered him.

"Come to the kitchen."

Taylor found Roah seated on the windowsill gazing into the backyard.

"You aren't scheduled to be here today," Roah said.

"Well, I want to practice. I'm going upstairs."

"Then I'll come with you." Roah followed as Taylor ran up the stairs and burst into the practice room. Before he had even stopped he fired off light daggers, scoring the target and tearing out large chunks of straw.

"Interesting," Roah said. "You have found a way to harness your anger instead of letting it cloud your focus. Let's see just how much you can control it." His Magelight blazed, and suddenly Taylor was shielding himself against Roah's light jets.

Taylor felt elated as every attempt of Roah's was thwarted by his shields. One of his yellow Magelights in particular seemed perfectly suited for this. It felt like Taylor could just let the Magelight do what it wanted. At last, Roah stopped.

"That was well done," he said. "Very well done."

"Thanks," Taylor said, panting. "I'm hungry."

"Go feed yourself, then." Roah left the room and Taylor followed him down the stairs. He seated himself back in the window as Taylor took out bread and cold cuts. He found containers of leftover Chinese food and took those out as well as a bottle of milk. He ate and drank his way through everything on the table, rinsed the dishes, and put them in the dishwasher.

"Do you always eat enough for three?" Roah asked.

Taylor belched. "That was just an appetizer." He glanced at the clock on the wall. "Hey, I better get home!"

Taylor waved and hurried down the hall and out the door. The rain had stopped and the sun was breaking through the clouds. He hummed to himself as he walked through town. When he reached his house, Taylor went to the kitchen and smiled at his mother. "What's for dinner?" he asked. "I'm starving!"

SEVEN: PARENTS NIGHT

Summer was ending and Andy looked forward to school starting. He was tired of having Mike and Becca make veiled—or not so veiled—remarks about making up with Goldeneyes and going back to the Compound. Neither of them knew he was training with Nafshi, and he wasn't about to tell them. They'd probably think he was crazy, anyway, talking to Nafshi's spirit. No, Nafshi was right. It was better that nobody else knew about it.

"Yes, it is better," she said from her perch on his bed. "And so are you, come to think of it."

Andy smiled at the praise and pushed his chair away from his desk. "Well, you worked me so hard this summer how could I be anything else?"

"True. Why do you keep looking at the clock?" she asked.

"It's Parents Night at the school and Mom's late, as usual."

"Is that important?"

"I thought you've been in my head all this time. Didn't you notice things like Parents Night?"

"No. Human affairs bore me."

"Ouch!" Andy said, grinning.

"I repeat: Is it important?"

Andy shrugged. "I have no idea, but it's something we have to do

PARENTS NIGHT

every year. Saunders usually gives a boring speech. Most of the time I run into Taylor and he says something nasty. And then we get to sit around while our parents meet our teachers and stuff."

"Sounds fascinating," Nafshi said, yawning. "Kindly leave me out of it. I'll take an imaginary nap on your very real bed."

"Knock yourself out," he said. "I'm going downstairs to wait for Mom."

Ten minutes later, Rachel Cohen hurried inside with a bag of hamburgers and fries from a fast food restaurant. "Eat fast," she said.

"We're late," Andy said in unison with his mother.

"I'm sorry, sweetie."

"It's okay, Mom. Sit down and eat. Becca always saves us seats."

Soon they were in the car on the way to the school. Andy texted Becca to find out where they were sitting and tell her when to expect them. They hurried through the corridors to the gym and found their friends. Teresa and Mike sat next to Becca. Her parents waved at them and Becca moved over to make room for Rachel next to her mother. Andy sat down between Becca and Mike.

"Who had five minutes past in the pool?" Greg Murdoch said.

"Sorry, I only had three minutes," Jake Jefferson said, grinning. "Say, how much is in the pool this year?"

"I had it, how much did I win?" Mike asked.

"Nothing, just like every other year," his mother said. "There is no pool. Leave Rachel alone, Greg, you big bully." Mike's dad laughed and pretended to fend off his wife.

"Next year you should come half an hour late," he said. "Then you won't have to listen to Saunders bore us to tears. Oh, joy, he's about to start."

Principal Saunders stepped up to the microphone, his tall, lean frame towering over the assistant principal, who had just finished introducing him.

"Good evening, parents. Thank you for being here as we wel-

CHAPTER SEVEN

come our newest students, and welcome back our returning students." He glanced straight at Andy and his friends. Andy expected it and stared stonily straight ahead. This year he wasn't going to let Saunders anger him. That went for Taylor, too. He was a junior, for crying out loud. It was time to start thinking past high school and toward his future, especially now that he was no longer involved with the Catmages. Andy realized he'd drifted away from whatever Saunders was saying and returned his attention to the principal.

"The road is sometimes long and hard, with bumps that will cause some of us to turn aside."

"Does he mean me?" Andy whispered to Becca. She shrugged.

"Know that the ones who turn aside will be forgotten. Only those with the strength to persevere will be etched in the books of memory. Only those who are strong and determined will achieve their goals."

Saunders kept his eyes on Andy as he spoke.

"That son of a—Andy, I think he *is* talking about you," Mike whispered. "How would he even know? Are they spying on you?"

"Maybe it's just a metaphor," Becca murmured. "We don't know for sure he means Andy."

"Then why is he staring at me?" Andy asked softly.

"Ignore him," Teresa said. "He's trying to make you mad. Don't let him."

"Turning away from the path is tempting for many. Life is hard. But only those willing to work hard will be rewarded. The rest will fade away to nothingness, and no one will remember their names."

Andy found himself clenching his fists. So much for not letting Saunders make him mad. He wanted to wipe that smirk right off his face.

The principal finished speaking and turned the mic over to the assistant principal, who started talking about fees and registration.

"He's such a jerk," Mike said. "You'd think he'd *want* Andy to quit. It helps his side."

Becca elbowed him.

PARENTS NIGHT

"What'd I do?" Mike asked.

"Shush," Teresa said.

When the assistant principal finished speaking, their parents headed off to their appointments.

"Meet us by the door when it's over," Mike's mother said as she stepped past her son.

"Where's your grandfather, Teresa?" Andy asked as they made their way through the crowd to a mostly empty hallway.

"Somewhere around. He always has stuff to do at events like this."

"We can take you home if you don't want to wait," Becca said.

"I might take you up on that offer."

"What offer?" Taylor asked. Andy turned to see him, flanked by Pete and Tommy, exiting the gym behind them. Andy was pleased to realize he had gained enough height this year to almost look Pete in the eye.

"Can I get in on that action if it includes two beautiful babes like you?" Taylor said.

"Excuse me?" Becca said coldly.

"C'mon, Becca, you're hot and everyone knows it. And Teresa is mighty fine, too!"

"Get lost, Taylor," Mike said, his face darkening with anger. He moved closer to Teresa.

"Yeah. Beat it, jerk," Andy said. "You're not wanted."

"So you say. What about these fine ladies?"

Becca and Teresa looked at each other, confused.

"Well, how about it?" Taylor said.

"What is *wrong* with you?" Becca said. She glared at him. There was something—different, somehow off, but she couldn't explain it. His eyes seemed almost glassy. Taylor didn't seem to notice her anger.

"I am overcome by your beauty. There has not been a female of such perfection in many, many generations."

Now Pete and Tommy were looking at each other in confusion.

"Get him out of here," Andy said to them between gritted teeth.

CHAPTER SEVEN

He clenched his fists at his sides. "I don't care if I get expelled, if he says one more word about Becca…

"C'mon, Taylor. No trouble tonight. You told us to stop you if these creeps tried to start up." Pete grabbed his arm and started pulling him away. Taylor shook his arm out of Pete's grasp.

"I don't want any trouble. I'm a ladies' man at heart, and my heart's as big as the moon!" He spread his arms wide and smiled at the girls. Pete and Tommy each grabbed an arm and forced him away, ignoring his protests.

"What the heck was that all about?" Andy said. "Is he hitting on you? Did he hit on you while you tutored him?"

"No! He's never acted like that before. I have no idea what's going on with him."

"Well, I don't like it. The less we see of him, the better. Taylor's probably in history class again this year," Andy said. "Are you going to tutor him this year?"

She shrugged. "I haven't spoken to Mr. Straight yet."

"Don't do it."

Becca's brows drew together. "You don't get to tell me what to do."

"Oh, but you can tell me to go back to the Compound and train with Goldeneyes again?"

Becca flushed. "That's not the point."

"It kind of is," Teresa said.

"Stay out of it," Mike muttered.

"Don't *you* tell *me* what to do."

Becca checked her watch. "I'm supposed to be helping Ms. Morris with some stuff." She glanced at Andy and the others. "I'll see you later."

"We may as well all go back to the gym," Mike said. He started out the door. Andy hesitated.

"Come on, Andy," Teresa said. "Don't be mad at Mike. He didn't do anything to you."

"Okay," he muttered, "but I'm getting really tired of them bugging me."

PARENTS NIGHT

Teresa nodded. "I know you are. But they're your friends. You know they mean well."

"Yeah, I guess. I'm glad you understand, anyway."

Teresa smiled and grabbed him by the arm. "Let's go!"

They hurried out of the studio to catch up with Mike.

EIGHT: JUNIOR YEAR

Junior year was shaping up to be different from the previous two years of high school. There was a noticeable distance between Andy and Mike and Becca. They didn't mention it much, but it was obvious they still thought he was wrong not to be working with the Catmages. Andy wished he could tell them about Nafshi, but of course he couldn't. They'd go running to Goldeneyes or Letsan and then where would he be?

"Exactly," Nafshi said to him as he dialed the combination on his locker. "Nobody but you is to know I'm around."

"No kidding," Andy muttered.

"Talking to yourself? You know that's the first sign of insanity," Mike said as he stopped by Andy's locker.

"Yeah? You know what the second sign is?"

"What?"

"Being friends with you," Andy said, grinning.

"You got a point there. I make it a policy only to befriend my fellow crazies. Hey, here are another couple of crazies now! Come join the insanity that is our social circle."

Teresa and Becca looked at each other and shook their heads.

"It's time for history class."

"Oh, joy, we get to see Taylor again," Mike said. "You know, the

JUNIOR YEAR

only reason he could get in again was because of your tutoring, Becca. Don't help him this year."

"If Mr. Straight wants me to tutor him again, I will. Don't be a jerk, Mike. Just leave Taylor alone and we won't have any trouble."

"I can't leave him alone. He is my sworn enemy, and I must destroy him!" He brandished a pen like a dagger. "Have at thee, foul miscreant!"

"Not funny, Mike," Teresa said, frowning. "Come on, Becca, let's get to class and pick seats."

The boys watched as the girls stalked off. "Was it something I said?" Mike asked.

"Yep. But I agreed with every word. Oh, well, maybe Taylor will flunk out this year and we won't have to see his face in class anymore."

"We can always hope! You ready?"

"Yeah." Andy closed his locker and they headed to class. They found the girls sitting together. Andy and Mike took seats directly behind them. Taylor came in after them, looked around the class, and took a seat in the front row.

"Looks like he knows his place," Mike murmured.

"So long as he's not near me," Andy said.

Mr. Straight entered the room as the bell rang, took a seat behind his desk and looked around the room as he took attendance. "Points for you being on time the first day, Mike," he said. "No doubt you'll lose them by tomorrow."

"It is my goal in life to be pointless," Mike said.

"Then you've peaked early," Taylor said to much laughter.

Mr. Straight's eyebrows rose and the class quieted. "Turn to page five," he said. "Let's see which of you gets the point of this lesson."

The day passed quickly. The four friends met again at lunch and in English class.

"We have a new teacher this year," Becca said.

"I'm not surprised. Miss Hoxie looked like she was a million years old. She probably had to retire before she keeled over." Mike said.

CHAPTER EIGHT

"You're terrible," Teresa said, laughing in spite of herself.

Becca shushed them hurriedly as she caught sight of the new teacher approaching the room. She nodded at the students and went to her desk, depositing an armload of paper and notebooks. When the bell rang a short time later, she asked the student nearest the door to shut it, waited until she sat down, and stood before the class.

"I'm Mrs. Ren Silvers, your new AP English teacher. I've had a chat with your last teacher and looked over the syllabus for the previous years. You'll find this year a bit more difficult and maybe a bit more interesting. Do we have any Shakespeare fans in the room?"

Mike's hand shot up, followed by Teresa and Becca and a few other students.

"Good. I've got a few of his sonnets to hand out." She passed the papers to the front of each row. "Who wants to start?" she asked. "It's going to take me a while to learn your names, so please say them when I call on you."

"Mike Murdoch, Shakespearean actor, at your service," he said, standing and taking a bow.

"An actor, eh? Then let's hear you interpret Sonnet 138."

Mike cleared his throat and began to read.

The first few weeks of school passed quickly. Mike and Andy got used to seeing Taylor in history class again. Andy did as the girls suggested and ignored him. Taylor did the same. Andy wondered if Taylor had been told by Saunders to leave them alone. Not that it mattered either way—it was nice to get through his classes without being bothered by him and his friends. Things were calming down as October arrived with the cool autumn days Andy loved so much.

Mike and Andy were already at lunch when Teresa and Becca joined them.

"The Halloween dance is only a few weeks away," Becca said. "We should get to work on our costumes."

JUNIOR YEAR

"What are we going to be this year?" Mike asked.

"Doesn't matter. Count me out because I'm not going," Andy said.

"What?" Becca said.

"Are you kidding?" Mike asked.

"Why not?" Teresa said.

Andy finished chewing a bite of his sandwich before he answered. "I'm tired of costumes. I'm tired of the dance. I'm tired of Saunders. And mostly I'm tired of what happens every year on Halloween."

"None of that has ever been your fault," Becca said.

"Really?" Andy looked around and lowered his voice. "I helped Goldeneyes plan the surveillance of Saunders' house and she almost died because I was late getting there, thanks to Taylor. I didn't do anything when Saunders showed up in his Magelight necklace two years ago. And I couldn't save Matti's fighters last year." He stared darkly at his plate.

"That's ridiculous," Becca snapped. "You *saved* Goldeneyes. You couldn't do a thing about Saunders. And you rescued Matti and a lot of other Catmages on Halloween last year." She looked around and lowered her voice. "Have you forgotten Saunders and his gun? Andy, how many lives have you saved by getting Catmages to Dr. Crane's when they couldn't help each other? How can you possibly ignore all the good things that happen when you're around?"

"It's easy. I just stack them up against all the deaths."

"Andy, you're being way too hard on yourself," Mike said. Teresa nodded at his words. "Becca's right. If it wasn't for you, who knows what might have happened? The bad guys might be in charge right now. Oh, wait. Saunders already is. Wow, I stink at pep talks."

In spite of himself, Andy smiled.

Mike grinned. "That's the spirit. Anyway, why do you think something's going to happen this year? Razor's back in charge again. I would *not* want to be going up against him."

"Yeah, well, I still don't want to go to the dance this year," Andy said.

CHAPTER EIGHT

"What's the matter, Cohen, did Becca finally get tired of your lousy moves?" Taylor said as he passed the table.

"Shut up, Taylor," Mike said.

"Classic. What, Cohen can't even speak for himself?"

"Shut up, Taylor," Andy said.

"Now you can't even use your own words? I'm surprised you can make a decision about the dance without help."

Becca glanced at Taylor and raised her eyebrows. He closed his mouth and frowned. "See you, Becca," he said and walked past the table, jostling Mike on the way.

"Jerk," Andy said through clenched teeth. "Why do you keep tutoring him? He'll never change. He'll always be a bully."

"What I do or don't do isn't your call. And for your information, Taylor's grades are improving in *all* of his classes. That's why I keep helping him. He's trying to be a better person."

Mike snorted. "Yeah? Gee, he's doing such a great job. He's changed so much!"

"That'll never happen," Andy said.

Becca glared at him. "No, it won't if you start up with him every time you see each other."

"What? But *he* started it just now!" Mike said.

"Today, yes. But lots of other times you say something first to try to get a reaction out of him."

"Always works, too," Mike said with a smug grin.

"And that's why Taylor's not the only jerk around here. Excuse me, but I think I'm going to finish my lunch somewhere else." Becca picked up her tray and walked over to a table of her friends from art class, leaving Mike and Andy staring, open-mouthed.

"But—what did I—"

Teresa shook her head. "Drop it, Mike. Let's just finish eating. Although you might want to ease off Becca about Taylor for a while."

Andy shrugged when Mike glanced his way. He turned his atten-

JUNIOR YEAR

tion to his sandwich.

The next morning, Andy was in front of his locker when Mike came by. He stopped short and grabbed Andy's arm pointing to a group of students by the door to Mr. Straight's classroom. Taylor, Pete, and Tommy were talking to a group of girls. Mike put his finger to his lips and Andy nodded. They eased themselves quietly toward Taylor.

"So are you going to the Halloween dance this year, Catherine?"

"Isn't it kind of early to be thinking of that?"

"It's never too early to ask a beautiful girl to go dancing."

Catherine and her friends looked at each other. One of them started laughing. "Well, maybe I'll go," she said. "If the right guy asks me."

The girls giggled.

"Maybe the right guy is asking," Taylor said.

The giggling grew louder.

"Are you asking me or telling me?"

"Asking. You're one hot-looking cat," he said.

"Cat?" she asked. The other girls roared.

Mike couldn't hold himself back any longer. "Geez, Grant, what are you, someone out of a 1950s movie? 'Cat'? Really? Is Catherine hep, too? Maybe even groovy?"

"Uh, Catherine. Cat. Short for Catherine," Taylor said as the girls roared with laughter. Taylor's face reddened.

"I can dig it man," Mike said, causing another eruption of giggles.

The girls walked off, still laughing. Pete and Tommy started forward. Taylor thrust his arm out to stop them.

"Class starts in a minute. Teacher will be here," he muttered. "You better get going." His glance fell on Andy as they moved down the hall. "What's the matter, Cohen, nothing to say?"

"I guess the cat's got my tongue," Andy said, grinning. "Smooth move, Grant. You'll have the girls eating out of your hand any year now."

"Yeah? You think you're doing so great? Who's Becca going to the

CHAPTER EIGHT

dance with? You're not taking her."

Andy grimaced. "She's not going with you either," he said.

"You sure about that, Cohen? I've got weeks to change her mind."

"Change whose mind?" Becca asked as she and Teresa walked up to the doorway.

"Never mind," Andy said.

"Yours," Taylor said. "Want to go to the Halloween dance with me?"

Andy turned scarlet with anger.

Becca glanced from Taylor to Andy. She shook her head. "I'm going with Teresa and Mike. So thank you, but no."

Taylor glowered as he turned and went inside the classroom. Andy tried to hide his relief. For a minute, he'd thought she was going to say yes. He started to follow Mike when Becca put a hand on his shoulder and pulled him to the side.

"This wouldn't have happened if you were going to the dance."

"It's time for class," Andy said, turning his back on her. He stalked over to his desk and sat down with a thump. Mike looked around the room, raised his eyebrows, and whistled.

"Looks like more than a few people could use some relaxation therapy," he said. "Repeat after me: O*wa*...ta*nah*...Siam!"

Mr. Straight came into the classroom and stopped at Mike's desk. "You certainly are if you think I don't know that one. Just once, Mike, I'd like to get to class and find you sitting quietly in your desk ready to start class, not starting up."

"I wasn't! I was trying to calm things down," Mike said.

"Uh-huh." Mr. Straight went to his desk and leaned against it, facing the class. "So, who wants to tell me what they thought about the latest chapter?" he asked. Mike's hand shot up. "Anyone but Mike," he said. "Graysen, let's see if you did the homework last night."

Another week went by and Andy was still adamant about not going to the

JUNIOR YEAR

dance with the others. They gave up trying to convince him, and history class settled back into its usual routine. They all groaned when Mr. Straight announced a pop quiz, but at least it was only ten questions. Andy scanned his answers as the last minutes ticked by.

"Put down your pencils, time's up," Mr. Straight said. "Pass your quizzes to the front and take out your books." He waited until everyone had done so and continued.

"It's project time," he said to scattered groans. "Two-person teams will be working together on a presentation due the end of next week. Your teammate's name is on your assignment." Mr. Straight went up and down the rows handing out papers.

"Hey Teach, it's you and me," Taylor told Becca.

Andy grimaced at the news.

"Looks like I'm with you, Teresa," Andy said.

Mike groaned. "I wanted to team up with Teresa."

"You're stuck with me," Max said.

"Well, you're not bad as a partner, but dude, you're nowhere near as pretty as Teresa."

Max snorted with laughter.

"You can use the rest of the period to discuss your project with your partner and figure out a distribution of work. I'll expect outlines by tomorrow. And believe me when I tell you I'll know if anyone is slacking," Mr. Straight said.

He went back to his desk as the students moved around the class and paired off. Andy tried not to look at Taylor and Becca, but he couldn't help himself.

"It's not like they've never worked together before," Teresa said.

"I know. But I still hate it."

"You need to forget about them and concentrate on our project. We have a week to explain the Silk Road, not Taylor Grant."

"Point taken. Sorry."

"Okay. Now let's decide who's going to do what."

CHAPTER EIGHT

By the end of class, they'd divided the work and agreed to get together after school and on Saturday, when Andy finished working at Coreyton Animal Hospital. "I'll bring my bike," he said. "I could use the exercise now that I'm not going out to the Compound."

Teresa looked around quickly.

"Oops," Andy said. "Probably shouldn't have said that here."

"No, especially with Taylor in the class," she said quietly.

Andy decided not to say anything more about Taylor and Becca, although sometimes it wasn't easy. Taylor was on his best behavior in history class or when Becca could see him, but the smirk he wore during PE and at lunch when Becca wasn't looking made Andy clench his teeth together to stop himself from saying or doing something he'd regret. The week couldn't end fast enough for him.

Saturday finally arrived, and Andy's mom dropped him off at Dr. Crane's. Three hours later, he'd finished his work and was on his way to Teresa's. He spent most of the ride distracted by thinking about the project, so he didn't notice Taylor Grant crossing the street behind him. And he didn't notice Taylor following him down the road, or ducking behind a car as Andy got off his bike and walked up to the Velez's front door and rang the bell.

"Hi," Teresa said as she opened the door. "Come on in."

Mr. Velez called out a greeting as they passed the living room. "Did you eat lunch, Andy?"

"No, Mr. Velez."

"Teresa will find something for you."

"Thanks!"

Andy followed her to the kitchen. The table was spread with books and papers. He shrugged out of his backpack and removed his books and papers. While he arranged them on the table, Teresa made sandwiches for them. They sat at the table eating and discussing the Silk Road. By late afternoon, their project was nearly finished.

"All we need to do now is read it over one last time. There, I've just

JUNIOR YEAR

emailed it to you. Call me after dinner and we'll go over it one last time."

"Okay." Andy stretched and yawned. "I can definitely use a break before I head home. I don't think I can focus my eyes yet."

Teresa laughed. "Let's sit outside for a while. It's not as good as your front porch, but it will do."

They went outside and sat down in plastic chairs on the small concrete porch. Andy took a deep breath. "I love this time of year. The leaves are turning, the sky is so blue—it's just perfect."

They sat in silence for a while.

"Can I tell you something without you getting mad about it?"

"Depends on what you're going to say."

"I've been doing a lot of thinking lately about, well, about Catmages. And Saunders."

Andy frowned. "Don't start."

"No, hear me out. You know, Andy, a lot of people want to be a part of something bigger than them. Like all the protesters we read about. They're looking for a cause they can believe in."

"What does that have to do with Catmages?"

"I'm getting there. Look at what we've learned in history class, how people came together to fight tyranny here in America and overseas. They did it because they believed their cause was right."

Andy's brows drew together. "I know the Catmages are right. That's not the point."

"Sometimes we get caught up in events that are bigger than we are. Sometimes the cause chooses us. I think you were chosen for this fight. I think you need to go back to the Compound. You need to start working with the Catmages again. This is your cause."

"I don't care! I don't want to hurt anyone again. I don't want to be like Saunders! He's horrible. You know what we never told you? I think Saunders arranged the accident that killed your mother. You want me to be a part of something like that?"

"What?" Teresa said, her breath catching. "Andy, what are you

CHAPTER EIGHT

talking about? A tree branch broke and fell on my mother's car while she was on her way to a meeting."

"Yeah. A meeting with Saunders. A tree in front of his house. On a sunny summer's day with no wind and no storm in sight."

"It had previous storm damage!" Teresa said. "The police found scorch marks!"

"Scorch marks like this?" Andy said, clenching his fist and thrusting it at the nearest tree. A flash flew from his Magelight and a two-inch-thick branch toppled to the sidewalk in front of them. Andy ran over to it and held it up to show Teresa the charred end.

"No," she whispered, "no. He didn't. He couldn't." She walked slowly to the end of the sidewalk.

"We have no proof. And Mike didn't want us to tell you. But you deserve to know. He had Wild Ones at the house. Any one of them could have done it."

"No," she repeated, tears sliding down her cheeks.

At the sight of her tears, Andy was overcome with remorse. "I'm sorry. I shouldn't have told you. But Teresa, I came so close to really hurting Taylor. I can't stand him, but I don't want him dead. I don't want to be like Saunders."

"You're not like Saunders. You're the opposite of Saunders," Teresa said, wiping her eyes. "You could never hurt someone on purpose. Oh, Andy, did he really kill my mother?"

She burst into tears, sobs wracking her body. Andy didn't know what to do. Teresa threw her arms around him. He stroked her back awkwardly while she cried.

"I'm sorry." *Idiot*, he thought. *Mike was right. You shouldn't have told her.*

Teresa finally cried herself out and took a step back from Andy, sniffling. "I'm really sorry," he said.

"You keep saying that," she said with a wan smile. "It wasn't your fault."

JUNIOR YEAR

"No. It was Saunders."

"That's why you need to go back."

"Can we not talk about it now?"

"All right," she said softly.

She looked so sad. Andy felt awful. He and Teresa both knew what it was like to lose a parent. The lowering sun glittered in the tears on her face and Andy felt—he didn't know what he felt, other than overwhelming emotion.

Before he knew what he was doing, Andy leaned toward her, his arms moving to her shoulders. At the last moment, she turned her face away. Andy's face burned and he stepped back, releasing her.

"Mike," she said softly. "Becca."

Andy felt like an idiot. "I should get going," he muttered. He turned and walked quickly into the house, followed more slowly by Teresa. Andy got his backpack and said goodbye to Mr. Velez. Teresa stood uncomfortably by the front door.

"Well, see you."

"I'll call you tomorrow about the project," he said without looking at her.

Andy got on his bike and rode away. Teresa closed the door behind her as she went back into the house.

Across the street, Taylor stood up and looked over the car he'd been hiding behind. "It was so worth coming back here to see what was going on," he said to himself. "Oh, I can't wait to tell Becca about what Andy and Teresa are getting up to. Monday is going to be one heck of a day." He laughed out loud and hurried down the block, a spring in his step.

Andy fretted all day Sunday. What was he thinking? Teresa was with Mike, and he'd tried to kiss her! He was so distracted that afternoon that Nafshi called off training after half an hour.

"You're useless to me until you settle yourself," she said sourly. "If you can't concentrate, get out of here and do something else."

91

CHAPTER EIGHT

"Fine," Andy said. "I don't want to practice now, anyway." He stalked off into his room and slammed the door behind him.

"Not very effective when I live inside your head," Nafshi said, though she didn't materialize in his room.

"Go take a nap or something," he sent. "I need to be alone. That means from you, too!"

"Fine," Nafshi said. "You're on your own until you call me back."

Andy sat down at his desk and started to review the Silk Road project. Thankfully, he could concentrate on that. When he was finished, he picked up the phone and called Teresa.

"Hi," she said.

Andy cleared his throat nervously. "Are you at your computer?"

"Yes. I was going over the project."

"Me, too." They spent the next fifteen minutes discussing the paper. When they were satisfied it was ready, Andy said, "So, about yesterday…"

"I don't want to talk about it. Ever."

"Okay."

"As far as I'm concerned, it never happened."

"Okay."

"See you tomorrow."

"Goodbye."

Andy hung up the phone, pleased. Okay, he'd done a stupid thing. But it was over, and nothing really bad happened. He and Teresa were still friends. His heart swelled with happiness.

"Okay, Nafshi, let's go train," he said.

"It's about time," she grumbled as he headed downstairs. "Neshama spare me from teenager trouble."

"Well, I didn't ask you to stick around," Andy said. "You're stuck with me."

"And *you're* stuck with me."

Andy shrugged. "Yeah, well, I like having you around most of the time."

JUNIOR YEAR

"Oh? And when do you not like it?"

"I'll be sure to let you know."

Andy took his usual position in the backyard, cross-legged on the ground.

"Let's begin," Nafshi said.

Andy didn't get a chance to talk to Teresa during math class on Monday, but she was friendly enough when he said hello. They met again in history class. Mr. Straight read down the list of teams who would present their projects that day. Andy and Teresa would go third, followed by Becca and Taylor. Mike cheered when Mr. Straight finished reading the list. "We're day two! We're day two!" he chanted, stopping when Mr. Straight frowned at him.

Their presentation went well. They took turns speaking about the different parts of their project, finished just shy of their allotted time, and heaved a sigh of relief that there weren't any questions. Andy and Teresa sat down and Taylor and Becca took their place at the front of the room.

"Break a leg," Andy muttered as he passed Taylor. "For real." Taylor smirked at him. Andy frowned through their presentation until Mike kicked him and whispered that if his expression got any nastier he'd use it as a model for a gargoyle in set design class. Andy took the hint and stopped glowering. He couldn't concentrate on the presentation, though. He couldn't stand Taylor spending time with Becca. At last the presentation was over, and class was nearly so. Then the bell rang, and the classroom filled with the noise of chairs scraping the floor, books being gathered, and students chattering.

"See you at lunch, Cohen," Taylor said brightly as he passed Andy's chair.

"And there it is again," Mike said. "Gargoyle face! I'm totally using that for the model Ms. Morris assigned us."

"Shut up," Andy grumbled. He picked up his books and headed out the door. "I have to stop off at my locker. I'll meet you in the cafeteria."

CHAPTER EIGHT

He hurried out of the room before Becca or Teresa could catch him.

Andy took his time going to his locker. The others were already seated and eating lunch by the time he joined them. He wasn't feeling very talkative, anyway. Between embarrassment at being around Teresa and anger at Taylor and Becca, Andy wished this day was already over. It couldn't possibly get any worse. And then he looked up and saw Taylor coming over, tray in hand.

"Hey, Murdoch, move over, I need to talk to you," Taylor said. He stood behind Mike, who turned his head and glared.

"Get lost, Grant. I don't have anything to say to you."

"That's fine, I'll do the talking. Hey, Teresa, Andy, you know, the funniest thing happened to me on Saturday."

"Take a hint, Grant. Get lost," Andy said.

"What he said," Mike added.

"No, really, Murdoch, you'll like this. It has all that stuff you like. Drama! Romance! Thrills! Intrigue! And—drum roll please—betrayal!"

"What are you talking about? Are you drunk or something?"

"Nope. See, I was on my way home on Saturday and I happened to see Cohen, there, riding his bike. Well, we were going the same way, only he didn't see me." Taylor shrugged. "You know, it really isn't smart, riding your bike without noticing your surroundings. You never know what might happen."

"So you saw me riding my bike. Big deal." He took a bite of his sandwich.

"Oh, that wasn't the big deal. The real big deal was what I saw when you were *off* your bike and in Teresa's front yard a couple hours later. Hey, Mike, are you and Teresa going out or what?"

Andy stopped eating. "Wait, are you saying you were *spying* on me?" he said.

"Are you saying there's something to be spied on?"

"What happens between me and Teresa is none of your business. Get to the point or get out," Mike said.

JUNIOR YEAR

"I'm getting there, I'm getting there. So I saw Cohen on the way to Teresa's, and I wondered what he was doing there. Then I remembered, oh yeah, they're both on the history project together. But you know what? It turns out they're doing more than history together, if you know what I mean." Taylor grinned broadly.

"No, I don't know what you mean. And I don't think I really care."

"Get lost, Taylor," Andy said, suddenly overwhelmed by fear. "Nobody cares what you saw."

"Oh, I think Mike and Becca will care. Really, they need to hear this. Trust me, Becca. So I'm coming back the same way, and I'm across the street from Teresa's house, and guess what I see? Andy reaching out to kiss Teresa. Ooh, I could have sworn Teresa was your girl, Mike."

"You're lying," Mike said. "Get out of here before I make you go."

"I'm not lying." He lowered his voice. "I can show you the Magelight picture. Yeah, I know how to do it, too," he said at Andy's sudden look. "And you know what Roah told me? He said you can't make up a Magelight picture. It can only show what really happened. So yeah, I'm telling the truth. I can prove it."

Mike and Becca looked at each other, then at Andy and Teresa. Andy couldn't hide the guilt he felt. "I can explain," he said.

Mike's mouth dropped open. "He—he's not lying?"

"Listen, I can explain. It wasn't like that."

"You kissed Teresa?"

"No! I tried to. I mean, no, that's not what happened." Andy's face flushed. "Look, I can explain, but not with this jerk hanging over us. Get lost, Grant!" Andy rose and clenched his fist. His Magelight grew warm.

"Andy!" Becca said. He turned to her and saw the pain on her face. His anger disappeared.

"Becca, let me explain."

She rose and picked up her tray. "I don't want to hear anything right now. Don't follow me." She left the table.

Taylor stepped back from Mike and Teresa, still grinning. "I guess

CHAPTER EIGHT

I'll go eat my lunch somewhere else. You three have fun now, hear?" Laughing, Taylor walked away.

"I didn't kiss her. We didn't kiss," Andy said.

"Then what happened?"

"It was kind of an accident."

"You accidentally fell into Teresa's face?"

"We—I—I sort of almost kissed her. But Teresa wouldn't let me. Nothing happened. I swear it!"

"Why would you try to kiss Teresa? How could you do this to me? And how could you not tell me?" he said, looking at her.

"It was nothing. It was just a stupid moment and it passed."

Mike stood up, knocking his chair over as he did. "A stupid moment? You're my best friend! Best friends don't kiss their best friend's girl!"

"I didn't kiss her!"

"You tried to. You know what? I can't look at either one of you right now." He righted his chair, picked up his tray, and left. Andy and Teresa's eyes met.

"I'm sorry," Andy said.

"So am I." Teresa said as she got up and walked away. Andy sat at the table by himself, staring at his plate, as students chattered all around him.

Taylor watched from across the room, a broad smile on his face. "Today was a good day," he told Pete and Tommy. "A very good day."

NINE: MISCHIEF IN THE NIGHT

The next few weeks were the worst of Andy's life. Mike stopped talking to him completely. Becca was stiff and formal with him in class and ignored him the rest of the time. Andy noticed that she was cool and distant with Teresa as well for a while, but the girls evidently made up because he saw them eating lunch together—with Mike, too. But they didn't seem to want to make up with him. Well, he reasoned, I was the one who tried to kiss her. He still had no idea why he had even wanted to.

He saw Mr. Velez one day in the locker room before PE class. Mike had just hurried off to the gym at the sight of him and left Andy to finish changing alone.

"Problems between you guys still?" he asked.

"Did Teresa tell you what happened?"

"Yeah. That was a dumb thing you did."

"I know. How come you're not mad at me?"

"Because you're a teenager. Teenagers do dumb things. I been telling Teresa that. Mike, too."

Andy's head drooped. "It's not working. They hate me."

"Nah, they're just hurt and angry. They'll get over it. Just be patient." He squeezed Andy's shoulder. "You're a good kid, Andy. Now go on

CHAPTER NINE

and get out of here. I got cleaning to do and you're in my way."

"Thanks, Mr. Velez," Andy said. He closed his locker and hurried to the gym, where he watched silently as Mike made sure he wasn't on Andy's team. Taylor smirked every time he came near. He was so full of himself he didn't even bother trying to rough Andy up when the teacher wasn't looking. In a way, it was worse. Taylor kept grinning and making kissing noises. Andy clenched his jaw, determined not to rise to the bait.

PE seemed to take hours. Andy sighed with relief when Mr. Getzler blew the whistle and told them all to go get changed. He decided to take his time getting back in order to give Mike enough time to get out of the locker room without talking to him. Besides, he was tired of watching Mike work hard to avoid talking or making eye contact. So he stopped at the water fountain and took a leisurely drink and walked as slowly as possible. He was the last one in the locker room and Mike was gone. Andy pulled off his gym clothes and changed into his school clothes, shut his locker, and picked up his books. He looked around and saw that the room was empty. Good. He didn't have to face anyone. Andy walked down a row of lockers and veered to the right. The room wasn't empty after all. Taylor was closing his locker and caught sight of him as he turned the corner.

"Cohen! How's my little kissing bandit these days?" he said brightly.

"Shut up, Grant."

"Isn't it amazing how a lifelong friendship can go *pffft!* over a silly little thing? Hey, you know what that song says, a kiss is just a kiss."

"I didn't kiss her!"

"Yeah, but it's the thought that counts, isn't it?" Taylor said, grinning from ear to ear. "Oh, Cohen, you have no idea how sweet this is. The amazing Andy, not so amazing after all. Guess when it comes down to it, you're not so great, are you?" Taylor's grin disappeared.

"Yeah? Well at least I've got girls who are interested in me. Nobody wants you. You're just one big loser, and everyone knows it."

Now it was Taylor's turn to get angry. "Loser, huh? Let's see, football team, special tutoring sessions with Becca—and boy, are they special!" he said.

MISCHIEF IN THE NIGHT

"What's that supposed to mean?"

"Figure it out, Brainiac. What did you think would happen after you hurt Becca's feelings like that? She just needs a shoulder to cry on. A big, strong, football player shoulder. Like mine."

"You're lying."

"Am I?"

Taylor and Andy glared at each other. The grin came back to Taylor's face. Then he pursed his lips and made a kissing noise again.

A wave of cold anger enveloped Andy. He felt as if he'd been drenched with ice water. *That's enough* sounded in his head. He didn't know if it came from himself or from Nafshi, and he didn't care. It felt right. His Magelight flickered and a jet of light flashed right at Taylor's face. Taylor's Magelights blazed in answer. A multicolored shield rose in front of him and Andy's light dagger bounced off harmlessly. An ugly expression came over Taylor's face.

"You want to start with me, Cohen? You got it." The lights from his Magelights played over both of them. Andy's Magelight roared to life, its green light flaring out of his wristband.

"Hey!" Mr. Velez called from across the room. "What the heck are you two doing?" His mop crashed to the floor as he ran over to the boys. "Are you crazy? You want people to find out what those things are?" He stepped in between them, forcing them back from one another. "What's wrong with you, Andy? How many times are you going to let this guy goad you into doing something stupid?"

Taylor laughed. "As many times as it takes."

"And you," Mr. Velez said. "You think you're such a big shot. You think you're in control. You're an idiot. You think Saunders gives a damn about you? Think again. The second he doesn't need you anymore, he'll drop you, or worse. You're on the wrong team, Taylor. Get smart. And get out of here. Now!"

Taylor flushed at the janitor's words, but he picked up his backpack and left. Mr. Velez and Andy faced each other. Andy's face was red and his

CHAPTER NINE

pulse was racing.

"Well?" Mr. Velez said. "What was that?"

Andy shrugged. "I got mad."

"No kidding. Mad and stupid. What if someone else had seen you guys?"

"Nobody saw us!"

"Pure luck. You won't be lucky all the time. Get a hold of yourself, Andy. You're going through a rough time. I get it. But that's no reason to act stupid."

Andy dropped his gaze. "I have to get to class."

"Go. But think about what I said."

"Yeah."

He shifted his books and hurried out the door. Mr. Velez went over to his mop, picked it up, and sighed. "Teenagers," he said with a snort.

A week before the Halloween dance, Andy sat on the front porch in the slanting sunlight of late afternoon, the sounds and smells of autumn all around. He heard the crunch of leaves in the yard next door and wondered what creature was walking around. Not a squirrel, he thought. Possum? Raccoon?

"Catmage?" the battered Maine Coon sent as he slipped between the hedge that separated Andy's house from his neighbor's.

"Razor!" Andy said out loud, clapping his hand to his mouth immediately after. "Oops," he sent.

"So you've forgotten everything you learned and made yourself an open target for any Wild One who comes near?" Razor said.

"Why would they come after me?"

"You think because you say you quit, they won't target you? Boy, you've gotten dumber since you left us."

Andy's face reddened. "Why are you here, Razor? I don't remembering asking you to visit."

"Well, you won't come to the Compound. So I came to you."

MISCHIEF IN THE NIGHT

"I'm not coming back."

"Yes you are. I know it, you know it, everyone knows it. You can't hide forever."

"I'm not hiding," Andy said angrily. "I'm protecting you and everyone else!"

"Hiding," Razor repeated. "I don't need protection. I'm the head of the Shomrim again. Did Letsan tell you they made Flathead take me back?"

"Yes," Andy said. "That's great! Congratulations."

"Look at you, smiling and everything. You miss me."

Andy's smile disappeared. "Doesn't matter. I'm not coming back. Every time I'm around, bad things happen. And then Catmages die."

"Bad things happen no matter who's around, Andy. These are bad times. The Wild Ones and Saunders are doing their best to make them worse. Yes, Catmages have died. That's what happens in war. And we're at war."

Andy looked away.

"We need every asset for this fight and you, boy, are one of our finest assets. Stop hiding here and come back to the Compound. Zohar has some pretty good strategies he and Mike worked out, but they need a boy with a Magelight, not a boy with a slingshot."

"Mike's been out to the Compound without me? He's not even talking to me now, but he's out with you?"

"He's been out a few times. You think we're going to stop preparing just because you're out here sulking?"

"I'm not sulking!"

"Okay. You're not sulking. Then what are you doing?"

Andy's thoughts went to his training sessions with Nafshi. He couldn't tell Razor anything about that. "Nothing," he said.

Razor watched him, eyes narrowed, as if he could read Andy's mind. *Did I let my guard down? Did he hear me thinking about Nafshi?*

No, she assured him. *I'm making sure you have a wall around your*

CHAPTER NINE

thoughts when there are any Catmages nearby.

Phew.

"Where did you go?" Razor asked. "You look—well, you look like you're talking to someone."

"I'm not talking to anyone," Andy said. Thinking wasn't talking. "I was just—distracted."

"So you won't come back to us yet, hey? All right. I can wait a while longer. But not too much longer. I have things to do that involve you."

"Well, you're wasting your time, then." Andy crossed his arms and propped his feet on the railing. "I'm not going anywhere."

Razor jumped onto the railing and stood facing Andy. "Let's make a bet. I like a treat every now and then, too. Next time I see you at the Compound, I want some of those little fish you give my brother."

"Sardines? Tuna?"

"Both."

Andy shrugged. "Whatever. I'm not going to lose."

"And I want you to feed them to me by hand."

Andy laughed. "Not going to happen. Thanks for coming by."

Razor grunted. "See you around, kid." He leaped off the railing onto the front lawn. "I'll let you know when I want you to bring the fish." He trotted through the gate and disappeared.

"You should practice your aura spell right now," Nafshi said when he was gone. "Go find Razor and his Magelight."

Andy straightened up and concentrated. He saw the orange light in his mind and felt Razor's aura moving steadily away from the house. "He's heading out of town. I thought he might stop by Saunders' house, but he's going straight for the road."

"See if there are any others around him."

Andy expanded the reach of his Magelight in his mind. *Pop, pop, pop, pop*—four more Magelights showed up.

"I think you're missing one. There are six in his squad."

Andy concentrated harder. There! There was the sixth. He recog-

MISCHIEF IN THE NIGHT

nized the feel of Zohar's aura and was immediately saddened. "He lost his leg because of me."

"He has his *life* because of you," Nafshi said sternly. "Andrew, your self-pity is beginning to wear thin."

His Magelight went out as Andy stood up abruptly. "It's getting cold. I'm going inside." He closed the door behind him with a bang.

Ari sighed with relief as he neared the West Woods. He and Lev led a squad of half-grown Catmages they'd managed to talk into leaving their Compounds. It wasn't hard. They were young males, tired of authority, and eager to start a new life out from under the thumbs of their parents and teachers. Ari realized he was starting to sound like one of those old-timers he used to laugh at when they spoke of the good days when they were young, but by the First, these young ones were tiresome. And none of them could hit a tree with a light jet if they were standing in front of it. He held back a laugh as he realized how long it would take to train these young ones up.

"Almost there," Lev said to the excited Catmages. They came within sight of a guard post and he called out his name to the listening Wild Ones. They emerged from the brush and watched as Lev and Ari led their charges to the center of the Compound. Kel came to meet them as the news spread.

"Hello and welcome!" he said. "Had a good journey? Tired? Thirsty? Dalet! Gimmel! Hay!"

His three Siamese siblings slunk out of a nearby bayit.

"Take these young Catmages to the stream and get them settled. There's an empty barracks near the birch tree." He turned to the new recruits. "These three will be happy to serve your every need," he said maliciously. "Do be sure to tell me if they don't."

He watched his siblings lead the way to the stream.

"This is the best you could do? This is only the second group you've found since summer!"

CHAPTER NINE

Ari examined his front paw. "All of the nearby Compounds have been turned against us by Razor and his allies. You do realize we need to be circumspect, don't you? We can't exactly go around shouting that we need fighters for a Catmage revolution. We had to travel quite a distance just to get these catlings."

Kel's tail beat the ground. "No females?"

"We couldn't talk any of them into leaving. You know how it is with females. They want a home, they want kittens. They're territorial. You need to give them a really good reason to leave."

"There are almost no female Seekers," Lev pointed out.

"Velvel found us females," Kel said.

"Yes, I know," Ari said. "We asked around before we left so we didn't waste our time going to the same Compounds. Velvel traveled very far and found overcrowded Compounds that wouldn't let many females breed," Ari replied. "We haven't been able to find any of those yet."

"Then look harder and travel farther."

"It will take us longer. Do you want Catmages now, or do you want them in the spring?"

Kel's tail whipped. "I want them now, but I acknowledge your point. All right, Ari. Do your best. I will tell my father."

Lev yawned widely. "Do you mind if we go rest? We've been on the road a long time."

"By all means. I'll go make sure my siblings are treating our new residents well." He trotted off toward the stream, tail held high.

Lev glanced at his father.

"Not now," Ari sent privately. "Sleep first." He led the way to their bayit and the two settled down to nap. It was dark when they awoke. Ari and Lev rose, stretched, and yawned.

"By the First, I could eat a rabbit," Lev said. "Let's go hunt."

As they left the bayit, they saw Kel and Roah coming their way.

"Well, they don't look happy," Lev said.

"Quiet."

MISCHIEF IN THE NIGHT

"Roah," Ari said as they met. "Good to see you."

"Kel has informed me of your latest finds. They are not enough."

"Did Kel also tell you how hard a time we had just finding those six young males?"

"He did. That is also not enough. You and Lev will go back on the road again and bring us females. This Compound cannot thrive if it has no kittens."

Kel looked sharply at his father, tilting his head.

"Is there something you want to say?" Roah asked.

"No sir. It's just an idea I got, I need to think it over a while. I will see you later." He left the three of them standing there and faded into the darkness.

"You will leave tonight," Roah said.

Ari bit back a reply. "All right. We'll go now. We need to hunt anyway. Might as well do it on the road."

"Bring back some females."

"If we can."

Roah stared at Ari. "I do not appreciate failure."

"We'll do our best. But we can't guarantee that we'll find willing females."

"Then find me more Seekers who will." Roah went down the path in the direction Kel had gone. Ari and Lev looked at each other.

"Let's get out of here," Ari said. Lev nodded and followed him to the edge of the Compound. They turned south when they reached the road, keeping to the brush so that oncoming cars couldn't see them. When they were far enough away from the Compound, Ari began to swear.

"I will *not* bring them any females," he said. "It's bad enough I have to leave those young males here to be influenced by their rotten ways."

"Maybe Razor will come up with a way to finish this before long, and they won't get a chance to ruin any more Catmages."

"Let's hope so. Come on, son, I'm famished. Let's get something to eat and get back on the road again. We'll think of something."

CHAPTER NINE

They headed into the trees.

Kel walked along the path. Roah's words had started a thought process that led to the beginnings of a plan that, he knew, would please his father. He jumped like a kitten as he realized how simple yet how devastating the plan could be. But Kel was smart. No need to be rash. He decided to think about it overnight and present it to Roah in the morning. Kittens. They would go after the kittens in the East Woods Compound. There would be no need to rely on Seekers.

TEN: HALLOWEEN

The autumn wind whistled through the branches of Hakham's bayit as the East Wood Council met within. Leaves blew past the opening as the Catmages took their places.

"Razor," Hakham said, "did you have any success with your visit to town?"

"Yes and no. Andy says he's not coming back, but I'm going to get two tins of fish when he does. I made a bet."

Letsan laughed. "Brother, will you be sharing with the rest of us?"

"No. Go to town and get your own."

Goldeneyes shifted uncomfortably. "We don't need fish. We need Andrew's Magelight and his powers. The Wild Ones haven't made a move in ages. I don't trust the quiet."

"Neither do I," Razor said. "This does seem to be one of their favorite times of year to make a move."

"How stand the Shomrim perimeter guards?" Hakham asked.

"Better than ever. We had a good number of new recruits after the Council meeting," he said, nodding at Hakham. "We know for a fact that we have a greater force than the Wild Ones."

"That doesn't mean they won't attack. It just means they'll be smarter about it," Zehira said.

CHAPTER TEN

"No doubt. Then we'll have to be smarter than the Wild Ones," Razor replied. "Don't worry, we're ready for them this time."

"Good," Hakham said. "Then I will rest easy the next few nights."

"I'll rest easy when the Wild Ones are all dead and the Tilyon is in our hands."

The first alarm came from Shomrim guarding the road. A large number of Wild Ones were heading toward the Compound, and the perimeter guards were under attack. They fought hard but were forced to retreat, overwhelmed by the flood of Wild Ones. Razor processed the message quickly and shouted to his captains. Shomrim awakened from naps, ran out of their homes, and hurried to join their squad leaders. In moments, dozens of fighters raced through the trees toward the attackers. Razor stopped at the edge of the wood, his ears twitching and his Magelight flashing as he scanned the area. Once he had an idea of the direction the Wild Ones were taking, he gave his lieutenants coordinates for their squads, watching as they hurried toward the enemy. He took one more quick look around, checked the Compound defenses one last time, then he and his squad sped to the scene of the battle.

Inside the Compound, Silsula called the kittens and younger Catmages to follow her to the meadow. She and Zehira kept them in a group as Patches and Leilei made sure none straggled behind. Silsula shot a worried glance at the Shomrim who ranged around them, wondering if she should summon more. She decided against it. Razor's warriors were needed for the battle. She and her team would be fine. The Wild Ones were cruel, but not so cruel as to attack kittens! When the youngsters were all seated nervously in rows before her, she had them separate into four groups and follow her and the others to the ma'on, the large shelter they used during the winter months. They went inside the structure as the adults took their positions at the three openings. Six of Razor's picked guards split up, two to each door, alert and ready.

"Is everything going to be all right?" Anat, one of the youngest

HALLOWEEN

kittens, asked worriedly.

"It will be fine, my lovelies," Silsula told her, trying to keep the concern from her voice. "Just stay here until we tell you it's safe to come out. You older ones, take care of the babies." She looked at Zev, one of the oldest members of the Teaching Rings, sitting confidently near the door. "You're in charge," she told him for all to hear. "Keep them calm and quiet," she sent privately. "Have them practice reciting the Laws. Make up something to keep their minds off things. Do whatever you have to. Just don't let them panic." Zev dipped his head in assent and Silsula joined Zehira, waiting and watching.

Razor and his warriors raced through the trees. He cursed the Wild Ones privately. Fighting in the woods meant they would be unable to join up in ranks. They'd have to battle in small groups. The Wild Ones would use the cover of trees to their advantage. Well, his fighters were superb, either in groups or singly. They'd prepared for many different battle scenarios. They'd handle this.

"Kill anyone you don't recognize!" he sent to his lieutenants scattered in the wood. They would relay the order to their fighters. Then he had little time to think, as the first wave of Wild Ones was on them. Razor fired, dodged, growled, and attacked. He saw Kfir in the distance. "What's the matter, Kfir, losing your touch? Did you think you could sneak past our watch?" he called.

Kfir closed the distance between them, firing light daggers. Razor dodged rather than shield himself.

"Saving your energy, Razor, or are you just weak?" Kfir said as he cast a shield in time to knock aside Razor's attack.

Razor laughed harshly. "No, just faster than you." He dodged another blade and flung one of his own. It scorched Kfir's shoulder and the big, cream-colored Catmage grunted in pain.

"Score one for you. My turn now." Kfir launched himself at Razor. The two grappled and bit and rolled and growled, hissing and yowling. The

CHAPTER TEN

sounds of their fight echoed through the wood.

Letsan and Hakham sped through the trees. They fell into a rhythm. Seek, attack, destroy. Find another group of Wild Ones, seek, attack, destroy. At one point they passed Zohar and his squad. Zohar raced around on three legs as if he'd been born that way. Letsan felt a thrill of pride as he saw his son chase and defeat a pair of Wild Ones. He didn't even need the backup his squad provided. Then Letsan swore as a light dagger glanced off his shoulder and the smell of singed fur rose in the air.

"Perhaps you should stick to admiring your son's fighting style on the practice field," Hakham said grimly, firing at the Wild One who had marked Letsan.

"Sorry, Master," Letsan said as his Magelight glowed and he joined his fire to Hakham's. His antagonist dropped to the ground and lay still. They looked around for new targets. Except for the ones facing Zohar and his squad, there were no Wild Ones near.

"We're awfully deep in the woods," Letsan said. "Where are the rest of them?"

"That is a good question," Hakham said. "There are some battles over that way, but there should be many more foes around us."

They reached the same conclusion at the same moment. Letsan's heart sank as he realized they'd been deliberately drawn into the woods. "They wanted us out here."

"Back to the Compound!" Hakham said. They turned and sprinted away. As they rounded a large maple tree, a group of Wild Ones rose from their hiding places and attacked. Letsan swore as his shield went up too late to deflect a barb from scoring his chest.

"Is it bad?" Hakham said, shielding them both.

"Give me a moment to stop the bleeding. Then may the First help the one who ruined my ruff."

Darts bounced off Hakham's shield as Letsan closed his eyes and performed the healing spell on himself. The cut stopped bleeding.

HALLOWEEN

"Now," he told them, rising and firing at the Wild Ones, "let us discuss how you must never harm my coat." Two of their enemies dropped as he and Hakham attacked. The rest ducked behind the trees, firing from cover. The Wild Ones outnumbered them. Hakham and Letsan dodged and shielded, firing light daggers when they could.

"This is going to take a while," Letsan said grimly. "Let's hope Zehira and Silsula have things under control."

Kfir rose to his feet, bleeding from several slashes, sides heaving. Razor spit out a mouthful of fur. Kfir and Razor circled one another warily. Razor had a gash opened along his ribs, but he was fresher than Kfir. "You're dead this time," Razor said. "You're not getting away from me."

Kfir laughed. "Oh, Razor," he said at last, "you are so predictable. While you and your Shomrim have been out in the woods seeking my Tzofim, who's been guarding your Compound? And what is the most precious thing inside a Compound? Or should I say, things?"

Razor hesitated as Kfir's plan began to unravel in his mind. "The kittens! You're after the kittens! No!"

"Yes. It's so much easier getting that lot from you instead of having our Seekers bring them in one or two at a time. They're young enough that we can reshape them without much trouble, don't you think? Treat them nicely, tell them about the lies you feed them, teach them the dangerous, exciting spells at a much younger age—well, it's worked nicely on all the kittens we've found so far, except for that idiot Patches. So, while you and your fighters have been chasing us through the trees, another team was tasked to fetch your kittens."

A message globe flashed out of Razor's Magelight. He had to warn Silsula!

"Too late," Kfir said. "You're not going anywhere, and your fighters are otherwise engaged. Look around you, Razor. See how far away we've drawn your Shomrim. Didn't you notice how hard it was to find us? Aren't you wondering where the other half of my fighters went?" Razor listened

CHAPTER TEN

sharply, trying to determine the number of enemies nearby.

"Fool," Kfir said. "They waited until we'd drawn your warriors far enough into the forest. One or two good fighters can keep quite a number of Shomrim busy if they have trees to duck in and around. It makes you think you're fighting a lot more warriors than you really are."

Razor glanced around the wood. Kfir was telling the truth. Razor's warriors were far away, fighting one-on-one or in twos and threes, but there were far fewer enemies within range than there should be. The feint had left the Compound nearly defenseless, and they'd fallen for it like a one-moon kitten trips over a stick. Fear chilled Razor as he realized that only a handful of fighters guarded the kittens. But he couldn't turn his back on Kfir. Fury filled him and he leaped forward with a roar of anger and frustration. Kfir rose on his hind legs and met the attack. They crashed to the ground, rolling over and over on the dirt. Even as he grappled with Kfir, Razor sent another Magelight message. The kittens must be protected!

"It doesn't matter," Kfir said as he backed off again. Drops of blood fell from his torn ear. "Your message won't do any good. There are squads of my Tzofim held in reserve heading for your precious kittens as we speak. That was the plan all along, Razor. That, and doing our best to destroy your forces."

"Yeah. About that," Razor said, leaping at Kfir once more. This time, Kfir dodged aside and took off running. Razor gave chase.

Goldeneyes battled two Wild Ones at once, ducking and leaping and shielding herself. She aimed a dagger for the eyes of one of her attackers. She closed her eyes as she made the dagger burst into a bright light, blinding the Wild One. Now it was single combat, and Goldeneyes was by far the better fighter. Her opponent fell. Breathing deeply, Goldeneyes turned her attention to the blinded Wild One. He turned tail and ran, blundering into trees and bushes. That one was no longer a threat. She looked around for the nearest battle to join, but an amber light globe zoomed through the wood and zipped into her Magelight to deliver Razor's message: The kit-

HALLOWEEN

tens were in danger! Goldeneyes turned toward the Compound and ran as if her life depended on it. As she ran, anger overcame her fear. They dared threaten the kittens! May the First help any Wild Ones who got in her way. But even as she ran she knew she needed more than her anger. She needed Andy and his friends. A message flared out of her Magelight and raced toward town. Goldeneyes could only hope he would get it in time.

She slowed as she neared the ma'on. She could hear the young ones crying in fear. Silsula, Zehira, and a handful of Shomrim guarded the entrances. Patches and Leilei fought furiously, their fur standing out stiffly and their Magelights flashing. Goldeneyes fired light daggers at the Wild Ones, and she fought to kill. Two fell before the others could turn to face her. Goldeneyes deflected their fire with a shield spell and then aimed at the Wild One who seemed to be the leader. She growled as she saw his face. Kel! Her dagger drew blood along his flank and he cried out in pain. Leilei used his distraction to good advantage.

"Traitor!" she shouted. "Coward! Attacker of the young and the weak!" As she spoke, she fired dagger after dagger at Kel and his fighters, forcing them back. Goldeneyes added her darts to Leilei's.

Silsula and Zehira, seeing the Wild Ones retreat, joined the attack. Two more fell. Goldeneyes was elated. The fighters were coming after them now and leaving the kittens alone.

"Second squad!" Kel shouted. "Imri! Inbar! Now!"

Goldeneyes gasped as two large Wild Ones emerged from the woods, firing at her as they ran. She could see more fighters behind them. Kel drew back behind the reinforcements. "Coward!" she called, drawing the attention and fire of his bodyguards. She hastily put up another defensive shield and retreated toward the ma'on. She reached the edge of the structure and moved to stand between Leilei and Silsula. Two Shomrim guards had fallen. The Wild Ones launched another attack and two more guards fell, wounded or dead. The defenders were tiring.

"Shields together, Leilei. Now!" she said. Leilei joined her shield to the one Goldeneyes still held. Now it was wide enough to cover them all.

CHAPTER TEN

The Wild Ones' darts bounced off the shield, but she and Leilei were tiring.

"We need help," Silsula said, panting as she fired at the Wild Ones.

"We'll have to hold on until we get it," she said grimly. "Sister, it is time to show these evil creatures that the blood of Nafshi runs in our veins. You remember our lessons with Methuselah?"

"Of course! Give the signal, Zahavin."

"As we practiced. Leilei, cover us when I give the word."

"I'll be ready."

She and Silsula moved closer to one another. She was comforted by the touch of her sister's flank against hers.

"Same here," Silsula said. "Don't worry, I won't tell Andy you're projecting your thoughts."

Goldeneyes couldn't suppress a laugh. She glanced around, taking in the positions of the Wild Ones, hearing the frightened voices of the kittens inside the ma'on. It sounded like Zev had started them chanting the Seven Laws again. Good.

"By the First, we're going to end this," she muttered. "Now, Leilei! Now, Silsula!" Leilei extended her shield to cover them as she and Silsula each created a large sphere of light, one gold, one green. The spheres glowed and glittered with rivers of undulating light. The Wild Ones, distracted, paused in their attack. Some of them stood transfixed. This spell was like nothing they had ever seen.

Leilei could hear Kel spitting with anger as many of the Wild Ones, hypnotized by the spheres, stopped in their tracks.

"Fire! Fire! What are you doing? We have the upper hand, don't stop now you idiots!"

As the Wild Ones gaped at the lights, the spheres merged. The rays of light intertwined, gold and green flowing in, on, and around one another.

"Patches, Zehira, *shield the kittens*!" Silsula cried.

From the corner of her eye, Goldeneyes could see Zehira expand a shield around herself and the door of the ma'on. The Wild Ones hesitated,

HALLOWEEN

still watching the balls of light. None of them had heard Silsula's command, but they were uneasy. Some backed away a few steps.

"Now!" Goldeneyes shouted. The sisters' Magelights blazed. Goldeneyes and Silsula quickly raised a shield to protect themselves as the two balls of light exploded. Jagged bolts of light flew in every direction, thudding against the shields, the walls of the ma'on, the ground, the trees behind the Wild Ones, at anything nearby—and also into the astonished Wild Ones. Three more fell. Goldeneyes saw Kel conjure a shield just in time, as had his two large guards. But the globe did its job. More than half the Wild Ones lay on the ground dead or wounded. They had given the East Woods Catmages a breather, but they were still in trouble. She could see more Wild Ones approaching to take the places of the fallen. Goldeneyes braced herself. They wouldn't be able to use that trick again. And the Wild Ones still outnumbered them. She didn't know how much longer they could hold out.

Andy grinned as he handed out candy to a group of four young girls, their parents waiting on the sidewalk. Every one of the girls was dressed in the same princess costume. He had gotten lost trying to keep track of how many princesses he saw tonight. As the last one took her candy and thanked him, he saw a golden globe of light heading his way. He gasped as he realized it was a Catmage message, and that color could only mean it was from Goldeneyes. The light flew into his Magelight and he saw images of the attack on the Compound. "The kittens! They're attacking the kittens! No!"

"What's that, Andy?" his mother asked.

"We have to go to them!" Nafshi said. She appeared on the table next to the door where he put the bowl of candy.

"How?" he sent.

"Andy? Is something wrong?" his mother said, coming down the hall. Nafshi tilted her head.

"Tell your mother. It's the only way to get there in time to help."

CHAPTER TEN

"Mom! Mom, I really need you to drive me somewhere. Now! A friend of mine is in trouble."

"Who's in trouble, Andy?"

"Goldeneyes!"

"What?"

"Mom, please! We have to go now. Please. Just trust me. If I don't get there in time, she'll die!"

"Are we going to the vet's? What's wrong?"

"No, it's not that. Please? I'll explain everything later, I swear, but we have to go now!"

"All right. Let me get my keys. Turn out the porch light and let's go."

Andy was in the car before his mother had time to grab her purse and keys. He gave her directions to the road near the Compound. Nafshi appeared on the dashboard as they sped out of town.

"Calm yourself, child. You need to concentrate if you're going to help my granddaughters. You're no good to anyone if you panic."

"I can't help it," he muttered.

"What's that, sweetie?"

"Nothing, Mom."

"Where are we going?"

"It's a place where Goldeneyes hangs out. It's in the woods outside of town."

His mother glanced at him and then back to the road. "And you know this how?"

Andy bit his lip.

"Tell her," Nafshi said. "You'll have to tell her later anyway."

"Goldeneyes told me," Andy said.

"Very funny, Andy."

"I'm not kidding. Goldeneyes can talk. Well, she can't talk like you and I can talk, not with her mouth. But she can talk with her mind. She spoke to me the day I met her."

HALLOWEEN

"I'm not laughing, Andy. If you don't tell me the truth, I'm turning this car around right now."

"Mom, no! You can't stop, she'll die! They'll all die! I swear I'm not lying. Why would I ask you to drive me to the woods in the middle of nowhere? I've been there lots of times. I'll show you. Just give me the chance to find Goldeneyes and you'll see."

She frowned. He'd been holding things back from her for ages. Of course it was ridiculous to think that cats could talk, but maybe at long last he would tell her what he'd been hiding. Rachel made up her mind. "All right. But Andy, I want the whole truth from you tonight. Understood?"

"Yeah. I'll tell you everything, I promise, as soon as I can."

His mother concentrated on driving. Andy's thoughts were racing. What if he wasn't enough? What if even with Nafshi around, he needed more help?

"I'm going to call Becca," he told her. He took out his phone and texted her that he needed to talk. She texted back.

Busy. I'm at the dance. And you're still a jerk.

Emergency at the Compound. Wild Ones attacking. Please help!

How can I get out there?

Your dad! Tell him. It's okay, it's an emergency. Need you!

OK. Be there ASAP. Mike and Teresa too.

Andy let out a huge sigh of relief. He watched the road carefully.

"Mom, we're almost there. Slow down, there's a spot on the shoulder you can park. It's hard to see at night."

She slowed down and pulled over to the side of the road when he found the shoulder. "Stay in the car," he said as he got out. "I'll be back as soon as I can. Please Mom, trust me."

"How are you going to see in the woods? They're pitch black."

"With this," Andy said. He held out his hand, concentrated, and his Magelight glowed brightly.

"What is that? How—how did you do that?"

"It's a Magelight. Goldeneyes taught me. I'll explain later. You'll

CHAPTER TEN

see. Just stay here, please, it might not be safe for you!"

His mother frowned. "What? Andy, I don't like this at all. If it's not safe for me, what about you?"

"I'll be fine. I have my Magelight. Mom, you have to stay, Becca and her father are coming. Just wait here for them."

"What?"

"Mom, I have to go! My friends might be dying!" Andy turned and ran down the path into the woods.

Rachel Cohen watched the green light disappear, her mouth slightly open. "Why not talking cats?" she said out loud. She leaned against the car, alternating between watching the road and looking toward the wood. "Maybe Becca will tell me what's going on." Then, as she kept watching the woods, she saw a rainbow of colored flashes of light in the distance. "Okay, maybe he's not making it all up. But that boy still has a lot of explaining to do."

Andy raced down the path to the Compound. He had to be in time! He had to. As he ran he could see flares of light arcing through the woods. That must be where the Wild Ones were battling the Shomrim. "Nafshi, I really need your help right now. I can't run into the middle of one of those fights."

"Keep running. Let me handle any Wild Ones we meet." Andy was startled as his Magelight glowed without his doing anything. Light daggers flew out and headed toward a group of Catmages and Wild Ones just ahead. He didn't know how she could tell which were the Catmages and which the Wild Ones, but Andy trusted Nafshi. Besides, he had no time to stop and help—he had to get to the ma'on. He hurried along, trying not to stumble over rough ground. Even with his Magelight, the path was fairly dark. At last the trees ended and he was in the meadow. His feet flew as he dashed across it. Nafshi was no longer controlling the Magelight. He could feel her inside him, mind questing ahead, searching for the Wild Ones and her friends and family. Andy ran toward the ma'on. Jets of light flashed all around it.

HALLOWEEN

"Stop now," Nafshi said. "We need to reconnoiter."

"What?" he said, panting as he obeyed.

"I need to survey the situation." They stayed out of sight of the Wild Ones. Andy could see his friends fighting furiously. Fear for their safety threatened to overwhelm him.

"You must put aside distractions," Nafshi said. "Concentrate. There are many Wild Ones, more than you could handle by yourself. But don't worry, Andrew. I'm with you this time. And," she said, her voice crackling in anger, "I am at my full power."

"I—can't—breathe—" he said. "Need a minute."

"You don't have a minute." She nodded toward the ma'on. "Get going, now! I need to see all of the enemy fighters. I don't have the energy to spare to find their auras!"

He ran toward the fight.

"Stay inside, catlings!" Silsula yelled, her fur standing on end and a growl suffusing her words. Her eyes blazed as she sent jet after jet arcing toward the Wild Ones, each one hitting its mark. Howls and screeches came from those Wild Ones unfortunate enough to be in Silsula's range. Andy only had time to marvel briefly at her powers before he found himself shielding Leilei and Patches, who stood to her right, from an attack that came from their side. Goldeneyes seemed twice her normal size, rushing back and forth along the ma'on, firing at the Wild Ones, flinging up shields as needed. But she was obviously nearing the end of her strength. A large tabby fighting next to Kel dropped as they watched. They could see the effort it was taking Goldeneyes to remain standing.

"Now!" Nafshi said. "Fire!"

Andy fired light daggers in quick succession at the Wild Ones. Several turned toward him to attack. Andy clenched his fist and brought his arm in toward his chest. A glowing green shield appeared before him and the attacks bounced harmlessly off.

"Here, have a taste of your own medicine," he shouted, firing back at the Wild Ones. Several of the barbs scored.

CHAPTER TEN

"Andy!" Leilei said. "Am I glad to see you!"

"Andy!" Goldeneyes said. "Thank the First!"

He had no time to respond. There were still too many Wild Ones gathered in front of the ma'on, and too few defenders. Andy quickly found himself in a frantic battle as the Wild Ones divided their force, some to deal with him, the rest continuing the fight for the kittens.

Patches hopped and hissed and fired, his fur completely fluffed out, shouting insults at the Wild Ones. "Patches is Nistar now! Wild Ones are bad, bad, bad! Picking on kittens! Leilei and Nistar will not let you have them!"

"That's my boy," Nafshi said to Andy. "I'm glad to see him take on the name I gave him in the Evil One's cellar. Here, let's do this in his honor." Before Andy could react, Nafshi had taken over the Magelight and Andy found himself firing light daggers so quickly they seemed to be coming from a strobe light. Many of them found a mark. More Wild Ones fell, but they were still outnumbered.

"No matter what your name, we will defeat you," Kel said. "We have plans for those young ones. Too bad you weren't smart enough to join the winning side. We could still use a Catmage like you, Patches."

"Patches is Nistar and he will never join bad Wild Ones. Kel is a liar! Kel was a false friend!" He fired two light blades quickly enough that the second one caught Kel on his paw. Cursing, Kel retreated behind his bodyguard.

Leilei laughed at Kel and fired at the large Wild One he hid behind. But their darts were fewer and farther between. None of them had any reserves of strength left, and Andy was busy battling his own squad of Wild Ones. They could use a little more help, he thought grimly as another Wild One fell to his light dagger.

"No!" Silsula screamed. "The kittens! They've reached the kittens!"

Andy turned quickly and saw that another bunch of Wild Ones had come around the ma'on from the rear and were driving toward the farthest door. The Shomrim guarding it had fallen and the Wild Ones were

HALLOWEEN

advancing. He could hear fearful mews from inside where the kittens and young Catmages were gathered. Silsula and Zehira ran to their defense. Patches and Leilei tried to follow.

"Stay where you are!" Zehira said. "Guard our flanks! We won't let anyone in that door!"

The attack on the kittens had brought out reserves of strength they hadn't known they had. Andy fought furiously to free himself to help Silsula and Zehira. A short distance away, Goldeneyes battled three Wild Ones at once.

A kitten shrieked in pain as a stray light dagger seared it. The sound pierced Andy to the core and every Catmage within earshot turned toward the crying kitten.

Andy lifted a fallen branch with his Magelight and heaved it at the Wild Ones in front of him. They broke and ran. "Leave those kittens alone!" Andy cried, running toward the ma'on, flinging spears of light as he ran. The Wild Ones split their attention. Some attacked Andy, some continued to try for the kittens. A Siamese Wild One fired wildly as he ran. Zehira threw herself in front of a light dagger headed straight for the kittens. She cried out as it hit her, dropped to the ground, and lay still.

Andy saw Zehira fall, and his heart felt like it would break in two. The world seemed frozen. He heard the Wild Ones cheering as they tried to rush through the door, saw the pain he felt reflected in Silsula's eyes, saw the kittens crouching in fear. Rage filled him, rage like he had never before felt. But instead of going hot, he went cold.

"You will never do that again," he said through gritted teeth. It seemed he could hear an echo of his words in his head. Andy narrowed his eyes in concentration and slowly closed his right hand into a fist. Then he flung it outward and opened his hand. A wave of green light left his fingers, a wave unlike any he had ever used before. It arced across the Wild Ones, ignoring any Catmages near, and where it touched, shrieks of pain followed. Some of the Wild Ones were flung onto their backs. Some ran away howling. When the arc ended, no more Wild Ones were left stand-

CHAPTER TEN

ing. The Siamese lay on the ground, dead or unconscious. Andy turned to the group of Wild Ones at the other end of the ma'on, who stood frozen in shock at what they had just seen. As Andy raised his arm to fire again, Kel fled and the rest followed, knocking into each other in their haste to get away. Chest heaving, Andy ran to Zehira and dropped to his knees on the ground beside her.

The kittens huddled around Silsula. Her Magelight flashed as she tended to the crying kitten. "There, Yoni. You're all better now. Stay with me, we'll get your *ima* as soon as we can. Come, catlings, all of you—let's get away from this place." She glanced up at Andy. "Are you all right?"

Andy wiped the sweat from his forehead. "If you mean am I hurt, no." He looked down at Zehira's lifeless body. "Not physically." His hand went out and he stroked her lifeless side. Silsula nudged his hand with her head.

"Don't be too sad, Andy. Zehira gave her life protecting our young ones. She would be the first to say it was a worthy fate."

"But I couldn't save her," he said, his voice breaking with unshed tears.

"No. But you saved the rest of us." Goldeneyes walked slowly toward Andy, her sides heaving. "Thank you for coming," she said. Andy sat down and reached out to her. She rubbed her head against his hand.

"I'm sorry," he whispered. "I wasn't good enough."

"Don't ever say that!" she said. "Of course you were! The First knows what would have happened if you hadn't gotten here in time."

"Your message scared me to death. Oh, Goldeneyes, I'm sorry! I'm so sorry for everything!" He picked her up and held her close. She purred and rubbed her cheek against his face.

"I'm sorry too, Andy. But we can talk later. We still have work to do. Look!" she said, her head turning to the wood. Colored flashes showed where the Wild Ones still attacked the Shomrim in the woods.

"We'll move the little ones to a safer place," Silsula said.

Andy glanced quickly over his shoulder and let go of Goldeneyes,

HALLOWEEN

who jumped to the ground. "Let's go help."

"Put the kittens in Hakham's bayit," Goldeneyes told her sister. "It's less exposed. Patches—Nistar—you and Leilei go with Silsula. Andy, come with me."

They hurried toward the lights. Andy could feel his phone buzzing in his pocket as he ran. There wasn't time to text. He sent Becca a Magelight message with a picture of Hakham's bayit. She'd know what to do. Now, though, it was time to see if there were any Wild Ones still stupid enough to come within range of Andy and Goldeneyes.

ELEVEN: DOUBLE EXPOSURE

"They tried to take the kittens," Andy said as they ran through the trees. "They're going to pay for that."

"They already have," Nafshi said to him. "I'm very proud of all my students tonight."

Andy glanced at Goldeneyes. "You should tell her that. I bet she'd love to hear from you, Nafshi," he thought.

"No. Trust me on this, Andrew. Tell no one I'm here."

His reply was interrupted as they ran into a fight. Andy saw Zohar and his squad fighting a pitched battle in a small break in the trees.

"Letsan's here, too," Nafshi said. Andy wondered how she knew. "Child," she told him, "when you get to be as old as I, and you've been around Catmages long enough, you'll be able to recognize their Magelights without any more effort than mine."

"Andy, pay attention!" Goldeneyes said as she shielded him from a Wild One's blast.

"Sorry," he muttered. He aimed and scored a hit on the Wild One and looked around for more. But the fight was mostly over. Andy's and Goldeneyes' arrival had been enough to turn the tide. Those Wild Ones who could get away were retreating.

"Zohar, where do you want me?"

DOUBLE EXPOSURE

"Stay here with Zahavin. My Shomrim will take it from here. Let's escort the Wild Ones to our borders," he said, "and make sure they never come back!" His fighters cheered and ran off after them, leaving Andy and Goldeneyes standing by themselves.

"There aren't any more nearby," Nafshi told Andy.

"I don't think there are any more Wild Ones around," he said out loud.

"Gather the Magelights off the bodies," Goldeneyes told him. She cut the leather straps off the nearest Wild One's collar with a dart from her Magelight. Andy looked around and saw two more bodies. He felt no more anger, only sadness.

"Why?" he asked. "Why can't they just be happy with what they are? Why do they have to keep coming after you?"

"They seek power," Goldeneyes said. "Or their heads were filled with lies and promises by Roah and Niflah. They have paid the price for their folly. Pick up the collars, please. We have to destroy the Magelights."

She stopped and gazed at one of the bodies, a small, black male with white feet. "I recognize this one. He was in my first Teaching Ring. His name was Gerev. What lies are the Wild Ones telling them to get them to fight on their side?"

Andy bent to gather the three Magelights. "I don't know. Why is Taylor fighting on their side? Because he's just a big jerk. Maybe this guy was a big jerk, too."

Letsan and Hakham came through the woods and stopped at the sight of the two of them.

"It is good to see you, Andrew," Hakham said.

"You too. Sorry it had to take another battle to get me here."

"You are here, and that's what matters. I'm sure you were a great help."

"Hey, Andy!" Letsan said as he twined himself around Andy's legs.

Goldeneyes told them all what Andy had done.

"I couldn't save Zehira."

CHAPTER ELEVEN

"But you saved the kittens," Hakham said. "Think of that, when you remember Zehira. Think of how happy she would be to know her teaching helped you save the little ones."

"I guess," Andy said.

Hakham turned to the others. "Back to the Compound, Zahavin. The Wild Ones are in full retreat. Razor has Shomrim squads scouring the woods to recover the enemy's Magelights. Saunders has enough of our Magelights. He will get no more."

Andy and Goldeneyes followed Hakham as he walked slowly back to the Compound.

"Oh, uh, I have to tell you something," Andy said. "I had to tell my mom about you guys. I needed the car. It was the only way to get here in time."

Hakham and Goldeneyes exchanged glances.

"You—you're not mad?" Andy asked.

"We knew it would happen eventually," Hakham said. "Where is your mother now?"

"I made her wait by the car on the side of the road. Oh, and I called Becca and Mike. They should be at your bayit helping guard the kittens. And, uh, they might have had to tell Becca's father."

"Andy, if you're waiting for me to make a fuss, I am too tired to care," Goldeneyes said. "I need to find my sister and make sure she's all right." She moved past him and hurried away, leaving Hakham and Letsan with Andy.

Andy took his phone from his pocket. He texted Becca that he'd be there soon. He kept his phone out and used the flashlight to guide him through the woods.

"We don't need that light," Letsan said.

"I do."

"Hakham, do you think we can find a way to help Andy see in the dark? Surely there's a Magelight spell that—"

Andy flashed him a look.

DOUBLE EXPOSURE

"Okay, okay," Letsan said.

As they reached the Compound, it was filling with Shomrim. Some limped out of the trees and collapsed. Many were bleeding or burned. Andy watched as the unhurt Catmages helped heal the wounded. He saw a knot of Catmages the others kept coming back to. Letsan saw him looking. "They're very good at healing spells. We keep them safe and bring our wounded to them, if we can."

"And if they can't? Do you need me to carry any of them?" Andy asked. "Should I call Dr. Crane?"

Leilei and Patches came across the meadow to them.

"Are you all right?"

"Yes," Leilei said. "I heard you. I'll ask Aunt Silsula if she needs your help," she said. "Have a seat, Andy, you look terrible."

"Gee, thanks." But he sat, realizing she was right. He was exhausted. It would be good to rest. It would be better to eat. He pulled out his phone to text Becca, stopped when he saw a flashlight coming down the trail. Of course she'd be smart enough to bring one. Andy waited until he could see Becca, Mike, and Teresa. "Over here," he called, waving and making his Magelight glow. They hurried over.

"Look," he said before any of them could say anything, "I'm sorry. I don't know why I did it. I was a jerk. It will never, ever happen again. I miss you guys!"

Mike tilted his head and frowned. "By Jove, I think he's got it!" he said. He flopped down on the ground beside Andy and stuck out his hand. Andy gripped it, smiling.

"Well, you're not wrong," Becca said, grinning. "You were a jerk. But you're forgiven. Now, are you all right?" Becca asked. "What can we do?"

He shrugged. "Sit tight until they tell us something, I guess."

The girls joined the boys on the ground.

"You look awful," Mike told him.

"That seems to be the consensus." He passed a hand across his

CHAPTER ELEVEN

sweaty forehead. "I'm tired and hungry, but that's about it."

"Andy, do you know why I'm your best friend?"

"Why?"

"Because nobody else takes care of you like I can. Here, pal." He dug into his jacket pocket. "I give you candy bars, lifted directly from the treats table at tonight's dance. See, Teresa, I told you they'd come in handy."

"As I recall, you said your ticket to the dance entitled you to take as much candy as you wanted. Then you stuffed them all into your pocket."

"Same difference," he said with a shrug. Mike gave Andy some of the chocolate bars and kept one for himself.

"Anyone else want candy? Not you, Patches, chocolate is bad for you."

"Patches does not want chocolate. Not unless it tastes like mouse."

"Nope, they haven't come out with mouse chocolate yet. I'll let you know if they do."

"Look, here come Silsula and Leilei now," Becca said.

"We can use your help," Silsula told them. "We have two or three Catmages that might benefit from seeing Dr. Crane."

"I'll call him. What's wrong with them?"

"Some really nasty gashes and broken bones. The Wild Ones decided that our rock-throwing stunt last spring was worth imitating. Our healers are worried there may be internal injuries."

"Where are they?"

"One of them is here. The others are still in the wood."

Andy phoned Dr. Crane, who said he would meet them at his office. "Mike, did you guys bring anything to carry wounded Catmages in?"

"There's a blanket in my car," Becca said.

"Never mind, it'll take too long to get it. We can use our jackets. Mike, come with me. We'll bring them back here. Becca, tell my mom we'll be out as soon as we can. She's probably going crazy by now."

"Yeah, my dad, too. He sent me ten texts so far."

"Well, it's almost over."

DOUBLE EXPOSURE

He and Mike followed Silsula into the trees. Soon they were heading back to the meadow, cradling two wounded Shomrim who seemed determined to prove their toughness by refusing to make a sound.

"Real stoics, huh?" Mike said.

"Dr. Crane says cats don't feel pain the way we do."

"Cats!" said Keren, the cream-colored tabby Catmage Andy was holding.

"Sorry, I mean Catmages." He rolled his eyes, wondering if they'd ever get over being called cats.

"Never," Silsula said. *Chirrup.*

"I'm projecting? Wow, I really am out of it."

"Then rest up after you get my charges to your doctor."

"I will."

Goldeneyes and Letsan were with the others when the boys got back to the meadow. Teresa held Becca's flashlight. Andy saw that Becca had bundled another wounded Catmage into a blanket and was stroking its ears. "Our parents are getting pretty antsy," she said, rising slowly with the Catmage in her arms. "I had to swear on my life that we'd get to the cars as soon as you came back."

"Are you going to come with us?" Andy asked Goldeneyes.

"We'll both come. I don't think your parents will believe you until we talk to them," Letsan said. "Besides, I can't wait to see the look on their faces."

"I can," Andy said. "I've been keeping things from Mom for more than three years now. She's going to kill me."

"Don't sweat it, Andy," Mike said. "What's the worst she can do? Ground you for life?"

"If I'm lucky. I guess we'll find out tonight. Goodbye!" he called to the others. "Take care of yourselves. And call me if you need me!"

Silsula twined around Andy's leg. "You take care too, Andy. Don't be too sad about Zehira. She wouldn't want you to be."

"I want to come to her memorial service."

CHAPTER ELEVEN

"We'll wait to hold it until you can be here. Send word."

They walked down the path that led to the road, carrying the wounded Catmages carefully. Their parents waited impatiently by the cars. Andy quailed a little at the frowns on their faces.

"We have to get to Dr. Crane's," Andy said. "I called. He's expecting us."

"Dad, we have to go, too. Will you take us there?" Becca said. Her father held open the door, looking none too pleased. His expression softened as he saw the wounded Catmage in his daughter's arms.

"Get in. We'll meet you there, Rachel."

Mike and Teresa got in the back seat carefully carrying their wounded Catmages.

"I'm going with you," Letsan said. "Zahavin can keep Andy company."

Mr. Jefferson's head jerked around as Letsan's voice echoed in his mind.

"You—you really do talk," he said. He got in the car and dropped the key as he tried to put it in the ignition.

"Here, let me," Letsan said. His Magelight flashed and the key rose through the air. Mr. Jefferson grabbed it.

"Your mouth's open, Dad," Becca said. Mike and Teresa exchanged glances.

"Don't you dare laugh," Teresa whispered.

"I better just drive," he said.

Goldeneyes jumped into the back seat of Andy's car. They drove in silence for a few minutes. Finally, Andy's mother spoke.

"So are you going to start talking or was that part not really true?" she asked as she glanced in the rearview mirror at Goldeneyes.

"I didn't know when I should speak," Goldeneyes said. "Andy, why don't you give me a proper introduction?"

"My God!" his mother said, jumping in her seat and nearly steering into the ditch.

DOUBLE EXPOSURE

"Mom, the road!" Andy said, holding tightly to Keren.

"I'm sorry. You weren't kidding. She really does talk." She gripped the wheel and glanced back in the mirror.

"I told you. She's a Catmage. They talk, and do magic, and a lot of other things."

"It looks like we're going to have a *long* talk later tonight," Rachel said. "Starting with why you've been lying to me all this time. I assume you knew Goldeneyes could talk the day you brought her home?"

"Yeah," Andy said. "Mom, I'm really sorry, but they wouldn't let me tell you until tonight. You have to understand, they'd be hunted and killed and dissected if anyone knew about them. No way would they be able to live in peace."

"Peace?" his mother asked. "They live in peace? Then why do they keep getting wounded? How did that one get hurt?"

"Uh—there's kind of a war on."

"A war!"

"Mom, I'll explain everything. I promise."

"I will, too," Goldeneyes said.

Rachel's breath caught as Goldeneyes spoke, but this time she didn't jump. "I suppose I'll get used to hearing your voice in my head. But it's strange."

"It gets easier, honest!" Andy said.

Dr. Crane and Maddie were waiting by the door when they arrived at Coreyton Animal Hospital. Andy got out of the car and put Keren on the counter.

"It's not as bad as last time," Andy said. "No dogs. But this one and the two Becca and Mike are bringing in got hit with rocks. They might have internal injuries."

Mike and Becca put their Catmages on the counter and stood back to let Dr. Crane examine them. "X-rays, this one first," he said. "Then get me X-rays of the other two. Andy, I'm not going to need your help tonight. I think it's a simple case of broken ribs and a few bruises, although I'm

CHAPTER ELEVEN

worried about this one."

"His name's Noam," Andy said. "Don't worry, Noam, Dr. Crane will fix you up. You can trust him. He's the one who saved Leilei and Zohar."

"And me," said Goldeneyes. Dr. Crane smiled at her voice inside his head.

"I'll stay with them, Andy," Letsan said. "The rest of you go home. I think you have a lot to talk about."

"Go, Andy. These cats are in much better shape than the ones you usually bring us. We can handle them," Maddie said. "We'll just keep pretending I don't know what's going on here if you like," she added, smiling. "Or you can leave knowing that I've known your secret and kept it for the past two years."

Andy was startled, but thinking about it, Maddie would have to be pretty thick not to have caught on. She was the vet tech Dr. Crane called every time Andy brought in a bunch of wounded Catmages. "Oh, uh, okay," Andy said. "But don't call them cats. They hate that. They're Catmages." He grinned at the nasty look Keren was giving them. "Thanks, Maddie. Thanks, Dr. Crane. See you later, Letsan."

"I've got to tell my wife we're going to be late. I'm not going anywhere until I've heard the whole story," Jake said. "Meet you at your house, Rachel. Teresa, do you need a ride home?"

"That would be great, Mr. Jefferson," she said.

"I'll drop you and Mike home, then."

"Wait, I don't want to go home. I want to be a part of this!" Mike said.

"You are going to have to explain this all to your parents, Mike."

"Not tonight," Andy said. "They're not going to believe him unless he has a Catmage to back him up."

"That's true. Your years of making stuff up is against you, Mike."

Mike shrugged. "Okay, I can wait. Or we can not tell them, and I won't get in trouble for not telling them."

DOUBLE EXPOSURE

"I think enough people have been told about Catmages tonight. And Kenny's too young to be trusted," Andy said. "Mr. Jefferson, Mike still needs to keep quiet about Catmages."

Jake Jefferson frowned. "I'm not his father. I don't know what to do," he said. "But I do know I'm bringing you two home. Do *not* start without me," he said, glaring at Andy as he ushered the others out the door.

Andy followed his mother to the car, held the door for Goldeneyes and got in after her. When he was settled, she jumped onto his lap. Andy wondered what to say. He hadn't really thought about what to tell his mother if she found out about Catmages.

"Neither have I," Goldeneyes said.

"Projecting again, huh?" he sent.

"Yes, but you're distracted."

"So are you, if you're not yelling at me about it."

"We have much bigger worries tonight, Andy," she said, rubbing her cheek against his face and purring.

"Wow," Andy whispered.

"I've missed you," she said.

"Me too." He scratched her ears and glanced over at his mother. She was looking at the road and frowning. That did not bode well. He decided the best thing for now was to simply keep quiet.

When they got to the house, his mother walked wordlessly to the kitchen and made herself a cup of tea. Andy sat down at the table and waited for her to speak. Goldeneyes took her place in his lap, peering over the table at Rachel. At last, his mother sat down, sipped her tea, and said, "Explain." Her voice was icy.

"Uh, aren't we going to wait for Mr. Jefferson?"

"No. Text Rebecca that she can talk to her father. I want to hear the whole story from you. Now."

Andy texted Becca quickly.

She called you Rebecca.

Yikes! She's really mad. Maybe we shouldn't come over.

CHAPTER ELEVEN

No, come! I need your help.
"Well?"

Andy ran his hand through his hair. "Um, let me think. Okay, the day I met Goldeneyes, Taylor and Pete followed me off the bus and pushed me to the ground…"

Andy was still filling his mother in about the events of the past three years as Becca and her father entered the kitchen. Their parents sat quietly as Andy finished his story, aided from time to time by Becca and Goldeneyes.

"And that's where we are now. The Wild Ones tried to kidnap all the kittens. They would have turned them into something awful, made them as evil as they are. I had to help."

His mother was still frowning. "So you've been hiding this from me for three years. Lying to me, putting yourself at risk, helping the Catmages fight, covering up when you were hurt. Is that about right?"

Andy couldn't meet her eyes. "Yes," he said.

"It was for a good cause, Mrs. Cohen," Becca said.

"You don't want to be talking right now, Rebecca," her father said.

"You were *kidnapped!*" Andy's mom shouted. "Hit on the head and kidnapped by that—that horrible Saunders! Andy, why didn't you tell me? I would have called the police, had him arrested—"

"I don't know, Mom. I guess I was afraid he'd do something awful to us. Or that nobody would believe me. He has so many people on his side! We called animal control on him last year and nothing happened. His neighbor calls the cops on him all the time and nothing happens! Mom, Saunders is powerful! The only way we're going to beat him is to help the Catmages get back the Magelights and the Tilyon."

"He's intimidating you because you are children," she said. "Jake and I are adults. We can take care of him."

"Mr. Straight can't, and he's Saunders' cousin!"

"Andy has a point, Rachel," Mr. Jefferson said. His glance fell on Goldeneyes. "Well? What do you think about it, cat?"

DOUBLE EXPOSURE

"Cat*mage*," Goldeneyes said stiffly. "I am a Catmage, not a dumb-cat. Kindly do not lump me in with an animal that can't think past its next meal."

Andy and Becca exchanged glances.

"This is so weird," Mr. Jefferson said. "I can't believe I'm hearing a voice inside my head that's coming from a ca—Catmage," he finished with a grin.

"To get back to my points," Goldeneyes said, "we can't alert the human authorities. Saunders' connections run very deep. We've tried, as Andy and Becca told you."

"He threatened my child with a gun!" Rachel said.

"Not exactly, Mom. He was threatening Goldeneyes. I picked her up so he wouldn't shoot her."

"I don't care! He could have killed you!"

"No, that's the one thing we have going for us," Andy said. "He has no compunction about killing Catmages. But he knows if he hurts me, he'll go to jail."

"I will remind you that he knocked you out and kidnapped you."

"Patches told me that was a mistake. He said Roah did it without permission. They were only supposed to get me to his house, not hit me on the head."

"Oh, so I should be glad they only wanted to kidnap you."

"Mom, I'm sorry. Really. But it's not like that anymore. It's not just us. Mr. Velez is helping a lot. If I'd been at the dance tonight, I would have got him to drive me to the Compound."

"And kept on lying to me," Rachel said. "I have a bone to pick with Mario, too."

"Mom, don't do that. He was only doing his best to help us."

"You're children!"

Andy lifted Goldeneyes off his lap, stood up, and leaned his hands on the table as he faced his mother.

"I'm sixteen!" Andy said. "I'm not a baby anymore. Mom, some-

CHAPTER ELEVEN

times you take risks to do the right thing. You know that. That's what police and firemen and soldiers do. Saunders is evil! He kills Catmages to get his way. He doesn't care how many he hurts. Someone needs to stop him. Goldeneyes came to me three years ago and said they couldn't do it without me. So what am I supposed to do? Stay here while my friends put themselves in harm's way? Stay here while Saunders gets more powerful and learns to use the Tilyon? You think he's going to stop at bossing around dogs and Catmages and people like Mr. Straight? What do you think he would do if he found a way to control people with it? I don't know about you, but I don't want to find out!"

Goldeneyes leaped onto the table next to him. "Andy is right. We need him. The prophecy states that we will not succeed without the Son of Aaron."

"So I've been told," Rachel said sourly.

"Then accept it and stop getting all worked up over something you can't change." Razor's voice echoed through all their heads.

"Razor?" Andy said out loud.

"Open the window, Andy. It's cold out here."

Andy raised the kitchen window. Razor leaped onto the sill and into the kitchen.

"You came all the way to town tonight? Why didn't you come with us?"

"I had things to do at the Compound," Razor said. "Now I have things to do here."

"Whoa," Mr. Jefferson said. "You have been through the mill. Is—is that blood on your side?"

"Yes."

"Who is this, Andy?" his mother asked.

"Razor, Letsan's brother. I told you about him. He's the Captain of the Shomrim, uh, the Catmage army."

"Your name is Rachel?" Razor asked. She nodded. "Well, Rachel, I came here tonight to make sure you don't take away one of my best warriors. Your boy did a great job tonight. Helped save the kittens. Probably

DOUBLE EXPOSURE

saved a dozen of my fighters. And look at him, not a scratch on him."

"That doesn't mean he's going to stay that way," she said. "I am not happy that my son keeps putting himself at risk."

Razor laughed harshly. "At risk? You haven't seen him fight. The Wild Ones haven't been able to touch him in years. If I didn't know better, I'd say he had Magus-level skills. I heard how you stopped the Wild Ones tonight," he said, looking up at Andy.

"What's a Magus?" Rachel asked.

"A really powerful Catmage, but they have to study for years and years," Andy said. "Nafshi was a Magus, and I'm using Nafshi's Magelight," Andy said. "That's probably why I can do those things." He listened in vain for a response from Nafshi, wondering why she wasn't talking to him tonight, when he needed her most.

"Don't sell your skills short, Andy. You've come a long way since the day we first started training and you couldn't float a leaf," Goldeneyes said.

"Thanks."

"You can make things float?" Mr. Jefferson asked.

"Yeah," Andy said. "Want to see? Hey, Razor, want to go for a ride?"

"Do it and you'll get your first scratch tonight, and it won't be from my Magelight," Razor said.

Becca and Andy laughed. Becca reached over and scratched his ears. "Mrs. Cohen, I've been with Andy nearly the whole time. We plan and practice, and believe me when I tell you the Catmages make sure none of us gets hurt. They think of us as older kittens, catlings, Silsula calls them," she said, grinning.

"That isn't a guarantee you won't get hurt."

"No, it isn't," Razor said. "There are no guarantees in life. You know that. Rachel, your son had a choice tonight. He could have stayed safe at home and let us deal with the Wild Ones on our own. But he didn't. He chose to come and help. He's not a child any more."

"Two more years and I'm legally an adult," Andy said.

"But not for two more years," Rachel said.

CHAPTER ELEVEN

"He saved my life last year," Razor said. "He'll probably do it again. And I'd give my life to protect him."

"We all would," Goldeneyes said. "Please don't forbid Andy to work with us. We need him, Rachel. And, to be honest—we've grown very fond of him."

Rachel looked from face to face. She glanced at Jake, who shrugged. "Maybe we should let things be for now," he said. He glanced at the clock. "It's late. Becca and I need to get home. Oh, Lord. I do *not* relish telling Danielle all this. Girl, you are going to have a serious talk with your mother tonight."

"Okay, Dad," she said softly.

"You can't let Saunders know you know anything," Andy said. "And you can't tell anyone else!"

"Nobody's going to believe me. I don't think Danielle is going to believe me."

"Razor, do you want to come home with me?" Becca said. "She'll believe me if you're there to back us up. And you look like you could use a soft bed."

"And a bath. Your mother is not going to like him getting blood all over your bed."

Razor stared at Mr. Jefferson. "Try to put me in a bathtub and you'll see what Magus-level power is firsthand."

Becca burst out laughing. "Don't worry, Dad, I'll clean him up. Come on, Razor. The car's out front." She leaned down and picked him up.

"I can walk."

"I know." She hugged him and he blinked at her.

"Just a minute, Becca," Razor said. He turned toward Andy. "You owe me fish. You came to the Compound tonight. I won the bet."

"Now?" Andy asked. "You want it now?"

"No. I'll let you know when the time is right."

"What bet is that?" Becca asked.

"I'll tell you all about it on the way home."

DOUBLE EXPOSURE

"I can't wait," she said, smiling. "Good night, Andy, Mrs. Cohen. Talk to you tomorrow. Bye, Goldeneyes."

"Bye, Becca," Andy said.

The phone rang as they were leaving. Andy answered it and spoke to Dr. Crane, who told Andy the Shomrim were resting comfortably in unlocked cages. One of them had a bruised kidney. The other was recovering from having its spleen removed. The third had three broken ribs. After Dr. Crane had made sure there were no internal injuries, Letsan had healed the ribs. Both of them were exhausted, and Letsan would be staying overnight with the wounded Shomrim.

Andy's mom was staring distantly out the kitchen window when he hung up the phone. "Dr. Crane says they'll all be fine," he said.

"That's good." She turned to him, her voice catching. "Andy, I'm frightened for you. You're all I have left. I can't lose you."

"Mom, I have to help. They can't win this war without me."

"War. There's that word again."

"We can't avoid it," Goldeneyes said. "We neither asked for nor wanted a war. But we have one and we must win it. Our very way of life is in danger. Maybe yours, too. We have no idea what would happen if Saunders finds a way to harness the power of the Tilyon. We must see this battle through, and Andy must see it through with us." She leaped onto the table and stood in front of Rachel, gazing up at her. "Would it help you to know that I would protect him as I would my own kittens?"

Rachel frowned. "No, not really."

"It better not come to that!" Andy said.

Rachel sighed. "We're not going to settle anything tonight. But I have to tell you, Andy, I'm very disappointed in you. I knew you were hiding something. I didn't know how big, or for how long. I wish you had come to me before."

"I couldn't, Mom. They made me promise not to. I'm sorry."

She frowned at him. "Go to bed. We'll talk in the morning." She stood up and pushed her chair back. "But first come here a minute."

CHAPTER ELEVEN

She pulled him into a long hug. "Be careful, my baby boy," she whispered.

"I will, Mom," he said. She kissed him and pushed him toward the door.

Goldeneyes followed Andy. She stopped at the doorway and turned to look back at Rachel. "I won't let Saunders harm him," she said to her privately. "You have my word on that."

Rachel nodded. Goldeneyes turned and hurried after Andy. When they got to his room, Andy put a spare pillow on his bed. Grinning slightly, he changed into pajamas, brushed his teeth, and got into bed without saying anything to Goldeneyes, who lay curled against the pillow he had prepared. Andy turned out the light and rolled onto his side facing her. Her eyes reflected the moonlight coming in the window.

"So now she knows," Goldeneyes said.

"It could have gone way worse," Andy sent.

"Do you think she'll stop you from helping us?"

Andy rolled onto his back and put his hands behind his head. "I don't know," he said. "She's really worried."

"She has good reason. Saunders may not want you harmed, but we have no such assurances from the Wild Ones. Roah was always cruel and vindictive. He left a wake of destruction in his path."

"If I ever see him again, I'll kill him," Andy said. His jaw clenched as he remembered the kittens crying in fear.

"You'll have to stand in line," Goldeneyes said, yawning. "Good night, Andy."

"Good night."

Goldeneyes fell asleep immediately. Andy lay staring up at the ceiling for a while, thinking about the events of the day. Well, at least one good thing came out of it. He was back with his friends again.

TWELVE: LICKING THEIR WOUNDS

Late that night, Stan Saunders sat back in a deep armchair in his living room, his favorite dog, Shadow, at his side, his hand occasionally reaching out to pat the dog. He waited, brows together, angry expression boding ill. Shadow's ears pricked up. Saunders glanced at the door. Roah and Niflah entered the room. The messenger they had sent cowered in fear at Saunders' feet. Roah glanced at him and he slunk away.

"So," Saunders said, "once again you have failed. Your brother and his supposed incompetents bested you in battle and you have no new kittens to show for it. How many did you lose?"

"Not many," Roah said. "It doesn't matter. We have two new Seekers and they will bring us more recruits."

"It doesn't matter," Saunders repeated. "You think not?" His hand moved away from the dog and slammed down on the arm of the chair. "Every defeat of ours strengthens our enemy! They were supposed to be demoralized by the loss of their young, and instead they are celebrating another victory! Did you even get the Magelights of your dead?"

"No. The Shomrim got them all before we could."

"They lost one of their best warriors," Niflah said.

Saunders turned his glower on the old tabby. "One. How very

CHAPTER TWELVE

good of your forces to kill *one* Catmage. At this rate, it will only take us a hundred years or so to defeat them!" Saunders rose and paced back and forth. The dog followed him. "And they got *all* the Magelights! What went wrong *this* time, Niflah?"

"The boy showed up. He has grown stronger. We still have no idea why he has the powers of a Magus. He and Zahavin turned the tide."

"The boy and Zahavin! Again! That boy thwarts me at almost every avenue! How is it that you have yet to discover a way to stop a child from ruining your plans?"

"You will not let us hurt him," Roah said. "You make us fight him without being able to use our powers to the fullest on him, but he has no such restriction."

"Then use your brains and outsmart him!" Saunders said. "Find a way to get his Magelight! Send your fighters to block him so that he can't help! Stand in front of him and trip him when he runs to the rescue, I don't care, just stop—that—boy!"

Saunders swept his hand along the mantelpiece and knocked pictures and knickknacks to the ground, sending the animals reeling backward.

"Get out of my sight. I need a respite from the stench of failure. Come to me tomorrow and we will try to salvage something out of this debacle."

Roah and Niflah hurried out of the living room, ears twitching in fear Saunders might be picking up an object to throw at them.

"We'd best find somewhere else to sleep tonight," Niflah said.

Roah looked at him. "I will not be treated like this for much longer."

"He has the Tilyon. And the dogs."

Roah did not answer.

When they came back the next morning, they saw Taylor riding up to the house on his bicycle. They waited until he dismounted and brought it inside the gate. The three of them walked up the steps together.

"Ready for our lesson?" he asked them.

LICKING THEIR WOUNDS

"We have business with Saunders," Roah said. "Begin practicing without me. I'll be with you when I can." Taylor nodded and followed them upstairs, separating as they reached the practice room.

They found Saunders sitting at his desk, frowning at the empty chair in front of it. His right hand grasped the Tilyon as the chair inched off the floor. When the legs of the chair were level with the desk, he set it back down slowly enough that it landed with a gentle thump on the floor.

"That was excellent control," Niflah said. "Are you calm now and ready to train?"

"That depends. These are still simple tricks any Catmage can do," Saunders said. "When am I going to be able to call on the full power of this amulet?"

"We don't know. It may be that only a Catmage can use the Tilyon to the fullest of its abilities. For that matter, it may be that only Neshama herself could do so. There are no tales of anyone other than the First using the Tilyon."

"There are no tales of everyday life in prerecorded history, and yet, we know that early man used tools and painted pictures on walls," Saunders said. "Spare me the tale of woe about the lack of information. Your job, and Roah's," he said, "is to train me in the use of the Tilyon so that I may harness its powers to move forward my agenda. So far, the only thing I've managed to do is lift things and make a few cuts on people and Catmages."

"Yet you've made great progress in that," Niflah pointed out. "This time a year ago you could barely use the Tilyon or a Magelight."

"I want to learn how to manipulate people. You say Catmages can make lesser animals do their bidding. I want to try making a person do mine."

Niflah's ears flattened. "We do not use our Magelights to influence other Catmages," he said.

"Why? Another of your precious Laws?"

"No. It isn't done for many reasons. Catmages are far more intelligent than any creature other than humans."

CHAPTER TWELVE

"Catmages can tell if another is trying to read their thoughts," Roah said.

"And there's the little matter of the glowing of the Magelight when you use it," Niflah added. "Even the least talented among us would know if we tried to control them."

Saunders' mouth thinned into a line. "I want to try it. Is Mr. Grant still downstairs?"

"Yes. He is practicing tasks I set him," Roah said.

"How would I go about influencing his actions?"

"When we want an animal to do something, we just picture it," Roah said.

Saunders half-closed his eyes and concentrated. "Come to my office. Now," he sent. He smiled slightly as they heard footsteps rushing up the stairs. Taylor hurried into the room and almost stepped on Niflah as he stood in front of the desk. His Magelight necklace lay on top of his dark sweatshirt.

"You called, sir?" he said, out of breath.

"Sit down in the chair, Mr. Grant. I'm going to perform some tests with the Tilyon, and you're going to help me."

Taylor gripped the Magelights. "I'm ready. What do you need me to do?"

"Put those away," Saunders said irritably. He waited until Taylor tucked the lights into his sweatshirt. "Now sit there and be quiet."

"Okay." Taylor tried not to fidget as he waited to see what Saunders was going to do.

Saunders decided to make Taylor tie his shoe. He closed his eyes, gripped the Tilyon, and built a picture in his mind of the boy leaning down in front of the desk and tying his shoe. He could feel the warmth of the Tilyon as the Magelight activated.

Taylor sat as still as he could, knowing the mercurial whims of Saunders well enough now not to annoy him. He had no idea what Saunders was doing, but if the man said to be quiet, then quiet Taylor would

LICKING THEIR WOUNDS

be, right down to making sure his thoughts didn't leak out to anyone in the room. Taylor erected the imaginary walls around his head that he pictured to help hide his thoughts from the Wild Ones while he practiced with them. Once they were in place, he watched as the principal gripped the Tilyon and closed his eyes. He felt a warmth emanating from several of his Magelights. He wondered why they were activating. He didn't need them to keep his thoughts to himself.

"Nothing is happening," Saunders said, sweat beading on his brow as he opened his eyes, still holding onto the image of Taylor tying his laces. The boy sat watching him curiously. Saunders frowned and tried again, gripping the Tilyon harder. The amulet grew hot in his hand as the Magelight glowed.

Taylor felt his Magelights heat up against his chest. He dared not stop concentrating on the imaginary walls. He couldn't risk his fear seeping into Roah's or Saunders' thoughts. But he knew something was happening. He wasn't sure what, but he had a feeling it wasn't good for him.

"Nothing!" Saunders spat.

"I am not surprised," Niflah said. "We warned you."

Taylor kept quiet. He recognized the look on Saunders' face. The principal was about to explode. He hoped he could get out of the room before it happened. It was definitely not time to mention that his Magelights seemed to be going off by themselves.

"This is useless. Let the boy go back to his practice," Roah said.

"Out! Out!" Saunders shouted, glaring at the boy as if it were his fault.

Taylor hurried out the door before Saunders could change his mind. He ran down the steps and stopped just inside the kitchen, breathing hard. "What was that all about?" he muttered. "I didn't cast any spells." He pulled the Magelight necklace out and looked down at it. "What happened to you?" he asked it, shaking his head as he realized he was talking to an inanimate object. He loosed the necklace and went back to the table to finish practicing the tasks Roah had set him. He felt a strange sense of

CHAPTER TWELVE

satisfaction in the back of his head. "This has been one weird day," he said.

Upstairs, Saunders paced restlessly. "That was a waste of time."

"Yes, it was."

"Can we get back to our lessons?" Niflah said.

"No. I want to try one more time." He stopped at the desk and picked up the phone. "I need you here," he said when Jack answered. Saunders hung up the phone without waiting for his cousin to respond. Jack would be over in a few minutes, he knew. He spent the time practicing moving objects back and forth across his desk.

"You've gotten much better at levitating objects," Niflah said. "Perhaps we should practice throwing them."

"Whatever for?" Saunders asked.

"It is a Catmage battle tactic. We sometimes throw stones and sticks at our enemies."

Saunders laughed. "If I need a weapon, I'll use my pistol. It is far more effective than sticks and stones."

Niflah's tail beat a tattoo on the chair. "Do not underestimate the value of using simple, nearby objects. For a Catmage, they can mean the difference between life and death."

"I am not a Catmage."

Niflah subsided irritably. Saunders always felt he was the smartest one in the room. It was a large part of why his lessons usually went so poorly. The boy, on the other hand, was eager to learn and listened well. When he put his mind to it, he was quite good. Well. Saunders wouldn't have the Tilyon forever. Niflah glanced aside at Roah and wondered if his former student was planning to take the Tilyon himself. Niflah couldn't see how. When Saunders wasn't using it, it was firmly locked in its metal box, and neither of them could get to it. But there was something going on. Of that he was sure.

Jack pulled his car to a halt at the curb outside Stan's house and sat there with the motor running. He hated having to report to his cousin like an errant child. Being in his house brought back memories of Stan bullying

LICKING THEIR WOUNDS

him throughout his childhood. He wished he could break the hold Stan had over him, but he didn't know how. Every time he tried, Stan made him regret it. He had the power to fire Jack. The one thing Jack loved more than everything else was teaching. He was good at it, the kids liked him, and he didn't know what he'd do if he couldn't do it anymore. Jack was sure that if he did displease his cousin enough to get fired, Stan would do his best to make sure nobody else hired him. He couldn't break free yet. Someday, though. Someday he'd find a way to stand on his own two feet. How different his life would be if his parents had lived! But wishing the past were different wouldn't get him anywhere. He turned the key in the ignition and got out of the car, walking briskly into the house and up the stairs, nodding at Taylor as he passed the boy in the kitchen.

"You called?" he asked as he entered Stan's office. Two of the cats were in the office with him. *Great, an audience.*

"Yes. Sit down," Stan said, pointing to the chair in front of his desk.

Jack sat. "Now what?" he asked.

"Just sit there."

Puzzled, Jack sat quietly and waited, watching his cousin and the cats. None of them spoke to him. Stan grew rigid and a look of concentration came over his face. The eyes in his pendant glowed. Jack wondered what they were doing but decided not to speak. Stan's mood was chancy at best. When he ordered you into his presence, his mood was generally bad and usually got worse.

"Nothing's happening!" Stan said.

"We told you it wouldn't," Roah said.

Stan glared at him. "*You've* done it!"

"Not on Catmages. On lesser creatures, with less complex thoughts," Niflah said. "We told you this probably wouldn't work."

"What wouldn't work?" Jack asked.

Stan turned his gaze to Jack. *Uh-oh. I don't think I should have said anything.* He flinched as Stan narrowed his eyes and frowned.

"Nobody asked you, *cousin.*" He made the label sound like an epithet.

CHAPTER TWELVE

"Nobody ever asks you. Your opinion, like yourself, is worthless. And weak."

Jack clenched his teeth but said nothing. He concentrated on a spot to the left of Stan's head so that it would look like he was listening.

"Do you think I don't know your tricks?" Stan said. "Jack, I am tired of your constantly disappointing me. There are consequences for that."

"Really, Saunders, Jack didn't—"

"Quiet, Niflah, this is between my cousin and me." Stan stood up behind the desk and grasped the Tilyon in his hand. "I wanted you to do something. You didn't. Now I get to do something." The Tilyon's eyes glowed and a jet of amber light sliced through the air and cut Jack's left cheek. He cried out in pain, his hand going to the cut.

"I didn't do anything!" Jack cried, rising from his chair. "Damn it, Stan!"

"Get out," Saunders said. "All of you! Out! Out!" The Tilyon glowed again. Jack ducked and ran through the door and down the stairs, past the kitchen where Taylor watched him with a shocked look on his face. Niflah and Roah were right behind him.

"Jack, wait!" Niflah said as he reached the porch.

"What?"

"Give me a moment. Hold still." Niflah's Magelight glowed and Jack felt warmth on his cheek. The bleeding stopped and the cut no longer stung. "I'm sorry," Niflah said. "That was wrong of Saunders. Fixing your cut was the least I could do."

Taylor reached the door just as Jack lowered his bloody hand.

"What happened to you?" Taylor said.

"Stan happened. You're playing with fire, Taylor. Watch out you don't get burned."

"You'd best leave too, boy," Niflah said.

"Yeah. Leave and don't come back, if you know what's good for you."

Jack hurried to his car and took off with a roar of the engine. Three blocks later, as he stopped for a red light, his heart still thudding, the tears began to flow.

THIRTEEN: A MIDWINTER'S NIGHT SCHEME

Winter set in, and Andy's visits to the East Woods lessened. He had expected Goldeneyes to pick up his training, but she stayed in the Compound more frequently, studying with Hakham or teaching Leilei. When Andy did have lessons, she was pleased with his progress and attributed it to his growth and experience. For the most part, Andy stayed home and worked with Nafshi when his homework allowed. She was happy with him and told him as much one Sunday morning.

"Thanks," Andy sent as he caught his breath after a difficult lesson. "It's been a lot easier to practice now that Mom knows and I don't have to hide as much from her. When am I going to be able to tell her about you?"

"Not yet," Nafshi said, pausing to groom her shoulder. "Don't you think she'd find it a little strange that you're working with my spirit?"

"Probably. But there doesn't seem to be much difference between believing in magical cats and believing in dead magical cats coming back to life through their Magelights," he said with a grin. "I don't understand why you won't let me tell Goldeneyes. She'd be so happy to hear from you."

"As I keep telling you, the time is not yet right. My coming back is unprecedented, Andy. We need to do this properly or we could devastate all of Catmage society."

CHAPTER THIRTEEN

"I don't see how."

"Really? Just imagine you had the chance to get the spirit of your father back through a possession of his. Would you not move heaven and earth to do so?"

Andy thought about what his life would be like if he had even the spirit of his father around. He barely remembered life with him, but the hole his father had left in his life felt like a hollow ache nagging at him on special occasions and sometimes on no occasion at all.

"Well, would that be so wrong?" he asked.

"Yes, it would. Think about it. Catmages would never allow the Magelights of their loved ones to be destroyed, hoping to keep their spirits alive. We have no idea how or why I am with you. What if only certain Catmage spirits could come back? Imagine the anger and strife among my people as they saw friends and neighbors bringing back loved ones but they could not. And that's before we even get to all that extra Magelight power there for the taking. Look at what Saunders has done with eleven Council Magelights, and imagine what someone like him could do with a far greater number. Believe me, nothing good will come of this if it gets out."

"Oh." Andy tried not to let his disappointment show.

"It may be that only you can know about me. Perhaps one day we can tell Zahavin and a few specially chosen others. I need more time, Andy. Time to decide what to do."

"Okay, I'll keep your secret. But I think you're wrong about telling Goldeneyes."

Nafshi gazed steadily at him until he looked away.

"I have homework," he muttered. "I'll see you later."

She disappeared.

"There are way too many mothers in my life," he said. Nafshi chuckled inside his head as he reached for his computer and turned it on.

The night was moonless as Razor padded silently through the snowy woods. Flurries swirled through the air and stuck to his long, orange fur. When

A MIDWINTER'S NIGHT SCHEME

he neared a small copse of young fir trees he slowed to a crawl and listened intently, sniffing the air. He heard nothing but the falling snow.

"We're here," Ari sent. "We've been waiting for you."

"Hurry up. I'm freezing my tail off," Lev added. "Not all of us have those marvelous Maine Coon coats."

Razor grunted and headed into the copse of trees, glancing around and pausing to listen. The night was quiet except for the wind rustling in the branches. "You're sure you weren't followed?" he asked.

"No. We were given another recruiting mission. We left the West Woods this afternoon," Ari said. "They think we're long gone."

"Then explain how you managed to miss any news of the attack on our Compound."

Ari dropped his gaze. "I'm sorry, Razor. We were out Seeking and had just come back when Kfir and his warriors were setting out. We couldn't get away to warn you. You know we can't send message globes unless we're far enough away that the Wild Ones won't see them."

"We need a better system of communication," Razor said.

"The minute you think of one, let us know," Lev said. Razor flattened his ears and glared at him.

"Any news?" he asked Ari gruffly.

"Not much," Ari said. "We've been told to recruit heavily. Roah made it plain he doesn't want us back without a large contingent of new Catmages. He was in a rage at the failure of their attack on the Compound."

Razor grunted. "I can imagine. I don't suppose we were lucky enough that he killed any of his warriors in his fit of pique?"

"No. Roah's cruel, but he's not stupid. There were punishments, but nothing more. He can't afford to lose any fighters and he knows it. Your Shomrim and Andy made quite a dent in their forces."

"Good. And these new recruits you spoke of?"

"We've been looking for half-grown Catmages who are dissatisfied with their lives."

CHAPTER THIRTEEN

"All half-grown Catmages are dissatisfied with their lives," Razor said.

"Kel gave us the idea," Lev said. "You should see his nonsense. He gathers them all outside the living area and they complain about how badly they were treated at their home Compound."

Razor grunted again. "Stupid. Waste of time."

"I don't know about that," Lev said. "They seem really devoted to him."

"Doesn't matter. Kel is on my list of Wild Ones who won't make it through this war. What else is going on?"

"Nothing, really," Ari said. "Saunders is going away with his dogs in a few days."

Razor cocked his head and his ears twitched back.

"He's leaving?"

"He's taking three of the dogs to a show next week."

"That was the excuse he used last year when they ambushed us."

"He really is this time," Lev said. "Roah and Kfir discussed it at length. They need to guard the dogs that stay behind. Apparently two of them are the special ones."

"Really? Saunders will be leaving them guarded only by a few Wild Ones? Ari," he said, "I do believe we can take advantage of this. Give me the details of when and where they're going. I'll get Becca or Andy to check for us and make sure it's not a ruse. And then, my friends—then we plan an attack *they* will not expect, and take out another Magelight. Or maybe two."

They gave him what information they could. They didn't know the name of the town, but Razor was confident he could get Andy or Becca to find it for him. He glanced up at the sky. The clouds were beginning to break.

"I'd better go," he said. "Good luck." He turned to go. "And make sure we know about the next attack," he said without looking back.

Lev and Ari said goodbye and watched Razor stride away.

A MIDWINTER'S NIGHT SCHEME

"Let's go find some more whiny catlings for Roah," Ari said.

Razor hurried back to the East Woods, ears twitching and senses alert. He heard nothing out of the ordinary as he reached the first sentries. They watched him pass without moving, their eyes scanning the wood. From time to time a sentry's Magelight glimmered. At least one guard per post had been chosen for their ability to cast the aura spell. There would be no more sneak attacks. The next time the Wild Ones came to battle in the East Woods, Razor would be ready for them. But maybe he could do something that would hurt them first. One message after another flashed out of his Magelight. By the time he reached Hakham's bayit, Katana waited outside and Letsan, Zahavin, Zohar, and Silsula were within. Razor felt a pang as he realized Zehira would not be coming, but he pushed that aside. Time for feeling later. Now was the time for action, or at least for planning the action.

"I have news," he said, shaking the snow from his coat at the door. "But first, I think Katana should take Zehira's place on the East Woods Council. Any objections?"

There were none. "Welcome, Katana," Hakham said. "The honor is well deserved."

She blinked at his praise. "Thank you, Hakham."

"Good. Now to the reason I called you here," Razor said. He told them what he had learned from Lev and Ari.

"We already tried attacking the house when Saunders was away and got our tails handed to us," Letsan said.

"I remember," Razor growled. "But that's not why I woke you in the middle of the night. I have a better idea than going after the dogs."

"Can we hear it, then?" Letsan said, yawning.

"I hate to say it, but Ruma had a point at the Council meeting last summer. Taylor has five Council Magelights. He's a half-trained boy without an aura. There's no reason why we shouldn't go after him. They may be expecting an attack on the house. They won't be expecting an attack on the boy."

CHAPTER THIRTEEN

"You can't hurt a child! We are not Wild Ones," Silsula said.

"We won't hurt him. We're just going to take his Magelight necklace and destroy it," Razor said. "But if he does happen to get hurt, too bad. He chose the wrong side."

"He is young and misguided," Hakham said. "We can't punish him for that."

Katana spoke up. "With all due respect, sir, we're not punishing him. We must retrieve those Magelights. If he puts up a fight, chances are he will get hurt. I see no other way to do this."

Hakham started to reply but Razor interrupted. "Oh, don't catch your tails in a thorn bush. We'll do our utmost to take the Magelights without hurting the boy. But this is our best opportunity in moons. Having Saunders out of town and extra Wild Ones guarding the dogs gives us a much better chance to catch him alone."

"Don't expect it to be a walk in the meadow," Letsan said. "Taylor was surprisingly helpful to Saunders last spring when we fought him at the school. We lost that fight."

"Then we'll make sure we bring more warriors this time. Two squads ought to do it. Zohar, Katana, I want your battle plan by mid-morning."

"Yes sir."

"We're going to need to hear those plans before we approve this mission," Hakham said. "Silsula is right. We cannot harm the boy."

"I tell you, he won't be harmed. We'll get the necklace from him and bring it where we can destroy the Magelights. Five Magelights! That's half our work done in one job."

"If we can do it," Letsan said. "Do we bring Andy in on this?"

"I think we should," Razor said. "Andy might be able to lure Taylor right into our paws."

"Andy has a tendency to lose his temper around Taylor," Goldeneyes said. "I think it's a bad idea to involve him."

"It's completely understandable," Letsan said. "Taylor's been tormenting Andy since before we met."

A MIDWINTER'S NIGHT SCHEME

"What's the worst that can happen?" Razor asked. "He helps us get the Magelights? Let the boy loose on the enemy! It's about time we went on the offense!"

Zohar nodded. "Andy will come through for us. He always does."

"I agree," said Hakham. "Razor, go and make your plans. Walk carefully with Andy, though."

Razor met Hakham's gaze unblinking. "Zohar, Letsan, Katana, with me."

They left the bayit. Hakham watched them go.

"I don't like it," Silsula said. "I don't like it at all."

Andy lay on his bed sound asleep, one arm dangling over the edge. He'd spent half the day before at his usual Saturday job at the Coreyton Animal Hospital. Then he'd gone home and worked on a school project until suppertime. After supper, he and Mike got involved in an online game that went on until the late hours of the morning. Now he slept as only an exhausted teenager could, dead to the world and twitching slightly as he dreamed.

Rachel Cohen knocked lightly at Andy's door. She grinned as she heard Andy's soft snores and quietly opened the door. "He's asleep," she whispered to the ragged Maine Coon cat at her feet. "I think we should wait until—"

Razor didn't let her finish speaking. He pushed into the room, jumped on the bed and shouted, "Get up, Andy!"

Andy opened his eyes. "What? Who?"

"Wake up. I need your help."

Andy rolled over and stared at Razor. "What are you doing here?" he said, yawning.

"I'm sorry, sweetie, I didn't know he'd barge in and wake you," his mother said, glaring at Razor. "He was just supposed to check and see if you were up."

"I need Andy's help," Razor said, unfazed. "Half the day is gone.

CHAPTER THIRTEEN

He shouldn't still be in bed."

"Teenager," Andy said with another yawn. "I'm going to take a shower. You can talk to me after I'm awake."

"I'll make you some breakfast," his mother said.

"Thanks, Mom," Andy said, rising and grabbing some clothes.

"I'll just wait here until you're ready," Razor said sarcastically.

"Feel free to come in the bathroom while you wait. I won't splash you. Much." He laughed at the look Razor gave him and closed the bathroom door behind him.

Fifteen minutes later, Andy was in the kitchen working on a plate of pancakes that his mother had set before him and listening to Razor, seated on a kitchen chair, tell him what he wanted.

"Sure, I can find out when the dog show is," he said with his mouth full. "If it's only a few days away, it's probably next weekend."

"Do I want to know why you need to know this?" Rachel asked.

"Probably not."

She shrugged. "All right. I'll get some work done while you talk to my son about putting himself in danger again."

"I told you, Rachel. I will protect Andy with my life."

Rachel nodded and went to her office, closing the door pointedly behind her.

"So let's find out about that dog show," Razor said.

"Do you mind if I finish eating first?" Andy asked. While he ate, Razor sat and stared at him. Andy refused to be intimidated. He finished his pancakes and put his dishes in the sink. "Come on up to my room," he said.

Razor followed him up the stairs and sat on his bed while Andy turned on the computer and searched for the information.

"There's a show in Boston next weekend." He scanned the entries. "Yeah, Saunders has three dogs in it." Andy turned to Razor, grinning. "You're going to attack again, aren't you? They'll never see it coming. This is awesome. I can't believe we're finally going to get the drop on them for

A MIDWINTER'S NIGHT SCHEME

a change." His smile faded as a thought struck him. "Hey! How did you get this information? How would you know about a dog show in Boston?"

"Never mind how I got the information. That's my job. Your job is to confirm it."

"Is that it? You woke me up for this?"

"Yes. And to tell you we're going after Taylor the night Saunders leaves. We're going to take back his Magelights while the Wild Ones are busy guarding the dogs. We make them think we're going to attack the house. They won't expect us to go after the boy at the same time. Get yourself ready. I want you there." He paused and laughed harshly. "You can get your revenge on Taylor. He's been a thorn in your side for ages."

Andy's eyebrows drew together and he frowned. "Yeah, he has. And no, I'm not going to help you. If you go after Taylor, you're doing it without me."

"What?"

"You heard me. I'm not going after Taylor."

"Why in the name of the First's left paw not?" Razor said, his mind-voice rising.

"Because I said no."

Razor was so angry he couldn't speak. His tail switched furiously and his tattered ears lay flat back on his head. After a long, angry pause, he said, "No is not an option. You are needed. Do your duty."

Andy clenched his teeth. "No. I'm not helping you fight Taylor."

"Letsan!" Razor roared. "Here! Now!"

Andy heard the downstairs door open and close, followed by swift footsteps on the stairs. Letsan hurried into the room and skidded to a stop.

"Tell Andy he will assist us in taking the Magelights back from Taylor."

"What?" Letsan asked. "Andy, what's the matter? You don't want to help us?"

"Yeah. But not with this."

"But—but we need you. You can help lure Taylor out so we can

CHAPTER THIRTEEN

attack him in force. All we have to do is get one good Magelight shot to the necklace chain and it falls off and we grab it!"

"Then you don't need me. Lure him out yourself." Andy crossed the room and pulled out his desk chair. He sat down with his back to them. Razor's tail still lashed. "You can see yourselves out," he said as he opened a game on his computer.

The two Maine Coons watched, speechless, as Andy proceeded to ignore them. A growl rose in Razor's throat. "We're not finished," he said.

"Come on, brother," Letsan sent privately. "Leave him be for now. I'll talk to him later and find out what's wrong."

Razor glared one more time at Andy and followed Letsan out of the room. His Magelight flashed and the door slammed shut behind him.

"What was that all about?" Nafshi asked.

"Don't you start on me, too."

"Why don't you want to help them?"

"You know why! You were there the night I almost killed Taylor."

Nafshi sighed. "You did not almost kill him. He took a little bump on the head. He's all better now."

"Doesn't matter. I couldn't control myself then. I can't trust myself not to do even worse next time!"

"Yes you can. I told you, you train with me, you'll bring yourself under control."

"Can you train me in time for this weekend? Can you guarantee me that Taylor won't get hurt?"

"No."

"Then I'm not going."

"Fine. Don't go. But you *are* training with me. Put away that game and do your breathing exercises. I want you calm when we start today's lessons."

"Fine," Andy muttered. He turned off the computer, swung his chair around to face Nafshi, closed his eyes, and took a deep breath. "Everything always seems to come down to breathing exercises."

A MIDWINTER'S NIGHT SCHEME

"Breathing, the stuff of life itself," Nafshi said wryly. "Now be quiet and concentrate!"

Razor was furious as they headed to the road that led out of town, their guards joining them as they passed their hiding places. He told Letsan just what he thought of Andy's refusal as well as some choice words for his brother's stewardship of the boy. Letsan stopped dead and growled at him.

Razor turned back and glared. "Shall we have at it, brother? You know I always win."

"Not always. I won't have you badmouth Andy. Or me. Stop it, or let's get to it."

"Sir," Tamar said, "Now is not the time or place. We need both of you healthy and fit for the next mission."

Razor dropped his gaze. "Tamar is right. Let's get going. I'm sorry, Letsan. The boy made me lose my temper." He grew quiet and Letsan left him alone to his thoughts.

"Right. We're not going home yet. We're going to Becca's," Razor said.

"I don't think she can talk Andy into it, either."

"Just be quiet and follow me." He led the way through town. As they neared Becca's block, he sent a Magelight message. Becca was out in front or her house waiting for them when they arrived.

"Inside," Razor said. She opened the door to let them in. Letsan and Razor went through the door. The rest of their squad ranged themselves around the house to keep guard.

"Are there Wild Ones around?" Becca asked as she led them to her room.

"Not close. But that's not why I'm here." He jumped on the bed and looked around. Letsan settled himself on the windowsill and kept an eye outside. Becca waited while Razor's Magelight flared. She knew his routine by now—he was scanning for any other Catmages or Wild Ones in the vicinity.

CHAPTER THIRTEEN

Once he was satisfied the area was secure, he said, "I want your help. We're going to take Taylor's Magelights away from him."

"How?"

"I'll be leading two squads of Shomrim to attack him while Saunders is away next weekend. The other Wild Ones will expect an attack on the house, especially because we're going to make sure someone is overheard talking about it. While they're off looking for us there, we'll gather at the boy's house. You'll lure him outside and we'll get the necklace from him while he's distracted."

Becca gaped at him. "You want me to what?"

"Lure him out. He trusts you. You told me you teach him every week. Have a lesson at his house but find a reason to get him outside. The Wild Ones are stupid. He's unguarded and vulnerable."

"How—how are you going to get his Magelight necklace?"

"We'll cut the chain and grab it as it falls."

"But what if he fights you?"

"Then we fight back. We win, we cut the chain, get the Magelights, and run. Then we destroy them."

"What if he gets hurt?"

"Then he gets hurt. Becca, he made his choice. He bears the consequences of his actions."

She frowned as she thought about what Razor wanted. Then she shook her head.

"I'm sorry, Razor, but I can't help you. You're asking me to betray Taylor's trust. I won't do that."

"That boy is the enemy!" Razor shouted. "How can you betray an enemy?"

"He's not the enemy, Razor. Yeah, he's on the wrong side, but don't you see how Saunders is using him? Taylor has a rotten home life. Working with Saunders makes him feel important. He gets picked on all the time by his stepfather and stepbrothers. I'm one of the only people in his life who doesn't hurt him. You're asking me to lie to him. The answer is no."

A MIDWINTER'S NIGHT SCHEME

"Letsan, you talk to her. Tell her we need her help!"

Letsan left his post in the windowsill and joined his brother on the bed. "Becca, he's right. We can probably do this without you, but it will be a lot easier with your help."

Becca shook her head again. "No. No, I can't do that to Taylor. He trusts me."

"By the First's whiskers, what is *wrong* with you humans?" Razor said. "First Andy won't help, now you won't, either? Are you in this battle with us or not?"

"That's not fair," Becca said. "You know we're on your side. But you're asking me to go against my principles and undo all the work I've done with Taylor. I'm trying to get him to our side, but through reason, not force! And I'm glad Andy agrees with me. If you want to get Taylor away from Saunders, you're not going to do it by attacking him!"

"Well, it's the only way to get back those Magelights!"

"If that's what you think, you've got another think coming. I'll do a lot for you, Razor, but I won't do this." She frowned down at them.

They stood glaring at each other. Then Razor twitched his ears and jumped to the floor. "I have to go. We have plans to make. Battles to win. Without your help." He couldn't hide the anger in his voice.

"Fine. You can see yourself out, then." She went to the door and held it open until Razor and Letsan left the room, shutting it loudly behind them.

"When this is over, I'm never working with children again," Razor sent to Letsan, knowing full well that Becca could hear him.

"Fine!" she yelled. Then she flung herself on her bed, exasperated. This was a bad idea. She felt it in her bones. Taylor reacted badly to brute force. She grabbed her pillow and threw it across the room. It knocked a picture on the wall askew. Becca went over to it and laughed. It was a sketch of Razor. She straightened it and replaced the pillow. Then she picked up her phone and pressed a button. "Hello, Andy? Hey, you want to come over for supper tonight? I'll ask my mom."

CHAPTER THIRTEEN

A few hours later, the remains of several pizzas lay on the kitchen counter and their parents were seated around the table chatting comfortably. Andy and Becca cleared the table and announced they were going to Becca's room.

"I'll call you when we're ready to leave," Andy's mother said.

"And we'll all pretend we don't know you want to speak in private," Becca's father added with a grin.

Andy smiled weakly and followed Becca to her room.

"Don't worry about Dad," she said as she closed the door. "They're just happy they know what we're doing now instead of wondering why you and Mike and I spent so much time with our heads together."

"So let's hear it," Andy said, sitting down in Becca's desk chair and swinging it around so it faced her bed. He listened quietly as she sat on the edge of the bed and told him what Razor wanted.

"He asked me to do the same thing," Andy said.

"Yeah, I know. He griped about it when I refused. Why did you? Turn him down, I mean."

Andy shrugged.

"Come on, Andy, it's me."

He couldn't meet her gaze. "I—I almost hurt him really bad last spring. I don't trust myself around him. What if I lose control again?" He raised his head, concern on his face.

Becca laughed. "So you don't have any problem at all going after Taylor, you're just worried you'll hurt him? Wow, Andy. After all he did to you. You're a mensch."

"No, I'm not. I just don't want to be like Saunders!"

"Well that's not a problem, because you never will be." Becca sighed. "Andy, what are we going to do? They're going to do this without us, you know."

"Yeah, I know. But we're not going to do anything. Don't you dare warn him!"

Becca frowned. "But—"

A MIDWINTER'S NIGHT SCHEME

"No! They're right about the Magelights. If they get them, it's better for our side."

"What if they hurt Taylor?"

Andy's brows drew together as he frowned. "Razor's right. He made his choice. If Taylor gets hurt, he brought it on himself. And you don't say *anything* to him." He studied Becca's face. "Promise!"

She thought it over, frowning. "Okay. I promise. He's on his own."

"Good. And while we're at it, let's not say anything to Mike. He's too ready to give Taylor a hard time and this is the kind of thing that could slip out."

"I won't if you won't," Becca said with a shrug.

"Andy!" his mother called from the kitchen. "Time to go!"

Andy rose, his chair scraping the floor as he stood up. "See you in school tomorrow. Don't worry, Becca. Razor's pretty good at what he does. By this time next week, the enemy is going to have five less Magelights for us to worry about!"

"Fewer."

"What?"

"Five fewer. Mrs. Silvers would correct you."

"It's Sunday night, Becca! Can't you give it a rest?"

She laughed. "Nope. See you tomorrow."

Andy left the room shaking his head.

FOURTEEN: FIVE FOR FIGHTING

In spite of his warning to Becca, Andy found that it was difficult to stop thinking about the raid. He saw Taylor in PE and in AP History, in the cafeteria and in the halls. Each time, he felt guilty and couldn't meet Taylor's eyes. He told himself he shouldn't feel that way. Taylor was a bully and a jerk most of the time, and he deserved whatever he got. He'd picked the wrong side in this battle. But still Andy couldn't bear to be around him. When he said as much to Becca in the halls on the way to lunch, she seemed unconcerned.

"Now I know why you said not to tell Mike. If you're feeling this guilty, imagine how he'd handle it—dropping hints, taunting Taylor—nope, it's a good thing we kept this to ourselves."

"Kept what to yourselves?" Mike asked from behind them.

"None of your business," Becca said.

"Aha! It's a foul plot to steal my lunch money and leave me to starve, isn't it? I warn you, Becca, these hands have been registered as deadly weapons," he said, holding his arms out in a karate stance. Becca yawned. Mike took the hint and changed the subject.

"Are you guys doing anything tomorrow? Maybe we can go out to the Compound," he said hopefully.

FIVE FOR FIGHTING

"I work on Saturdays, remember? And I have a paper due Monday, so I need to get that done."

"I'm tutoring Saturday afternoon," Becca said, ignoring the look Andy flashed her. "Don't even start," she said as Mike opened his mouth. He snapped it shut with an audible click.

"Then I guess it's just Teresa and me. Action movie, here we come! Hey, there's Teresa! See you at the table." Mike hurried over to the food line, leaving Becca and Andy to join them at their own pace.

"Don't you start, either," Becca said.

"I wasn't going to. But you know what's happening Saturday night," he said, dropping his voice. "Make sure you don't get stuck in the middle of it."

"Not a chance. I'll be long gone before dark. Can we not talk about it anymore? Especially here?" she asked, nodding to the left where Taylor was watching them.

"Okay, okay. We'll just talk about food or something."

Becca glanced at the dish of the day. "Or maybe we can talk about something else," she said, wrinkling her nose.

Becca's father dropped her off at Taylor's Saturday after lunch. "Text me when you want me back."

"Bye, Dad," Becca said as she closed the car door. Taylor was waiting for her as usual. The door opened before she had a chance to knock.

"Hi," he said.

"Ready to learn everything you never wanted to know about the Crusades?" she asked.

"I am if you're the one telling me. Come on in, Mom made cookies for us again."

"Where are your stepbrothers?" she asked cautiously.

"At the mall or something. Mom finally made them understand that they need to leave me alone during tutoring sessions. You should have been here. It was awesome." He grinned.

CHAPTER FOURTEEN

Becca didn't smile back. Taylor's stepbrothers bullied him worse than he used to bully Andy. "Are you sure they're not going to take it out on you?"

"I'd like to see them try," he said. "Now that I have my Mage—" He stopped short.

"Lights," Becca finished for him. "Let's not pretend I don't know you have Magelights, Taylor. You know what I think about that."

He frowned. "I don't see why I can't have them. Andy has one."

"Because he's the Son of Aaron."

Taylor laughed. "Yeah, right. That's what they *say*. Doesn't mean it's true."

"I don't know why you want to work with Saunders and the Wild Ones. They're horrible. Look at all the horrible things they did."

"Yeah? You mean like Andy throwing me to the ground and almost giving me a concussion last spring? Boy, that was really nice of him."

"That was an accident. Oh, never mind. Let's not argue. I'm here to teach you about history, not talk about Magelights."

"Fine by me," Taylor said. "Let's go to the kitchen, Teach." He led the way and sat down at the table, where a plate of cookies lay in the middle of his books and papers. "Any chance you might have time to help me with my math homework today?"

"Let's see how much we get through in history first. The faster you work, the more likely we can get to the math."

They sat down at the table and got to work.

A few hours later, Becca stood up and stretched. "Well, I'm all tutored out. You better get a good grade on the math test on Monday. I don't want all that effort to have been for nothing." She glanced at the kitchen clock. "Whoa! My dad's probably wondering what happened to me. I'd better text him."

"I'm surprised he's not banging down the door to make sure I haven't kidnapped you," Taylor said. "He doesn't like me."

"He'd like you more if you would stop hanging out with Saunders."

FIVE FOR FIGHTING

"I thought you said we weren't going to talk about that."

Becca shrugged. "I saw the opening and took it."

In spite of himself, Taylor laughed.

She glanced at her phone. "Dad will be here in a few minutes. Did you leave me any cookies?"

Taylor walked Becca to the door when they heard the car horn. He stood in the doorway and watched her leave. He felt a pang of sadness when she was gone. He shook it off and stepped back, shutting the door behind him. There was time to watch a game on TV before dinner. And then there was more homework. High school was a lot harder since he had started studying with Becca. But maybe one day she'd start paying more attention to him and less to that loser, Andy. And if not, well, there were lots of other cats in the Compound. The oddness of the turn of phrase in his thoughts didn't even register with him as he went to the TV room.

Razor, Zohar, and Letsan gathered in a hollow under a hedge down the street from Taylor's house. The moon was a thin sliver that cast little light. Zohar's warriors were scattered around the block awaiting word to attack.

"You're certain he's the only one home?" Razor asked Zohar.

"Yes. I saw the father leave a short while ago. The mother is out. Shamir says she went to work and that she often works into the late hours of the morning. Our spies report no one has entered the house since Becca left late this afternoon."

"And how do you intend to lure him out of there without Becca or Andy?"

"My father came up with a great plan that doesn't involve them."

Letsan laughed. "It's so simple I can't believe we thought we needed them. As soon as our Shomrim are in place, I'm going to ring the doorbell."

Razor grunted. "I'd prefer having him far enough out of the house that he can't shut the door on us."

"Shamir has door duty. Once Taylor is outside, it's his job to make sure that door doesn't close unless we want it to," Letsan said. "We don't

CHAPTER FOURTEEN

have much choice here, Razor. We've talked this to death. Do you trust Zohar and me or not?"

"I trust you."

"Then let's go."

"All right. Give the signal."

Zohar and Letsan sent word to the warriors waiting nearby. Letsan went to his position near Taylor's front yard. He hid behind the wheel of a car on the street and concentrated. His Magelight flashed and a stick rose from the ground and flew slowly through the air. Letsan moved it carefully into place and jerked the stick forward into the doorbell. The door opened and Taylor looked around. His Magelight necklace was tucked under his sweatshirt, but the chain around his neck glinted in the light from the hall.

"Hello?" he said. "Is anyone there?"

Shamir took a few steps in the yard next door, deliberately walking on dead leaves. Taylor heard the rustling and his head jerked to the right. "I can hear you," he said. Shamir took a few more steps. "Very funny. Come out and show yourself!" Frowning, Taylor moved out onto the porch.

"Now!" Zohar shouted to his Shomrim. "Aim for the chain! Cut it! Quickly!" Two squads of warriors concentrated fire on the chain. Light daggers zoomed in from everywhere.

Taylor raised his arm in front of his face to shield himself. As he did so, all five of his Magelights flared and a shield appeared over his torso. The light daggers bounced off harmlessly. Taylor had no idea how he'd done that, but he smiled grimly.

"Again!" Zohar called.

Letsan, Razor, and two full squads of Shomrim repeated fire. Taylor's heart beat faster as adrenaline coursed through his body. He laughed as the next batch of light daggers bounced impotently off his shield. Now that the first shock of the attack wore off, he was enjoying this. He'd been waiting a long time to get into the battle, and these stupid Catmages were bringing it right to his doorstep. Try to attack him, eh? Well, two could play that game. He remembered his training and decided to show off what

FIVE FOR FIGHTING

five Magelights could do. He fired off light jets in quick succession just as he had trained. Orange, green, yellow, green, yellow. A mix of emotions ran over Taylor. He felt proud in his own abilities as he flicked the light daggers at the Catmages, angry that they dared to attack him, and after a few rounds, he found himself tired and hungry. Well, that wouldn't do at all. He needed peak energy if he was going to fight off—how many were out there, anyway? Once again, without conscious effort, he felt the answer. Three paws' worth plus the two leaders. *What?* Oh, fourteen. Taylor frowned and brought his attention back to the Shomrim ringing his front yard. It was time for some trash talk.

"Give it up, losers," he called. "Look how many of you there are, and the best you can do is bounce your lights off my shield?" He laughed. "And it's only me right now. Should I call in some reinforcements and show you a really good time?"

"How?" Razor said. "How is he doing this? He's just a child with no aura! There is no way he should be able to hold off you and me and two squads of Shomrim!"

"I don't know!" Letsan said, as angry as Razor. "This is not good. Not good at all." He ducked as a dagger from Taylor came too close and flung up a shield as another four headed their way. Taylor was grinning at them as he fired his Magelights. "Something is very, very wrong. Can you feel it? Those Magelights feel—wrong."

"I don't have time for feelings," Razor growled. "We need to get those Magelights. Together, brother, on my mark."

The two of them waited until Taylor was busy defending himself against Zohar and his squad. Then they attacked in unison. Razor tried to distract Taylor with a shot near his eyes and Letsan aimed for the chain. They watched in shock as one of the light daggers Taylor aimed at Razor actually changed course—and color—and blocked Letsan's shot.

"That's impossible!" Letsan said.

Taylor laughed loudly. "You guys couldn't hit the side of the house if you were standing in front of it. Got anything better? I'm getting bored."

CHAPTER FOURTEEN

As the Catmages gathered for another attack, a car rolled down the quiet street, startling them all. Razor ordered the Shomrim into hiding, hoping their Magelight daggers hadn't been seen by whomever was in the car. Taylor swore as it pulled into the driveway and the engine cut off. His stepfather got out and slammed the door behind him. He walked unsteadily toward the open front door.

"What do you think you're doing?" he asked, his words slurring as he spoke. "Shootin' off fireworks? That's illegal. And dangerous."

"So's drinking and driving," Taylor muttered quietly enough that his stepfather couldn't hear him.

"Get in the house! Door open in the winter, what do you think, I'm made of money?"

"No, because Mom pays the bills." Taylor couldn't stop himself from retorting. His stepfather hurried toward him, fist raised.

"You want this?" he said.

Taylor winced but he stood his ground and said nothing. His stepfather stopped and glared down at the boy, his breath reeking of beer. Taylor felt his Magelights grow warm against his chest. Not now, he thought frantically. He can't see the lights!

His stepfather growled and shoved past him. "Out of my way," he said. "I need the bathroom." Taylor heaved a quiet sigh of relief as his stepfather staggered into the wall on the way into the bathroom. He'd probably pass out in his chair the moment he sat down. Best if Taylor got out of sight quickly. He hurried to his room and closed the door. As soon as the door shut, he was overcome with weakness. Taylor collapsed against the wall and slid down to the floor, exhausted. "What was that?" he wondered out loud. "What the hell happened?"

He pulled the necklace out from under his sweatshirt and over his head. The gems lay dormant now, though they were warm to the touch. "What did you do?" he asked them. Then he laughed again. "Now I'm talking to a bunch of rocks. Taylor, you have rocks in the head." He waited until his breathing slowed to near normal, then he stood up shakily, feeling

FIVE FOR FIGHTING

famished. He listened carefully at the door, but heard nothing. He went silently down the stairs toward the bathroom. His stepfather hadn't even made it to the living room. Taylor carefully stepped over him as he lay on the floor in the hall, open-mouthed and snoring. Taylor shot him a disgusted look and walked quietly to the kitchen. He opened the refrigerator and took out bread and peanut butter and jelly, then ate his way through half the loaf before he felt better. As he took a pack of cookies out of the pantry, he decided that he wasn't going to tell Roah and the others anything about what had just happened. There were too many weird things that he didn't want to share with them. He had a feeling they had never heard of anything like Magelights shooting off by themselves. He bet they wouldn't like it. And maybe they'd take his Magelights away. Anger surged at the thought. No. These were his Magelights. Nobody was taking them from him. Nobody. And he hadn't needed any help fighting off Razor and Letsan and their warriors, had he? No, Taylor was better off on his own, as usual. He grabbed an energy drink from the fridge, tucked the cookies under his arm, and went back upstairs to his room. He shut the door behind him and locked it. Yeah, this was not the sort of thing he could share with anyone.

Outside the house, Razor and Letsan had withdrawn to a safe distance, still shocked to their core. "What happened?" Razor asked. "What was that?"

"I don't know, brother, but I have a bad feeling that when we figure it out, we're not going to like it."

"I already don't like it. Zohar! Shamir!"

"Sir," they said as they hurried to his side.

"You will tell your warriors to keep their mouths shut about what just happened until we know more. Understood? They tell no one. No one!"

"Yes, sir."

"We're going back to the Compound. Now."

"Sir."

Razor and Letsan led the way out of town. The Shomrim ranged

CHAPTER FOURTEEN

themselves around their officers.

"Hakham will want to know about this immediately. And he's not going to be happy," Letsan said.

Razor dismissed the Shomrim when they reached the Compound and gazed stonily at Letsan. "No need to wake Hakham," he said. "This can wait until morning."

"Agreed," Letsan said.

They walked wearily to their bayits, lost in their own thoughts. As Razor turned to go inside his home, he paused.

"By the First's whiskers, brother, you were right. Something is very, very wrong."

"I'm starting to think it was a good idea we didn't have Andy along after all."

"So am I."

FIFTEEN: THE ENEMY WITHIN

Andy pulled cautiously into the Coreyton Animal Hospital parking lot, tires crunching on spots of ice and snow. His mother sat in the passenger seat, nodding as he maneuvered the car into a parking space and put it into park.

"Nice job," she said.

"Thanks." Andy released the seatbelt and got out, grabbing his backpack from the back seat while his mother walked around the car to the driver's side.

"See you later," she said as he waved and hurried inside. It was a bright, chilly Saturday morning. January was nearly over and as much as Andy liked the snow, he was getting a little tired of winter.

"Morning, Andy," Maddie said as he headed to the back room to deposit his coat and backpack. "You're on litterbox duty," she said. Andy groaned. "Oh, come on, you must be used to it with all those cats in your life."

"Don't let them hear you call them cats," he said softly.

"They're not here now, are they?"

Andy grinned and went to clean the cages.

It was a busy morning. Andy cleaned exam tables after Dr. Crane and Dr. Lipstock were through with their patients. Dr. Crane called him in

CHAPTER FIFTEEN

to observe a cat that had swallowed an extremely long string, and Maddie had him help with some cat toenail trimming.

Andy was bringing a chart to the front desk when the front doorbell rang as it opened. He glanced up and his breath caught. Principal Saunders was holding the door for one of his Dobermans. Andy didn't need Nafshi's voice inside his head telling him it was one of the specials. He could sense it in the way the dog looked directly at him, in the way Saunders was grinning—that smug smile that set Andy's teeth on edge. Andy's glance went to the dog's collar. The stud in the middle was larger than the ones surrounding it. Yeah, that was one with a Magelight all right.

"Hello, Mr. Cohen. I had no idea you worked here," Saunders said.

Andy knew Saunders was lying. Nothing he did was coincidental. This was his third year working here. All Saunders had to do was look in his file, or maybe not even that. Who knew what the Wild Ones had told him about Andy?

"Can I help you?" the young woman behind the counter asked.

"Stan Saunders. I have an appointment to trim Shadow's nails," he said.

"Is this your first time here?"

"Yes."

"I'll need some information from you."

"Certainly. Oh, may I request Mr. Cohen's help? We're very—familiar with one another. He's a student at my school. I'm sure he would be most careful. He knows the value of a good dog…don't you?" He turned his gaze to Andy, a slight smile lifting the corners of his mouth.

"Of course," Stephanie said.

Andy wanted to wipe that smirk off his face. He would rather have done anything else than go into an exam room with Saunders and his dog, but he didn't see a way out of it.

"Why don't I go see if Dr. Crane is ready while you give Stephanie your information?" he asked. He slipped around the desk and into the back, where he found the vet looking through a microscope.

THE ENEMY WITHIN

"No parasites," he said with a smile. "That's one less thing to worry about." His smile faded at Andy's expression. "What's wrong?"

Andy told him quickly about his new patient and its owner.

"The dog has a Magelight?" Dr. Crane asked. "How is that possible? Wait, tell me later. Don't worry about it, Andy. There isn't much mischief your principal can cause while I'm clipping his dog's nails."

"That's not what I'm worried about. He's here for a reason. He never does anything without one."

"Well, he can't do anything to you in front of me. So we'll just go in there together."

"I am with you too, Andy. Saunders will do nothing to you," Nafshi said.

Andy took a deep breath.

"Come on," said Dr. Crane. "Let's go trim those nails and get him out of here quick."

"Okay."

Andy followed Dr. Crane to the exam room. Maddie gave him the chart and said, "This is Shadow."

"Champion, eh? I'm surprised you didn't take him to your regular vet."

"He was booked solid today and it needed to be done."

Dr. Crane looked up from the chart and glanced at Saunders. "Have we met before? You seem familiar to me."

"I don't recall meeting you."

Dr. Crane shrugged. "Right, let's see to those toenails. Maddie, give me a hand here."

Nails don't need cutting, said a strange voice inside Andy's head. *I don't want to be here. Let's go home.*

"Is—is that the dog speaking?" Andy asked Nafshi.

"Yes," Nafshi said. Andy could feel the disgust she felt. "It can talk! By the First, it's an abomination!"

"Why is Shadow talking to us?"

175

CHAPTER FIFTEEN

"He isn't. He's talking to the Evil One but he can't direct his thoughts. He's projecting everywhere. Listen."

Yes, I remember what you said. I will do it. But I don't like it here. Am I going to get stuck with that sharp thing?

"Wonder what Saunders asked him to do," Andy sent.

"Nothing good."

"So, Mr. Cohen, do you intend to help, or is your role to stand there staring while Dr. Crane and his assistant do all the work?" Saunders said.

Dr. Crane frowned. "Well, he mostly observes cases, Mr. Saunders. He's not a qualified vet tech. Andy waits until he's directed by me or Maddie to help, mostly to hold animals while we work on them. He knows better than to take part in a procedure without permission."

Andy tried not to grin as Saunders narrowed his eyes. That was the first time he'd ever seen someone correct the principal, let alone stand up to him. And Dr. Crane *totally* schooled him.

"*Principal* Saunders." His voice was even, but he couldn't hide the annoyance in his tone.

"Oh. Sorry. *Principal* Saunders," Dr. Crane said in the exact same tone. He turned his head away from Saunders and winked at Andy, who cleared his throat. "Shadow seems calm enough. Andy, come on over here and help Maddie. You hold the collar."

"Shadow is perfectly well behaved. You don't win dog shows with an animal that doesn't know how to follow orders."

Don't want to follow orders. Want to get out of here.

Saunders eyes flashed as he looked toward the dog.

"He's talking to the dog," Nafshi said.

"Probably telling him to shut up," Andy sent.

"I wonder if I could poke the animal in his cage, so to speak," she said.

"Do it! Saunders is always poking *me*."

Nafshi laughed. "Watch and learn, Andrew. Watch and learn."

THE ENEMY WITHIN

Before Andy could wonder what she meant, Nafshi started meowing. Shadow's head jerked up and he looked around, whining, trying to find the cat in the room. Andy could barely hold in his laughter as he watched the dog strain in Maddie's grip.

"Whoops," he said, taking a stronger grip on the collar. "Doesn't seem to be as well behaved as you thought," Andy said to Saunders.

"Shadow, sit!" Saunders said.

There is a cat in here. Where is it? Why can't I smell it or see it? Not one of your good cats. Let me go. I will find it!

Nafshi's laugh echoed inside Andy's head. "No you won't, you big dumb thing," she sent to Shadow, adding another meow. Shadow's feet scrabbled against the metal exam table as he struggled to get free.

"Maddie, come on, get a good grip!" Dr. Crane said.

"It's not her fault," Andy said. *Oops. Probably shouldn't have said that.* Saunders glance flashed at Andy and his lips thinned.

"Somehow, Mr. Cohen, trouble always follows in your wake. Why do I think you are to blame for my dog's misbehaving?"

Andy gazed innocently at Principal Saunders. "I'm not doing anything. Ask your dog what the problem is."

"Dogs can't talk," Saunders said with a sneer.

"Yeah. They can't."

Dr. Crane looked at him curiously, sensing something was going on. "Well, if you can't control your dog, Principal Saunders, we're going to have to muzzle him. I can't take the chance on having my people hurt."

"Shadow, sit!" Saunders said harshly. The dog whined and sat, quivering. "There. I don't know what got into him, but it's passed."

"No it hasn't," Nafshi said, laughing again. "Put me in a cage and starve and torture me, eh? Payback time." She meowed again. Andy felt his Magelight warm and quickly hid his hand behind his back.

"Don't!" he sent.

"Too late," Nafshi chuckled. Andy saw a tiny bolt of light fly into Shadow's right rear. The dog yelped and leaped forward. He slipped out of

CHAPTER FIFTEEN

their grasp and launched himself off the table straight at Saunders, who was standing in front of him. Shadow pushed Saunders across the room into the counter. He bounced off and fell to the ground, knocking down a metal tray that clanged when it hit the floor, scaring Shadow even more. The dog was running and jumping everywhere. Andy backed away as Dr. Crane managed to grab Shadow's collar and yank him to the ground. Maddie rushed in to help restrain him. Saunders raised himself, his face suffused with anger.

"That was for me. And Zahavin," Nafshi said.

Saunders' head whipped around.

"Nafshi!" Andy sent, shocked. "Did you let him hear you?"

"Indeed I did," she said. "It's about time the enemy knows to be afraid of us."

"On second thought, perhaps his nails are fine the way they are. Clearly your staff isn't up to the task of caring for a champion show dog," Saunders said, not taking his eyes off Andy.

"My hat's off to your vet if he manages to control that dog on a regular basis," Dr. Crane said, frowning. "Maddie, let's get to the next case. Andy, come on." He pulled the door open and left the room, followed by Maddie. Andy hesitated a moment.

"Why do I think there's so much more here than meets the eye, Mr. Cohen? Hm?"

"I have no idea. You know, Dr. Crane is right. You really ought to learn how to control that dog, Principal Saunders."

"And you should look to yourself, Mr. Cohen." His voice dropped so that only Andy could hear him. "I will get to the bottom of this. Count on it." Andy turned and followed the others, leaving Saunders and his talking dog to show themselves out.

The rest of the morning passed quickly. Andy was gathering his things, getting ready to go, when Dr. Crane called him over.

"Now I know why Saunders seemed so familiar to me," he said. "About five years ago, I was working late, running some tests after everyone

THE ENEMY WITHIN

else had gone. Someone knocked on the door. I tried to tell him we were closed but he said he would only take a minute. So I open the door and this guy walks in. He tells me his dogs have a show coming up the next day and his prime champion is nervous and can't seem to sleep. There's nothing wrong with him, he says. I tell him to take the dog to an emergency clinic. He says no, taking the dog to a vet would make him more nervous. He asks me for a sedative. Says he'll pay cash and flashes a big wad of hundred dollar bills. I tell him that I can't do that and say again he should go to the emergency vet. He gives me a dirty look and leaves. I never knew who he was until now. He probably thinks I forgot about it."

"No, that's not how he operates," Andy said. "He knows you remember. He doesn't care. You don't have any proof he tried to buy drugs from you illegally. It's your word against his."

Dr. Crane's eyebrows rose. "Well, if he got those drugs, he didn't get them from me or anyone here."

"He got them," Andy said glumly. "He used them to keep Nafshi a prisoner all those years ago."

"I'm not a prisoner now, Andy. And I intend to get him back for every moment I spent imprisoned in his house," she said. Andy shivered at the menace in her tone.

"Cold?" Dr. Crane said.

"I guess. My mom's probably outside waiting for me. I'll see you next week."

"Have a good one. And Andy?"

"Yeah?"

"Be careful around that guy."

"Always."

SIXTEEN: RID ME OF THIS TROUBLESOME CATMAGE

Winter was over. A fresh spring breeze blew inside the open porch door as Stan Saunders sat glowering at his kitchen table. But he wasn't interested in the weather. He was interested in stopping the constant interference in his plans. He had no idea what Andrew Cohen had done to Shadow at the vet's, but that irritating boy had done *something*. That voice he had heard—he knew it, but he couldn't place it. It had been bothering him for months, and he was still no closer to the answer. And that wasn't the worst of it. Nothing was going right lately, and it hadn't been going the way he expected for—thinking about it—years. Those insufferable children and cats had thwarted him at almost every turn. They had almost gotten to the Tilyon before he had! The thought struck him oddly. How had they known where to find him that night? He had never been able to discover the reason for it. If someone had betrayed him, they would pay dearly.

Saunders' frown deepened. The Tilyon was supposed to be the tool he needed to further his plans. He was supposed to have achieved far more by now. He gripped the amulet around his neck and felt it grow warm at his touch.

"Damn it!" he shouted, rising and knocking his chair to the floor. He kicked it across the room. "Why can't I do more with this? Niflah!

RID ME OF THIS TROUBLESOME CATMAGE

Roah! Here! Now!"

He heard two thumps from upstairs as the cats leaped down from wherever they'd been napping. Probably the guest room bed. His frown deepened at their laziness.

Niflah was still yawning as the two Wild Ones entered the kitchen.

"What is it?" Roah asked.

"Was the bed comfortable enough? Would you like me to have the maid add turn-down service to your room?"

"It is midafternoon, Saunders. We are cats when all is said and done. We need our sleep," Niflah said.

"Well, I need you to rid me of these troublesome Catmages," Saunders said. "Or to be precise, one Catmage in particular—our precious Zahavin."

"What do you mean?" Roah asked, ears twitching.

"I've been thinking about the events of the past several years. She is the key to the Catmage resistance. Remove her, and you remove their heart and soul. Nothing can survive without a heart."

"Our opponents have many strengths," Niflah said. "I wouldn't be too hasty to assign this big a role to any one Catmage."

"Oh, really?" Saunders said. "Let us review Zahavin's actions since the, ah—unfortunate—deaths of the Council four years ago. She was the reason Hakham was late to the meeting. Because of that, he survived to create a new Council and interfere with our plans. She and Hakham were alive to hear Razelle's prophecy, which resulted in her finding and training Andy Cohen, the precious Son of Aaron." His tone made the title sound like an insult. "Mr. Cohen has interfered with us for three years, including saving Zahavin's life so she could continue to destroy our plans. Each time, through his interference or through Zahavin and Hakham's, our forces are turned back from their goals. I had her in my sights last spring, and she somehow managed to get that idiot Matanya to sacrifice himself for her! She defeats us at every turn! Who stopped your warriors last Halloween, Roah? And the one before that?"

"The boy," Roah said bitterly. "The boy and Zahavin. Their powers

CHAPTER SIXTEEN

have increased each time we have faced them. Why don't you go after the boy, Saunders? He is young. You are bigger and stronger. You can easily destroy him even without the Tilyon."

"I can't touch the boy," Saunders said. "You don't understand our laws. I can do nothing to harm him. I have no wish to go to prison. But," he said, eyes glinting with malice, "Zahavin is under no such protection. No one would care if something were to happen to a mere cat." His lips thinned as he finished.

"You know," Niflah said, "I believe you are right, Saunders. Eliminating Zahavin might also take the boy out of the fight."

Saunders looked at him keenly. "Explain."

"Andy was badly demoralized after Matanya was killed. Just imagine how much more Zahavin's death would affect him."

A smile slowly spread across Saunders' face. "Yes. Yes, I think you're right. Eliminating Zahavin will take care of two problems at once. Get on it right away!"

"It will not be easy," Roah said. "She has Letsan and Razor and many warriors on her side. And her powers grow stronger. Zahavin is beginning to fight like Hakham."

"They're training her to be a Magus," Niflah said. "It's the only explanation."

Saunders' eyebrows rose. "A Magus?"

"We told you about them before. They are the most powerful Catmages alive," Roah said. "Nafshi was one. Why do you think we got so little out of her? She was strong, maybe the strongest Catmage of her time. You haven't seen Hakham fight. He is very powerful. And he is Zahavin's teacher. Niflah is right. They are training Zahavin in the ways of the Magi."

"He trains his apprentices this way, yet when I approached him he turned me down. Me! His own brother!"

Saunders narrowed his eyes at Niflah. "Spare me the tales of your sibling rivalry, and help me hurt your brother. This training is all the more reason to remove Zahavin! We have been foiled at every turn by her med-

RID ME OF THIS TROUBLESOME CATMAGE

dling. Eliminate her, and we rid ourselves of the biggest thorn in our side."

"Yes," Roah said. "She is an important piece of the resistance. Take her away and they will lose spirit. A dispirited enemy is a defeated enemy."

"How do you propose we do this?" Niflah asked.

"I don't know," Saunders snapped. "Are you or are you not my war leaders? That is your job. I want her taken care of, and I want it done soon."

"We must consider. Let us think about it and get back to you."

"I am tired of waiting, Roah."

"Yet we must discuss this with the ones we trust, and come up with a plan. It will be difficult. Our enemies are always on guard these days. They do not even travel to town anymore without at least a squad of fighters."

"Do what you need to do. But find a way. And make it soon."

"I will think about it and return within the week," Roah said. "In the meantime, we shall return to the West Woods."

"Do that," Saunders said. "In the meantime, I'll sit here twiddling my thumbs."

The sarcasm in his tone annoyed Niflah. "If you want this done sooner, you can always bring your precious gun to Andy's house and try to catch Zahavin going in or out," he said.

Saunders went scarlet with anger. "You watch your tone with me, Niflah," he said, contempt dripping from his voice. "I am not one of your apprentices."

"No. And neither are we your servants. We are partners, Saunders. You have assigned us a complicated task. We will consider it and come back to you with a proper plan." He swept out of the porch door and down the stairs, not looking back to see if Roah followed.

Saunders and Roah glanced at each other, then Roah headed out the open door. Saunders watched him go, frowning. He was still angry. He took a deep breath, grasped the Tilyon, and concentrated. The amulet flashed and the door slammed shut. Saunders smiled grimly. Then he righted the chair he'd been sitting in, slid it against the table, and went up

CHAPTER SIXTEEN

the stairs to his office. He looked out the window into the yard, where he saw Shadow and Gunner sitting alertly in their run. "I think," he muttered, "that Niflah is outliving his usefulness."

Three days later, Roah, Niflah, and a group of Wild Ones arrived on Oak Street after dark.

"There are no Catmage spies in the vicinity," Kfir said.

"That you know of," Alef replied. "Did you do an aura check?"

"No," Kfir told him. "I used my senses. Are you questioning my abilities?" His tail switched.

Kel, who was at the rear of the party, perked up at the thought of Kfir going after Alef. "I think, Captain Kfir, what Alef meant to say was that although your prowess at tracking is well known, you would be better served to make sure with an aura check—just in case you missed something."

Kfir's ears laid back on his head. "That's what Alef thinks, is it?" he asked.

Kel could barely keep from laughing out loud. This was almost too easy.

Alef glared at them both. "*Kelev* does not speak for me," he said, knowing Kel hated the use of his full name. "Everyone knows and admires your abilities, Kfir. But our enemies are crafty. It never hurts to make double sure."

"That's enough from all of you," Niflah said. "There is the house. We have arrived. It doesn't matter anymore if Razor knows we're here. Now get inside and stop arguing!"

Kel marched along behind Roah with his tail arched over his back. Roah turned to look at him. "You will stand beside me at the meeting," he said privately. "But do not dare to stir up Kfir again when I need him to have his wits about him. Are we clear?"

"Yes sir," Kel said, a little chagrined that his father could read him so well.

Roah told the guards to stay downstairs and went upstairs with Ni-

RID ME OF THIS TROUBLESOME CATMAGE

flah, Kfir, Alef, and Kel. Saunders sat waiting for them in his office behind his desk, his long legs stretched out beneath it.

"Well?" he said.

"There was much discussion about Zahavin's weaknesses. We think we can lure her into a trap if we take something precious to her."

"And what do you know that is precious to her?" Saunders asked.

"The boy. Andy."

"We tried that before," Saunders said. "He lit my cellar on fire. And that was before he even had a Magelight. I have no intention of risking a kidnapping charge. The boy is off limits."

"We don't have to actually *take* the boy. We make her *think* we have him."

"And when she sends him a message and he answers? Idiot! Is this the best you can do?"

"We thought of that. If you would let us use force, we could keep the boy occupied while we set the trap for Zahavin."

"No! I've told you, Mr. Cohen is off limits. If he is harmed, the first one they'll come to is me! Those wretched children know too much already. They'd head straight to the police if Andy turned up missing."

"There is another who is precious to her," Niflah said. "Velvel told us much about the East Woods before they caught him. Zahavin has a niece she's very fond of."

"Leilei," Kel said. "Her name is Leilei."

Saunders looked at him. "You're one of Roah's, aren't you?"

"Yes sir," Kel said, flattered that Saunders remembered him. "Zahavin thinks the world of her niece."

"Then we will use that. Find this Leilei and take her. Roah, can you make this happen?"

"We must discover a way to draw her out of the East Woods. Razor set strict rules on travel to and from the Compound after our attack last fall."

"I know a way," Kel said. "Zahavin adores Leilei. And Leilei adores Patches. Get hold of Patches, and you can lure Leilei right into our trap."

CHAPTER SIXTEEN

"Patches!" Alef said with a bark of laughter. "That idiot?"

"Yes. He may be an idiot, but they are close. Closer even than you and Bett," Kel said with a glint in his eye. Alef's ears went back.

"How do you know this?" Saunders asked.

"I spent some time with them last year, sir. I spied on them until the attack on the Compound."

"Why are you still not spying on them?"

"I was seen during the attack on the Compound last spring."

"That was a waste of an asset," Saunders said. He frowned at Roah. "Why didn't you keep Kel away from the East Woods?"

"There wasn't much more he could have learned. Razor was getting too suspicious. Besides, it was time my son took his place by my side."

"I learned enough before they found me out, sir. If we take Patches, Leilei will try to rescue him. She is impetuous and overconfident in her powers. It has gotten her in trouble before. She was attacked by your dogs when she tried to spy on you some time ago. Patches saved her life that night."

"You learned this much while you were with them," Saunders said. "And nobody felt it worthwhile to pass this information to me?"

"We do not bother you with details," Niflah said. "I remind you that those are your own instructions."

Saunders frowned. "All right. I like the plan. Implement it."

"It will be done," Roah said. "Kel, you will find a way to lure Patches out of the Compound."

"I have already thought of it, Father. I shall set a trap for him. And if he doesn't fall for it, all I have to do is show myself to him. He hates me and wants me dead."

Saunders smiled. "I like your son, Roah. I like him very much."

Roah arched his tail over his back. "Thank you."

"Let me know when it is done."

Roah and the others recognized the tone of dismissal and turned to go. As he turned, Roah's shoulder brushed lightly against Kel's. Neither of them saw the look of pure hatred on Alef's face.

SEVENTEEN: CATSOVER

Mike sat down at the lunch table grinning from ear to ear. "Best news ever!" he said.

"What's better than spring break starting tomorrow?" Andy asked.

"Kenny's got a soccer tournament out of town over spring break, and my parents are both going. They're asking your Mom tonight if I can spend the weekend with you. So no Kenny at the Passover Seder!"

"Excellent!" Andy said. "I mean, about you staying with me, not about your brother. Teresa's right. You are kind of mean to him."

"Think about it, though. This means everyone at the Seder will know about you-know-what, so we can have all our friends there. Just imagine Razor sitting in a chair during the Four Questions!"

Andy and the others burst out laughing. "You know, that's not a bad idea. Maybe we should invite him."

"Invite who, Cohen? Me? Aw, you shouldn't have," Taylor said as he elbowed Andy in the back. He was flanked, as usual, by Pete and Tommy.

"I wouldn't invite you to your own funeral," Andy said. "Get lost, Grant."

"Speaking of funerals, how are your, ah, friends?" Taylor asked. "Safe and secure out there in the woods, I hope?"

Becca kicked Andy lightly and he bit back a retort. "Taylor, I

CHAPTER SEVENTEEN

thought you were past this," she said with a frown.

"I guess you thought wrong, Becca." He glanced away, unable to meet her gaze. "Let's go," he said and pushed Andy as he left, followed by Pete and Tommy.

"You're still tutoring him?" Andy said, his face scarlet with suppressed anger. "I told you he'd never change."

"You're wrong. He's definitely changing. But sometimes—" she hesitated.

"Sometimes what?" Andy asked.

"Nothing."

"Forget about that jerk, Andy. You and me, three whole days, and no schoolwork!" Mike said. "High five!"

Andy ignored Mike as he watched Taylor go through the food line, piling every inch of his tray with plates of food. The look on his face made Mike and Becca follow his gaze. Mike whistled.

"That," he said, "is a lot of food."

"He's on the football team," Becca said.

"It's springtime. No football."

"Baseball, then."

"Nuh-uh," Andy said.

"Oh, why do you care?" Becca said, exasperated.

"Because it's weird," Andy said.

They watched in awe as Taylor ate his way through what looked like enough food for three people.

"I'm getting sick just watching him," Mike said.

"Then stop watching," Teresa told him.

"Good idea!" Mike turned away and looked down at his half-eaten sandwich, shrugged, and took a bite.

"Weird," Andy said again.

Mike's parents dropped him off after dinner the night before the tournament. Andy and Mike set up an air mattress in Andy's room and settled in

CATSOVER

for a long gaming session.

"Try and get *some* sleep," Andy's mother told them both as she headed off for bed. "And no excess noise. I still have to work tomorrow."

"Okay, Mom," Andy said.

"Don't worry. We promise to go to bed while it's still dark out," Mike said. "So what time is sunrise again?"

Rachel Cohen shook her head, closed the door behind her, and headed for her bedroom. "Don't forget I'm a light sleeper, Mike," she called.

Mike nodded. "I remember. So Andy, you'd better not make so much noise this time."

"Pretty sure that was you yelling when you lost your last life," Andy said.

"Oh, yeah, it was." Mike grinned and handed Andy a controller. "I promise not to yell tonight."

It was still dark out when they went to bed, but they rose much later than the sun. When they yawned their way downstairs for breakfast, Andy found a note with chores that needed to be done before they could get on with their gaming session. Mike grumbled, but he and Andy got the Passover dishes out of storage and loaded them into the dishwasher. They straightened up the dining room and played video games while they waited for each load to finish. By the time Andy's mother got home from work, the dining room table held piles of gleaming china, glass, and silverware.

"Nicely done," she said. "The Jeffersons will be over tomorrow to help cook. What do you say to pizza for dinner tonight?"

"Farewell to bread? Absolutely!" Mike said.

"It's not 'farewell' for you," Andy grumbled.

"No, but I promise to feel your pain for the whole week while I'm eating bread and you're not."

"Thanks, bud."

"*De nada.*"

They had a pleasant evening and went to bed at a reasonable hour after they were warned that they would be woken up early regardless of

CHAPTER SEVENTEEN

what time they went to bed. After breakfast, Mike and Andy set the table and took the Haggadahs out of their box, putting one book by each place.

"Who all is coming today?" Mike asked.

"Well, Teresa and Mr. Velez and the Jeffersons."

"I know *that*," Mike said. "I mean which Catmages are coming? You did ask your mom, didn't you?"

Andy shrugged. "Yeah. I'm not sure who's coming. Mom said Goldeneyes and Letsan could definitely come, and that they could decide who else to bring. I think she's torn between wanting to talk to more of them and still not really believing they can talk."

"But she's talked to them, right?"

"Yeah, a few times."

"Weird. So you don't know who's coming? What if Goldeneyes invited the whole Compound?" Mike looked around the dining room with a critical eye. "Nope, not enough room for them all," he said, grinning.

"The whole Compound? Seriously? Have you *met* Goldeneyes?"

"Good point. Okay, I'm guessing Leilei and Patches."

"Maybe. We'll find out in a few hours. I told them to be here before sunset."

"We should show your mom how we play Catmage catch."

"Sure, if you never want to be able to play it again."

"Another good point. Andrew Cohen, you are the smartest guy in this room."

Andy laughed. "You're right. Let's go see what else Mom wants us to do."

They spent the morning straightening up Andy's room and being called on for individual jobs as his mother thought of them. They were taking a break when Becca and her mother arrived.

"Soup time!" Mike called as they came into the kitchen. "Great, I'm starving."

"The table's all ready, Becca," Andy said. "There's not much left for us to do."

CATSOVER

"Well, we need to eat lunch," Mike said.

"It's on the porch. I cleared out the last of the bread this morning and made you sandwiches," Andy's mom told them.

"Thanks!" Mike said, heading out the door, followed by Andy.

The afternoon passed quickly. Becca stayed busy in the kitchen. The boys came and went as needed, and the house filled with delicious aromas.

"If you need someone to make sure that chicken soup is good, I'll volunteer to taste it," Mike said as he stopped in the kitchen for a glass of water.

"Why not?" Becca's mom said. "It's ready. Who wants some?"

Mike, Andy, and Becca sat down to steaming bowls of chicken soup while the two women joined them.

"I need to put my feet up for a while," Rachel Cohen said.

"Aren't you going to taste the soup, Mom?" Andy asked.

"Already did. It's excellent, as usual, Becca."

"Yeah," Andy said. "The matzoh balls are great!"

Becca smiled.

"Well, that's no surprise," a gruff voice said. "Becca's a girl of many talents."

Razor stood in the open kitchen window. Andy's mom raised her eyebrows and fought to keep her jaw from dropping. "I'm still not used to that," she said. "Hi, Razor."

Razor dropped to the chair nearest the window. "Hello," he said to Becca's mother.

She smiled at Razor and raised her eyebrows as she glanced at Rachel. "I've only spoken to him once before. It really takes some getting used to."

"Yes. Yes, it does," Rachel said.

"Are we too early?" Letsan called from outside just before appearing in the open window.

"Um, no," Rachel said. "It's just you two?"

CHAPTER SEVENTEEN

"Not quite. Mrs. Cohen, thank you for your hospitality. Andy, open the back door, would you? Hakham is getting on in years, I'm not sure he can make it to the window sill."

Andy hurried to the door and pulled it open. Half a dozen Catmages sat on the ground waiting for him.

"They're all Catmages?" Becca's mom asked. "They can all talk?"

"Talk, talk, yes! Patches has been speaking since he was a kitten, now everyone hears him. You hear me too, human mom? DO YOU HEAR PATCHES?"

"Ow, Patches, not so loud!" Andy said. "We hear you, we hear you." He glanced at the two moms, who were staring at Patches and the others. "I'll introduce you. Mom, you know Goldeneyes, but Mrs. Jefferson doesn't. You guys come inside as I say your name. Goldeneyes is also called Zahavin." He waited as she crossed the threshold. "Next is Hakham. He's in charge of everything. He even taught Goldeneyes and Letsan." Hakham said hello, came inside and moved over to Letsan, who he swatted. "Too old to leap into that window? I'll show you, you cheeky thing." He jumped effortlessly onto the windowsill and started grooming his shoulder. Andy's mom laughed.

"You look like you're in great shape," she said. Hakham blinked at her.

"This is Silsula, Goldeneyes' sister. She's a Nanager."

"What's a Nanager?" his mother asked as Silsula wound around her legs, purring.

"I take care of the little ones." *Chirrup.* "Andy told me my job is a cross between a teacher and one of your daycare workers."

"So you take care of Mike when he visits, then," Mrs. Jefferson said with a grin.

"Oh, dear, no. Nobody can handle him. He's beyond my abilities, I'm afraid." She laughed along with the two moms while Mike pretended to look offended.

"This is Zohar, Letsan's son," Andy said. His expression hardened.

CATSOVER

"He lost his leg after a fight at Saunders' house."

"Yes, but I think the dog that did it broke a couple of teeth on me," he said cheerfully. "I'm glad to meet you, Andy's mother."

"Rachel," she said. "I can't believe I'm talking to—Catmages."

"Rachel, then. Thank you for having us in your home."

"Last, but not least, these are Leilei and Patches. Patches is the crazy one who can't stop hopping," he said, laughing as Patches did his signature four-legged hop into the house. "C'mere, Patches." Andy leaned down and picked him up. "Behave yourself tonight or Mom will never let you come back."

"Patches always behaves! Patches is a good Catmage."

"You sure are," Mike said as Andy deposited Patches into his arms with an admonition to take care of him.

"Andy, why don't you show them all into the dining room. Oh—where will they sit?"

"On the extra chairs, Mom. I'll take care of it."

"Well, we're not quite ready. We have an hour or two before we start."

"Don't worry, Mike and I will babysit them. Come on, guys. This way."

Andy and Mike led the Catmages into the dining room. Andy told them to sit on the chairs lined against the wall on either side of the table. He made sure Patches and Leilei sat together and told Patches to stay put. "I'm going to have my eye on you all night," he said.

"I'll sit next to them," Silsula said. "Patches and I get along very well, don't we, dear?" *Chirrup.*

"Yes! Silsula is a good, good, good Catmage! She is always nice to Patches!"

"Mind if I wander around?" Razor asked. "Your house has never been surveyed for defensive purposes, has it?"

Andy rolled his eyes. "Razor, the Wild Ones aren't going to attack my house."

CHAPTER SEVENTEEN

"You can never be too careful."

"Do what you want, then. Just don't get in my mom's way or she'll let you have it." Razor jumped down from the dining room chair and waited expectantly until Zohar joined him. He looked up at Letsan, who was settling himself down in one of the extra chairs.

"Suit yourself, brother, but I'm staying here," Letsan said. "I know this house from top to bottom. It's safe."

Razor grunted and led Zohar out of the room. A few minutes later, Letsan caused a shout of laughter by lying in wait behind the window curtain and leaping out as Razor returned. "Wild One attack!" he shouted as Razor rose on his hind legs to meet him. The two wrestled and growled and rolled into the wall. They broke apart laughing, and went back to their perches on the chairs.

When Jake Jefferson arrived, he stopped briefly in the kitchen before hurrying to the dining room. "All right, let me see them," he called as he came through the door. Andy introduced him to the Catmages he hadn't yet met and he stood grinning hugely, listening to their excited chatter. Even the normally aloof Razor couldn't hide his delight at taking part in a millennia-old ritual that was part of Catmage history as well as human.

By the time Teresa and her grandfather arrived, the cooking was done, the table set, and they were ready to begin.

"Aren't you going to introduce the Catmages to Mario and Teresa?" Andy's mother asked him, taking the cake that Teresa held out and nodding her thanks.

"Nah, we already know them all," Mario said. "We're old friends, Razor and me," he said, nodding at the Catmage behind him and reaching out a hand to scratch behind Razor's ears. Razor blinked at him. "We been out to the Compound a few times."

At last they were ready to begin. The Seder plate lay at the head of the table in front of Rachel Cohen. Wine and grape juice was passed around and wine glasses were filled as everyone took their seats.

"Andy, we should probably explain everything to the Catmages who've never been to a Seder before," his mother said. "Will you hold up the Seder plate, please?"

As he did, she explained the significance of the hard-boiled egg, the shank bone, the bitter herbs, the parsley, the matzoh, the *maror*, and the *haroset*. The Catmages listened attentively. Even Patches was quiet.

"We read from a book called the Haggadah," Andy said. "It means 'telling' because we tell the story of Passover every year. This is the Passover Seder. Seder means 'order.' We do it in the same order every year."

"And you have been doing this since the First received her Magelight?" Silsula asked.

Andy shrugged. "I don't know exactly how the ancient Hebrews celebrated the Passover, but we've been doing it this way for a long, long time. Maybe I can look it up for you on the Internet later. But right now, we need to begin. There's a lot to do before we get to the dinner break and I'm starving!"

Mike nodded in agreement as everyone picked up their books.

The Catmages watched in fascination and listened intently as Andy, his friends, and their parents took turns reading passages from the Haggadah, drinking the ceremonial cups of wine and eating the ritual foods. When they passed around the matzoh, Patches couldn't restrain himself. "Can Patches have some, too?" he asked.

"Why not?" Rachel said, grinning. "Andy, give some matzoh to the Catmages."

"They're not going to like it," he said.

"Patches wants to try it!"

"I'll help!" Mike said, grabbing pieces of matzoh in both hands and jumping up from his seat. Andy shrugged and joined him. Soon the Catmages were crunching away on the dry, cracker-like pieces. Patches ate his with relish.

"It's, ah, it's very different," Goldeneyes said after a small taste. Most of Letsan's remained on his chair. Not many of the Catmages seemed to care for it.

CHAPTER SEVENTEEN

"I like it," Razor said. "Good move for once, Patches."

"You should try the horseradish next," Mike said. "You'll love it."

"Don't you *dare!*" Teresa said. "Don't listen to him, Patches. The horseradish will burn your throat."

"Mike is mean!" Patches said.

"Spoilsport!"

"Michael," Rachel said. "Just because your parents aren't here doesn't mean you can't be punished."

"Sorry, Mrs. Cohen."

Razor stared at Mike. "Oh, don't worry. If Mike tricked any of us into eating something bad, we'd take care of him ourselves." His Magelight glowed.

"Okay, okay, sorry, Razor," Mike said hastily. "I get it. I won't do it again."

Mr. Velez laughed out loud. "Mike, you're not too bright if you think you can get away with pranking Razor. That is one cat who can look after himself."

The Catmages watched the rest of the first half of the Seder in relative quiet. In spite of the warnings, Patches did want to try the horseradish but Andy stopped Mike from giving him a piece. "Here, try the parsley instead."

"Tastes like grass. Patches is not sick. No more grass!"

"Just hang on for a bit more and we'll give you something really good. Turkey dinner!" Andy said.

"Patches will wait. Patches is hungry."

Now that the first half of the Seder was complete, they removed the extra glasses and Haggadahs and got the table ready for dinner. The humans ate soup and hard-boiled eggs while the Catmages got pieces of chicken, some of it removed surreptitiously from the soup bowls.

"Really, Andy, there's chicken in the fridge you can give them," his mother said.

"I know, but this is easier."

CATSOVER

She sighed and shook her head. When the main course was served, Rachel decided to give each Catmage a small plate of turkey. "You're going to give them scraps anyway, and this will protect my dining room chairs," she told Andy.

A chorus of purrs greeted the gift of turkey. "Patches likes turkey very much," he said. "Andy must bring this to the Compound!"

"Are you kidding? There's way too many Catmages. I'd have to bring a truckload."

"Then Patches will visit Andy more often."

"That would be fine," Andy said, grinning.

"No it wouldn't," Razor said. "There's a war on, remember?"

Everyone fell silent at the reminder.

"Yes, there's a war on," Becca said, "but that doesn't mean we don't do normal things. There's no reason why Patches can't visit if he takes the proper precautions."

"Patches will be careful!" he said.

"We'll see," Razor growled.

They finished dinner and Andy and Mike helped clear the table while Becca and Teresa put the desserts on the sideboard.

"You know, Razor," Mike said, "it occurs to me that Catmages need more expressions."

"What are you talking about?" Razor asked.

"Well, you know how you say 'By the First' and stuff like that? You're going to run out of things to say. It's not varied enough. Now, I am a renowned Shakespearean scholar—"

Becca snorted with laughter.

"Okay, I'm a renowned Shakespearean *actor*—"

"At Coreyton High," Andy said, grinning.

Mike turned to glare at him. "If the peanut gallery is finished? Yes? Well, since I have read many Shakespeare plays—" He looked around as if daring someone else to interrupt him. "I have some suggestions."

"Uh-oh," Becca whispered to Teresa, who grinned.

CHAPTER SEVENTEEN

"Like, here's one: By the darkness of my nostrils, I smell a rat!"

"Rats are tasty," Patches said.

"Ew," Teresa said.

"For the love of cats?" Mike asked. "Wait, wait, I have it! I swear on my ragged left ear, I will end you!"

"Both his ears are ragged, Mike," Letsan said.

"I have a million of them. How about: My tail! My tail! Wilt thou dare to pull my tail?"

Everyone burst out laughing, but Razor sat unmoving.

"Here it comes," Becca said quietly as the laughter ended.

"I think you're right, Mike. I think I *should* change things up a little."

"You do?" Mike said.

"I do. Here, how's this? By the power of my Magelight, let us have no more of this." Razor's Magelight flashed and a Haggadah rose from the breakfront behind Mike and started hitting him around the head. Humans and Catmages laughed long and loud as Mike made futile attempts to shield himself. When Razor finally stopped smacking Mike with the booklet, the laughter died away.

"You should know better than to mess with Razor, Mike," Becca said. Andy nodded, grinning broadly.

Mike shrugged.

"He's never going to learn," Mr. Velez said.

"Probably not," Teresa agreed.

The dishwasher was loaded and food put away. Dessert was served, and shortly after that they got to the second half of the Seder. More than one of the Catmages curled up on the chairs as the humans made their way through the grace after the meal, the last two cups of wine, and the ceremonial songs.

"Next year in Jerusalem!" they all said together as they reached the last page, and the Seder was over. Andy and Mike collected the Haggadahs and put them away.

CATSOVER

"Time to go," Becca's mother said, rising.

Patches yawned hugely. "Time to go to sleep! Patches is tired," he said. "We don't have to walk back to the Compound tonight, do we?"

"No," Razor said. "We can stay here. If that's all right with you, Rachel."

"That's fine," she said as Patches spread out and curled up on his chair, bumping Leilei over to the next one.

"I'd invite you to come home with me, but you should probably stick together for the walk back tomorrow," Becca said.

"I can drive them to the Compound before work," Andy said. "Would that be okay, Mom? I could use the hours for my permit."

"All right. Then you and Mike had better not stay up too late tonight. We'll need to leave early in the morning."

"Patches likes riding in cars!" he said.

"I like it too, when it means I don't have to walk as far," Leilei said.

"I'll walk you all out to the door," Andy said to his friends.

"Tonight was great," Becca said.

"Thanks for having us," Teresa said, her grandfather echoing her words.

"Thanks for coming," Rachel told them.

"It was a night to remember," Mr. Velez said. "Passover with a bunch of Cat—mages," he said, grinning wickedly at Goldeneyes as he paused in the middle of the word.

"I'm tired," she said, yawning. "Andy, I'm going to stay down here and sleep. See you in the morning." She lay down on her chair and curled her tail around her legs. The other Catmages followed suit.

"Good night," Becca called to them as she left the dining room. The tip of Razor's tail lifted and fell as she turned off the light.

Mike, Andy, and Becca stood on the front porch watching the Velezes and Jake Jefferson get into their cars and leave.

"Well, another one gone," Mike said. "I'll meet you upstairs, Andy. Time for a game or two before we have to go to bed?"

CHAPTER SEVENTEEN

"Yeah, I'll be up soon."

Mike closed the door behind him. A light breeze rustled through the still-bare branches. Becca shivered.

"Are you cold?" Andy asked.

"A little."

"We could go inside."

"No, I don't mind. It's nice being out here with you."

"Yeah. It is nice."

Andy couldn't help notice how pretty Becca looked in the moonlight. Her double-curved smile seemed particularly attractive tonight. He found himself staring into Becca's eyes.

Say something, he told himself, but no words came. He felt like an idiot, not knowing what to do.

Becca reached over, grabbed him by the lapels of his shirt, pulled him close, and kissed him. When it was over, Andy still had no words.

"I figured it would take you another year if I didn't," she said. "Tell my mom I'm waiting for her." She turned and walked to her car.

Andy pushed open the front door feeling dazed, a slight grin on his face. He made his way down the hall and gave Mrs. Jefferson Becca's message. He went through the kitchen and up the stairs, still wearing the grin.

Rachel and Danielle waited until he left the kitchen before exchanging amused glances.

"Do you think—?" Rachel asked.

"Uh-huh," Danielle said, rising. "I better go."

"I'll walk you out."

Mike sat in front of the computer as Andy entered the room.

"What took you so long?" he asked, pausing the game. "Hey, what's with your face?"

"Huh?"

"You look goofy."

"Gee, thanks."

"There you go, all better now. I never saw you smile like that before."

CATSOVER

"Probably because I never kissed Becca before."

Mike jumped out of his chair. "What? Awesome! It's about time. Teresa and I were starting to think you'd be an old man before you finally kissed her!"

Andy said nothing, but the grin came back.

"Okay, if you're going to look like that the rest of the night, I'm going to bed." Mike reached out and turned off the computer. He and Andy got into their pajamas and brushed their teeth. Andy turned out the light and stepped over Mike on the air mattress. As Andy got into bed, he lay there thinking about the moonlight reflecting in Becca's eyes.

"I can hear you making that goofy face," Mike said.

"Shut up, Mike."

"Good night, Andy."

"Good night."

EIGHTEEN: MOUSE TRAP!

It was a warm spring evening. Lev and Ari padded slowly through the brush on the side of the road. Lev was in the lead. Behind him trotted four small tabby kittens about three months old. Every so often one of them wandered to the side chasing a blowing leaf, or a leaping or flying insect. Ari would run after the kitten and gently head it back in line.

"You're sure they're going to meet us?" Lev asked.

"I sent the message. Hakham will be there."

"You should have told him to bring Silsula," Lev said grumpily.

"You've found kittens before," Ari said. "What's the matter?"

"Never like this. Four half-breeds in one litter? It's unheard of!"

"And all females. What a shame the West Woods isn't going to get them." Ari laughed. "Silsula will be over the moon. I wish I could see her when these little ones arrive."

"Me too," Lev said. "When *can* we visit our family?"

Ari paused to think. "Not until the war is over, Lev. Razor needs us on the inside."

Lev sighed. Then he jumped after one of the kittens who was running into the brush after something he could only guess at. "Hey! Haven't you ever seen a butterfly before? Leave it! Come back here!"

Ari laughed and made sure the other three stayed put. "Come on,

MOUSE TRAP!

little ones," he said. "We don't have much farther to go. Let's all get together now." The two of them shepherded their charges along until they reached a grove of trees. Ari stopped and told Lev to keep the kittens quiet. He moved stealthily ahead and settled himself in the brush before examining the area for auras. "Excellent," he said. He hurried back to his son. "They're here. Let's go."

They led the kittens to the Council Wood. Waiting for them by the oak tree were Razor and Hakham. The kittens seemed delighted to meet more Catmages, and they ran happily to them.

"You look like me!" one of them told Hakham. "Are you my father?"

"No, little one," he said.

"Are you my father?" another asked Razor. Razor stared down at the kitten for a moment. He blinked at her. "No. I would never leave anyone as pretty as you. Or your sisters." He leaned his head down and licked her ear.

Lev and Ari exchanged a glance and looked away.

"You girls need to go with Lev for a little while. Hakham and I need to talk to Ari," Razor said. Lev shot him a look and sighed.

"This way, little ones," he said. "Who wants to race me to that tree?" The kittens scrambled to rush ahead of him.

"We found an entire litter," Ari said.

"So I see."

"We couldn't bear to turn them over to the Wild Ones. My daughter will raise them well, and they'll learn all they need to be good Catmages."

"How do we keep them quiet about your finding them and bringing them to us?"

Ari shrugged. "I have no idea."

"They're too young to be circumspect," Hakham said. "Kittens at that age tell everyone everything they know."

"I couldn't leave them, Hakham, and I can't sentence them to a life with the likes of Roah and Kfir!"

CHAPTER EIGHTEEN

Razor grunted in agreement. "I wouldn't, either. But if the Wild Ones get word of this, your cover is at risk."

"Life is risk. I'll take my chances. We've brought them enough young males to keep them happy. Last run, we got the biggest whiners we could find, made sure they're all under a sun cycle old, and took them there, where they can stand around every day and gripe to Kel how terribly they were treated by their elders. It turns out that Lev has a talent for finding the disaffected youth of our kind."

"If you start talking about how much better the old days were, I'll notch your ear," Razor said.

Ari laughed.

"So have you anything to report?"

"No. We've been on the road for the past moon. We need to get back and find out what's going on. Things have been quiet for too long. I'm sure Kfir has something in mind. Before we left, there were a lot of private meetings."

"You haven't been able to penetrate his inner circle yet?"

"No. They've made it clear the only thing they want us for is our Seeker abilities," Ari said. "Lev's been trying to make friends with Kel, but so far no luck. That one keeps his counsel close."

Hakham's hackles rose. "Still, it doesn't hurt knowing you two are on the inside. You'd better get going. How are you going to explain being away for a moon and not having any half-breeds to show for it?"

"Easy. We're blaming you. We met up with some of your far-ranging patrols and you took them from us."

Razor gave a short bark of laughter.

"So, you really do want that ear slit, don't you?"

"No. But you're going to have to singe some fur. My tail, if you please, and make sure you don't hit anything *but* the fur."

Razor laughed again. "It will be my pleasure." Ari turned around and held his tail still and flat on the ground. Razor sent a light dagger along the top and the smell of burned fur filled the air.

MOUSE TRAP!

"Not bad," Ari said, curling his tail around to look at the burn. "It should be enough to get them to believe us. How many did you steal from us?"

Razor looked over at Lev and the kittens. "At least four," he said. He glanced at Hakham. "It's going to be a long walk home."

"Why don't you leave them in the Council Compound? It's closer," Ari said.

"Can't trust Kharoom. It's okay, I can handle kittens. Just because I don't have any doesn't mean I don't know what to do with them."

"I'd hunt for you for a week if I could go on that journey with you," Ari said. "But Lev and I had better get back." He called his son, who came racing over followed by the kittens.

"We have to go, little ones. Razor and Hakham will take you to your new home. Listen to them, and be well!"

The kittens jumped around Lev and Ari, crying their goodbyes.

"Will you come visit us?" the smallest one asked.

"Someday," Ari said. "Goodbye! Be good!"

He and Ari made their way down the path and melted into the underbrush.

The atmosphere in the West Woods Compound seemed charged. Something was up. Several of Kfir's warriors guarded a large bayit. Ari could have sworn that had been a barracks before. The guards watched them balefully as they passed.

Kel met them on the path to their home. "Good to see you both! I'm glad you're back. What have you brought us this time?" he asked brightly.

"Nothing," Ari said. "Razor has started long-range patrols. We ran into a squad and had to run for it. They took our half-breeds! And look! Look at my tail!" He curled it around to show the burn.

To his surprise, Kel laughed. "Don't worry about Razor. He's not going to be trouble for very much longer."

"Why? Is there something we should know about?" Ari asked.

CHAPTER EIGHTEEN

"No. This doesn't concern you—yet. We may have use for your skills later on. In fact, I'm sure we will. Go to your bayit, rest up, and be ready to come to me at a moment's notice."

"All right," Ari said, careful to block his thoughts. He and Lev went to their bayit and settled down on the bed of leaves.

"What was that all about?" Lev asked.

"I don't know. But I expect we're going to find out before long. Careful, son. Guard your thoughts and be *very* careful of anything you say to me."

"I will." Lev yawned and put his head down on his paws. "At least we can rest up. Watching kittens is exhausting." He was asleep moments later.

The next morning, Niflah, Kelev, and Roah gathered in Roah's bayit the morning before to set the plan in motion to capture Patches. Kfir and his lieutenant Oren were in attendance as well. Alef and Bett sat behind Roah. Alef glared daggers at Kel when nobody was looking. Kel laughed to himself. His siblings were not at the meeting. Alef's standing had fallen as his own had risen, and it felt wonderful. He turned his attention to his father as Roah began to speak.

"I am concerned about one aspect of your plan, Kel. How do you intend to get within range of Razor's guards without their picking up your Magelights? We have known for months that they scan regularly for Magelight auras to prevent another sneak attack."

"They scan regularly, but they can't scan constantly," Kel said. They need to preserve their energy. Also, my spies report that there are certain hours of the day when they are less attentive. Midafternoon is one of those times."

"We have a squad of Tzofim ready to draw off the guards if Kel needs it," Kfir added. "But I don't think we will. We have noted their weakest guards. That's where we'll slip through." He laughed harshly. "The Shomrim have gotten soft again. Razor thinks we're still licking our wounds

MOUSE TRAP!

from the failed assault last fall." His tail whipped back and forth along the ground. "He will learn how wrong he is."

Roah turned his gaze to Kfir. "You had better be right. Saunders is not the only one tired of failure. You came here making great promises, yet Razor and his Shomrim keep blocking us at every turn."

"Not every turn," Kfir growled. "We took out Matanya and many of his warriors."

"That was last cycle," Roah said. "This cycle is a different story—one filled with failure."

"Roah, is this the time for argument?" Niflah asked. "Can't you at least wait until the plan is at least underway before you start the berating?"

"No. Kfir knows his duties. He is not a kitten and doesn't need you to defend him."

Niflah's ears flattened. "Perhaps not. But neither does he need to be insulted before starting an important mission."

Kel watched with great interest as his father stared angrily at Niflah. Would he have the pleasure of seeing two of the three leaders fight? Would he see Niflah taken down in front of him? Kel could barely contain his glee. To his dismay, Kfir stepped in between them.

"It's fine, Niflah. Roah is right. I haven't given us a victory in far too long. Today we start the process to reverse our fortunes and hand Razor and his Shomrim their tails."

"Since he cares so much about you, perhaps Niflah should go along with you and Kel. He hasn't been in the field since autumn."

"We don't really need—" Kfir started to say.

"I'd be delighted," Niflah said. "I want to make this work as much as you do, Roah."

Kel looked from one to the other. That was a surprise move. No matter. It was important to guard himself. Kel walled off his thoughts and spoke.

"I welcome the aid of one so powerful, and of such reputation."

"Yes, he is most powerful," Roah said. "Perhaps Niflah can use those

CHAPTER EIGHTEEN

powers to help you capture Patches." His words dripped with sarcasm.

"I have just the spell for the job," Niflah said cheerfully. "It's the one I used to get Nafshi."

Kel's ears pricked up. The old one had just made his addition to the team worthwhile. He had never explained to anyone how he'd managed to capture a Catmage as powerful as Nafshi. All Kel knew about it was what he'd been told. Saunders had come home one day with Nafshi drugged and in a cage, a very smug Niflah at his heels. Perhaps he could get on the old one's good side and learn the spell.

"I'd love to learn how you did that," Kel said.

"Perhaps you will. After we get Zahavin."

"How do you plan on luring Patches to us?" Roah asked.

"He hunts in the same area of the woods most afternoons," Kel said. "A simple mind calls for a simple plan, sir. We're going to lure him away with a mouse."

"A mouse?"

"A mouse. I promise you, Father, you're going to enjoy the tale."

Kel and Niflah met Kfir the next morning at the edge of the Compound. They walked together to the East Woods as his Tzofim spread out behind them. Kel led the way, checking from time to time with Kfir to make sure their approach was unseen.

The captain looked up at the sun in the sky. "They change the guard in a little while. Get into position and wait. If Patches is going to hunt today, he will be here soon."

"Oh, he'll hunt. He's predictable, our old friend," Kel said. Niflah grunted and made his way into the underbrush near an old oak tree.

"Positions, everyone!" Kfir sent. Soon there was no noise and no movement from the Wild Ones lying in wait except for the twitching of ears and whiskers. Kel searched the woods and found a nearby mouse. He directed it to the path that Patches would follow.

Kel had time enough to grow nervous waiting for Patches to arrive.

MOUSE TRAP!

It was all very well to say he was certain the fool would be out in the woods today. He was not nearly as sure as he appeared. But just about the time he thought the mission would be a failure, they all heard soft paws treading on the dirt path ahead. Patches was on the hunt. Kel was right. He steered the mouse toward Patches. They could hear its progress and then the slow, careful steps of a Catmage on the prowl.

"I can't believe it. It's really working," Niflah said.

"I told you it would. Patches likes to think otherwise, but he is predictable."

Patches moved quietly down the path after the mouse, step by careful step. The mouse halted and so did Patches. He gathered himself to leap, moving his hind legs silently until he was ready to spring. He pounced. The mouse darted too late and Patches knocked it over with his paw, grabbed it by the neck and crunched down until it was dead. Then, his mouth full, Patches broke into his four-legged hop and started to sing.

"Mousey, mousey, come to Patches' housey!" he sang. He dropped the mouse on the ground and pushed at it with his paw. "Patches will take you home and share you with Leilei!" he said. He bent to pick it up again.

"Or," Kel said as he walked out from the brush where he'd lain hidden, "Patches will come home with Kel and Kel will eat the mouse that Patches caught."

Patches growled, his ears back and his tail lashing. "Don't come near Patches. Kel is a bad, bad Catmage. No, not Catmage. Kel is Wild One! Bad Kel. Kel lied to Patches!"

"I did indeed. And now I'm going to capture Patches and bring him home with me."

"No you won't!" Patches said, his Magelight glowing. "You will not defeat Patches. I am Nistar! Nafshi taught me!"

"And I was taught by the ones who taught Nafshi," Niflah said as he stepped out from behind the oak tree. His Magelight blazed. "This is one of my favorite spells. Go ahead. Try to send a message to your friends."

"Patches cannot! He cannot move! He cannot use his Magelight!"

CHAPTER EIGHTEEN

Patches tried to open his mouth to yowl, but couldn't. "What did you do to Patches? Bad Niflah! Leave Patches alone! Let Patches go!"

"Oh, be quiet," Kel said. But he looked interestedly at Patches, who could do nothing more than twitch his ears. His tail curled down between his legs. "What did you do? How did you do that? I've never seen such an effective spell. You cast it so quickly, and just look at him! He can't move a whisker! How, *how* did those fools choose your brother instead of you to head the Council?"

Niflah dipped his head at Kel's flattery. "My brother knows nothing of this," he said scornfully. "It's a scruffing spell. It's related to the way a mother picks up her kittens. I saw the potential for it ages ago. I practiced immobilizing small creatures and worked my way up to Catmages. Patches will go nowhere until I want him to."

"It's brilliant!" Kel said. "How many more of these spells are you keeping to yourself?"

Niflah chuckled. "I can't give away *all* of my secrets, young Kel. Now, if you will be so kind as to take his Magelight, we need to get Patches back to the Compound before Razor's Shomrim wander by. Kfir, would you send a message to Saunders, please?"

Kel practically skipped over to Patches as Kfir sent a message globe. He cut the leather strap securing Patches' Magelight. Another flash and the necklace soared through the air to land at his feet. Kel leaned down and picked up the Magelight with his teeth. "Well, this is a bit awkward, but it will have to do. How are you going to get that one moving?"

"Watch and learn, youngster." Niflah moved forward, and Patches stumbled along with him, tail still tucked between his legs.

"Patches does not like this! Let Patches go!"

"Be quiet or I'll let Kel beat you with that mouse."

"Oh, I almost forgot. Go ahead, Niflah, I'll catch up. Patches was kind enough to supply my dinner." He bent to the mouse as Niflah forced Patches through the wood toward their Compound, followed by Kfir. Kel caught up with them, licking his chops.

MOUSE TRAP!

Over in Coreyton, Principal Saunders sat behind his desk, frowning at his computer screen. His mind wasn't on the words in front of him, however. He was waiting for news. He slid his chair back and swung around to the window. He glanced at his watch. They should have told him something by now. He was very tired of working with animals. He couldn't wait until he mastered the Tilyon. Once he did, he would have no need for the kitties. His brow smoothed as he thought of not having to deal with Niflah and his insufferable attitude for much longer. Saunders turned back to the computer screen and began to type.

Some time later, he pushed his chair back from the desk and stretched. A bright green globe zoomed into the Tilyon and a grin spread across Saunders' face. Excellent. They had the idiot. He pressed a button on his phone and spoke to his assistant. "Ms. Jaskow, get Taylor Grant out of class and bring him to me," he said.

When Taylor arrived, Saunders strode out of his office and said, "Follow me." He led the way to his car. Taylor waited in silence as they drove through the streets. Saunders turned onto the road that led out of town and said, "You'll find a leather shaving kit in the console. Take it out when we arrive. Then you will go into the Compound and administer a sedative to Patches. Kel's plan worked very well. You will come back to the car as soon as you are finished. I'll excuse you to your teacher when we return."

"That's great, Principal Saunders!" Taylor said.

"Not yet, it isn't. Patches is only the first step on the path to destroying Mr. Cohen's will to fight."

"I could destroy him myself," Taylor muttered.

"You haven't so far," Saunders said, his brows lowering.

Taylor kept quiet for the rest of the ride. A few minutes later, Saunders pulled over to the side of the road. He grasped the Tilyon and sent a message flashing out of it.

"Run," he said to the boy. Taylor took off down the path.

CHAPTER EIGHTEEN

When the Wild Ones arrived at the West Woods with their captive, Patches was greeted by laughter and jeers. Niflah marched him to a low bayit with a wide doorway. Kfir and his warriors stood behind, blocking the doorway. Niflah, sides heaving, released Patches. "I'd forgotten how much energy that spell takes," he said. Patches crouched on the ground, cowering as he looked from face to face.

"Where is Taylor?" Niflah asked.

Kfir's ears twitched. "He's coming. Roah just received a message from Saunders. The boy is on his way."

Moments later, Taylor came running down the path clutching a small leather bag. He paused outside the bayit to catch his breath.

"You know what to do?" Niflah asked.

"Yeah. Principal Saunders explained it pretty clearly. Plus, he had me practice on Dalet last night. I think she's still a little doped up," he grinned.

"Then do it."

Taylor bent to enter the shelter and moved toward Patches, who backed away growling. Niflah cast the scruffing spell once more and Patches froze. Taylor knelt next to Patches and removed a hypodermic needle from the kit. He took hold of the loose skin on the Catmage's neck between two fingers, pushed the needle through the skin and depressed the plunger.

"Bad boy! What are you doing to Patches! Niflah, let Patches go. He will run away from here and never come back. Never tell. Patches promises!"

"You're not going anywhere," Taylor said. "You're going to be a big help to us, Patches. In fact, with your help, We're going to beat Andy and all his friends."

Patches felt suddenly tired. His head spun and his eyes unfocused.

"You drugged Patches," he said. "Patches remembers this feeling. You are a bad, bad, bad boy." His voice faded and his legs began to wobble.

Niflah watched as Patches sank to the ground. "You know what to do, Taylor."

"Got it." He picked up Patches. Just inside the door were several

MOUSE TRAP!

steel cages. Taylor opened one and put Patches inside, closing the door and locking it with a combination lock.

"No hidden Magelights this time," Niflah said as he caught sight of Kel coming up the path with Patches' collar. "I'll take that," he said.

Kel dipped his head and dropped the Magelight at Niflah's feet. He looked inside the bayit. "Well done. That's step one. Now we get to work on the next."

"Your father will be pleased."

Kel blinked at Niflah. He couldn't wait to see Alef's expression when Kel reported the first part of the mission accomplished. Everything was going perfectly.

"So we do this again when you get Leilei?" Taylor asked.

"Perhaps. Having Patches makes it that much easier to get her. It is Zahavin who will be the most difficult to catch. I'm sure we'll need you for that operation."

"Just remember to give me enough time to get here," Taylor said. He glanced at the clock on his phone. "And speaking of time, I better go. Principal Saunders is waiting." He waved cheerfully and hurried back toward the road.

"We should drug Leilei anyway," Kel said.

"Do you think she'll be able to fight her way past Kfir and his warriors? Are you that afraid of her powers?" Niflah asked, sarcasm dripping from his voice.

"No," Kel said. "I am trying to anticipate all possibilities. She is one of Nafshi's line, as you know."

Niflah stiffened. "Hers is not the only line of strong Catmages. We can handle a single Catmage, regardless of her heritage."

"As you say, sir. I was just being cautious."

"I have taken her abilities into account. You may go," Niflah said, dismissing him. Kel seethed inwardly, blinked at him, and left.

I'm going to remember that, Old One. Kel hurried down the path to his bayit.

213

CHAPTER EIGHTEEN

Leilei awoke from a nap in the late afternoon still tired. Hakham had worked her very hard in their lesson today. But that's how Magi are made, she thought. And why shouldn't she aspire to that level? Nafshi was one. Auntie Zahavin was on her way to becoming one, and so was Auntie Silsula. *They* had private lessons with Methuselah last season. Now it was her turn. She was the latest in the line of Nafshi to push her powers to their limits. And power was needed! The Wild Ones were still out there, still plotting against Catmages. Saunders still had the Tilyon.

Thoughts of Saunders still disturbed her. She glanced at her side where her many-colored fur covered the scars from the time she had been caught in a dog's jaws and nearly killed. Patches had saved her. She purred softly. She was very fond of him, quirks and all. Patches made her laugh every day. Others in the Compound might think him foolish, but she knew better. Patches was a lot smarter, and a lot more powerful, than most Catmages realized. She rose, stretched, and decided to go find him. Strange that he wasn't napping at her side as he usually did when he found her asleep in their bayit. Well, maybe he was playing with the kittens. She yawned and stretched again, shook herself, and hurried out of the bayit.

Not long after, Leilei sat in the meadow, puzzled. She had checked the entire Compound and Patches was nowhere to be found. She'd asked the guards along the path if he'd left, but they'd said that no one had left or entered the Compound all day. None of the kittens or catlings had seen Patches. Something was definitely wrong. Silsula didn't seem too worried, though.

"Have you tried sending him a message, dear?" *Chirrup.* "You know how he can be. For all we know he's sitting under a tree trying to talk to a squirrel because he likes the look of its coat."

Leilei laughed. "You're right. He's probably just distracted somewhere. I'll find him." She concentrated, and a green globe of light emanated from her Magelight and zoomed away. She watched it go, puzzled. That was the direction of the enemy compound. Patches wouldn't—no, that was silly. He was probably near the border, that's why the globe had gone

MOUSE TRAP!

toward the west. She sat down to wait for an answer.

At the West Woods Compound, Patches gazed groggily out of his cage. Roah, Alef, and Bett sat with Niflah, Patches' collar at his feet. Leilei's message flashed into the bayit and entered the Magelight. Niflah put his paw over the Magelight. "It's from Leilei," he said with satisfaction. "Shall we send her an answer?" The others laughed and watched as the old Catmage concentrated and conjured a globe from the Magelight beneath his paw. "Now," he said, "we wait until she comes to us."

"It's like old times," Alef said, "only it's the idiot in the cage, not Nafshi. But Nafshi's heirs will be here soon enough. And then we will have what we need to defeat them."

Patches couldn't gather his thoughts. His eyes were closing. "Leilei?" he said weakly. "What about Leilei?"

"Leilei is coming here," Bett sneered. "And she'll never leave."

"N-no," Patches said. "Must tell her not to come." His head drooped as the drugs overcame him, and he passed out.

"After our plan is complete, Patches is ours," Bett said. "You promised," he told Roah.

"Yes, I did. You may have the imbecile. His punishment is long overdue."

"There's no need for that," Niflah said. "We have what we needed. Patches has done us a favor after all."

"He betrayed us. He fought for the other side. He must be punished," Roah said. They stared at one another. Finally, Niflah dropped his glance.

"Do what you will, but don't expect me to watch," he said with disgust. He turned his back on them and left.

"You heard him," Roah said. "Do what you will."

Leilei drowsed while she waited for Patches to respond, her eyes half-closed and her mind empty. When the return message entered her Magelight,

CHAPTER EIGHTEEN

she jumped up, her heart pounding. She saw Patches lying on the ground by the side of the road, his back to her. No! Had he been hit by a car? He needed her help, and fast! She tore off down the path that led to the road, ignoring anyone who called out to her. The guards tried to stop her when she reached the post at the end of the wood. She bowled them over with spells Hakham had taught her, racing to the road that bordered the West Woods. There, there was the spot where Patches should be. She prayed to the One Above Us All that her healing skills would be up to the task. She'd stop the bleeding and then call Andy. Yes, that would work. Heal first, though. Patches might need all of her strength.

Leilei stopped at the side of the road, sides heaving. Where was he? What in the name of the First was going on? She reached out with her Magelight for his aura. A chill ran over her. She turned to run.

"Hello, Leilei," said Kel, emerging from the brush by the side of the road. Kfir and a dozen other Wild Ones stalked out from their hiding places, closing off every direction of escape. "Oh, were you looking for Patches? Step forward, Nava." One of the Wild Ones, a Calico that looked much like Patches, moved to the front of the group. "A good match, don't you think? Especially if you have her lie down with her back to you. Which is what we did before we sent you that message." Kel laughed. "Patches isn't here. But I know where he is. In fact, we'll take you there."

"I'll never go with you!"

"Oh, my dear Leilei. You think that was a request. How sweet."

Leilei was still panting from her mad dash to the road and exhausted from the day's lessons. But she wouldn't let them take her without a fight. Her Magelight glowed.

"If you strike us, we kill Patches," Kfir said. "We have him. Go ahead, check for his aura. We can wait."

Leilei looked at him suspiciously.

"It's in that direction," Kel said, nodding. "Not far, just few minutes' walk on the other side of the road. He is, ah, enjoying our hospitality." The Wild Ones laughed.

MOUSE TRAP!

Leilei was suspicious, but she concentrated and cast an aura spell. They weren't lying. She sensed Patches and his Magelight. And not far from Patches, she sensed—something familiar. She couldn't place it. Were there Catmages she knew among the Wild Ones? No! More traitors? She hissed.

"I presume this means you know we're telling the truth?" Kel asked.

Leilei glared at him. "Patches was good to you. And this is how you repay him."

"Patches is weak!" Kel said. "The strong take. The weak are taken, as we have done to him, and now you. Fight us, and he dies. Disbelieve me at his peril. We don't need both of you to accomplish our purpose. Only you."

Leilei growled, her fur fluffed. "I hate you," she said. "You're going to pay for this."

The Wild Ones laughed again.

"It would be nice to think so, wouldn't it? But I assure you, Leilei, if there is any payment to be made, it won't be by me. Patches, now—he'll pay dearly for your misbehavior. So you'll want to think twice before trying anything." His Magelight flashed and her collar dropped to the ground, the leather sliced through. She held herself in check as he signaled one of Kfir's Tzofim to pick it up. She was sure Kel meant what he said.

"This way, if you please," Kel said with exaggerated politeness. Several of the Wild Ones chuckled. Kfir's Magelight flared and a jet of light struck the ground near her rear legs, causing her to jump.

"Move it!" he said. "We're not sticking around to see how many of Razor's guards followed you. Get going!"

Leilei stepped forward. Half of Kfir's guards closed in behind her. Several more flanked her and the rest joined Kel in the front. Leilei walked along in a circle of her captors, seething inwardly. The only good thing, she realized, was that she would be with Patches. And it wouldn't take long at all for Razor to realize what had happened. She was glad she had charged through the guards. Her friends would come rescue them soon. The thought cheered her as she was forced along to the West Woods Compound.

CHAPTER EIGHTEEN

They reached the Compound all too soon. Leilei was surprised to see how much like her own it was, except there were so few kittens. There were fewer females as well. Maybe that's why they were attacked last fall. If they were only attracting the dissatisfied males, that would explain a lot.

Her musings were cut short as her captors led her into a large bayit. Inside were several steel cages, and in one of them lay Patches.

"Patches! Patches, are you all right?" she asked, her voice full of concern.

Patches raised his head wearily. "Leilei? Are you here to rescue Patches?"

A roar of laughter greeted his words.

"Wild Ones are mean," Patches said.

"Rescue you? Oh no, Patches. She's not here to rescue you." Roah swaggered into the bayit, followed by Niflah. "She is here to accomplish a larger goal. Neither of you, actually, is our target. We're far more interested in Zahavin."

"What?"

"A trade. We never did get Nafshi's Magelight, and the boy who wields it has done much damage to us. I think it's only fair that we trade you for Zahavin. Oh, and a guarantee that your fellow Catmages leave us alone from now on."

"They'll never agree to that," Leilei said.

"Perhaps not. But the Son of Aaron will have a difficult time attacking us if all he can do is worry about his friends, don't you think?"

"That's why you took us? So you can try to stop Andy?" She laughed. "You have no idea what you've done. They'll come for us."

Roah stared at her. "We'll see. In the meantime—get in the cage." His Magelight flickered and a light jet creased her back, sending the smell of singed fur throughout the bayit. Leilei flinched and stepped into the empty cage next to Patches. Another flare of his Magelight slammed the door behind her. She watched helplessly as Niflah chuckled and floated a lock through the air, pushed it through the latch and clicked it shut. Even

MOUSE TRAP!

if she had her Magelight, she wouldn't be able to open a combination lock. Without it? Fear and sadness were beginning to overwhelm her, but she was determined not to let them see. Leilei sat down on the cold, hard steel and stared at her captors.

"You won't win. You never do."

Another shout of laughter erupted.

"Yes, tell us how we're losing—tell us from behind the bars of your cage," Kel said. "You're delusional, Leilei. And you're wrong. We have you. And soon we will have Zahavin. And after that—well. The Son of Aaron won't be a problem for very much longer."

The Wild Ones left. Patches was asleep. Leilei lay down and tried to get comfortable. She told herself to take heart. Yes, their Magelights were gone. But not their powers. She didn't have a focal point, true. But was she not of the line of Nafshi? And did that line not go all the way back to Neshama, the First Catmage? Kel was a fool. And she'd prove it. *Sleep. Rest,* she told herself. *When you wake, you'll think of something.* She sighed. *I hope.*

Kel practically strutted as he followed the others outside. His plan had worked perfectly. Roah blinked at him as they gathered in a knot outside his bayit. "Well done, son," he said. Kel thought his heart would burst with pride. He glanced smugly at Alef, who dared not say a word.

"What next?" Kfir asked.

"We go to the East Woods and make a deal," Kel said. "But first, I need our Seekers. Kfir, make sure your guards keep watch for any movement from the other side."

"They already do," Kfir growled.

"Good. Father, I'll be back soon." He hurried off and made his way to Ari and Lev's bayit. It was time to let them know what he needed.

"Excellent, you're awake," he said as he found them sunning themselves outside their home. "I have need of your skills. We have a couple of visitors from the East Woods."

"What?" Ari said, jumping up. "Are we under attack?"

"No. We've captured two Catmages."

CHAPTER EIGHTEEN

Lev and Ari exchanged glances. "Which ones?" Ari asked.

"The half-breed, Patches, and one of Nafshi's line—Leilei."

Lev's heart beat so fast and loud he found it amazing the others couldn't hear it. His daughter, a prisoner! Now they knew why that big bayit was being guarded.

"What do you want us for?" Ari asked.

"We don't intend to let Razor launch a rescue attempt. You will both be on guard duty until further notice. We want you to make periodic checks for any auras heading our way."

"That's a lot of work for just the two of us," Lev said. "How do you expect us to do that without burning out?"

"You're Seekers," Kel said. "Aura detection is what you do. It's easier for you than for the rest of us."

"Yes, but we still have to expend energy if we're constantly searching. Don't you know how Seekers work?"

"Not really, and I don't care. You have your orders. Report to the guard post near the road."

"Are we allowed to eat first? We'll need our strength if you don't want us to be useless in half a day."

"Fine. Go hunt. Report to the forward guard post as soon as you're finished." Kel stared at them until they lowered their heads, blinking. Ari waited until Kel left before leading Lev to the trees. They went a long way into the wood, pretending to hunt. When they were they were alone, they stopped.

"They have Leilei!" Lev said. "Father, what can we do?"

"I don't know. I don't dare send a message. Any stray globe would raise suspicions. I think we have to do what Kel wants until we find a way to help."

"Father!" The anguish in his son's voice was enough to make Ari close his eyes. He moved close to Lev and rubbed his shoulder against his son's.

"We'll think of something. In the meantime, let's find some food. We really are going to need our strength."

NINETEEN: CAT TRAP!

Katana picked herself up from the ground, listening to Leilei's footsteps disappear in the distance. She didn't know what spell Leilei had used, but it was powerful enough to have knocked over both guards. "Zofi," she said to the grey tabby shaking herself as she struggled to her feet near the tree trunk she'd been flung into, "Stay here. Stay alert. I'm going for help."

She ran to the Compound, scanning for Razor or Hakham, anyone in charge. She found Zohar at the edge of the meadow drilling a squad of young Catmages, new recruits Ufara had sent.

"Have you seen Razor?" she said, interrupting him in mid-order.

"Katana," he said so that only she could hear, "you're setting a terrible example for these young ones." Out loud, he said, "Everyone sit and take a break for now."

Katana glanced at the recruits and blinked apologetically. She said privately, "Leilei just bowled over Zofi and me and ran out of the Compound toward the West Woods. We need to scout the woods and be ready for anything. Where's Razor?"

Zohar turned to the young Catmages who sat in formation, waiting for his next order. "Dismissed," he said. "Go enjoy yourselves." They cheered and left. "Razor was with Hakham a little while ago. Come on."

CHAPTER NINETEEN

He took off running.

"There he is," Katana said as they neared Hakham's bayit and saw Razor outside talking to Hakham and Silsula. They skidded to a halt a few steps away.

"What is it?" Razor said.

Katana explained quickly. Before she'd finished, Razor was shouting for his captains.

"Razor," Silsula said, horrified, "Leilei came to me earlier today looking for Patches. I didn't think anything of it, you know how Patches is. But now I think the Wild Ones took him, and Leilei—she—"

"She went to rescue him. The fool! She should have come to us. Let's hope we can catch her before the Wild Ones do!"

Shomrim converged from every direction. Razor barked out assignments, and the captains and squad leaders hurried to follow his orders. Katana and Zohar went to their own squads to pass along commands. Soon the wood was filled with Shomrim racing to the border, Razor in the lead with Zohar and Katana on their flanks. Silsula and Hakham sprinted behind the leaders.

They reached the road and halted, scouts separating and hurrying along the road to do their tasks. Razor set up a command post just inside the cover of the woods and listened silently as reports came in one by one. Before long, every squad had checked in. There was no sign of either Leilei or Patches, but one squad had found signs that a large group of Catmages had passed near the road. Razor and the others hurried over to the site. Silsula bent her head to sniff around the footprints. She lifted her head, her mouth open to process the scent more deeply.

"Leilei!" she said. "She was here not long ago. They took her. They have my niece!"

"Then they must have Patches, too," Hakham said. "I can't think of any other reason Leilei would have assaulted Katana and Zofi."

"Well, that's a comfort," Katana said wryly. "At least it wasn't personal."

CAT TRAP!

"Cut the comedy," Razor said. "This isn't the time." He paced back and forth, sniffing the ground and swearing. "Kfir was here," he growled. "Why did they take them? To what end? What are they going to do with Patches and Leilei?"

"I don't know," Hakham said. "But it can't be anything good."

"Zohar!" Razor barked.

"Sir?" he said, hurrying forward.

"Set a guard. A strong one. Wild Ones are not entering our woods again. Move our forward guard posts to within sight of the road. Tell them to be wary of humans but stay in sight of the road at all times! Understood?"

"Yes, sir." Zohar sped away to carry out his orders.

"Katana, put more Shomrim in the guard posts we're taking warriors from. This could be a trick by the Wild Ones to get past our guards and attack the Compound."

"I'd rather use our Shomrim here, sir. Some of the recruits Ufara sent are promising. They're not ready for a fight yet, but they can do guard duty."

"Then get them."

"The rest of you who haven't been ordered to guard duty, back to the Compound!" Razor shouted. "Zohar's squad, to me! Fall in behind." Five Catmages rushed to form up on Razor's orders. "No more traveling alone in the woods."

"We are not alone," Hakham told him.

"No, but we are only three, and Silsula's concentration is off."

"All I would need is a Wild One in front of me and you'd find out how good my concentration can be," she said angrily.

"Back to the Compound," Razor said.

He led the way through the woods. Silsula was silent, turning occasionally to look back as if she expected to see Leilei. Hakham and Razor glanced at one another.

"I know you're thinking about Lev and Ari," Hakham said private-

CHAPTER NINETEEN

ly. "We will discuss it later."

"Don't you think keeping their cover is less important than retrieving our own?"

"Of course I do! It's also possible that Lev and Ari can help us and still stay unknown. But I will take no chances. We will speak about this later."

Razor grunted and quickened his pace. Letsan and Goldeneyes joined them when they arrived at the Compound. They followed him as Razor found his Shomrim organized in neat rows on the practice field.

"By now your captains have filled you in on what's happened. Two of our Catmages have been taken by the enemy. You are on alert from now until further notice. Any questions?"

There was a short pause, then one of the Shomrim shouted, "When do we go after them, sir?"

"When I tell you to," Razor said over the cheers that erupted. "Don't worry, you'll get your chance. The Wild Ones have something planned, that's for sure. Captains, to my bayit. All warriors not on duty, dismissed!"

The mustered Catmages broke apart, some heading to the guard posts, the rest going back to their bayits or to hunt. Goldeneyes and Silsula followed Hakham while Letsan stayed with his brother as Razor led the captains to his bayit and waited until they were inside.

"Right. Plans, ideas, suggestions—it's brainstorming time. We're getting our Catmages back."

By the time Kfir and Roah had hashed out their next move, the night was gone and dawn was breaking. Kfir and a strong contingent of his fighters led the way, with Kel just behind. He could barely contain his glee as he trotted toward the East Woods Compound with Gimmel and Dalet at his heels. Oh, this parley was going to be so much fun. He couldn't wait!

"Get ready, we're getting close to their guard posts," Kfir said. His fighters took their positions. Three of Kfir's fighters stood in front, followed by Kfir and Kel. Gimmel and Dalet were at the rear.

CAT TRAP!

"That's close enough!" Razor's guard called out.

"Is that you, Katana?" Kfir said, moving forward to stand out from his fighters. "Good. Go tell Razor we want to talk."

Katana growled. "He's already on his way."

"Will we have long to wait?" Kfir yawned widely. "I missed my afternoon nap."

Katana ignored him and watched warily, ears twitching.

"If you're counting my Tzofim, don't bother. We came to talk, not fight."

Katana said nothing. She watched Kfir and his fighters steadily until Razor appeared. Zohar, Letsan, Hakham, and Goldeneyes stood with him. Many of Razor's warriors emerged from the woods to flank the Wild Ones.

"Good afternoon," Kfir said pleasantly. "So good to see you all! How long has it been?"

"What do you want?" Razor growled.

"Actually, it's more what you want," he said. "Are you missing any Catmages?"

Goldeneyes exchanged glances with Hakham.

"Stop playing games, Kfir. Why are you here?"

"Oh, let me, please," Kel said, stepping forward. Razor growled at the sight of him.

"What do you want?" he repeated.

"I want many things, but we're here with a specific purpose in mind. You are missing a couple of Catmages. Patches and Leilei, I believe?"

"Get to the point." Razor said.

"We have them. They are our…guests."

"What proof do we have that you're not lying?" Goldeneyes asked.

"I'd show you with my Magelight, but why expend unnecessary energy? This is just as good." He turned his head to his siblings, who moved forward. "Do you see what my two *Kelevim* are carrying?" The guards stepped aside to show Gimmel and Dalet each holding a Magelight collar

CHAPTER NINETEEN

in their teeth. "These are your missing Catmages' Magelights. I'm sure you recognize their auras."

Goldeneyes gasped as she recognized Leilei's Magelight.

Kel's voice dripped with malice. "You see? Even I tell the truth sometimes, Zahavin. We have your niece and her idiot friend."

"What do you want?" she asked.

"You," Kel said. "We will return Patches and Leilei—unharmed—and possibly even give them back their Magelights. In return, Zahavin will be our, ah, guest. Saunders so very much wants to see you. There is much he can learn from you, he says."

"No!" Letsan said. "They'll never keep their word. Zahavin, don't fall for it. It's a trap!"

"Of course it is," Razor growled. He stepped forward until he was opposite Kfir. "Give me one good reason why I shouldn't give the command to take all of you, and the Magelights, too. And then go get our friends."

Kfir laughed. "Only one reason? How's this: My Tzofim will kill Leilei and Patches if all of us don't return by the time the sun is high. Is that a good enough reason?"

Razor growled long and low. "It will do. By the First, Kfir, one day you will pay in full for everything you have done."

"Perhaps. I have made the same promise about you. Time will tell which of us will keep his vow." He twitched his ears, his tail lashing. "Well, Zahavin? Are you coming with us?"

"She is not," Hakham said, standing beside her. "Zahavin, they will betray us the moment they have you. Stay right where you are. Kfir, take your warriors and get out of our wood before I have Razor give the order to destroy you all."

"We've just been over that. You hurt me, your precious Leilei pays the price."

"Go!"

"You have two suns to decide, Hakham. If we don't have Zahavin

CAT TRAP!

by moonrise of the second sun from now, the others die. And then we have two more Magelights for Saunders. Kel here tells me that Leilei's is a very powerful one. Saunders been asking particularly for more of those."

Hakham's Magelight glowed and his fur crackled with electricity. "Leave now, Kfir, before we decide that we can rescue our missing Catmages before your companions will know of your deaths."

Razor and his warriors moved forward as one. Kfir backed slowly until the underbrush was between him and Hakham. "Two suns. We'll kill the idiot first. Then the scion of Nafshi." Kfir and his warriors disappeared into the trees.

There was little talking on the way back to the Compound. The leaders of the Compound gathered in Hakham's bayit.

"I have to go," Goldeneyes said. "They'll kill Leilei and Patches! You heard Kfir!"

"Absolutely not," Hakham said. "Now I understand why they took Patches and Leilei. They were bait. You are their true prize, but don't think the Wild Ones will keep their word. They won't return the others to us."

Razor grunted. "Hakham is right. We'll get them back, but not by sacrificing you. We have resources the Wild Ones know nothing about."

"What kind of resources?" Goldeneyes asked. "Because if ever we needed them, we need them now!"

"Never mind what. Trust me, Zahavin. I promise you, we'll get them back safe and sound."

"So I'm to rely on vague promises and your assurances? Razor, this is my niece we're talking about!"

Razor bristled at the criticism. "My word has been good enough until now. Nothing has changed."

"Everything has changed! It was my failure that led to Nafshi's death. I won't have Leilei suffer as well!"

"There's more than enough blame to go around for that. I didn't gauge Roah's strength well enough. Hakham didn't know his brother was feigning death the night the Council was killed."

CHAPTER NINETEEN

"You forgot Andy," Letsan said. "He still thinks he's to blame for getting hit on the head and captured." He chuckled at the look Goldeneyes gave him. "Oh, save the dirty looks for someone they work on, Zahavin. And save your breath. We're not letting you give yourself up to the Wild Ones. We'll find another way to get Patches and Leilei back."

"How?"

"That's what we're here to discuss."

Goldeneyes laid back her ears and switched her tail. "I can't stay here. I can't think. I need to be by myself for a while." She bolted out the door and ran down the path to the meadow. She veered around the corner and doubled back along the meadow's edge, ignoring the calls and surprised looks from Catmages and kittens. Some of the kittens tried to follow her, thinking it was a game. She shrugged them off, veered around the meadow again and sprinted down a path that led through the woods. She knew the guards would stop her, but she just had to run.

When she reached a guard post, she halted, breathing heavily, ignoring their questions as she thought of Leilei and Patches, frightened and caged, in the midst of the Wild Ones. Andy had told her a few stories about how Nafshi had been treated, and Patches had told anyone who would listen that the Wild Ones were "bad bad bad bad *bad* Catmages" who had been very mean to him.

Tears, she thought. *If only we had tears like humans. The One gave us much, but he never taught us how to cry.*

Soft footsteps behind her made her turn. It was Letsan. He moved beside her and rubbed his cheek along hers. "We can still feel deep sadness, Zahavin. I'm as worried as you are. But I have faith in my brother. And in the Catmages all around us. We'll get them back."

She closed her eyes and lay down, tucking her front paws beneath her. Letsan lay next to her, his shoulder and flank touching hers. They stayed together in silence. At last Letsan rose, stretched, and yawned. "We should go back. Razor will have the beginnings of a plan by now."

Goldeneyes stood and gazed at him. She dropped her head and he moved closer and licked her ear.

"All right," she said. "Let's go back."

They walked slowly side by side down the path.

That week Taylor reported to Niflah at Saunders' house after school to learn the scruffing spell. Niflah ended their Thursday night lesson in an excellent mood. Taylor came through the kitchen door smiling. Not even the sight of Saunders seated at the table frowning at the newspaper could dim it.

"The boy has made great progress," Niflah told Saunders. "I'd like to finish up with one more session tomorrow, but it would be better if we had more time than an hour or so after school. Can I have him during the day?"

"All right. But Mr. Grant, two things: You'd better perform that spell perfectly by tomorrow afternoon."

"I will, sir. What else?"

"Don't fall behind in your classes. You need to stay in the class with Mr. Cohen."

"No problem, sir. I've got a B average this year."

"Good."

"Want to see me cast the spell, sir?"

"Yes. I would like to see a good result for all the time being spent on your training."

"Dalet!" Taylor called. "We need you here!"

The Siamese Wild One crept warily down the stairs and into the kitchen. Her fur was ragged in a few places, and she approached the others hesitantly.

"Show me," Saunders said.

Taylor narrowed his eyes in concentration. Two green and one yellow Magelights lit and Dalet's tail curled down between her legs.

"Try to cast a spell," Niflah said.

"I can't."

CHAPTER NINETEEN

"Try to move."

"I can't do that either," Dalet snarled. "How many times are you going to make me sit through this?"

"As many as it takes. Taylor, move her forward a few steps."

Dalet's legs jerked and she shuffled toward the refrigerator. She was inches away from it before Taylor released her. Dalet glared at the boy and shook her legs one at a time.

"Next time, cast that spell on Niflah and see how he likes it."

"We all have our parts to play," Niflah said cheerfully. "Right now, yours is to be Taylor's test subject. We could always return you to the Compound to be with your brother Kel."

"No, it's fine here," Dalet said hurriedly.

Saunders narrowed his eyes, and the others fell silent.

Taylor held still for fear Saunders would turn his gaze on him. He'd made it clear that he only wanted them to concentrate on the battle. Saunders didn't care about their personal lives. Some of the Catmages did. Dalet may not get along with Kel, but she seemed friendly enough to Taylor, and sometimes he even thought Niflah liked him. Roah was more interested in only those parts of Taylor's life that pertained to what he needed. But it was a working relationship. He helped Roah, Roah helped him—to a certain extent. He refused to help Taylor directly with his stepfather, but he had told Taylor stories of what he'd done to Catmages who had gotten on his bad side, and Taylor had learned from them. He was, Taylor realized, a bad Catmage to cross. He was starting to understand why Roah had gotten kicked out of the Compound in the first place. But all of them paled compared to Principal Saunders in a rage.

"You may leave, Mr. Grant. Niflah, I want to talk to you. You, out!"

Dalet scrambled away, and Taylor hurried down the hall and out the front door. He got home just in time for dinner, preventing another outburst from his stepfather for being late. But Taylor wouldn't care if he did get yelled at. He was finally getting a big part in the fight against Cohen and his friends. The Wild Ones were appreciating him more and more.

CAT TRAP!

And the more they liked him, the more he learned. One day, he wouldn't back off from his stepfather. And he wouldn't even have to touch him. But he would teach the old drunk a lesson he'd never forget.

The next morning, Taylor left the house at his usual time, but instead of heading for the bus stop, he turned toward Saunders' house. He hurried across town. The day was warm enough not to need the jacket Taylor wore over his t-shirt, but wearing it hid his Magelights from view. Lately he had found that he was happier when he was wearing them. Carrying the necklace didn't feel quite right, even in his pocket. He wanted the stones resting against his skin. He could see them in his mind's eye. Orange, green, yellow, green, yellow. Those were his Magelights, that was their order. Orange, green, yellow, green, yellow. He found it relaxing to chant mentally as he stepped along.

Niflah was waiting for him on the porch as he came through the front gate and closed it behind him.

"It's a fine day," he said.

"Yeah," Taylor told him. "Are we going to work outside today?"

"No. Open the door for me, will you?"

Taylor stepped up on the porch.

"Not that way."

"Oh. Yeah." The orange Magelight flashed and the door swung open.

"Nicely done. Now let's go find Dalet and perfect the scruffing spell."

An hour later, Niflah sent Dalet out of the room and declared that Taylor had learned the spell to his satisfaction. Taylor grinned and made a half-bow.

"I'd like to thank the members of the Academy—well, actually, no, just you."

"What I don't understand," Niflah said, ignoring Taylor's clowning, "is why you're not at all tired. The scruffing spell takes a lot of energy if you have to cast it for any length of time, and even more if you try to make

CHAPTER NINETEEN

the scruffed Catmage move. Yet here you are, not even winded."

Taylor shrugged. "I'm not a Catmage. Maybe it's easier because I'm human."

"Perhaps," Niflah said. "Well, no matter. You have performed well, and as your teacher, so have I. What do you say we go to the kitchen and raid the refrigerator?"

"Are you picking up human slang?" Taylor grinned.

"Apparently so."

"Yeah, I could use a snack. Let's go see what Saunders has in his pantry."

They were just sitting down to eat when a green message globe flashed into the room.

"It seems fortune favors us," he said. "Zahavin has been spotted outside the Compound. She must be trying to sneak in and free her niece. Bring that with you, child. We're going to the West Woods."

Taylor's face lit with pleasure. "Great! If we stop by my house on the way, I can grab my bike and we can get there faster."

"Then we shall do so. Give me a moment, I need to send a message back." He concentrated and sent a globe zooming out the window. "There. They'll leave her be until we get there. Go get the sedative, Taylor. Zahavin is nearly as powerful as her grandmother. We'll take no chances."

Taylor ran to the office and was back quickly with the leather case. The two of them hurried outside.

"This is going to be a great day," Taylor said, grinning as they sped to his house.

The day after the ultimatum, Goldeneyes was heartily sick of the endless talk and arguments among Razor, his captains, and the Council. They still had no valid plan of action and the deadline was drawing near. They hadn't told Andy yet. Razor thought Andy would probably do something rash if he knew Leilei and Patches were being held. He refused to budge when Goldeneyes and Letsan reminded him how valuable Andy had been during

CAT TRAP!

the attack on Halloween.

Goldeneyes also thought that Razor and Hakham were holding something back from the rest of them, and it bothered her that she wasn't entrusted with it. She found herself wandering over to Leilei's bayit, even napping in the bed of leaves that still held her scent.

The morning was filled with birdsong and the rustle of leaves and brush on the forest floor. Goldeneyes ignored a field mouse that practically ran right into her as she walked along the path. She wasn't hungry. She wanted only one thing—Leilei and Patches back home again. As she made her way down the path, she made up her mind. If Razor wouldn't make a move to get them, she would.

She slipped silently through the trees, treading carefully as she approached the nearest guard post in the wood that led to the road. Luck was with her. The guards were relatively young—and better still, inexperienced recruits. She moved silently to position herself for flight, careful to keep downwind. She searched the area with her Magelight until she found a rabbit. She concentrated again and found a second rabbit a few dozen yards away. Perfect. Just one more, she thought, reaching out. She found a squirrel. It would do. Goldeneyes closed her eyes and breathed slowly and deeply. Her Magelight glowed and the three animals headed straight for the guard post, making as much noise as they could. The guards came instantly alert. Her Magelight flashed again, and the animals broke into a run. The guards huddled together, staring in the direction of the footsteps.

"Wild Ones!" one said. "What do we do?"

"Use your Magelights!" she heard one urge the others. "See what's coming. I'll send a message to the captain!"

While the guards watched anxiously where the noises came from, Goldeneyes hurried away in the other direction. She ran with her head down, careful to avoid any dry leaves or twigs. If she knew Razor's captains, the guards would be too busy explaining why they called him to the guard post over a couple of rabbits to do anything else. It was possible the captains might search the woods anyway, but she'd be long gone by then.

CHAPTER NINETEEN

Goldeneyes ran quickly and quietly and finally came to a halt beneath a fallen maple tree. There was a hollow in the earth near its roots. She stopped there and caught her breath, listening intently. She hadn't been followed. Good. She sped toward the West Woods. The Wild Ones might think they had the upper hand, but was she not of the line of Nafshi? She would get Leilei and Patches released. And then she would find her way out of whatever the Wild Ones had in store for her.

An hour later, she lay silently in a thicket near a Wild One outpost. The two guards seemed bored and inattentive. Goldeneyes wondered if the small animal trick might not work a second time. She searched the area for rodents and was rewarded with a squirrel in a nearby tree. She moved it down the trunk while she searched for something already on the ground. A mouse napped in its burrow not far away. Perfect. She woke it and directed it toward the outpost. Then she made the squirrel and mouse jump simultaneously and run away from the outpost, making as much noise as they possibly could.

The guards sprang to attention and looked in the direction the noise was coming from. Goldeneyes made sure the wind carried the scent to the guards.

"A mouse," Goldeneyes heard one say. "I'm hungry."

"We're on guard duty, Tal."

"I'll share it with you. You stay here, I'll go get it."

Tal hesitated.

"Come on. It won't take more than a minute or two. There's something wrong with that mouse, making so much noise. Let's put it out of its misery."

"Maybe it's sick. Maybe you shouldn't go after it."

"Or maybe it's just stupid. Let me go catch it. If it smells funny, we won't eat it. Come on, Tal. Aren't you even a little hungry?"

"Okay. Go get it. But be quick! If Kfir or Roah catch us—"

"Are you kidding? They don't bother with nobodies like us. It's Kel you have to watch out for. That one you just don't want to cross. Ever."

CAT TRAP!

"Then hurry up and get that mouse, Danit!" Tal said.

Goldeneyes watched as Danit ran off into the underbrush. She drove the mouse away, watching Tal follow the action with his eyes. She pushed it one last time. As it darted into the trees, unable to control itself, she crept past the guard post on silent feet, eyes and ears open for the sight and sound of any Wild Ones. When she reached the cover of another thicket, she sighed inwardly and hid herself deep inside it. Now to survey the area and discover how many more guards she needed to get past. She glanced at the sun, still climbing toward noon. She was beginning to regret being so hasty. It was easier to avoid being seen at night. Perhaps she should stay here for the rest of the day, finish looking around when darkness fell Maybe she could even find a way to rescue her niece and Patches herself. Well, it didn't hurt to hope. In the meantime, she'd stay hidden here, out of the way of any Wild Ones except the nearby guards. She'd be perfectly placed to hear any new orders or catch any comings and goings. She settled herself to wait.

Hours later, Goldeneyes awoke from a nap, sniffing the air and watching the late afternoon sunlight filter through the leaves. The nap had restored her strength and composure. Having to be constantly on edge and on guard had wearied her. All was quiet around her. The guards were at their post, and she heard only the ordinary sounds around a Catmage Compound. That was a good sign. They hadn't found her hiding place, and Razor apparently hadn't yet sent anyone looking for her. Goldeneyes decided to take advantage of the quiet to look for Leilei and Patches. She closed her eyes and relaxed, concentrating on Leilei's aura. Patches would be wherever her niece was. Her Magelight glowed as she combed through the many nearby auras, skipping over the ones she knew were at guard posts. They would be well inside the Compound. Goldeneyes soon grew weary. Looking for a single aura in a large group of Catmages was a lot harder than being able to pinpoint one when looking in a narrow area. If only she could risk sending a message. But no, that wouldn't work. They didn't have their Magelights. Panting with the exertion of searching for the

CHAPTER NINETEEN

auras, Goldeneyes stopped until she felt revived to try again. At last she found what she was looking for. Now she knew where they were, though she didn't know what she'd do with that information. Exhausted, Goldeneyes went back to sleep.

Ari and Lev lay quietly in the brush of the guard post. The time had gone by slowly, one monotonous search after another. They dared not talk too much in private for fear of being noticed. Kel had strengthened the guard post's staff. They were surrounded by Kfir's loyal warriors. All Lev and Ari could do was search, rest, and eat. There was no time to plan an escape—or find a way to contact Razor.

Kel and Kfir came to the post just after Ari and Lev had finished eating and were grooming themselves.

"Have you found anything today?" Kfir asked.

"No," Ari said, pausing in the middle of washing his face.

"When did you last search?" Kel asked.

"Not long ago."

"Well, search again. I don't trust Razor!" Kfir said.

Ari flashed him a look and settled down to check for Catmages. Lev joined him. Their Magelights glowed steadily as they closed their eyes and looked with their senses.

"Guard post…guard post…guard post," Lev said. "Nothing to the south."

"Nothing but guard posts to the north," Ari said. His breath caught he felt another aura near one of the guard posts. *By the One, no! Not Zahavin!* He tried to contain his emotions, but Lev could tell something was up. He scanned north. His head jerked toward his father as he sensed his sister's aura.

"What is it?" Kel asked. "You see something! What do you see? Is Razor coming? Are we under attack?"

Ari had no choice. If he and Lev were to maintain their cover, he had to betray his daughter. Kel had other Wild Ones searching. It was only

CAT TRAP!

a matter of time before they found her.

"There is an unfamiliar Catmage not far from the forward guard post, on the near side toward us. Only one."

"Excellent! Kfir, get a couple of squads. I'll get the boy and Niflah!" They ran off to get the others.

Ari and Lev gazed at one another. The guards had all moved to the front of the brush, watching eagerly for whatever was going to happen next.

"What have I done?" Ari whispered to Lev. "What have I done?" He closed his eyes in anguish.

Letsan sat blinking in the late afternoon sun. He was tired of the endless discussions on how to get Patches and Leilei back, tired of the arguments, tired of doing nothing. In fact, he was just plain tired. He stretched himself and yawned hugely. He was hungry. Maybe Zahavin would join him for a hunt. Now that the thought of it, he hadn't seen her in hours. He stretched again and headed toward their bayit to see if she was napping there. When it turned out to be empty, he went to find Silsula, who said she hadn't seen her sister all day.

"Why?" she asked. "Hasn't she been with you in the meetings all day?"

"No. I thought she was with you."

The realization dawned on them both at the same time.

"She wouldn't have," Silsula said.

"She couldn't have," Letsan said.

"Hakham. Hakham will know," Silsula said. They took off running. They found him near the edge of the meadow and told him hurriedly of their suspicions. They waited silently while he half-closed his eyes and cast the aura spell.

"She is nowhere in the Compound," he said.

"Check—check the West Woods," Letsan said, fear twisting in his guts.

CHAPTER NINETEEN

It seemed ages before he finished casting the spell this time. Letsan and Silsula watched anxiously. At last, Hakham opened his eyes. "I—I am sorry, Silsula. Letsan, Zahavin is with the enemy."

Something woke Goldeneyes from a deep sleep. She blinked, trying to remember where she was. Oh, yes. Hiding near the West Woods Compound. She yawned and stretched, rose to her feet and emerged carefully from the brush. She stopped short. Surrounding her from every direction was a large group of Wild Ones.

"Hello, Zahavin," Kel said.

Her head jerked from side to side. There were at least two squads of Wild Ones standing all around. And there was Niflah and Kfir. She hissed at them.

"Save your breath," Kel said, laughing. "And thanks so much for saving us the trouble of making the trade. Taylor!" he called. He waited while Taylor ran out of the woods. "We kept him back until we were sure we had you. No sense letting those noisy human feet wake you before we were ready."

Taylor skidded to a stop. He was carrying a brown leather case. "Scruff first?" he asked.

"Absolutely. Let's see how you fare against the great Zahavin," Niflah said.

Taylor concentrated. His Magelights glowed. Goldeneyes tried to back a step and found herself unable to.

"What are you doing to me?"

"Making sure you don't fight me on this. Niflah, what if she breaks free while I give her the shot?"

"I'll back you up. But that was well done, Taylor." He strode forward and added his scruffing spell to Taylor's. "You can let go now."

Taylor's Magelight faded. He kneeled down beside Goldeneyes, took a hypodermic needle out from the pack, and gave her a shot. Goldeneyes could do no more than growl.

CAT TRAP!

"Her Magelight," Niflah said.

"Oh, please, let me," Kel said and sent a light dagger to cut her collar. Taylor picked it up and put it in his pocket.

"You can keep scruffing her and make her walk," Taylor said, "or I can just wait for the drug to take effect and pick her up and carry her."

"Don't touch me!"

"Carry her it is," Kel said to a shout of laughter.

Taylor waited until Goldeneyes wavered and fell. She could do nothing but growl weakly as he leaned down and picked her up.

Taylor followed Kel through the woods. Wild Ones greeted the sight of their enemy lying limp in his arms with hoots and jeers. When he reached the bayit with the cages, Taylor bent low to go inside and placed Goldeneyes in an empty one. Alef and Bett waited inside the bayit, eyes glittering with malice.

"Auntie Zahavin!" Leilei said. "No! They got you, too?"

Goldeneyes tried to focus her thoughts to respond. She tried to get up and fell down. "Leilei," she said faintly.

"Auntie Zahavin!" Leilei repeated.

"*Auntie Zahavin,*" Bett mocked.

"Bett is mean," Patches said. "Bett was always mean."

"Quiet, you half-breed traitor," Alef said. He launched a light dagger at Patches, singeing him in the flank. Patches cried out in pain.

"Leave him alone!" Leilei said. They laughed at her. "You wouldn't laugh if I had my Magelight," she said angrily.

"But you don't have it," Alef sneered. "And so, all you can do is talk. Just like Nafshi. Not only do you look like her, but even with all your powers, you're going to come to an end in that cage just like she did. Little Nafshi," he said, his voice dripping with venom. "You and your Auntie Zahavin, too."

Leilei watched Taylor close and lock the door on her aunt's cage, and heard Patches whimpering next to her. Anger overwhelmed her. "If I had my Magelight," she said, "I'd make your feet burn like they'd been dipped in fire."

CHAPTER NINETEEN

Alef and Bett laughed at her words. Leilei pictured the two of them standing in flames in her mind's eye. Their laughter cut off suddenly, and they leaped into the air, crying out in pain.

"What did you do? How did you do that without a Magelight? My feet! They burn!" Alef said. He held up a paw. The pad was red and blistered. Bett yowled in anguish.

Leilei felt exhaustion overwhelm her. "I don't know, but I'm glad I did! I'll do it again if I can!"

Niflah looked at her thoughtfully. "I don't think we should let you," he said. "Clearly you are stronger than I had realized." His Magelight glittered and Leilei found herself immobilized.

"Taylor, if you would administer the sedative to Leilei," he said. Taylor opened her cage door and gathered a fold of her skin for a shot. Leilei was helpless to prevent it.

"There," Niflah said as her muscles relaxed while the shot took effect. "Now you're going to be much easier to deal with. I'm quite impressed, though. You must be a strong Catmage indeed, if you could cast a spell without a Magelight to focus your powers. There aren't many who can."

Leilei swore at him as he let the spell lapse. But the drug soon overcame her and her head drooped.

"Get out," Niflah said to Alef and Bett. "Your cruelty earned you that punishment."

Alef glared at him but they dared not disobey. "We'll remember this," Bett told Alef privately. "They both will pay." The two of them walked away limping.

"Now for Zahavin's Magelight," Niflah said. "Give it to me, Taylor."

Taylor took the collar out of his pocket and tossed it to Niflah, who caught it with his Magelight and floated it to the ground. He placed his paw on the golden stone in the middle of the leather straps and reached out to sense its aura.

"What?" he said, shocked. "This stone has no aura. It's glass. Just like Nafshi's was!"

CAT TRAP!

"Glass? I don't get it," Taylor said. "I thought all Catmages have to use Magelights to focus their powers."

"We do. But we never found Nafshi's Magelight—and after she died, the next we heard was that Andy Cohen had it."

"Maybe she hid it somewhere and told him where it was hidden," Taylor said.

Niflah ran over to Goldeneyes, who lay at the bottom of her prison, laughing weakly.

"Where is your Magelight, Zahavin? Where is it?" Niflah was livid.

"On my collar," Goldeneyes said, giggling.

"That's what Nafshi always told us. She lied. You're lying, too."

"Not lying. Zahavin is not a liar. Niflah is the liar. You are all liars!" Patches growled softly.

Niflah looked thoughtfully at Patches. "She's not lying, eh?" he said.

"Niflah, Patches is an idiot. Why would you take anything he says seriously?" Kel asked.

"We underestimated Patches once, to our regret. I think he knows more than he lets on. Patches, where is Zahavin's Magelight?"

Patches half-closed his eyes and rocked sideways. He tried to hop but his legs gave out underneath him. "Nafshi told you. On her collar," he said. He laughed weakly.

"On her collar. On her collar," Niflah muttered. The others looked at him like he was crazy. He stared long and hard at Goldeneyes. She raised her head and blinked, trying to concentrate. Suddenly Niflah leaped in the air. "Kel! Get me the Seekers!" Niflah said. "I should have thought of this ages ago. On your collar, eh? We'll see about that. Yes, we'll see all right. Quickly, Kel!"

Kel hurried away from the bayit, calling for his brother as he did. When Gimmel arrived Kel ordered him to the guard post with a message for Ari and Lev. Then he sought out his father. He found Roah in his bayit listening to Kfir's report of the capture. Roah looked up when Kel arrived.

"Sir," Kel said, "there's a problem with the prisoners."

TWENTY: PARENTAL CONSENT

"Happy Friday!" Andy called as he came downstairs. He jumped the last four steps and grinned at his mother, who sat at the table in her pajamas drinking coffee.

"Aren't you going to work today?"

"No. I finished my big project and I'm taking a mental health day. I'm going to lounge around in my sweats all morning and then get my hair and nails done this afternoon. Maybe I'll hit the spa. In fact," she said, stretching luxuriously, "you may be on your own for dinner, kiddo. There are so many things I've been putting off and I feel like treating myself today."

"Go for it, Mom," Andy said, sitting down and pouring a glass of orange juice. "You work too hard. Don't worry about me. I can order a pizza without your help." His grin grew wider. Andy had been ordering pizza for them since at least the fourth grade. His mother had been a workaholic his entire life.

"Thanks. I'll text you if I'm not going to be home for dinner." She watched Andy pile French toast on his plate. "Leave some for me."

"Are you kidding? French toast on a weekday? I'll fight you for it!"

She laughed and took the last two slices. "Hurry up and finish your

PARENTAL CONSENT

breakfast. I'm not driving you in if you miss the bus."

Five minutes later, Andy rushed out the door waving goodbye, and Rachel hummed as she cleared the dishes off the table.

Later that afternoon, Rachel sang along to a song on the radio as she pulled into the driveway. Her hair was done, her nails were shiny and pink, and she felt more relaxed than she had in ages. Wait, wasn't that Letsan on the front porch? It was. He jumped down the steps as she exited the car.

"Rachel! Rachel! Where's Andy?" he said, his voice in her head sounding anxious.

"He's in school. What's the matter?"

"Zahavin! The Wild Ones have her!"

"What?"

"They have Patches and Leilei, too. Rachel, we need Andy! They took Zahavin!"

Letsan was frantic, pacing back and forth. Rachel's mouth dropped open. "I—I don't know what to do."

"Take me to Andy!"

She glanced at her watch. "He's just about done with school. Get in the car." She hurried to the door and held it open as he jumped in. She backed the car out of the driveway and turned down the street. "Get on the floor and hold on," she said grimly, "and hope I don't get stopped for speeding."

Andy caught the bus and brightened the minute he realized Taylor wasn't on it. A day without Taylor was always a good one for him. Not having him in history class or PE made the day go by much more quickly. He and Mike were extra cheerful at lunch, causing enough of a ruckus that Mr. Straight found it necessary to come over to their table and tell them to quiet down.

"Sorry, Mr. Straight," Andy said while Mike grinned and didn't look the least bit apologetic. Andy poked his friend. "Mike's sorry too. Right, Mike?"

CHAPTER TWENTY

"That sounds like a good name for a song. Mike's sorry too. Give me a minute, I haven't led a group song in the cafeteria since—wait, when was the last one?"

"No," Mr. Straight said. "Sit down and be quiet, or you'll have detention today. Right after school. I have a lot of papers to grade, Mike, I can keep you here all the way to dinnertime."

"Okay, okay. I'll be good." Mr. Straight looked doubtful as he left the table.

When the bell rang for the last class on Friday afternoon. Andy closed his book with a sigh, put it in his backpack and slung it over his shoulder. He went to his locker to pick up his history book before catching the bus. As he walked out the door to the parking lot, he stopped short. His mother was standing on the sidewalk. She saw him and waved urgently. Puzzled, Andy ran to her.

"Come on. Get in the car," she said, urging him toward it. He opened the passenger door and his mouth dropped open. Letsan was sitting on the seat.

"The Wild Ones have Zahavin. She went to them. We told her not to. Andy, she's gone!" His mind-voice was as full of worry as Andy had ever heard.

"What? Mom?" Andy said.

"I don't know what I can do, Andy. You tell me."

Andy tried to think. "I—I'm not sure."

"We need Becca, Mike, Teresa, Mr. Velez. Everyone! We have to get them back!" Letsan said.

"Where's Razor? Where are the others?"

"I don't know. I didn't wait. I just ran to town to find you. I didn't know what else to do."

Andy looked anxiously at his mother. Letsan had never lost his composure before, not even when Goldeneyes had been shot. Andy bent down and picked him up.

"We'll get them back, Letsan. All of them," Andy said. He got in

PARENTAL CONSENT

the car and pulled Letsan onto his lap.

"Yes, we will," Nafshi told him. "Tell that oaf to calm down and start thinking like a member of Avdei Ha'Or before I tell him for you!"

"Give him a break!" Andy sent. "He's allowed to be upset for once."

"But not for long. We need him. Fix it, Andrew, or I will."

"Let me make a few phone calls," he said out loud. "Letsan, Becca's always got great ideas. She'll help. We'll have our own council meeting, with Catmages and people. Mom, is it okay if I have everyone come over to our house?"

"Of course."

Within minutes Becca, Mike, and Teresa were heading for their house. Andy told Becca to use the spare key. "Don't go home yet," he told his mother. "Let's go to the Compound. Letsan, tell Razor and the others to meet us. We'll pick them up and bring them here—uh, if Mom says it's okay."

Rachel nodded. "It's fine. But you drive." She pulled over to the curb. "You know the way better." They switched seats. Letsan jumped into her lap as she settled into the passenger seat. She held him close. "Don't worry, Letsan. We'll get your friends back."

"We'd better," Andy said.

"We will," Nafshi told him. "And then may the First help the Wild Ones who took my granddaughter and Leilei."

Andy drove carefully down the road that led to the East Woods Compound. It was great not having to lie to his mother anymore. She seemed to understand how important the Catmages had become to him. And to be honest, it was nice being able to ask for help for a change. If only they could think of a way to stop Saunders altogether.

He slowed as he neared the entrance to the Compound, pulled the car to the side of the road, and turned off the engine. A message light flashed out of Letsan's collar, and soon Razor, Hakham, Silsula, and Zohar emerged from the guard post. Katana and Sami trotted behind.

CHAPTER TWENTY

"Brother," Razor said, "if you ever run off like that again—"

"Oh, be quiet," Andy said. "Not everyone's an emotionless robot like you."

"Andy!" his mother said.

There was a long silence. Razor said nothing, though his tail switched quickly from side to side.

"Sorry. It just came out," Andy said, puzzled. If he didn't know better, he'd say that his words sounded like Nafshi, not him. Chastened, he opened the back door and they jumped into the car. "Mom, you take the wheel. I need to talk to Razor and the others." Rachel nodded. As soon as he settled into the passenger seat, Letsan jumped into his lap and rubbed the side of his face against Andy's. He closed the car door and put his arms around Letsan as his mother pulled onto the highway. "We'll get her back, Letsan. I promise."

"Yes," Nafshi said to Andy in a cold, steely voice. "We will. And then—then we will take care of the Wild Ones."

When they pulled into the driveway, Mr. Velez's SUV and Mr. Jefferson's car were already parked in front of the house. Becca, Mike, and Teresa waited on the porch.

"We brought everyone up to speed and came right over," Becca said.

Rachel shook her head and hurried inside. Mario Velez and Jake and Danielle Jefferson sat at the kitchen table.

"Andy, no matter what you all are doing, you're not doing it without me," Jake said.

"We could really use the help."

"Yes. Thank you," Letsan said.

"I made tea," Danielle said, holding cup out to Rachel. "I thought you could use some."

"Thanks," she said and looked around the kitchen. "You know, it's getting a bit cramped in here. Let's go to the dining room."

PARENTAL CONSENT

Everyone followed her to the other room and settled down around the table. Andy couldn't help but notice the gathering seemed like an eerie echo of the Passover Seder, except now the Catmages sat in chairs next to the table—and Patches, Leilei, and Goldeneyes were absent.

When everyone was settled, Razor spoke.

"We need to rescue our friends. Any ideas short of an all-out assault?"

"An assault might get them killed," Letsan said. "There has to be a better way."

"Not necessarily," Hakham said. He glanced at Razor. "We have two spies inside the West Woods."

"Zahavin told me she thought you were hiding something! Who? Do we know them?" Silsula asked.

"I should think so. They're your father and brother. They've been with the Wild Ones at the West Woods Compound since summer."

"Here? They've been here all this time? Why didn't they tell us? Why didn't *you* tell us?"

"That would defeat the purpose of their being undercover agents now, wouldn't it?" Razor said.

Silsula was overjoyed at the news. "They can help rescue Leilei and the others!" *Chirrup*.

"There's a problem," Hakham said. "We haven't heard from them at all since Patches was taken. If they could have communicated with us, they would."

"Where exactly is this Compound?" Mr. Jefferson asked. "We only got the one glimpse of where you all live. Where are these other guys?"

"In the woods outside of town," Andy said. "Wait, I have an idea. Mom, can I use your laptop?"

"It's on my desk."

Andy ran out of the dining room to his mother's office, and came back with her laptop. He sat down and brought up a browser. Then he turned the screen toward the adults. "This is where the Catmage Com-

CHAPTER TWENTY

pound is," he said, pointing to the map on the screen. His finger moved across the road. "This is the West Woods Compound. It's where the Wild Ones live and where they're keeping Goldeneyes and the others."

Mr. Jefferson looked thoughtfully at the screen. "Can you zoom in a bit, Andy?" he asked. Andy obliged him, and he laughed. "That's what I thought. Hey, Becca, how'd you like to go camping this weekend?"

"What? Dad, are you crazy? They need us to help get Goldeneyes back!"

"Nope, I'm not crazy. See this?" he said, placing his finger to the left of where Andy had pointed. "That's the campground we used to go to when you were younger. It's right near their Compound. Andy, we've just found the perfect place to set up camp, so to speak."

Andy grinned. "That's a great idea, Mr. Jefferson!"

"Explain," Razor said.

"A campground is a place where people go to sleep out in the woods. We bring tents and trailers and cook over campfires and stuff. Mr. Jefferson brought Becca and me camping there a bunch of times. We can go to the campground and the Wild Ones probably won't even know we're there."

"You may be right," Letsan said. "They don't think much about humans at all, except for you, and that's only because you have Nafshi's Magelight. I'd bet they'd keep far away from this…campground…if it's full of people."

"That *is* a good idea," Razor said. "We can use it as a base for a strong force of warriors. They don't know Andy has new human allies, and they won't expect an attack from a place where humans are gathered. We go after the Wild Ones with a multistage plan. Stage one, set up near their Compound. Stage two, get into their Compound and free the prisoners. Stage three, escape."

"Stage four, kick their butts," Mike said.

Razor growled. "For once, I agree with you."

Mike smiled. "Sorry it took something like this to get us on the same page. So who all is going with Mr. Jefferson and Becca? Besides me,

PARENTAL CONSENT

that is."

"Me," Mr. Velez said. "I'll go. Teresa too, I'm sure."

"Try and stop me," she said.

"I'm going, too," Rachel insisted. "Danielle and I want to be part of this," she said, glancing at her best friend. Danielle nodded.

Andy shook his head. "Mom, you're not going to like this, but I don't think anyone else but me should go."

"But I want to help. Isn't that why you finally told me about Catmages? So I can help?"

"You will be helping. You and Mrs. Jefferson can be our Catmage taxi service. If they need to get somewhere fast, we can text you to come get them. We have more than enough people. Any more and we may as well wear a sign saying we're on our way to get them."

His mother frowned. "So we're supposed to stay behind and do nothing but worry?"

"No. You're supposed to stay behind and be our backup. You have no idea what a relief it will be to know that you and Becca's mom can come at a minute's notice with anything we think we might need. We can pack the cars with supplies."

"What kind of supplies?"

Andy hesitated.

"Rocks!" Mike said. "Baseballs, tennis balls, bats, weapons!"

"I was thinking more along the lines of towels and first aid materials for the Catmages," Andy said.

"Oh. Those too. And rocks. Which we can throw at the Wild Ones."

"Mom, will you do it?"

She thought it over. "All right. But I don't promise to stay here if you get in trouble!"

"Fair enough," Andy said.

Danielle Jefferson nodded. "We'll be your backups."

"That will keep them out of the battle," Letsan sent privately.

CHAPTER TWENTY

"Good thinking, Andy."

"Yeah. Don't tell Mom," he sent back. "No way I want her anywhere near those dogs or Wild Ones when the Magelight daggers are flying."

"Neither do I. They won't hear it from me."

"That's still only one small portion of a plan," Razor said. "We have a lot of work ahead."

"Maybe I should make a pot of coffee," Danielle said.

"I'll order pizza."

"I'll ask my mom if I can sleep over," Mike said.

"Andy, can you make a printout of that map for us?" Mr. Jefferson said.

They each attended to their tasks and soon were gathered around a large version of the map in the middle of the dining room table. The Catmages walked around the edges of the paper as they discussed possible strategies. The pizzas arrived and they ate in the dining room, still working on the plans. Andy and Becca got food for the Catmages. Somewhere around eleven Andy looked wearily away from the laptop screen and saw Teresa dozing off at the end of the table. He stretched and yawned.

"Mr. Velez, you should take Teresa home. It's late. I'm pretty tired, too."

"You have work tomorrow, Andy. You need to go to bed," his mother said.

"I texted Dr. Crane already. I'm not going into work."

"Oh. Well, you still need sleep. Mike, don't keep him awake playing video games."

"I won't," he said, yawning in his turn. "How about you guys?" he asked, looking at the Catmages. "Where are you going to sleep, Razor?"

"Nowhere. We're not finished. We'll stay here until we are."

"Okay. See you in the morning. I'll walk you to your car, Teresa," Mike said.

Andy went to the front door and watched everyone leave. Mike

PARENTAL CONSENT

came back and whispered that he'd asked Mr. Velez to bring his slingshot with him to the campground.

"Good idea," Andy muttered, watching Mike as he headed up the stairs. Andy turned out the porch light and closed the front door, leaning his forehead against it. He shut his eyes and thought of his friends caged, frightened, tormented by the Wild Ones. "Not again," he whispered. "Not this time, Saunders."

Andy pushed himself away from the door, his resolve hardening. He touched Nafshi's Magelight and felt its comforting warmth. "They have awakened the sleeping giant," he muttered.

"What's that?" Nafshi asked.

"Something I heard in history class. Something the Wild Ones are going to find out."

Andy walked slowly up the steps to his room. Mike was already in a pair of Andy's sweatpants and filling up the airbed. Andy changed out of his clothes and went in the bathroom to brush his teeth. He stopped short on his way back. Mike had moved the airbed directly in his path.

"Every time," he muttered. "Do you always have to be in my way?"

"Yes. It's my way of showing affection."

"Show affection by giving me a hug or something. Move."

Mike chuckled and move the airbed out of Andy's way. "Wait, do we hug?"

"Not generally." Andy settled into his bed. Mike lay down on the airbed and yawned. "Mike, they have Goldeneyes," Andy said softly. "What if—?" He couldn't bring himself to finish the sentence.

"Not gonna happen. We have Razor, and Letsan, and all the good guys. And we have you. Who do the Wild Ones have?"

"Taylor," Andy said sourly.

"Yeah, that would be the guy you flattened around this time last year." Mike grinned at Andy. "My money's on you, pal."

"Thanks," Andy said. He was glad Mike was with him. It kept him from staying awake all night worrying.

CHAPTER TWENTY

"And you have me," Nafshi said. "The Wild Ones have no idea what they've done. We *will* get my kin back. And Nistar, too," she said, using the name she had given Patches.

Heartened, Andy turned off the light and lay back, closed his eyes, and smiled. "That's right," he told her. "We have Nafshi. Boy, are they in for a surprise."

TWENTY-ONE: FATHERS AND DAUGHTERS

Ari and Lev were worried and frustrated. Their daughters were drugged and caged, and there was a very good chance they'd be killed by the Wild Ones. They were helpless to do anything at the moment. Roah ordered them to keep scanning the perimeter in case Razor and his Shomrim attacked. The morning passed slowly as the two Seekers scanned, rested, ate, and then repeated the process until the sun was high in the sky. Ari bided his time, waiting until he was sure the Wild Ones that kept watch with them were distracted. At last, two Wild Ones came to relieve the ones that had been with them all day. Ari's tail flicked his son and they changed their line of sight to the Compound, looking for their daughters. A few minutes later, both of them felt relief as they sensed Leilei and Zahavin's auras, strong and bright. They turned their attention back toward the East Woods. The new guards took their places, oblivious.

The day wore on. During their next rest break, Gimmel came to them with a message. "Niflah wants to see you. Report to the prison bayit," he said. Ari's pulse quickened. He and Lev couldn't be seen by their daughters. How could they manage this without being discovered? He glanced worriedly at Lev, who blinked at him.

"Lead the way," Lev said. "I'm really tired of scanning for auras."

CHAPTER TWENTY-ONE

They found the bayit heavily guarded by Kfir's strongest warriors. The fighters watched Lev and Ari as they halted near the door, deliberately keeping out of sight of the cages they knew were inside. Ari's heart ached as he thought of his daughter and niece lying in cold steel prisons. Roah, Niflah, and Kel waited for them outside.

"We have a problem," Niflah said. "Zahavin's Magelight is missing. The one on her collar is glass."

"What does that have to do with us?" Ari asked.

"We want you to find her Magelight."

"Then why are we here? Shouldn't we be looking where you found her?"

"No!" Roah said. "This is exactly what happened with Nafshi. She somehow hid her Magelight from us and then gave it to the boy. Zahavin's Magelight is here somewhere. Find it."

Lev laughed harshly. "You want us to search for a single Magelight in an entire Compound of Catmages? That shouldn't take more than half a moon."

Roah glared at Lev. His ears twitched and his tail thumped the ground. "Do not take that tone with me, Seeker, or you will have one less ear on that thick head of yours."

Ari stepped forward. "Forgive him, Roah. We've been working hard recently. We're going on very little rest and still trying to protect the Compound from sneak attacks by Razor."

"Get in that bayit," Roah said. "Find me that Magelight."

Ari and Lev looked at one another. They had little choice but to follow Roah's order. As they stepped inside, Lev saw Leilei try to get up and fall. He gasped.

The three captives turned their heads at the sound of his voice. Goldeneyes tried to focus her eyes on the newcomers. "You look familiar," she said. She turned her gaze to Ari. "So do you."

At Roah's glance, Ari said gruffly, "Hmph! A tabby Catmage looks familiar. Can't be because the world is filled with tabbies, can it?"

FATHERS AND DAUGHTERS

"No, that's not it. You look like—"

"What exactly do you want us to do?" Ari said, cutting across her words.

"Scan Zahavin."

"And what am I supposed to be scanning for?"

"Just do it and tell me what you discover."

Ari bit back a retort and concentrated. He decided to put on a show for them. He made his Magelight glow brightly and he closed his eyes and feigned concentration. He didn't know what Niflah was looking for, but there was no way he'd get any information out of Ari. He almost laughed when he realized that Niflah had given him a perfect way to contact Zahavin. Now he concentrated for real as he built walls around his thoughts.

"Zahavin, it's me, Aryeh. Levavi and I are under cover. We'll get you out of this, but *don't let them know who we are.*"

Goldeneyes opened her eyes, her head nodding. She looked at him and blinked. "All right, Father," she murmured. "I won't tell anyone who you are."

Leilei lifted her head and gazed at Lev. "That's where I saw you before!" she said. "You look just like my father!"

"What's wrong with them?" Ari said. "Are they insane?"

"No," Roah said, looking keenly at the two of them. "They are drugged. How interesting that they both think you are their fathers. Niflah, did you ever meet Zahavin's father?"

"If I did, it was many cycles of the sun ago. I don't remember him."

"Quiet, Leilei!" Ari sent privately. To the rest he said, "What does that have to do with us? Tabby markings are among the most common of our kind. These two are drugged! You would take the word of two of the enemy who are obviously out of their minds?"

"I'll be quiet, Father, I promise," Leilei said out loud. "Will you get me out of here soon? I've missed you."

"That did it," Lev sent to Ari. "Run!" They turned and dashed for the door.

CHAPTER TWENTY-ONE

"Take them!" Roah shouted a moment too late as Ari and Lev rushed the doorway, firing light jets and forcing their way past the guards. They darted in between the bayits, Kfir and his warriors in hot pursuit.

"Stay close to me," Ari said, zooming past a surprised pair of guards at the end of the row of bayits. They rounded the last one and doubled back, losing half their pursuers. The others were closing. "This isn't going to work," Ari said as jets of light flew thick and fast. One grazed his hind leg and he grunted in pain. "We can't outrun them."

"No," Lev said as they ran, "but we can outsmart them. Let's get to the downed tree by the latrine and into the hollow under the roots."

"Follow me, then. And run like your life depends on it!"

They reached the tree and dove into the hollow. There was barely enough room for the two of them inside. Kfir and his fighters wouldn't be able to squeeze in to get them out. But neither could the two of them leave without being captured.

"I hope you know what you're doing, Lev."

"Trust me."

"You can't escape us, traitors," Kfir growled. "We'll dig you out if we have to, but you're not going anywhere."

"Oh, shut up, you great oaf," Levavi said. "I'm so glad I don't have to pretend to like you anymore. Honestly, this dead tree has more personality than you."

Kfir growled and fired jet after jet into the hole. Levavi laughed as he deflected them with a shield. "Keep them busy," he whispered to Aryeh. "I have work to do."

"Move over," Aryeh whispered back. They edged past each other until Aryeh was near the opening of the hollow. He fired a light jet out and heard a yowl. "Got one," he said.

"Dig them out!" they heard Kfir growl. "Come on, in squads. Form up!"

"We don't have much time," Aryeh muttered.

"Quiet."

FATHERS AND DAUGHTERS

Levavi closed his eyes and calmed himself, extending his senses out into the forest, blocking out the sound of his enemies scrabbling in the earth on the other side of the tree. Finally, he found what he was looking for. "Excellent," he whispered. The sounds of digging grew louder.

Jets of light came flashing into the hollow. Aryeh huddled behind a shield, trembling with effort. "I hope whatever you're doing happens soon," he said to his son. "We can't hold out much longer."

Levavi's Magelight flashed. Something was running toward the tree. Leaves rustled outside the hollow. Then the air was full of shrieks and curses and the sound of footsteps running away. A powerful stench engulfed them. Aryeh struggled outside, retching, followed by Levavi. They could hardly breathe, but they ran full-tilt away from the Compound. There was no sign of the enemy behind them. Levavi was fairly sure that none of the Tzofim could find their scent through the overwhelming stink. When they felt comfortable they hadn't been followed, they paused to catch their breath.

"You called a skunk," Aryeh said, breathing hard and laughing. "By the First, you called a skunk into the middle of the battle. Levavi my boy, this is a story that will be told on long winter nights for many cycles to come."

"What now?" Levavi asked. "What do we do about Zahavin and Leilei?"

"Now we have to get to the Compound and find Razor. Kfir has more fighters to send after us while these recover from the skunk spray. Let's get our bearings and get away from here."

They looked around the wood for landmarks and calculated the distance they'd come.

"I recognize this place. We're close to where the humans like to sleep outdoors," Levavi said.

"We'll hide out here. As soon as we're settled in, I'll contact Razor."

Levavi growled assent. They took off for the campground at a brisk pace. Every so often, Aryeh chuckled as they ran. "You called a skunk," he

CHAPTER TWENTY-ONE

said as they jogged along.

Kfir walked wearily back to the West Woods Compound. Half his fighters had been sprayed by the skunk and were desperately rolling in mud and leaves to rid themselves of the clinging stench. He set some of the rest to help clean the affected ones. They'd be no use to him at all until they were free of the smell. They may as well broadcast their positions to Razor's Shomrim. He entered the prison bayit hesitantly and found Roah and Niflah staring at Zahavin, who seemed sound asleep in her cage.

"You lost them?" Roah asked. "Yours is not the walk of a victor."

"Yes," Kfir said. "They called a skunk. It took out many of my Tzofim."

"A skunk," Roah said. "Your fighters could not wrest control of it and send it on its way?"

Kfir couldn't meet Roah's gaze. "It surprised us. When we heard it coming, we thought it was more of my warriors coming to help. By the time we realized it was a skunk, it was too late. And then nobody thought of anything but escape."

"Which is what Lev and Ari did, of course."

"Yes."

"Idiot! Fool! Incompetent!" Roah's Magelight blazed.

"Stop," Niflah said. "What's done is done. Punishing him will do nothing. Kfir, go make sure your warriors are in fighting shape as soon as possible. We need to be ready for anything."

"Yes sir," Kfir said, retreating hastily before Roah could use his Magelight.

Roah turned a baleful gaze to Niflah. "He deserved punishment."

"Perhaps. But I am far more interested in Zahavin at the moment. Tell me, Roah, have you scanned her for her aura?"

"No. Why should I?"

"Because if you do, you will find something very interesting."

Roah was suspicious, but he did as Niflah said. "Why does it seem

FATHERS AND DAUGHTERS

wrong?" he asked.

"Look near the great vein in the neck."

Roah scanned her again. "By the One," he gasped, "there is a separate aura there. Her Magelight is in her neck! It is under her skin! No wonder we couldn't find Nafshi's. We never thought to look for a Magelight in her body!"

"I've heard rumors, stories, about a secret society of Magi who wielded their Magelights in a way the rest of us could not. I never quite believed it. This, now—this explains much."

"How do we do this thing?" Roah said. "Why do they?"

"Isn't it obvious? They are more powerful when the Magelight is bolstered by the heart's blood. And you can be sure that if Zahavin has embedded her Magelight, she was taught how by my brother," Niflah said bitterly. "Of course Hakham would do this for his precious apprentice and not for me."

"Then we will do the same. Let us become as powerful as they."

"It's not that simple," Niflah said. "Her Magelight is quite close to the vein. One nick, one mistake, one wrong placement by even a tiny margin, and you will die."

"Then I will not make a mistake."

Niflah shook his head. "I have a better idea, Roah. They want their daughters back. We want to know how they do this. Let us make a trade. For real, this time."

Roah gazed at the old tabby. "All of them?"

"Well, we'll certainly *say* we'll give back all of them. But I think we should keep Zahavin anyway. Tell her that if she shows us how to embed our Magelights, we will let her friends go. Then give them Patches and Leilei."

Roah laughed. "We can have a messenger at the East Woods in an hour."

"No. Send one in the morning. I will stay here and wait for Zahavin's head to clear. Station guards on every side of this bayit as well as at

CHAPTER TWENTY-ONE

the door. Let's not take the chance that as the drugs wear off, she tries to escape."

"We should have the boy here ready with more sedative if need be. He can give her just enough to make her weak, not enough to make her sleep."

"Excellent idea! Make sure Taylor comes to the Compound early tomorrow."

"What about Saunders?" Roah asked.

Niflah paused in thought. He made sure that no one but Roah would hear his next words. "I don't think he needs to know that we have found a way to gain more power, do you?"

Roah blinked in acquiescence. "I will tell the boy to be ready. Call me when Zahavin can be questioned." He turned and left the bayit.

"Under your skin, eh?" Niflah muttered. "If you can do it, so can I."

TWENTY-TWO: CAMPFIRE BOYS AND GIRLS

Levavi and Aryeh made their way cautiously through the wood, checking frequently to make sure they weren't followed. Aryeh was greatly relieved when he heard the sounds of people nearby. They kept out of sight as they surveyed the campground for a hiding place. Levavi found a thorn bush on the border of the campground that was thick enough to provide cover but had an opening they could slip through.

"This will have to be comfortable enough. Mind the thorns as you enter."

Aryeh followed his son and settled himself on the ground. "Keep watch," he said. "I need to send a message to Razor."

"Father, what about the humans? They'll see the light."

"Humans have been seeing our message lights since we first discovered how to send them. These will think the same as the others: Swamp gas, or fairy lights, or fireflies, or their eyes playing tricks on them. And if we get in trouble for it, so what? Our daughters are worth it. Now be quiet and let me concentrate!"

Lev blinked at his father. He watched as a yellow globe of light formed at Aryeh's collar and zoomed out of the thicket and out of sight. Now all they could do was wait.

CHAPTER TWENTY-TWO

When Andy woke the next morning, Letsan was lying at his feet. Andy swung out of bed, stepped around Mike, and headed to the bathroom. He left Mike asleep on the airbed, took his phone from the night table, and went downstairs to forage for breakfast. Halfway down the stairs he heard the thump on the floor that indicated Letsan was awake. He went to the pantry and took out a can of food for the Catmages and a box of cereal for himself.

"Hey," he said as Letsan joined him in the kitchen. "Breakfast is over there," he said, nodding.

"I can smell it." Razor padded into the room and joined Letsan at the bowl. "You're going to need more," he said as the other Catmages came in from the dining room. Andy hurried to get two more bowls and fill them. Soon the kitchen was silent except for the sound of Andy eating his cereal and the Catmages eating tuna.

"Becca says her dad reserved a campsite for us," Andy said between bites, reading the texts on his phone. "He wants to go out there around lunchtime. How soon can you get a rescue mission ready?"

Razor lifted his head from the bowl. "My Shomrim are already on their way. We received a message from Aryeh and Lev last night. They were exposed and had to flee for their lives."

"Are they okay?" Andy asked, half-rising from his chair.

"They're fine." Razor bent his head to the bowl. "We're going to need transportation."

"Where to?"

"The campground. Zohar and his force are going with you. Zohar will wait with you until we call him. Then he'll lead a strong flanking movement from the campground. In the meantime, Katana and I will come straight at them with most of our warriors. Lev and Ari will join Zohar. They know the West Woods well, and even better, they know where the Wild Ones are keeping Zahavin and the others." He laughed harshly. "The Wild Ones won't expect it. They think so little of humans. They have no idea how useful it is to have friends with cars."

CAMPFIRE BOYS AND GIRLS

"Now that would be something Danielle and I can do." Andy looked up to see his mother leaning against the door of the foyer that led to her office. "And it would keep us out of danger," she said to Andy. "Oh, don't look so surprised. I'm your mother. I know what you're thinking *some* of the time. Who's coming with me?"

"Katana, Zohar, and me," Razor said. "After you take the Shomrim to Becca's, I need a lift out of town. I need to coordinate with my captains at the Compound."

Rachel grinned. "All right. But I'm stopping for coffee on the way." She looked around the room. "Is Mike still sleeping?"

"I guess so," Andy said.

"I'll wake him," Razor said wickedly. "There's no time for laziness." He slipped up the stairs. Moments later they heard an outraged shout from Andy's room.

"Not cool, Razor! Not cool!"

"I don't even want to know," Rachel murmured. "Tell Razor to meet me outside. Come on, the rest of you." She led them to the garage.

Razor came downstairs quickly, followed by Mike. When Andy raised his eyebrows, Mike said, "He jumped on my stomach."

"Don't sleep so late next time," Razor said. "Where's your mother?" he asked Andy.

"Garage."

"See you later."

Mike sat down at the table. "What's for breakfast?"

By mid-morning, the day's plans were set. The two moms had already left with Razor and the rest of the Catmages to ferry them wherever Razor directed. Mike and Andy waited on the porch for their rides to arrive. Mike would go with Mr. Velez and Teresa. Andy would join Becca and her father, who were bringing the tent and equipment they needed to give the appearance that they would be camping for the night. Mr. Jefferson had a long phone conversation with Andy, making him tell everything he

CHAPTER TWENTY-TWO

remembered about Nafshi's captivity and asking a lot of questions Andy couldn't answer about how and where the Catmages were being held in the West Woods. Andy had his sleeping bag and backpack ready. Mike would be using his mother's sleeping bag which, he pointed out, was thankfully not covered with puppies or kittens or cartoon characters.

"Wait, didn't you have a cartoon-themed sleeping bag?"

"Yes, but that was when I was a kid."

"Yeah, like two years ago," Andy said, grinning.

"So are we really going to camp, or is it just pretend?" Mike asked. "Hot dogs and hamburgers and s'mores would be excellent."

"I don't know. We'll have supper there for sure, but I don't know if we're going to stay overnight. We're kind of hoping to rescue them tonight."

"If we don't, we try again tomorrow morning?"

"No," Nafshi said. "We'll get them out tonight. Count on it."

"Nafshi says we'll do it tonight," Andy said.

"What?" Mike asked. "A dead Catmage is talking to you? Andy, I think you're losing it."

"Uh, I mean, we'll do it for Nafshi!"

Mike shook his head. "Weird." Becca's father pulled into the driveway as Mike was about to say more. Relieved, Andy picked up his things and brought them to the car. Mr. Jefferson popped the trunk and Andy stowed his sleeping bag in it. He put his backpack on the floor of the back seat.

"I'll see you later," Andy said.

"Kick some Wild One butt," Mike told him.

"You, too."

Goldeneyes woke from a restless sleep filled with Wild Ones and fighting. She could swear she'd seen her father and brother. But no, it must have been a dream brought on by the drug she'd been given. She shook her head. It seemed clearer than the day before. Perhaps she would be able to

CAMPFIRE BOYS AND GIRLS

concentrate and use her Magelight to get them out of their cages. Then she remembered the locks were numbered locks. She couldn't open them, and there were no tools around she could use to break the locks or the cages that held them. Her spirits fell. She saw Leilei sleeping in the next cage. Patches snored away in the cage nearest the door. No, there was no way they would escape without help. It's too bad she had only dreamed about Levavi and Aryeh.

Goldeneyes heard soft footsteps outside. Her hackles rose as Niflah and Roah came striding through the door.

"Ah, you are awake," Niflah said. "Did you enjoy your brief meeting with your father and brother?"

"It wasn't a dream? That was really them?"

"Yes," Roah said sourly. "Now I know why they were such failures as Seekers. Your kin were spying for Razor."

"Where are they? Have you harmed them? Niflah, what have you done to them?"

Niflah chuckled. "Nothing, my dear, nothing. They gave Kfir the slip yesterday."

"But we should thank you and Leilei for exposing them," Roah said. "If Kfir had been more competent, they'd be sharing those cages with you. Or they'd be dead."

Goldeneyes thought back to the day before. By the first, she *had* exposed her father. She thought she was speaking privately but the drug had made her unable to hide her mind-voice. But they got away. Thank the One Above Us All, they got away!

"What do you want?" she asked as the two Wild Ones sat down before her prison.

"We want to make a deal, my dear," Niflah said. "Information for the release of your friends. And Zahavin—your Magelight? We know where you're hiding it."

Taylor turned his bicycle off the road, squinting in the morning sunlight.

CHAPTER TWENTY-TWO

Roah had only told him to come to the Compound, not why he wanted. Taylor shrugged as he walked his bike through the trees. He had stowed food and water in his backpack, having learned the hard way that sometimes Roah required his attendance for extended periods. Just because cats could go long hours without food didn't mean Taylor had any intention of going hungry.

He parked his bike near a tree and walked the rest of the way to the Compound, nodding at the Wild Ones he knew. He found Kel waiting for him at Roah's bayit, flanked by his sister and brother.

"Where's Roah?"

"With the prisoners. He wants you there."

"Oh. Are you coming?"

Kel's tail twitched.

"No. He only wants you." His mind-voice sounded sulky. Taylor kept his face blank. He had no desire to get in the middle of a cat fight. The thought almost made him lose his composure and laugh. As he left Kel and went to find Roah, Taylor thought he could hear the echo of loud, uproarious laughter in his head. So many weird things seemed to be happening these days. He stooped to enter the bayit. Roah and Niflah sat in front of Goldeneyes, who was sitting up and looking far more alert than she had yesterday.

"Good, you're here," Niflah said. "Did you bring the kit?"

Taylor held up the leather bag that held the needle and sedative. "Which one needs a refresher?"

"That depends on Zahavin," Roah said. "Tell us what we need, and your friends go free. Refuse, and they will suffer." His Magelight blazed and he fired a jet that barely missed Leilei's ear. "I could just as easily have blinded her," he said as Leilei's head rose sleepily at Goldeneyes' cry.

Goldeneyes growled. "You won't release them. You will never keep your word."

"Perhaps he won't," Niflah said, "but I will. Zahavin, you know what we want. Tell us how to embed our Magelights, and your niece goes free."

"What are they talking about?" Leilei asked. "Auntie Zahavin? Where's my father?"

Roah's tail thumped. "He ran away, Little Nafshi. Your father was afraid."

"My father isn't afraid of anyone!" she said, trying to stand. She fell on her side.

"Sleep, Leilei. Or talk to Patches. We'll talk about this later," Goldeneyes said.

"Are you going to run away like my father did?"

Goldeneyes' heart leaped as she thought of the last sight of their fathers. She knew what to do now. She would stall for time. If her father and brother were here, Razor and Letsan couldn't be far away.

"No, Leilei, I'm not going anywhere. Sleep."

Leilei sighed and closed her eyes.

"Perhaps we can come to an accommodation after all," Goldeneyes said. "But not without a show of good faith first."

"A show of good faith would be excellent," Niflah said. "But I trust you no more than you trust me. We do it together or not at all."

Andy surveyed the campground as Mr. Jefferson maneuvered his car along the winding dirt road to their campsite. He was glad to find the Knotty Pine Campground nearly empty. There was only one other family in an RV on the other side of the campground. He wasn't surprised. Prime camping season wouldn't start until school let out next month.

"This is perfect," Mr. Jefferson said, smiling broadly as he stopped the car. "Nice and private, but close to where we need to be. All right, everyone out. Let's get set up."

A short time later, they were nearly finished unpacking the car. Andy and Becca lifted the cooler from the trunk and carried it between them, putting it on the ground near the picnic table. The only thing left was a large plastic box that Becca's father told them to leave in the trunk.

CHAPTER TWENTY-TWO

He was carefully building a charcoal pyramid on a portable grill.

"There," he said when he finished. "We're all set for dinner." He glanced over at the adjoining campsite, where Mr. Velez, Mike, and Teresa were setting up their equipment.

"Almost done, Mario?" he called. Mr. Velez nodded and waved.

"Be right there." He stowed a large duffle bag in the tent and walked the short distance between the campsites, followed by Mike and Teresa.

"You kids take a walk and look around the area while Mario and I discuss a few things. Don't go too far."

"That's a great idea," Mike said. "Come on, Teresa!" He grabbed her hand and pulled her along. Andy and Becca shrugged and hurried after them.

"Mike, wait up!" Andy called.

Mike and Teresa stopped to wait for them. The four of them followed a winding path that led through the woods. Birds flew in and out of trees and squirrels scampered around them. Flowers were blooming and they disturbed a few chipmunks as they passed. Mike picked a daisy for Teresa and presented it to her with a bow. She smiled and tucked it into her hair. Andy hesitated and then picked one for Becca, who did the same.

"I wish this was a real camping trip," Andy said. "I wish we could just sit around the campfire tonight and roast marshmallows and tell lame ghost stories."

"My scary stories aren't lame," Mike said.

"They really are," Becca said, grinning.

"If you want a scary story, just let Razor hear you talking like that." Zohar's voice sounded in all their heads. Andy scanned the woods and saw nothing.

"Zohar, where are you? I don't see anyone," Mike said.

"You're not supposed to see us."

Andy scanned the woods with his Magelight. He left the path and stopped in front of a deep drift of leaves with a small, cat-sized entrance at one end. "Nice cover," he said as he noticed the lattice of sticks beneath a few of the leaves. Zohar and several squads of Catmages were hiding in a large, shallow hole.

"We dug it this morning after your mother dropped us off," Zohar said. "It took you long enough to get here."

"Razor told me to wait for someone to contact me."

"Which is what I'm doing." He turned his head to the Catmages behind him. "Lev, Ari, come meet the Son of Aaron."

"Andy," he said. "My name is Andy."

Two tabbies emerged from the hole. "Andy," Ari said. "I'm Aryeh, Zahavin's father. This is her brother, Levavi."

"Hi. This is Becca, Mike, and Teresa," he said, pointing to each in turn. "They're going to help us get Goldeneyes and the others."

"Lev and Ari have been briefing us on the layout of the West Woods," Zohar said. "You need to know this, too. And share the information with your friends."

"If you give me a few minutes to run back to camp and get a notebook," Becca said, "I can make a map."

"Or we can come with you," Aryeh said.

"You know, they can. There's nobody near our campsite. Is that all right with you, Zohar?" Andy said.

"I'll come with you. Sami, keep an eye on things. Contact me if you spot anything out of the ordinary."

Sami nodded and stood watch as Andy and the others returned to the campsite. When they arrived, Mr. Velez and Mr. Jefferson were sitting in canvas chairs drinking sodas.

"That was quick," Mr. Jefferson told Andy. His glance fell on the Catmages coming out of the trail behind Andy. "You've found them already?"

"Mr. Jefferson, this is Goldeneyes' father and brother. They're going to help Becca make a map of the West Woods Compound."

"Excellent!" he said, rising. "Mario and I have been discussing what we're going to do tonight. Becca, Mike, Teresa, you three are staying back."

CHAPTER TWENTY-TWO

"What?"

"No!"

"We want to help!"

"Now hear me out," he said. "We don't want you kids anywhere near the kind of battle it's going to take to free Goldeneyes and the others."

There were more cries of protest.

"Let me finish!" he said. "Becca, you told me that you and Mike and Teresa did a good job last year helping defend the Compound. But you weren't on your own. You had the Catmages helping you. I don't want you in the thick of the attack. Mario and I think you kids ought to be the rearguard. You stay far back, you take care of anyone trying to sneak up on our forces, and you pull out any wounded Catmages who need attention."

"Oh," Becca said. "Okay, that's fair."

Mike was sullen. "I want to go with Andy."

"Don't be stupid," Mr. Velez said.

"You are sixteen years old," Mr. Jefferson said. "You don't get to make that decision. We do."

"I don't want Mike to come with me," Andy said.

"What?"

"They're right. Those light daggers can be deadly. Can you make a Magelight shield?"

"Well, no, but I can duck really fast."

"Yeah? Want to try it now?" His Magelight pulsed with light.

"Uh, no, that's okay," Mike said, backing away. "I get your point. Okay. We'll stay back. But I'm bringing my slingshot."

"I want you to," Andy said. "But don't think this is a game. And don't think the Wild Ones will stop in the middle of a battle and say, 'Oh, it's just a kid, I won't try to hurt that one.' They're either terrible themselves or they've been totally brainwashed. Go ask Patches how they treated him."

"I can't. That's why we're here, to get Patches and Leilei and Goldeneyes!"

"Yeah, I know," Andy said. "That's why I'm here, too."

CAMPFIRE BOYS AND GIRLS

"Quiet, you two," Mr. Velez said. "Now what's this about a map?"

Becca led the Catmages into the tent and took a sketch pad from her backpack. They described the Wild Ones' Compound and watched, fascinated, as she drew a map of the woods, the paths, and the bayits and clearings. When she was finished, she put the pages on the picnic table, weighed down with rocks. They gathered around it as she traced the route they would take to get to the bayit where Goldeneyes and the others were being held.

"There's still a big problem," Ari said. "The cages are locked with number locks. We can't open them."

"Number locks?" Mr. Jefferson said.

"Combination locks," Andy said. "Catmages generally don't count higher than seven. And they don't get the concept of combination locks."

Mr. Jefferson grinned. "Don't worry about that, Andy. Becca and I had a long talk last night. I can get your friends out of those cages. Trust me."

"Okay. Zohar, can you get this information to Razor?"

"I can. Give me a moment."

They watched as he walked up and down the table gazing at the maps. His Magelight blazed and a message globe went flying toward the East Woods Compound. He turned to Ari and Lev. "You should contact Razor and reinforce that with pictures from your experience at the Compound," he said.

"We'll do that," Ari told him. "This might take a while. I'd like to send enough messages for Razor to know the Compound inside and out. But Lev and I haven't had anything to eat since yesterday and messaging takes a lot out of you."

"We brought food," Teresa said. "I'll get some. Go send those messages." She and Mike ran off to her tent to retrieve cans of chicken and fish for the Catmages. By the time they'd finished, the afternoon sun was slanting low over the trees and it was almost dinnertime. Mr. Jefferson started the grill while Mario removed hot dogs and hamburgers from the cooler.

CHAPTER TWENTY-TWO

The rest of them got the table ready and pulled out condiments and side dishes. Mike got his hand slapped by Teresa for trying to eat the potato chips while the rest of them were setting up the table.

As they sat down to dinner, Zohar told Andy he was going back to the Shomrim. "Join us after you eat," he said. "Razor will be giving the order to go soon after sunset."

Andy nodded. "We'll be ready." He swallowed a mouthful of hamburger and tried not to show how worried he was about Goldeneyes. *What if our plan doesn't work?* he asked Nafshi.

"It will. We'll have my granddaughter back tonight. Count on it."

I hope you're right.

"Thinking hard about tonight?" Becca asked.

"Yeah."

She put her hand on his arm. "You can do this."

"I couldn't save Nafshi."

"This is different. You're older, more experienced, and you have a Magelight."

"And us!" Mike said.

"Do you ever mind your own business?" Andy asked, exasperated.

"Nope. I have 20-20 hearing, so I always know what's going on. You can hide nothing from me. Nothing!" Mike brandished his plastic fork at Andy.

In spite of himself, Andy laughed. "All right. But yeah, I'm worried. We only have to get to the Compound without being spotted, fight our way through their warriors, and then get three Catmages out of steel cages. No biggie."

"I told you, Andy, don't worry about those cages. I'll be right back," Mr. Jefferson said, getting up from the table and walking to his car. He came back carrying the large box he'd left in the trunk. He dropped it on the ground with a loud thump and clanking noise.

"What's in there?" Andy asked.

"This," Mr. Jefferson said, grinning as he removed a large bolt cut-

CAMPFIRE BOYS AND GIRLS

ter from the box. "And this." He brandished an aluminum bat. "I may not have a Magelight, but I'm pretty sure this bolt cutter will take care of those locks. And this bat will take care of any Wild One dumb enough to come near me or mine."

Andy smiled broadly. "That's awesome, Mr. Jefferson."

"I got one, too," Mr. Velez said. "But I'm staying in the back with the kids to make sure they're all right."

"Thanks, *Abuelo*," Teresa said.

Mr. Jefferson shouldered the bolt cutter and bat. "Time to go, Andy. Mario, give us a ten minute head start and then come after us." He reached out and pulled his daughter into a one-armed hug. "You take care of yourself, baby girl. Your mama will kill me if you come back with so much as a stubbed toe."

"I'll be fine, Dad."

"You all take care," he said.

Andy stood and faced Becca. "Be careful," she said.

"You too."

With a sideways glance at her father, Andy leaned forward and gave her a swift kiss, then walked away, his face burning. He looked back before they disappeared into the wood and waved. His friends waved back.

"It's this way," he told Mr. Jefferson and led him to Zohar's hiding place. Zohar was waiting outside for them, flanked by Ari, Lev, and Sami.

"Ready, Andy?" Zohar asked.

"Yeah. Everything set?"

"Yes. Time to go." He turned to Sami. "Form up." Within moments, the Shomrim were assembled in squads. Zohar gave the squad leaders their orders and the Catmages melted into the woods, padding silently toward the West Woods Compound. "Ari and Lev will be your guides. I'm going to join my warriors. May the First shine on all our paths tonight."

"Find my girls," Ari said. "In Neshama's name, bring them home."

"We will."

Zohar turned and ran off into the dusk.

CHAPTER TWENTY-TWO

"Ready, Mr. J.?" Andy asked.

He swung the bat off his shoulder and through the air one-handed.

"Yep. Let's go. We got some friends in need."

Ari and Lev led them through the woods.

TWENTY-THREE: EAST VERSUS WEST

Dusk fell. Razor stood in front of his assembled warriors on the practice field, who sat in rows behind their captains and squad leaders. Letsan, Hakham, and Silsula stood to the side. Katana stood next to her commander.

"You all know your parts," Razor said. "The Wild Ones have three of our own. We're getting them back. Are you ready?"

Dozens of voices sounded as one. "Yes!" they shouted.

"Then let's go. Make me proud!"

The warriors separated into squads and melted into the woods. Hakham, Silsula, and Letsan followed Razor.

"Are you ready for this, brother?" Razor asked Letsan as he drew near.

"Yes. I'm in control now."

"Good. Because there's no one I'd rather have beside me in battle. Except maybe your son."

Letsan laughed grimly. "Let's hope Zohar and his Shomrim do their part well."

"He will," Hakham said. "He has the Son of Aaron with him."

"And my father and brother," Silsula said proudly.

CHAPTER TWENTY-THREE

There was no more talking as they jogged toward the West Woods Compound.

Goldeneyes tried to hide her impatience. She'd been arguing with Roah and Niflah on and off for hours, trying to work out the details of releasing Patches and Leilei. At least they weren't still drugging her or the others. Taylor had been sent away and told to bide his time until they needed him. But every time she thought she'd gotten them to let one of them go before having to show them how to embed a Magelight, Roah brought up another objection. It didn't matter that Niflah grew impatient as well. They'd gotten nowhere.

To make matters worse, the sedatives were wearing off and they threatened to have Taylor come back and inject all three of them. Goldeneyes fought desperately against that, pointing out that she couldn't teach them a thing with her mind muddled. She could barely concentrate on talking to them half the time, she said. It was true—whatever they'd given her made her light-headed and drowsy.

"If you make a mistake while embedding the Magelight, you will die. You want me clear-headed."

"How do we know you won't give us false information on purpose?" Roah asked.

Goldeneyes bristled. "Because unlike you, I keep my word."

"We're getting nowhere, Roah," Niflah said. "Make a decision and stick to it."

"You may release Patches, then."

"No! Leilei first!" Goldeneyes said.

"Patches agrees. Leilei should go free," he said.

"Quiet, idiot," Roah said.

"Roah is mean to Patches."

"Please be quiet, Patches," Goldeneyes said.

Patches subsided into mumbling.

"Very well," Roah said. "Little Nafshi may leave. I will call the boy and have him release her." He turned his head toward the door. A minute later, Taylor came running up to the bayit. He slipped through the entrance.

"You called?"

"Open Leilei's cage. She will be leaving us. You will escort her past the guard post and let her return to her people."

"Leilei, run home as fast as you can when they let you go!" Goldeneyes told her.

"But what about you and Patches?"

"We'll be fine. Just do it!"

"All right, Auntie." She backed away from the entrance.

As Taylor dialed the combination, Roah sent him a private message. "Take her out of the bayit, but do not release her. Bring her to the main guard post and wait for my call."

Taylor opened the lock and swung open the door. He concentrated and cast the scruffing spell on Leilei and removed her from the cage. He left the lock dangling in the latch and the door hanging open.

"What about her Magelight?" Goldeneyes asked.

"She can make another," Roah said indifferently. "*Nistar* did," he said, sarcasm dripping from his voice.

"How did you become so twisted?" she asked. "Niflah, how can you bear being around someone as horrible as Roah?"

Roah glared at Goldeneyes. "Perhaps you should learn to be more civil," he said and shot a light dagger at her. It grazed her flank, singeing the fur and cutting the skin.

"Enough!" Niflah growled. "Zahavin, tell us what we want to know and all three of you will be back with your friends before dawn."

"All right," she said. "I can't fight you any longer. But I'm so tired and my head is still so unclear. I need to rest."

Niflah peered at her. "Very well," he said. "Roah and I have things to attend to, so we'll give you some time. But when we come back, you had better tell us what we want to know, or it isn't just you who will suffer." He

CHAPTER TWENTY-THREE

glanced meaningfully at Patches as he and Roah left the bayit.

They walked side by side to Roah's home.

"She'll never tell us," Roah said.

"I think she will. Frighten her enough about Leilei and Patches, and she will tell us what we need to know."

"Perhaps we should just try it ourselves without waiting for her."

"If you want to risk it, go right ahead. Doubtless we can find someone to take your place."

Roah glared at the old tabby, ears back. "Do not test me, old one."

"I am not. I am merely stating the truth. Don't get reckless at this stage. We are close to getting everything we want."

They arrived at Roah's bayit. "I'm off for a meal and a nap," Niflah said. "Shall we meet back at the prison bayit at dusk?"

"Yes."

Roah watched Niflah as he headed into the trees. "*I* am close to getting everything *I* want," he murmured.

Niflah yawned hugely and stretched when he awoke. It was later than he expected. Night had fallen. He was surprised Roah hadn't sent someone to wake him. Well, it didn't matter. Zahavin wasn't going anywhere. Niflah stretched again and sent out a call to Taylor. He heard the boy's footsteps shortly after and exited his bayit.

"What do you want?" Taylor said. "I have to leave soon if I'm going to make it home by curfew."

"Where is Leilei?" Niflah asked.

"I got tired of watching her. I gave her another shot and left her sleeping it off with the guards. Don't worry, she's not going anywhere."

"That was not what you were told to do!"

"Yeah? Well the next time *you* sit around for hours watching a doped-up cat giggle and say stupid stuff while you're trying to concentrate on your homework."

Niflah growled and his eyes grew wide. "Do not take that tone with me, young man."

Once again, anger overwhelmed Taylor. He felt an inner voice raging, wanting to hurt Niflah, to punish him for what he had done. One of his green Magelights blazed. Taylor's heart beat faster and his blood pounded in his ears. Just as he was about to do—something, he didn't know what—a yellow Magelight brightened and he felt suddenly calmer.

"What in the name of the First is wrong with you?" Niflah asked. "Were you about to *fire* on me?"

Taylor took a deep breath. "No. I, uh, don't always have control of my Magelights. Sometimes they just light up like that," he said.

"Then you need to control them better."

"Well that's only the second time it ever happened," Taylor lied.

"Then you had better make sure there isn't a third. Now. I need you to take something to Saunders for me," Niflah said. His Magelight glowed and the two captured Magelight collars floated through the air to Taylor, who grabbed them and put them in his pocket. "Saunders was asking for more Magelights. Give him those. The owners will soon have no use for them."

"You're going to kill them?" Taylor asked.

"Why do you care?"

"I don't. I was just—Andy really likes them. It's going to hit him hard."

"That's exactly the point, my boy. We want him on the sidelines. He's been far too much trouble for too long."

"I can take care of Cohen," Taylor said. "You don't have to kill his friends to sideline him. Let me do it!"

"Out of the question. Now stop arguing and get going."

"Are you coming with me?"

"Not tonight. Zahavin has some knowledge to impart before she is no longer of use to us."

"Whatever. I'm out of here." He turned and hurried down the path, lighting his way with a flashlight.

CHAPTER TWENTY-THREE

As Taylor's footsteps faded, Niflah made his way to the prison bay-it. Roah was already there.

"Perhaps we should just try ripping out your Magelight for practice putting in ours," he said as Niflah walked in.

"That would be a terrible idea," Niflah said. "Zahavin would die, and we'd be no closer to finding out how to do this ourselves."

"Still, better her than us."

"True. But I think we should wait until—"

Roah's head jerked around as he and Niflah both heard the shouts from outside.

"Attack! Attack! Razor is coming!"

"Tzofim! Join up, get into your squads!" roared Kfir. "Form up, you fools!"

"This isn't over," Roah snapped as he hurried outside, followed closely by Niflah.

Goldeneyes and Patches looked at each other. "A rescue?" Patches asked. "We're saved!"

"I think you're right," she said.

"I think you're wrong," Alef said as he swaggered in. "Bett and I have a score to settle with Patches. Don't we?"

"You would harm Patches when your own Compound is at risk?" Goldeneyes asked, hoping to divert their attention.

"It won't take long," Alef said. "Who's going to tell? You? You won't be around much longer, either."

"We'll just have to see about that," she said. Alef and Bett hadn't been around since they'd been thrown out the day before. Goldeneyes was fairly sure they didn't know that she'd not been given any more mind-fogging drugs. Patches didn't have his Magelight—but she had hers.

"Patches, I have an idea," she sent privately. "Listen carefully and do as I tell you."

Andy and Mr. Jefferson followed Zohar and the Catmages as quietly and

EAST VERSUS WEST

quickly as they could. They wanted to be in position before it got too dark to see without a flashlight.

"Wish I had cat eyes," Mr. Jefferson whispered.

"It's all right, we're almost there."

"How do you know?"

"I can feel the auras."

Ari heard Andy's whisper and looked back sharply. "Your Magelight isn't lit and you feel the auras?"

"Yeah, I learned how over the summer."

"That's a Seeker's talent!" Lev said.

"Quiet!" Sami said.

They hushed and trod softly after the leaders. At last the Shomrim halted and gathered together. They were close to the West Woods guard post, Andy guessed. That was the plan, anyway.

"Yes," Nafshi told him. "I can feel the auras."

Andy bit back a laugh.

"Now we wait," Zohar told them.

Razor gave the order to halt as they neared the launch point of their attack. He glanced around to make sure everything was ready. There was a risk they'd be sensed before they charged, but that was a risk worth taking. He waited until the squads were in formation. He nodded at Katana, who gave the order to charge. Within moments, squad after squad of Shomrim sprinted toward the West Woods, firing at the guard posts and rushing into the Compound. Razor sent a message globe and hurried to the fore, flanked by the Council members. He thought of Kfir's reaction to having his own Compound attacked. "I told you you'd pay," Razor said. "Now to find you and finish you once and for all." He sped on, firing light daggers at any Wild One hapless enough to cross his path, looking for Kfir.

Patches cowered and backed up against the rear of his cage.

"Don't hurt Patches. Leave Patches alone. Patches is not hurting

CHAPTER TWENTY-THREE

anyone."

"You hurt us by existing," Alef said. "We didn't get the chance to finish you off when we all lived at the house in town. Now we're going to rectify that."

"Leave him alone!" Goldeneyes said.

"Quiet, Zahavin. You won't live through this night, either. You'll pay for what you did to our son."

"What are you talking about?"

"You killed Hay on the night Kel tried to take your kittens. You and your sister and that fancy spell of yours," Bett said bitterly.

"First we kill Patches. Then we kill you," Alef said, a low growl starting in his throat.

"Together?"

"Together."

Their Magelights flared, and two sets of bright blue daggers flew toward Patches, who screamed "No! You will not kill Patches today!"

The light daggers bounced off the shield in front of him.

"How? How are you doing that? You have no Magelight!" Alef sputtered.

"Patches does not need Magelight. Patches is a Nistar, a student of Nafshi! You can't touch Nistar! He has Nafshi's protection!"

"Excellent," Goldeneyes sent privately. "Just keep pretending it's you doing the shielding and you'll be fine. Sooner or later, the Shomrim will come and rescue us."

"That's impossible," Bett said. "How can a half-breed idiot have that much power?"

Taylor was annoyed that he had to ride home in the dark. Niflah should have figured out what he wanted hours ago. He hadn't gone far from the Compound when a message globe zipped into his Magelight necklace. The Compound was under attack!

Taylor leaned over and made a U-turn in the road, pedaling furiously back to the Compound. If Cohen was there, he was in for a big surprise. Taylor grinned nastily as he sped down the road.

Zohar gave the signal to the Shomrim and Andy. "Time to go, Mr. Jefferson," Andy said, hurrying after the Catmages. They poured into the Compound from the side and came upon fighters hurrying to join the main assault at the front of the Compound. With a cheer, Zohar's warriors bore down on the reinforcements. Soon the sound of Catmages fighting, yowling, and screaming filled the air. Andy flung up a shield around himself and Becca's father. "Let's go find Goldeneyes," he said. They hurried toward the bayits.

Razor found Kfir near the main guard post, shouting orders while standing over something Razor couldn't make out. "Waiting for me?" Razor called.

"Among others," Kfir said. The battle raged on either side of them. Hakham, Silsula, and Letsan caught up to Razor.

"What are you waiting for?" Letsan asked. "Kill him!" He fired a dagger that Kfir easily deflected.

"I wouldn't do that if I were you," Kfir said. "Look what I have here." He stepped back, leaned down, and bent his head. When he raised it, he was holding Leilei by the scruff of her neck. Her head lolled to one side.

"Leilei!" Silsula shouted. "Is she alive? If you've killed, her, Kfir—"

"Oh, she's alive. For now. Call off the attack, Razor, or this one and your precious Zahavin will die. We warned you."

"Not on your life," Razor growled. "If she dies, you die. And we both know that's not what you want."

"We appear to have a stalemate," Kfir said. "However will this turn out?"

"Do you give up?" Patches said as Alef and Bett tried again and again to kill him. Their daggers bounced harmlessly off the shield Goldeneyes maintained.

CHAPTER TWENTY-THREE

Alef and Bett were furious. Bett snarled as another of her light daggers fell to the floor and fizzled out.

"No! By the One, there's no way he could do this without his Magelight! Where are you hiding it, Patches? It must be here somewhere." She looked frantically around the room.

"Patches is not hiding it, Patches is not hiding it," he said in a singsong voice.

"Shut! Up!" Alef said, charging up to the cage and leaping on top of it. "Stop talking, you halfwit half-breed!"

"Alef is rude and mean."

"Yes, he is," Goldeneyes said, trying to deflect Alef's attention. But she was tiring and the drugs and lack of food had taken a toll on her. She wasn't sure she had the strength left to shield Patches from two directions. If Alef fired a Magelight from the top of the cage…

Andy and Mr. Jefferson ran as quickly as they dared, making a winding path through the Compound. Andy didn't dare drop his shield while they ran. "Nafshi," he told her, "find me their auras. Point me in the right direction."

His Magelight glowed, and a wave of relief flooded him as he sensed Goldeneyes not far away. "That one," he said, pointing. Mr. Jefferson nodded and scanned the darkness. "I don't see any Wild Ones," he said.

"Follow me." Andy ran for the bayit and ducked, diving through the door. He knocked into something and realized he'd just rolled over Bett, who apparently had the wind knocked out of her. Alef stood on top of the cage that held Patches. His Magelight flared and he fired a dagger at Andy's face. Andy didn't have time to react.

"No!" Goldeneyes said, throwing a shield over Andy. The dagger bounced off and landed in the cage, hitting Patches in the shoulder. Patches yowled in pain.

"So," Alef said, "it wasn't you after all." His Magelight flared as he prepared to end Patches once and for all.

EAST VERSUS WEST

"I don't think so," Mr. Jefferson said as he swung the bat, knocking Alef into the wall of the bayit. He fell to the ground and lay still. "What about that one?" he said, nodding toward Bett.

"Check it out," Andy said. "There's an empty cage with a lock on it." Andy lifted Bett and tossed her in the cage while Mr. Jefferson did the same with Alef. He shut the door and closed the lock, spinning the wheel. "Try getting out of that one, jerks," he said.

"Andy, can you get me out of here?" Goldeneyes said.

"Yeah, just a sec."

He stood back while Mr. Jefferson used the bolt cutter to cut through the locks in no time. Patches stumbled out of his cage.

"Thanks, thanks, thanks, thanks, thanks, Becca's father," he said. Mr. Jefferson laughed and picked up Patches as he staggered around. "Can you hold onto my shoulder?" he asked. "I still got two heavy metal things to carry in case some more of these bad boys get any ideas."

"Patches will try."

Mr. Jefferson moved Patches to his shoulder and picked up the bat and the bolt cutters.

Meanwhile, Andy rushed to get Goldeneyes out of her cage. He pulled the door open and she leaped into his arms, purring.

"Thanks. But there's no time to waste. The Wild Ones have Leilei! Taylor took her out to the main guard post early this afternoon, and we haven't seen her since!"

"Then let's go find her. Give me a second. Mr. J., keep an eye on the door. Smash anything that tries to get inside." Andy closed his eyes and concentrated, reaching out for Leilei's aura. Before he could search for her, he heard a shout.

"Look out!" Mr. Jefferson said as two Catmages tried to enter the bayit. He swung his bat.

"Hey! It's us!" Ari said as he leaped aside.

"Father!"

"Zahavin!"

CHAPTER TWENTY-THREE

"Where's Leilei?" Lev asked. "Zahavin, where is she?"

"Taylor took her to the main guard post earlier."

"I was just looking for her aura," Andy said.

"I'll do it," Lev said. "I could pick my daughter out of a sea of Catmages without even needing my Magelight."

Lev's Magelight flared. "She's still at the guard post. It's awfully crowded out there. And Father—Kfir is with her."

"Then we will deal with him. Let's go." He and Lev rushed outside. Andy and Mr. Jefferson came out more slowly, ducking to get through the door. They straightened up and stopped short as they came face to face with Taylor. Andy scowled at him.

"What are you doing here?"

"Payback time, Cohen. Payback for last year."

"Taylor, don't do this. Come on, son, you're better than them," Mr. Jefferson said.

"I'm not your son."

"Becca's been saying good things about you for months now. Come on, Taylor. Make her proud."

Taylor hesitated.

"Don't waste your breath, Mr. Jefferson. Taylor made his choice. He's never going to help us."

Taylor's brows drew together. "Right you are, Cohen. At least, I'm never going to help *you*." His Magelight necklace lit and Andy shoved Mr. Jefferson to the side. "Get out of here. Go help find Leilei. I'll catch up with you later."

Now it was Mr. Jefferson's turn to hesitate.

"Move!" Andy shouted.

"We'll come back for you after we find Leilei," Goldeneyes said as she ran after her father and brother.

"It's just you and me now, Grant. Hit me with your best shot."

Taylor obliged with a Magelight barrage. Orange, green, yellow, green, yellow. Andy deflected them and fired off three jets in a row that

EAST VERSUS WEST

bounced off Taylor's shield.

"Looks like it's an even match now, Cohen. Maybe I should hit you with a different shot." He charged Andy, drawing back his arm and folding his fingers into a fist. Andy was caught by surprise and hesitated.

"No," Nafshi said, "I don't think so." Andy's Magelight smoldered and Taylor stopped still as if he'd just run into an invisible wall. Andy sighed with relief. "Am I going to have to knock that boy over again?" Nafshi asked.

"No!" Andy said out loud.

"No, what? No, don't hit me?" Taylor laughed. "You just never change, do you? Scared of me in middle school, scared to face me now. Chicken Cohen." He laughed again and fired off more light daggers. Orange, green, yellow, green, yellow, all in quick succession. Andy raised a shield, deflecting the daggers. He fired back and soon the air between the two boys was filled with many colored daggers bouncing off their shields and landing on the ground. The smell of charred dirt and plants filled the air.

"Looks like it's a stalemate," Taylor said. "Figures. You really aren't so hot without all your friends around, are you? Hey, if you want, we can drop the Magelights and fight it out the old-fashioned way. Except I'm still bigger and stronger, and I'll beat you to a pulp."

Taylor took a swaggering step forward. Before Andy could stop himself, he took a step back, memories from middle school flashing through his mind. He saw Taylor and Pete and Tommy picking on him on the bus, following him to his house, waiting for him in the hallways and after school. As he took the step back, Taylor's derisive laughter sounded in his ears.

Andy felt a cold anger envelop him. He could feel the blood rushing in his ears, his heart beating faster. His Magelight blazed so brightly it nearly blinded him. Now it was Taylor who hesitated and stepped back.

"Shut up, Taylor," Andy said in a cold, hard voice that seemed to be coming from somewhere else. "You're smart to back away. But you're too

CHAPTER TWENTY-THREE

late. Does this bring back any memories?" Power pulsed through his Magelight as rage flowed over him. The Magelight glowed brightly and Andy flung out his arm. A green light enveloped Taylor. All five of his Magelights blazed in response, pushing the light outward so that it looked like Taylor was silhouetted in green, yellow, and orange light. Andy could feel Nafshi adding her strength to his, her rage to his. A blinding flash filled the space between them, and Taylor dropped like a stone. Andy stood watching, breathless, shaking. The rage ended abruptly and Andy felt drained.

"Is—is he—what did we do?" Andy asked. He knelt beside Taylor and saw his chest rising and falling.

"He's fine," Nafshi said contemptuously. "He's been knocked out cold again. He'll wake with a headache, no more."

"You shouldn't have done that!" Andy said. "You said you wouldn't hurt him!"

"*We* did that, Andrew. You wanted it as much as I did. And I told you, he's not hurt. Much."

Andy drew a shaking hand across his forehead. "I don't have time to argue with you now. Goldeneyes needs us." He got to his feet.

"Wait! The Magelights, they're in his pocket," Nafshi said.

Andy bent down and took the Magelight collars out of Taylor's pocket, stowing them in his own. Then he reached for Taylor's Magelight necklace. "That was the last time you'll ever use this on anyone," he said. As his fingers closed around the stones, a jolt of multicolored energy flared out and knocked him backward.

"What was that?" he said. "How did Taylor do that?" He was still out cold. Andy rose to his knees and reached for the Magelights again. The necklace glowed and he hesitated. He heard leaves rustling in the wood around him.

"Never mind, Andy, we have to go," Nafshi said. "Wild Ones are coming this way, too many for us."

"But the five Magelights!"

"Go!"

EAST VERSUS WEST

Andy leaped to his feet and hurried away. Let the Wild Ones find Taylor. He had to make sure Leilei was all right.

"And if she's not," Nafshi said, "they'll pay. They'll all pay."

Kfir and Razor faced each other. Kfir let go of Leilei, who fell to the ground and lay still.

"Thank the One," Silsula said. "She's still breathing!"

"I can kill her with a thought," Kfir said. "It's still a stalemate."

"What do you want?"

"First, call off the attack. Now."

Razor twitched back his ragged ears.

"Do it!"

He sent word to his captains. Soon the sounds of battle had died down as the Shomrim withdrew from the Compound.

"Let us have her," Razor said.

"Not yet. All of you but Razor, leave."

Letsan growled. "He intends to kill you, brother."

"He can try."

Hakham glanced at Kfir and Razor. "If Razor doesn't come back, you will answer to me. One way or another, this will end."

"Perhaps, old one. Or perhaps your brother will win."

As if on cue, Niflah emerged from the darkness to join his guard captain. "Hello, brother," he said.

Hakham said nothing.

"Am I interrupting the negotiations? Have you discussed Zahavin? She's locked up tight, you see, and we have terms you must meet before you can have her back."

"I reject your terms," Goldeneyes said from behind them as she fired daggers at the guards surrounding Kfir.

"So do we," Ari said, adding his fire to his daughter's. Kfir turned to face the new threat as Niflah shielded them.

Razor laughed harshly. "Looks like you lost your bargaining chips."

CHAPTER TWENTY-THREE

"Not all of them," Kfir said, moving to stand over Leilei. Before he could touch her, Lev launched himself into the air and knocked Kfir aside.

"Get away from my daughter," he growled.

"I'm with him," Mr. Jefferson said, brandishing his bat. "Who's next?"

Niflah and Kfir looked around, took stock of their situation, and fled into the darkness.

Lev leaned over his daughter. "Leilei! Leilei!" She raised her head groggily.

"Hello, Father," she murmured. "Are you here to take me home?"

"Yes. Yes, Leilei. We're here to take you home." He leaned down and licked her ear.

Andy walked slowly out of the darkness. He brightened when he saw Leilei, who struggled to rise. "I'll take her," he said, lifting her and cradling her in his arms. "I have your Magelight. Yours too, Patches."

"You found them?" Goldeneyes asked.

"Sort of. I took them from Taylor."

"What about his Magelights?" Razor asked.

Andy shook his head. "Didn't get them. I'll explain later."

"Is he all right?" Mr. Jefferson asked.

"Yeah. He's fine."

"We should go," Razor said. "Katana, does anyone need assistance?"

"Not this time, sir. Nothing but the kind of wounds we can deal with ourselves. Nice to catch the Wild Ones flatfooted for a change."

"Then set a rearguard and let's go home."

Andy carried Leilei and let Mr. Jefferson light the way with his flashlight. Lev, Ari, Silsula, Letsan, and Goldeneyes followed along. Patches purred loudly from his perch on Mr. Jefferson's shoulder, occasionally rubbing his face against him.

"You're something else, Patches," he said.

"Becca says so, too."

"Are you sure Leilei's all right?" Lev asked.

EAST VERSUS WEST

Andy shrugged. "I think so. But if she's not okay by tomorrow I'll bring her to Dr. Crane."

Teresa, Mike, and Becca saw their light and met them in the wood. Becca smiled with relief as she saw Patches on her father's shoulder. "I see you found a new friend," she said.

"Becca's father is a good, good, good, good man," Patches said, purring loudly. "Patches likes Becca's father."

"We took down the tents," Mr. Velez said. "We figure it will be more comfortable sleeping in our own beds tonight."

"Not to mention safer," Becca said. "I don't like the idea of being so close to the Wild Ones after what we just did."

"Which reminds me, what did we just do?" Mike asked.

"I'll tell you when we get home. I'm beat."

"Okay. We'll meet you there." He and Teresa got into the Velez SUV. "Any of you Catmages coming with us?" he asked.

"Looks like everyone's going wherever Goldeneyes and Leilei are going," Becca said. "Dad, I'll take Patches."

"Thanks. See you at Andy's."

They climbed wearily into their cars and left the campground.

Andy and Becca's mothers met them at the door, relieved at the sight of the Catmages and the lack of visible wounds on any of them. They went into the dining room and ate sandwiches while Mr. Jefferson did most of the talking. Andy shrugged and avoided any details about his fight with Taylor. "Look, I got the Magelights back. Didn't have time to do much else."

Becca watched him curiously. She knew there was something he wasn't saying. But she didn't press. She reached over and fed a slice of turkey to Patches, who ate it eagerly.

Silsula insisted that Leilei go upstairs and rest. Lev went with her, father and daughter walking side by side contentedly. Goldeneyes watched them go, glancing at her father, who sat in a chair next to her and Letsan.

"I'm sorry I almost got you killed," she said wryly.

CHAPTER TWENTY-THREE

"I'm sorry it's been so long since I came to visit." He stepped past Letsan and rubbed his cheek against his daughter's.

"This chair is getting awfully crowded," Letsan said.

"I can fix that," Aryeh told him. Without warning, he shoved Letsan off the edge of the chair. Everyone burst into laughter. "You've spent plenty of time with my daughter. It's my turn now."

"All right," Letsan said. "Then I'll take this chair." He leaped onto Andy's lap.

"Here we go again," Andy said, pushing Letsan's tail out of the way as he reached for a glass of soda. "Cat hair. Always with the cat hair."

TWENTY-FOUR: EXULTATIONS AND LAMENTATIONS

Taylor hurried through the empty halls. School was out as of yesterday, but Principal Saunders had summoned him to his office. Taylor wondered what was in store for him. It wasn't his fault they lost the prisoners. That was all on Roah and Kfir. And as far as Taylor knew, they were still out in the West Woods.

He passed by Mr. Straight's classroom and saw his teacher pulling down decorations from the wall behind his desk. Taylor almost said hello, but stopped himself. There wasn't time. Saunders hated it when you were late. He kept going and stopped in front of the open outer office door. None of the office staff was around. He drew a deep breath and let it out before heading for the closed office door.

"Enter," Saunders said at his knock. He sat behind his desk, frowning, his hands clasped on the desk in front of him. Taylor stepped forward to stand in front of him and wait. You didn't sit unless Saunders told you to.

Moments ticked away as Taylor stood silently in front of the desk.

Neither of them heard Jack Straight enter the outer office. As he saw the tableaux before him, his mind went back to the many times Stan had done something similar to him. It would be a very bad thing to walk

CHAPTER TWENTY-FOUR

in on. He stood behind the door, out of sight, listening.

Taylor tried to remain calm and still. *Fine. He's done this before, too. I can wait.* But for all his bravado, Saunders' silent stare unnerved him. He cleared his throat.

"You are growing impatient?" Saunders asked. "Am I taking up too much of your valuable time?"

"Yes. I mean, no, my time isn't valuable. I mean, uh—"

"Be quiet, Mr. Grant."

Taylor was quiet.

"What did I tell you when I first gave you those Magelights?"

"You told me to learn how to use them. You said I could keep them as long as I did well. I'm doing well, aren't I?"

"You were."

Taylor noticed the past tense and readied himself. "Are you saying I'm not doing well anymore? I almost beat Cohen. I was doing fine until—well, I don't know what happened. One second we were fighting it out and the next second I was on the ground."

Saunders paused again and locked his glance on Taylor's. The boy fell silent.

"I thought you told me you could handle Mr. Cohen. I thought you told me you were ready to take your part in this battle. That I could count on you."

"I did! I did all of that!"

"No, you did not!" Saunders said, slamming his hands on the desk and standing to lean across the desk. "Where are our three Catmage prisoners? Do we have them still?"

"They—they got away. But sir, they had help! There were those two spies and Becca's dad—"

"SILENCE!"

Taylor froze.

"We had a deal, Mr. Grant, and you are not keeping up your end of it. Perhaps it is time you returned my Magelights."

EXULTATIONS AND LAMENTATIONS

A range of emotions washed over Taylor, fear the uppermost. "No! Please, Principal Saunders, you can't do that!"

"Can't I? I told you when I gave them to you that those are *my* Magelights. That they are on loan to you. That I would take them back if you didn't do your very best."

"I did do my best! I swear it! Ask Roah, he saw me, he saw what I did! He'll tell you!" Taylor glanced around the room. "Is he here? Can you call him? He'll vouch for me! Please don't take the Magelights back. Please, sir."

The edge of Saunders' mouth rose in a smirk. From his vantage point in the outside office, Jack could tell his cousin was enjoying the boy's terror. His heart went out to Taylor—he remembered all too many similar scenes between Stan and himself.

"I'll do anything you want. Tell me what to do!"

Saunders said nothing. He stood staring at Taylor, watching the boy's agony. Jack shut his eyes and tried to will himself to walk away. He couldn't get involved. It would just make things worse. Taylor only had to put up with Stan for another year. Jack was stuck with him for life. So what if he lost the Magelights? It wasn't the end of the world.

Tears slid down Taylor's cheeks. Jack watched in shock as the boy drew a shuddering breath. "Tell me what I need to do to keep these Magelights. I'll do it. You want me to go after Cohen today? I'll do it. You want me to take out a Catmage? I'll do whatever it takes. But please—don't take them from me."

Saunders smiled. "Now you understand, Mr. Grant. Now you know the consequences of disappointing me. The next time I rely on you, you will do what needs to be done. Won't you?"

Taylor brushed his arm across his eyes. "Yes, sir. I'll do whatever you want. We'll beat them next time, no matter what it takes."

"Now get yourself out of my sight before I change my mind. The sight of you is beginning to sicken me."

Jack eased himself back a step to make sure Taylor wouldn't see him

CHAPTER TWENTY-FOUR

as he rushed out of the office. He looked through the crack in the door and waited until Stan turned to look out the window. Then he hurried to the edge of the outer office and pretended he had just walked in the door.

"Do you need me for anything else today? I'm taking off."

"No, you are useless to me, as usual," Stan said.

"Right. Later." He strode quickly out of the office and to his car. He pulled onto the street, and halfway down the block he saw Taylor with his head down, hands in his pockets. Jack pulled the car over to the curb next to him.

"Want a lift, Taylor?" he asked.

Taylor shrugged.

"Come on, get in." Taylor moved stiffly, not making eye contact. His eyes were red. Taylor shrugged again and got into the car. He looked out the passenger window as Jack drove toward his house.

"You did good this year, Taylor."

"It doesn't matter."

"What do you mean, it doesn't matter?"

"Saunders wants to take away my Magelights," he said. "They're the only reason I managed to pass your class. They're the reason I did so well in math class."

"That's ridiculous! Becca told me you worked extra hours with her to improve in math, and you've worked hard for the last two years to stay in my history class. Who told you it was the Magelights?"

Taylor shrugged again. "I don't know. It just—feels that way."

"Well stop feeling that way. You did all this, not those stupid stones." They stopped for a red light and Jack turned to face Taylor. "Promise me you'll stop saying that."

Taylor shrugged.

"And stop that damned shrugging!" Jack said, exasperated. "Talk to me, Taylor."

"There's nothing to say. Saunders gave me these Magelights, and he can take them back. He wasn't wrong about that."

The sound of defeat in the boy's voice cut Jack to the core. How

EXULTATIONS AND LAMENTATIONS

many times had he felt just like that after Stan had gotten through with him? He wanted to say something, but he didn't know what—or how.

They drove the rest of the way in silence. Jack stopped the car in front of Taylor's house. Taylor got out, muttered a brief thanks, and hurried inside. Jack stayed where he was, the motor idling, thinking. Remembering.

Damn it, Stan. When is it ever going to be enough?

"This is the last of it, Dad," Becca said as she and Andy each placed a box of her ceramic pieces in the trunk. "Don't make any sharp turns on the way home," she said sternly, though her wide grin belied the tone of her voice.

"Yes ma'am," her father said, "but we have one more trip to make."

Andy had the car door open and was about to get in. "We do?" he asked.

"Yes," Mr. Jefferson said. "There's something inside the school I need to take care of. And I'm going to need you both there." He closed the trunk of the car and walked back to the building.

Andy and Becca exchanged puzzled glances as they followed him. "Do you know what he wants?" Andy sent to Becca. She shook her head.

As he led them through the halls, Andy stopped as he realized Mr. Jefferson was taking them to the principal's office.

"Mr. Jefferson, I'm going back to the car. I don't want to see him."

"Dad, I don't think this is a good idea," Becca said.

"Yeah, it is. It's time we confronted Saunders, Andy. I'm tired of him thinking he's immune to any consequences."

"Well, he is," Andy said.

"No one is immune. No one."

"We have another year of school, Mr. Jefferson. You know he can make trouble for us."

"He won't. Trust me, this will work. Come on, Andy. Let's go tell him off. You'll feel so much better."

"No I won't. He still has the Tilyon and most of the Magelights. I won't feel better until we have them all back."

CHAPTER TWENTY-FOUR

Mr. Jefferson put his hand on Andy's shoulder. "Andy, come on. You don't have to say anything. I'll do all the talking. But it will do you a world of good to be there to see someone push back on Saunders. He gets away with terrorizing kids. I'm not a kid."

Andy thought it over.

"He's got a point," Nafshi said. "And I won't let any harm come to any of you. Go ahead, Andy. Mr. Jefferson is right. You need to confront the Evil One."

"Okay," Andy said. "I give up. Let's go."

He followed Mr. Jefferson down the last hall to the principal's office, Becca at his side. The door to his office stood open. Principal Saunders sat behind his desk. He looked up at the sound of their footsteps and smirked. Roah sat in the window behind the desk, staring balefully as they entered. Andy suppressed a burst of rage that may have come from Nafshi as she encountered the Wild One who had tormented her for months while she was a captive in Saunders' cellar.

"I didn't think he'd have any Wild Ones with him. Checking for more," Nafshi murmured as Andy stiffened.

"Well. To what do I owe the honor of this visit? School is over. Will you miss me so much that you wanted to say goodbye, Mr. Cohen? If you like, I can arrange for plenty of visits over the summer."

Andy said nothing but his face turned scarlet. Becca put her hand on his arm.

"He wants to make you mad," she whispered. "Don't let him."

"He does it so easily," Andy sent.

Becca's father stood in front of the desk and looked down on Saunders as he sat behind it. "You're pretty tough on a kid. Did you ever pick on anyone your own age or were you always just a big bully?"

The smile on Saunders' face thinned as he stood and drew himself up to his full height. He stepped around the desk and stood close to Becca's father, looking down at the shorter man.

"Why, Mr. Jefferson, you're not trying to pick a fight with me,

EXULTATIONS AND LAMENTATIONS

are you? A man of your age and, ah, intellect? I'd have thought that was beneath you."

"Dad," Becca said.

Her father laughed. "Pick a fight? No. But I want to put you on notice that you're not just facing kids anymore. I got your number, Saunders. I had it three years ago when I spoke to you about Taylor picking on my daughter, and you didn't seem to find his actions worth punishing." He crossed his arms and smiled back at Saunders.

"Oh, and it's Mr. Cohen who needs protection now? I've always known he was a bit of a coward, allowing Mr. Grant to bully him over the years. And wasn't it your fault Nafshi died?" he said. "If you hadn't lit that fire in my basement—"

Something snapped inside him and Andy leaped forward. He didn't know what he was going to do, but he couldn't stop himself. Roah leaped from the window to the floor and up onto the desk beside Saunders. Andy's Magelight began to glow.

"Andy, no!" Becca shouted as her father thrust his arm in front of Andy, blocking him from moving forward.

"You have another year of school left, Andy. I'd rather you didn't spend it all in detention."

"Or in jail for assaulting his principal. Listen to the man, Mr. Cohen. I have been quite patient with you and your friends and all your—interference—over the years. You have no idea what I am capable of," Saunders said. "But keep on bothering me, and you will find out. I promise you that." His eyes glittered as his hand went to the Tilyon beneath his shirt. Andy's Magelight grew warm and he felt Nafshi's presence soothing him. He drew a deep breath, glanced at Becca, and raised his eyebrows, nodding at the door. She shook her head and shrugged, pointing at her father, who was now staring silently at Saunders. To their surprise, the principal broke the tableau first and looked away.

"Okay, that was worth it," Andy sent to Becca. She nodded.

Her father took a step closer to Saunders. "*You* have no idea what

CHAPTER TWENTY-FOUR

I'm capable of," he said softly. "I'm tired of this game. I'm tired of you coming after my daughter and her friends. You leave these kids alone, or you'll have to deal with me."

Saunders laughed. "I have dealt with you, and I am the victor. I retain the Tilyon." His smug smile returned. "I have beaten your friends at every turn."

"Really?" he asked. "Where's Goldeneyes? And Patches and Leilei? That's right, we got them out of your hands, and our spies were with you for nearly a year. Oops. Oh, and how many dogs have you got left again?"

Now it was Saunders' turn to get angry. "So you got the kitties back—for now. You won a battle. But the war isn't over. And would you like to know what the most wonderful thing about all of this is? You can't go to the authorities. Nobody will believe you. Magical necklaces? Talking cats? Oh, it's delicious. You can't touch me," he hissed. "Nobody will believe I can do magic. Like this." The amulet around his neck glowed through his shirt. "Would you like a sample of what I can do?"

"No!" Andy shouted. His Magelight shone as Nafshi prepared a defense.

"Yeah, not this time," Mr. Jefferson said between gritted teeth. Before Saunders could use the Tilyon, he swung his arm. His fist connected with the principal's face and Saunders bounced against the desk and fell to the floor. Jake Jefferson stood over him, eyes narrowed. "Looks like a good right cross trumps magic," he said. "Oh, and since nobody saw me punch you, I guess you can't go to the authorities, either."

Saunders sat up, holding his eye. "There are two witnesses here. They both saw it. I'll sue you, Jefferson. You'll regret this!"

"Andy, Becca, did you see what happened?"

"Principal Saunders tripped and fell into his desk," Andy said, barely holding back a laugh.

"I saw it, too. So clumsy!" Rebecca said, grinning.

"Go ahead, Saunders," her father said. "It's your word against the three of ours. Or would you like to bring that cat with you to the police

EXULTATIONS AND LAMENTATIONS

and have *him* tell them what happened?"

Becca and Andy laughed out loud.

"See you in the fall. Come on, kids." He turned and swept out of the office, Becca and Andy on his heels.

They hurried away. By the time they got outside, they were running.

"I can't believe you did that, Dad."

"In the car!"

"That was awesome. I can't wait to tell Mike," Andy said.

"He's going to be so mad he wasn't here."

They got into the car and pulled on their seat belts. As the car pulled out of the parking lot, Andy started laughing.

"I can't believe you just clobbered Principal Saunders."

"I told you you'd feel better."

"Well, if you told me you were going to hit him, I wouldn't have put up an argument."

"I didn't intend to. Oh, no," he said.

"What?" Becca asked.

"Your mother is going to kill me."

Laughing, they headed home.

Andy glanced over at Becca as he drove down the road to the Compound. "It's great having a full license," he said.

"Don't rub it in. I have two months to go."

"It's a shame Mike can't be here to see this," he said, grinning. "His mom caught him being mean to Kenny again and grounded him."

"That's not a bad thing," Becca said. "I'm surprised you're letting me come for it."

Andy shrugged. "Razor insisted."

He pulled over to the shoulder and they got out of the car. Andy picked up a shopping bag that clanked as he swung it. They waved to the guards at the outpost and made their way down the path to the Compound.

CHAPTER TWENTY-FOUR

"Perfect!" Becca said. "All the Teaching Rings are getting out. You'll have a huge audience!"

Andy groaned. "That's just great."

Moments later, Patches and Leilei came running toward them. Patches hopped around the two of them, nearly tripping Andy. Laughing, Becca leaned down and scooped him up. "Hi, Patches," she said.

"Hello, Becca, hello! Hello, Andy!"

"There he is," Andy said, nodding to the other end of the meadow where Razor and the rest of their friends stood waiting. "Looks like he brought everyone."

"Well, it's your own fault for making such a stupid bet," Becca said.

"Thanks so much."

"Andy!" Razor said as they approached. "I believe you have something for me?"

"Two cans of fish, as promised."

"Then let's have it. I'm hungry."

Andy sighed as a large crowd of Catmages gathered to watch. He opened the two cans, one of sardines and one of tuna. He picked up a sardine and held it out to Razor. "This is so gross," he said. Razor laughed and took the sardine from him, placing it on the ground to eat it.

"Did you bring enough for everyone?" Letsan asked.

"No, I'd need a truckload."

"Now the tuna," Razor said.

Andy put his hand in the can. "This is even more disgusting," he said to waves of laughter. Razor licked the tuna off his fingers and then licked his chops.

"That's enough. You can give the rest to the little ones." Cheering, the kittens who had been crowding near the front charged up to Andy and Becca, who doled out bits of the fish to each of them. Becca gave Patches the can to lick.

"And that," Razor said, "is why you should never doubt me."

"Trust me, I won't ever make that mistake again."

EXULTATIONS AND LAMENTATIONS

Razor went up to Andy and reared up on his hind legs, steadying himself on Andy's knee. "You did good, Andy. And I'm glad you came back."

Andy smiled and scratched Razor's ears.

"Can't you go any faster?" The long-haired mackerel tabby stood on his hind legs with his front paws on the dashboard and was watching the road.

"Go faster, he says? So, he's a driver now? Get down, Methuselah, you'll hurt yourself if I have to stop short."

"At this speed, Harry, if you stop short, all that will be hurt are your feelings because you should be embarrassed at driving so slowly!"

"We'll get there when we get there. I'd rather get there in one piece. Neither one of us is getting any younger."

Methuselah sighed and sat back down on the seat. "Hakham needs to know what we've found."

"And he will, in good time. Just be patient."

Methuselah looked up at Harry, who gripped the steering wheel tightly as he drove. Harry was right, they had time. But he was worried. Last year he had told Hakham about his concerns regarding Andy and Nafshi's Magelight. Now he had proof that he was right to be concerned.

"I think we're getting close. Look out the window again and tell me if that's the place I should park my car."

"Oh, now it's okay to look over the dashboard?"

"Be quiet and tell me if we're here, wise guy. Always with the sarcasm."

"Yes, that's it. Pull over, Harry," Methuselah said. When the car stopped, Harry leaned over and opened the door for him. "Are you coming?"

"Ach," Harry said. "I should go walking in the woods at my age? You'll be calling 911 to take me out after I trip and fall and break my hip," he said. "I'll wait here. You be careful!"

Methuselah jumped to the ground. "Always," he said as he trotted to the path leading to the East Woods Compound.

"Stop and identify yourself!" a cream-colored Catmage shouted as

CHAPTER TWENTY-FOUR

he neared the path.

"Methuselah. Who are you? Where's Hakham?" he said irritably. "He'll vouch for me. Or Zehira, if he's not around."

A tabby Catmage came out from her hiding place. "I recognize him, Keren. It's all right. You can go, Master Methuselah. I'll let Hakham know you're here." A message globe flashed out of her Magelight and zoomed down the forest path. Methuselah followed it much more slowly. About halfway to the Compound, he saw Hakham loping toward him. Methuselah stopped and waited.

"Welcome, old friend," Hakham said. "What brings you here? And how did you get here?"

"Harry. He's waiting for me by the road. We found something that requires your attention. Something about Nafshi's Magelight," he said, his mind-voice dropping to a whisper.

Hakham sat down next to Methuselah and scanned the woods. "We are alone. Or do you want to go somewhere else?"

Methuselah ignored the question. "Last night Harry was reading through an old Safran's journal. It was from the same time as the note we found last year warning against using another's Magelight. It was only a few words: *Buni went mad. He is dead.*"

Hakham waited expectantly. "And? Is there more to this story?"

Methuselah's gaze dropped and his voice grew soft. "Hakham, Buni is the Catmage who used another's Magelight as his own."

"Oh. Oh. This—this is not good."

"No, Hakham. This is not good at all."

Late that night, Taylor lay in bed staring at the ceiling. The feeling of helplessness had given way to rage. *He won't take my Magelights. By the light of the First's eyes, he'll take them over my dead and buried body.*

ABOUT THE AUTHOR

Meryl Yourish attended the Clarion Science Fiction and Fantasy Writers' Workshop at Michigan State University, which led to her first fiction sale.

After spending most of her life in northeastern New Jersey, Meryl moved to Richmond, Virginia in 2002. She spent her first six years in Richmond teaching fourth graders in religious school at a local synagogue. Although a teacher really shouldn't play favorites, the hero of The Catmage Chronicles was named after one of her students.

Today she spends her time writing and lives with her two cats, one of whom looks suspiciously like Letsan.

Find out more about Meryl, her writing, and her cats at www.merylyourish.com.

ACKNOWLEDGMENTS

Once again I would like to thank Sarah Getzler, who was always there for me when I got stuck, and always ready to slap me upside the head and tell me everything is fine when I wasn't so sure.

Thanks to Janet Platt and Chris Hlatky for their friendship and assistance.

Thanks to the great caretakers at Bon Air Animal Hospital, not just for the medical advice from Dr. Tom Haney (a.k.a. Dr. Crane), but for their efforts in keeping Tigger 3.0 around to be my Letsan for another year.

To my beta readers: Cathy Henry, Janet Platt, and Rene Sartor Enders.

To Mike Scher and Drew Wheeler for catching my mistakes.

As always, I'm very grateful to Neil Clarke for his friendship, support, and ebook formatting. And to my editor, Bridget McKenna.

Thanks to my fellow writers Larry Felder, Anna Erishkigal, Kate Berry, and Margaret McGraw for their support and encouragement, and to my new coworkers, especially Andy, Hema, and Tandy.

A very special shout-out to my loyal Facebook fans: Gian Cagampan, Kathy Pritchard, Robert Gunter, Vicki Reed, Debra Franklin, Cindy Lopez, Dave Mac, Dave Roberts, Ryka George, Kathy Greathouse, and Michelle VanWiggeren.

Cover revised by JW Manus
Cover design: Camille Murphy Bugden